I0764549

A Cloak of Red

A BOOK OF UNDERREALM

Brenna Gawain

A CLOAK OF RED

Brenna Gawain

The author greatly appreciates you taking the time to read this work. Please leave a review wherever you bought the book or on Goodreads.com.

Interior Design: Legacy Books, Inc.
Publisher: Legacy Books, Inc.
Editors: Garrett Robinson, Karen Conlin, Cassie Dean
Cover Artist: Miguel Mercado

1. Fantasy - Epic 2. Fantasy - Dark 3. Fantasy - New Adult

First Edition

Published by Legacy Books

To my cousin Dean,
who gave me my first ever fantasy book to read

To all the cats who sat on me while I honed my craft

To the family and friends
who are the reason I'm here today

CONTENTS

THE BOOKS OF UNDERREALM

THE NIGHTBLADE EPIC

NIGHTBLADE

MYSTIC

DARKFIRE

SHADEBORN

WEREMAGE

YERRIN

THE ACADEMY JOURNALS

THE ALCHEMIST'S TOUCH

THE MINDMAGE'S WRATH

THE FIREMAGE'S VENGEANCE

THE TALES OF THE WANDERER

BLOOD LUST

STONE HEART

HELL SKIN

THE TENTH KINGDOM

A CLOAK OF RED

THE BOOKS OF UNDERREALM

CHRONOLOGICAL ORDER

NIGHTBLADE

MYSTIC

DARKFIRE

SHADEBORN

BLOOD LUST

THE ALCHEMIST'S TOUCH

WEREMAGE

THE MINDMAGE'S WRATH

STONE HEART

THE FIREMAGE'S VENGEANCE

HELL SKIN

YERRIN

A CLOAK OF RED

THE BOOKS OF UNDERREALM

THE CHRONICLES OF UNDERREALM

TAVERN CROSSINGS
THE NIGHT OF TWO KINGS
A NIGHT ON THE SEAT
THE MAN AND THE SATYR
THE BEAST WITHIN
CHASING MOONSLIGHT
BLOOD ON THE SNOW
THE HAMMER OF THE KING
THE TIDES OF WAR
THE LEGEND OF CABRUS
THE SUNMANE PASS

FELDEMAR
DULMUN
THE GREAT BAY
WADELAND
Boende
Kindu
Gurumo
Mua
Umera
Thelua
The Greenmarsh
Vennrig
Motburg
Kuangu
Bumba
Situ Lake
Rice Farming Terraces
Maiko
The Langhale
Amot
Ammon
Caravan Attack
Destor
Hallrand
Kuangu Lake
Isangi
Handelsen
Ikela
Arod
Ulande
Bandar
Flametongue
Dulmish Raiders
Brekkur
The Birchwood
The High King's Seat
Garsec
Kendal
The Melnar
Malo
Klagetoh

A Cloak of Red

A BOOK OF UNDERREALM

Brenna Gawain

PROLOGUE

THE MAGESTONES GLITTERED UNDER THE TORCHLIGHT like twinkling stars in the night sky, but Armod of the family Kallis found them ultimately unsatisfying, and not worthy of their reputation. He had been expecting something more. Something magical, mayhap, like colors for which no one had a name, or an unnatural chill against the balmy summer air. Instead, he saw only a long, thin sliver of what looked like rutilated glass. He picked one up, examining it curiously between his be-ringed fingers, and then tossed it into the air, unimpressed.

"Are you sure these are genuine?"

It was late at night upon the High King's Seat, so late as to be nearly blending into early morning—the perfect time for such business affairs, since anyone awake would be too weary to be suspicious. Many merchants conducted less-than-honest dealings at an hour such as this, particularly around this time of year, when even the nighttime was swelteringly hot. Not many were undertaking deals quite so unscrupulous as he, however.

Armod was no stranger to this underhanded kind of practice. A lifetime of handling his family's affairs on the High King's Seat under the noses of some of the most diligent constables in the nine lands had honed his sense for trouble to a knife's edge. This plain wooden chest full of stones did not seem nearly remarkable enough to be worth such a fuss, and he would be a horse's ass before he would let these Yerrins cheat him. If they expected him to be cowed by the strength of their family's reputation, then they would be disappointed.

He heard the creaking of leather behind him as his guard-captain, Norrik, shifted slightly, no doubt set on edge by the suspicious undertone in his question. Armod made no move to tell the guard-captain to subside, but left his gaze fixed upon the seller of the forbidden wares, a tall, black-skinned man in customary Yerrin green. The merchant drew in a sharp breath, also noticing Norrik's movement, and Armod was gratified enough by the concern in the Yerrin man's eyes to smile thinly.

It was long since Armod had paid a visit to his family's homeland of Dulmun, as he could not abide the abysmal climate, but lately having a bodyguard who hailed from the region had been a real boon to Armod's business. Norrik was already as tall as a bear and as broad as an ox, but it was his distinctly Dulmish lamellar armor that drew the most nervous glances here in the south.

"You need only wave one before the nose of a wizard, and you will know it as genuine," the Yerrin replied, coolly, though his eyes still darted between the two men. "But that would rather give the game away, would it not?"

"Do not take offense, my friend," Armod cajoled him, setting the chest of magestones down and strolling casually over to the edge of the balcony. "I work in the trade of jewels and pearls, and every other deal contains at least one counterfeit. But the family Kallis prides itself on . . . *honest* business."

"As does the family Yerrin," the man countered, but he bowed. "A guarantee, then. We will honor a reversal of the trade freely, if you should decide you have been cheated. But I think that neither you nor your illustrious relatives will be disappointed."

Satisfied more by the capitulation than the guarantee itself, Armod waved magnanimously towards the lockboxes full of gold weights and black pearls that he had prepared as payment. One of the merchant's clerks began examining the contents of each of them thoroughly, while Armod turned his attention to the view of the Seat below. They were in the rooftop garden of the Kallis family's manor, surrounded by the waving boughs of flowering trees and marble pillars all entwined with leafy vines, and he drank in the comfort and familiarity of the setting, knowing that he would soon have to travel and leave it all behind.

The clerk finished her inspection of Armod's goods and nodded quickly to the merchant, who in turn inclined his head politely in Armod's direction and began making preparations to leave. Several manservants staidly collected the stacked lockboxes, and soon the Yerrins were gone into the night, as quietly as they had arrived. Sighing, Armod turned away from his perch overlooking the city and wandered over towards the pavilion, where his castellan waited for him along with his current dalliance.

She was plump and pretty, and made a fine model for his jewelry whenever his customers wished to see what his goods would look like when worn, but their relationship was strictly casual. She was not privy to much of the Kallis family's shadier business, and Armod certainly did not intend to tell her about this current act of high treason. His castellan, Hargrim, had no doubt told her that the Yerrin family were here selling fabrics (or some other such lie) while she waited for Armod to finish with the deal.

"I fear you may as well return to your apartments, Onila," he told her, in not entirely feigned disappointment. "I will likely be preoccupied with planning for our journey for the rest of the night."

She sighed wistfully, and then kissed him on the cheek, smelling of sea salt and cedar. "Very well . . . but be sure to make time for me before you leave!"

He promised her that he would, and then, once she was gone, signaled for Norrik to hand the small chest full of treasures over to Hargrim, who had the most experience with this particular commodity.

"Excellent," the castellan said, his dark blue eyes glinting fiercely as he inspected the stones. "This is slightly more than I expected for the price."

"Tell me again: how did you come to know so much about these stones?" Armod asked him, dropping heavily onto a nearby bench. "You are no mage, unless you have hidden it quite well."

Hargrim shrugged, closing the chest with a snap. "I did not always work for the esteemed family Kallis, sir. Before your mother's time, I once dealt briefly with those among the Mystic order who trade in information about such things. The Yerrins would wish you to believe that it is they alone who facilitate the transport of their stones across the nine kingdoms, but truly, without a sympathetic redcloak, they would get nowhere. An old friend of mine in the Mystics spoke to me often about the stones, and about ensuring they were not stopped at borders."

"Let us hope your knowledge in that regard will not be needed," Armod replied, sighing. "I would be happier to make the trip without encountering either Yerrins *or* Mystics, if we can help it."

"Have you decided when we shall sail, sir?" Hargrim asked, and Armod shrugged.

"Within a day or two. It is quite easy to secure sea passage to Selvan, so we need not worry overmuch about a specific day."

Norrik stirred slightly again, the deep, gravelly rumbling in his throat betraying his concern. "With respect, master, would it not be wiser to sail directly for Dulmun? Surely, the longer the stones are in our possession, the more risky the journey will be."

Armod grunted sourly, wishing it were that simple. "We could sail for Dulmun only if we wanted our every item of cargo turned upside-down and inspected four or more times by the trade officials here before leaving. And that will not do. No, I must take my pearls and fine jewels to the shores of Selvan to pawn off on Garsec noblemen, as I have done countless times in the past. This way there will be no need for them to be suspicious of me—at least, not until I have ridden north into Feldemar, beyond the High King's reach. The journey may take some months, but I expect we will also make some fine coin along the way, so it will be more than worth it."

"I will begin making preparations for the trip immediately, sir," Hargrim said smoothly.

Armod waved him away to his work, uninterested in the finer details. "Yes, yes. Make sure to remember to pack winter clothing. The colder months in Dulmun are *frightful*, or so I have heard."

"Guard that chest with your life," Norrik told Hargrim gravely, as the castellan turned to leave. "Its contents will change the course of our war against the High King!"

Privately, Armod had much less interest in what King Bodil might plan to do with the magestones, preferring to think instead on the coin she would no doubt pay for them. His family was constantly preoccupied with the pastime of trying to win her favor, but it was an unending errand, for she was largely uninterested in the jewelry and other fine metalwork that made up most of their trade. Like her famously utilitarian father before her, Bodil did not even wear a crown.

But now, with battlefields across the north soaked in blood and the king's raiders harrying the coastlines of Feldemar and Selvan, Armod could see an opportunity that had opened up. Any merchant of sufficient cunning and boldness to bring her such a potent weapon for her war as the forbidden magestones would find themself in the unique position of having not only her attention, but likely also her gratitude. And given what the power of this weapon could win Dulmun, King Bodil would surely be in a position to be quite generous indeed, once the smoke had cleared.

Some might have called it war profiteering, but Armod simply called it business.

ONE

The sound of children's screams interrupted the humdrum bustle of the midmorning marketplace, piercing equally through barriers of curtain, stone wall, and sleep. Before Theren could even register what was going on, she tumbled out of bed, snapping alert with the speed of a guard suddenly under inspection, her arms up and ready to defend herself. Her heart thundered in her chest, and her gaze jerked around the room, searching every corner and evaluating every object before her for a threat.

Her empty apartment seemed unimpressed with the display.

The fire of the instincts that had carried her to her feet was doused unceremoniously by the mundaneness of reality, like a cold bucket of rainwater to the face. The sounds floating up to her window from the markets beneath were banal; the jingling of coins and loud barking of merchants carried none of the panic or hush that would accompany some terrible event. She wondered, dully, if she had imagined the screams entirely. Even as she stood listening, though, another rang out—but this time she also heard the smaller nuances in the sound that her sleeping brain had glossed over: the splashing of water, and the giggling of children, and the notes of delight rather than fear in the shrieking.

She sighed wearily and then rubbed at her eyes with her hands, frustrated that she could work herself up into such a state over nothing more than a few children playing in a fountain. She remained there for a moment, directionless, not knowing what to do, while her heartbeat gradually calmed and the tension left her limbs. Of course, now that her brain no longer thrummed with misplaced alarm, it had apparently decided to remember that she had drunk far too much wine last night and proceeded to chastise her by causing her head to ache tremendously.

Groaning, she resolved to remedy that with more wine, but then remembered hazily that she was supposed to be meeting Lilith that afternoon.

A wave of embarrassment swept over Theren as she imagined what Lilith would say if she were here now. The elusive part of Theren's mind that still knew how to be gentle with herself told her that Lilith of all people would understand, but she pushed it aside, ashamed. She did not care if her other friends saw her like this, wretchedly in need of a drink and miserable, but Lilith . . . Lilith was different. Lilith was almost the only reason that Theren could manage to crawl out of bed these days.

Stirred finally, she made to trudge over to her pantry in search of food but stopped as an empty bottle clinked against her booted foot. The thick, smoked glass was just dark enough to show a glimpse of her reflection as she set it on the shelf beside all the others, her own scowling eyes staring back at her in accusation. She ignored them, as she always did; at this point there was nothing left to say to herself. What was done was done, and she would have to live the rest of her life with that, for good or for ill.

A year ago, she would have been waking up in her dormitory at the Academy, the foremost institution for magical education in all of the nine kingdoms, preparing for what would likely have been an ordinary, boring day of schooling. Back then she had longed for adventure, itching every day to escape from the cloying routine of lessons and study sessions, old dusty instructors who had neither time nor patience for her, and older dustier books in which she had little interest.

But when adventure had found her at last, it had been less glorious than she had always hoped. The Seat being invaded by an army of traitors to the High King had been perilous enough, but it was the series of grisly murders that had plagued her school that had truly changed her mind about the lure of what she would once have called "excitement."

She still had nightmares, sometimes. Still felt her heart stop every time she heard a scream. Stories of the heroes of old never spoke of this kind of lingering fear, so Theren wondered if it was a sign that she was unsuited for a life of anything more strenuous than sorting books and performing parlor tricks.

Her mouth twisted sourly at the thought. Her childhood had been spent sleeping in gutters, orphaned and penniless, with nothing to her name but the clothes on her back. She had only been able to attend the Academy thanks to the sponsorship of a wealthy patron from her hometown of Cabrus—but that sponsorship had come with a price. Her patron, Imara, had stipulated that once Theren's training was complete, she would return and enter Imara's service, no doubt to perform magical tricks for amusement and be paraded around at parties like a particularly well-bred hound.

No matter how difficult a life of adventure had already proven to be, Theren would still have rather died than accept the alternative that awaited her.

And therein lay the problem. Up until the mess

that was the murders and the eventual capture of the culprit, Isra, Theren had been very successful about delaying her graduation and staving off her eventual vacuous fate. But everything had swiftly gone wrong, and despite the pointed meddling of the Mystic order and her instructors, it had taken the efforts of Theren's friends to solve the mystery, while she herself had suffered under the Mystic's knives.

Suffering. Her right hand twitched involuntarily to her other elbow, cradling the remembered scar of a knife wound, and she glowered sullenly at her reflection, feeling ashamed once again. She had wrought more suffering than she had ever received. She had no right to feel sorry for herself. For the Mystics had acted within the King's law, had they not? But she—well, she had broken one of the highest laws of all. It was a crime that would likely have carried the sentence of death had she been any older than she was, and it was said that she had gotten off lightly with the punishment of expulsion from the Academy instead.

For her, however, expulsion meant the immediate end of her safety from Imara, and the gradual slipping away of her freedom. News seemingly traveled fast, for several sorties of guards had already been sent to retrieve Theren and take her home to Cabrus; those guards were why she slept in her boots with a knife to hand under her pillow, ready to flee at a moment's notice. They were also why she was here at all, hiding in a dingy apartment paid for by Lilith's coin, hoping to avoid being found in the first place. She knew, however, that trusting in Lilith's ability to divert Imara's increasingly persistent lackeys was becoming dangerous for the both of them.

The longer she stayed in one place, the tighter the net would close around her, and the more favors Lilith would have to call in to attempt to keep her out of trouble.

Thinking of Lilith again, Theren at last was galvanized, and pulled herself up to her full height. She would have to deal with all of this later; for now, she had an appointment to keep. Still stumbling slightly under the pressure of her headache, Theren went to work making herself presentable, bathing and washing her hair and trying to scrub away the dark shadows from under her eyes. She hurriedly downed enough food to keep herself upright, and then dressed in her cleanest shirt and breeches, slipping her knife inside one of her boots and wrapping herself in a thick grey cloak to hide her face.

She made her way outside, wincing at the assault of daylight, and then began her walk across the city towards Lilith's lodgings. The bustle of the midday markets made it easy for her to slip quietly through the streets, though she did attract a few looks for her heavy cloak in the height of the summer heat. All in all, however, it still seemed safer than leaving her face uncovered.

In a small courtyard tucked between two stone

buildings, Theren spotted a cheerful stall selling flowers, and was drawn towards it. Among the rows of yellow and red roses and the purple splashes of violets and irises, there was a tightly bound bunch of bright pink zinnias, which the lady merchant explained were from Feldemar, just as Lilith was. Staring sightlessly at the flowers, Theren wondered how Lilith must feel, being so far away from her family and her home. Especially after everything they had both been through recently, Theren thought that Lilith might be happy to have even a small piece of her homeland.

Her last few pennies clinked in her coin purse, and she handed over all but one to pay for the zinnias. It was a small thing, a *tiny* thing, really, but hopefully it would go some way towards showing Lilith how much Theren appreciated her aid, undeserved as it was. The merchant, smiling knowingly, told her that she was sure the recipient of the flowers would love them, but Theren felt her cheeks grow hot with embarrassment in response and scurried away, the zinnias a brightly colored secret beneath her cloak.

Not two streets away from Lilith's home, however, Theren found herself filled with a strange unease, and looked around warily for the source of it.

She found it quickly, her ears picking up on the creaking of leather and slight jingle of chain that meant guardsmen were nearby. This was a much fancier marketplace than the ones closer to her apartment, filled with goods that were far too expensive for her to buy, but she nonetheless picked up a random trinket from a stall and pretended to examine it with interest, in order to appear inconspicuous while she surreptitiously observed the guards. There were more than half a dozen, moving stolidly from stall to stall and speaking with all of the merchants—a fact that gave Theren immediate cause for concern. This was not an ordinary security detail.

Bending down as if examining something stuck on the sole of her boot as one approached the next stall over, she heard the crinkling of paper.

"Have you seen this girl? We believe she may have passed through here occasionally over the past several weeks. Dark brown skin with straw-blonde hair?"

Theren's pulse pounded as the merchant hemmed and hawed, but she knew she was not safe no matter what his response might be. That description was almost certainly of her, as she rarely saw her hair color on anybody on the Seat, let alone on those with her color of skin. This square certainly offered the easiest access to the street where Lilith's lodgings were, but she had never thought that Imara would send guards *here* instead of where they suspected Theren was living. She had not even considered that Imara might know about Lilith; however, she realized now, interviewing any number of students or instructors at the Academy could have revealed that they were important to each other.

She stood up, grateful for the cloak to hide her

hair, and looked around for some way to distract the guards. Across the marketplace from her, there was a stall selling wines and beers with a cart full of barrels sitting nearby. Yoked to the cart was a drooping, bored-looking mule. Theren grinned, ducking her head to hide the glow of her magic from any onlookers, and then reached out with her mind and flicked the reins, smacking the mule on the hindquarters for good measure. Startled, he launched forwards into a jolting trot, and quickly made off with the merchant's entire back stock of goods.

As she had hoped, the panicked shouting immediately drew the guards' attention, and she was able to slip away into an alley.

Sobered despite her victory, Theren put her head down and hurried the rest of the way towards Lilith's lodgings. It was clear that hiding here on the Seat was no longer an option; indeed, it seemed she should have left some time ago. Fleeing to the southern kingdoms was out of the question, as Selvan, Wadeland, and Dorsea were too close to Imara, and she had no love for the customs of either Idris or Hedgemond. But if she could escape to Feldemar, or even Calentin—yes, she had heard wondrous tales of the beauty of Calentin, and it was not known as the Far Kingdom for nothing—Lilith could come and visit her, and she could start a real life.

She rounded the final corner and then stopped dead in her tracks, breath freezing in her throat. Less than ten paces away, purposefully approaching the heavy wooden door that led to Lilith's home, was the red cloak of a Mystic, worn by a stout blonde woman. Clearly it was this woman who had sent the guards to investigate the marketplace, while she went to speak with Lilith directly.

Every thought in Theren's mind screamed of panic. Imaginary knives played along her skin like fingers of ice, and she could no longer control her limbs. What she was doing barely even registered with her, but in a desperate attempt to pull the Mystic's attention away from Lilith's door, she flung whatever was in her hand at the woman's back. The bouquet of zinnias bounced harmlessly off the bright red cloak, and its wearer turned around to see what had hit her.

They locked eyes for a moment, Mystic and fugitive mage, and whatever the woman saw in Theren's eyes, it led her to step away from Lilith's apartments.

"Hey! You!"

Theren fled, not even bothering to look back. Heavy footfalls let her know that the redcloak was following, which filled her with conflicting feelings of relief and terror. She was torn; if she escaped, the woman would no doubt return to Lilith's home, but being captured was not an option, either.

"Stop! In the name of the King's law!"

The words made Theren shudder, and she picked up her pace, ducking into the open door of a warehouse on instinct. She snaked through room after room, the thunder of her heartbeat not quite drowning out the sounds of continuing pursuit behind her. Though she was quite fit, the heavy cloak she had worn for her disguise amplified the heat immensely as she ran, and she could almost feel herself wilting. At this point, she thought distractedly, the best plan of action was to gain some distance on the Mystic somehow, and then double back to warn Lilith.

Rounding a corner, she skidded to a halt, confronted by a dead end. She cursed, looking around urgently for a way out, any way out. The only option seemed to be breaking through the walls or ceiling with her magic, so she tried to regain her breath as she gathered her will.

"If you looked at me and thought that I would be in any mood for games, girl, you were wrong."

She swung around abruptly, not wanting to leave her back exposed, and saw the Mystic fully for the first time. Though slightly shorter than Theren, the woman was broad across the shoulders, and her arms were obviously muscular even under her chain mail. She had the golden-blonde hair and high cheekbones of a woman of Hedgemond, and she looked out of place, clutching a long, heavy spear and standing in full armor amid barrels of salted ham and sacks of vegetables.

Theren opened her mouth for a moment, but closed it again, bitterness stinging in her heart. What could she do? Tell this woman of her patron's greed and conniving ways, and hope for "the King's justice?" No, there was no point in words, not with the twice-damned *Mystics*.

Instead, she spat at the woman's feet and pulled down on the roofing above her with her magic, creating an opening through which to leap upwards and escape. Before she could jump, though, the Mystic swung her spear in a wide arc. Theren moved to dodge, but the spear tip cut through a sack leaning against the wall and flicked its contents—heavy, blinding white flour—in the direction of Theren's face, clouding her vision and filling her lungs.

She tried to wave some of it away, but the grit had gotten into her eyelashes and stung at her eyes, forcing them closed. Wildly she flailed her arms, reduced to panic by her inability to see; as a mindmage, Theren needed sight to be able to use her magic, and the lack of it left her practically helpless. The wild lashing of her fists, however, connected only with empty air. Before she could regain her senses, the butt of the Mystic's spear caught her squarely in the stomach, and she doubled over in pain. The wind knocked out of her, she struggled feebly against her assailant, but it was to no avail. The woman wrapped something around Theren's face and trussed her arms and legs, before lifting Theren across her shoulder like a prize stag at the end of a hunt.

Utterly helpless, she was carried through the city to whatever fate awaited her, wrapped in the folds of that hated red cloak.

TWO

The breeze that blew in across the High King's Seat from the harbor carried with it the scents of saltwater and tar in equal measure, making Vivien's nose wrinkle in displeasure. The Mystic garrison in the city had always been in unfortunately close proximity to far too many of the Seat's wharves, and today in particular a large number of them were packed tightly with as many ships as could find berth in each. The smell was acrid enough to distract her from the matter at hand, but only momentarily, since the fugitive whose transport she was overseeing was making a great deal too much noise to be ignored.

"Please!" The young man was begging once again, holding out his cuffed hands towards Vivien in a gesture of pleading. "Please, mistress, it was an honest mistake! How was I to know the ring I lifted was a signet ring? I thought it was just a bauble!"

Vivien hefted the item in question—an exceptionally heavy gilded pewter ring that was in fact the official seal of the family Thanian, a middling-rank noble family from Idris who were in a complete uproar over the theft—in the palm of her gloved hand. How anyone could have mistaken it for a simple ring was beyond her, but then she was used to the trappings of nobility. It was possible that he really had been unlucky and oblivious enough to believe that it was merely another piece of jewelry, but it was also possible that he had been sent by one of Thanian's enemies or competitors, as the family themselves seemed to believe. From this point onward, the truth, to Vivien, was irrelevant; her job here was done, and needless mercy was not an oft-quoted quality of the Mystics, or indeed of hers.

"I fear it is not me who you will have to convince," she told him, with a sweet smile that was at odds with the harsh rasping of her voice.

The look of terror elicited by her words ignited a small, cold fire of hatred within her heart, and with great satisfaction she watched two guards drag him bodily across the square towards the garrison's back entrance. It was only within the past few months that she had recovered the ability to speak at all, having suffered a series of terrible burns down the side of her face and neck, and already she was utterly sick of everyone's reactions to her voice and disfigurement. The gasps and looks were almost, she mused bitterly, worse than the injury itself had been.

With him out of the way, she tucked the seal safely into a small concealed pocket inside her tunic, where it would stay until she could return it, at whatever time seemed the most beneficial to her. She would ordinarily have considered letting the family fret over it for a few more days, but she was under orders to leave the city tomorrow night, so it would be better done today than during tomorrow's bustle of final packing. Keeping the seal hidden from her fellows was a simple task—the folds of their red cloaks lent themselves well to keeping secrets—but a necessary one. After all, it would not do to let some young recruit with no knowledge of the courtesies of the merchant families deliver it, would it? Certainly not.

Too few of their order truly understood the art of trading favors and reputation as currency. Vivien considered herself among the best, especially here on the Seat, but there were always more favors to be stockpiled, more names to be added to her arsenal, more strands to be woven into her web.

The wind troubled her once more, whipping her loose black hair in front of her eyes, and she frowned again, turning towards the garrison's twin iron front doors. Inside the entrance hall was a veritable sea of red, capes and cloaks of all shapes and sizes adorning the many Mystics present as they bustled about packing in preparation for their upcoming journey. Conscious of the attention she had attracted on entering, Vivien tossed her hair back over her shoulders and drew herself up to her fullest height, determined to stand tall under their scrutiny.

Let them see her scars. They would know then what she had lived through.

Fewer heads turned as she continued onwards through the mess hall; the Mystics here knew her better. No doubt they also knew that she was uninterested in the food served there, as Vivien neither ate nor slept in the garrison, instead preferring to reserve a room at an inn with considerably better food *and* beds than what the order provided. After all, what was the point in acquiring coin in service to the High King if you did not spend at least some of it to make your life better? And she would rather have died than deal with lice.

Beyond the ordered corridors that divided the barracks into neat squares, she came at last to the tiny, cramped room that served as the office for the custodian of their cells, only just large enough to contain a desk and a chair. On the desk was the thick, leather-bound book that had brought her there, the ledger into which the prisoner's details would need to be entered—but it was unattended, so she leaned forwards and rang the small brass bell that would hopefully summon the custodian back from whatever errands he happened to be seeing to. The scraping of footsteps across the floor told her that it had indeed done so, but as the other door opened and the custodian on duty entered, it was not the short, rotund man that Vivien had been expecting, but instead a tall, brown-skinned Mystic named Naro.

Though Naro was younger than her by a number of years, his eyes always seemed to be tired enough for a man twice his age. She found him peculiar, and unnervingly so: despite being handsome enough to catch the eye of any number of young people in the city, and at least reasonably intelligent, he was a habitual loner, rarely spending time with even the others in the garrison. He was also among the few Mystics whose regard for her had not changed since her injury, and that worried her for a reason she could not quite pinpoint. The way he had of looking at her as though he knew all her secrets did not help, either.

She should not let him worry her, she told herself firmly. Her secrets were far too well-hidden for anyone to know about them. Of that, she was almost certain.

"Vivien." He greeted her curtly, kicking the chair out from the desk and flipping the ledger open. "I assume our newest arrival belongs to you?"

"Not for long, but yes."

He nodded, picking up a battered quill and making a note in the ledger. "Charge?"

"Theft and trespass," she replied carefully, made

cautious by his brusqueness. “I expected to see Aizo here, rather than you. Is he called to duties elsewhere?”

“He requested leave to spend the afternoon with his grandchildren before the journey tomorrow,” he answered, somewhat reproachfully, as though speaking of personal matters was an affront to him. “You said theft. Status of the items in question?”

“Already returned,” she lied glibly, holding her peace through the long, cool look that he gave her. “House Thanian may seek further reparations, however.”

He grunted sourly, making a face as he noted this all down in the book. “Make your mark, then.”

As he pushed the book towards her, heavy footsteps echoed down the hallway behind him, and another Mystic slammed her way into the room, stalking past Naro.

“Any luck?” he asked the newcomer, a blonde-haired, rosy-cheeked woman from Hedgemond who Vivien knew much better and did not like at all.

The woman, Ilya, threw her hands up in a gesture of exasperation. “Not a word when first I found her. Now she cannot be silenced! She insists—ceaselessly—that she is under the protection of the family Yerrin and that we have no right to hold her, even though multiple witnesses confirm she is the mage we sought. This patron of hers cannot take delivery of her fast enough!”

The mention of the Yerrin family name made Vivien’s ears prick up, despite her distaste for Ilya. She had just recently done some favors for several of the Yerrins here in the city, but it could never hurt to do more.

"A mage, you say," she interjected smoothly, as she finished signing her name. "Has there been another incident at the Academy?"

Ilya turned to face her, still glowering in irritation, and shook her head. "She is a runaway. She surely has nothing to do with the family Yerrin, before you ask, or they would simply have paid her patron to release her. There will be no need for you to go fishing around."

Vivien smiled courteously, marveling at the fact that despite her perpetually pink-flushed cheeks, Ilya more closely resembled a bull than the Hedgemond milkmaids to whom such complexion was usually attributed. "I will, of course, take your deductions into consideration when I question her."

Snorting, Ilya whirled on her heel and left the room, heading back towards the mess hall. Vivien opened her mouth to seek permission from Naro to speak with this mage prisoner, but he just waved a hand, clearly not interested in arguing.

Once she had crossed the threshold into the jail area itself behind the thick, oaken door, Vivien could indeed hear distant yelling from one of the farthest cells, and also managed to pick out the occasional repetition of the word "Yerrin." Her interest piqued, she quietly made her way down the row towards the young woman's voice. Despite what Ilya seemed to believe, Yerrin was a powerful and dangerous name to invoke without cause. It was true that the girl could simply have been exceptionally desperate, but it was best never to discount possible avenues of influence. Who knew what secret lovers or unlikely friends the merchant families kept?

By the time she reached the girl's cell, the shouting was nearly deafening as it echoed off the stone walls.

"Let me go! Darkness take the lot of you! You redcloaks *love* the goldbags! Go ask them! You cannot keep me here! The Yerrins will come for me if you only tell them my name! You go and find Lilith of the family Yerrin and tell her that you have Theren locked up! She will see that you regret holding me here! Do your jobs and let me go!"

Vivien was impressed. The girl—a mentalist, by the blinders of iron and leather that had been strapped over her eyes—was lean and looked somewhat malnourished, but with every word she struggled fiercely against the iron chains that held her. She seemed to be tall for her age and had cool, olive-tinted brown skin, almost as dark as Naro's, with a thin, flat nose and prominent cheekbones. Most peculiarly, her hair, which was cropped short so that it fell in feathers framing her face, was an unnaturally bright white-gold color, like straw shining in the morning sun—dyed by alchemists, no doubt.

It was this hair that made Vivien realize that she had actually seen the girl once before. Sometime last year, a member of the family Yerrin—Lilith, in fact, the very name that this mage-girl was now trying to invoke—had been accused of several murders, and was detained and questioned by the Mystics at the time. Vivien, of course, had taken it upon herself to watch closely over the investigation, for the ease of mind of her Yerrin contacts, and so had been present when several of Lilith's friends were brought in to speak with her.

One of them, though she had been less slim and a little less tall at the time, had certainly been this girl—Theren, she had called herself. There was no longer any doubt whatsoever in Vivien's mind that Theren truly did have at least some connection with the Yerrins.

Suddenly, the girl's head jerked in Vivien's direction, obviously sensing her presence, and Vivien felt self-conscious for a moment, thinking that she must breathe much louder now than she had before her injury.

"Ah, finally!" Theren declared, attempting to sound brazen, though her voice was full of undisguisable relief. "At last, someone listened! I am not sure your Yerrin masters will be pleased by how long you made me wait, but I will put in a good word for you if you hurry and let me loose!"

So, she is not sure that they will come for her, Vivien thought to herself, frowning. But she *is* sure enough to call on them, at least.

"I am certain that Lilith will be pleased to see me!"

Theren continued, her tone almost pleading in its desperation.

Vivien smiled and shook her head at the girl's foolishness, deciding not to enter the cell and speak with her. Not yet, at any rate. Theren was clearly scared, and that fear could prove to be a useful bargaining chip with either the family Yerrin or the girl herself, if encouraged skillfully enough. Vivien would have to make some inquiries first, of course, but she believed that she could turn this situation quite handily to her advantage.

"Let me out! *Please*!"

Chuckling hoarsely to herself as she considered the boon that had just fallen into her lap, Vivien left on quiet feet through the door by which she had entered, and went out onto the High King's Seat to seek information on Lilith of the family Yerrin.

THREE

It took all of the energy that Theren had left to heave once again on the chains securing her wrist irons to the floor. She had no idea how long it had been, as the blinders on her eyes meant that she could see no changes in the light outside to gauge the passing of time, but she felt like it must be a new day by now. Her shouting had not seemed to attract much attention, and a gnawing fear had been set in the pit of her stomach that her captors intended to simply leave her there to rot. It had kept her awake despite the long hours that she had been there, almost as potent a worry as the terror that the Mystics would once again deign to have her tortured.

She shivered uncontrollably, her chains jingling, as she was overcome once again by the memory of their knives. They had been quick with such hospitality on her last stay in a Mystic dungeon, but they may have decided that there was no information worth carving out of her this time. Or they might simply have wanted to let her stew for a while.

"I know you can hear me!" she ventured again, her voice trembling from overuse. "You will regret it if you leave me here to die! The family Yerrin will see you suffer for it!"

Inwardly, she cringed, aware that this was a glaring lie. With the exception of Lilith, the Yerrin family's attitude towards her would be ignorance at best, and at worst outrage that one of their own was associating with such gutter trash. But she had no choice—she had no other cards to play, nobody else to ask for aid. Nothing else stood between her and the end of everything that she knew.

She also had to hope that any Mystics listening to her would consult Lilith first, for asking a more important family member instead would bring the Yerrin family ire down upon her. Theren wondered suddenly if that was what had happened: that the Yerrins had been annoyed by her claims and commanded the Mystics to leave her to die.

The horror of it hit her like a hammer blow, and

she redoubled her efforts against the chains. She strained against them until her muscles screamed, tiny stars appearing against the blackness that was all she could see, as her blood pounded in her ears and she felt herself growing faint.

Head swimming, she collapsed back to the floor, and managed to curl herself up with her head between her knees as she waited for the dizziness to pass. After so long deprived of sight, she experienced every tiny noise in the cell amplified tenfold as her hearing attempted to compensate, and each clink of the chains made her shudder. This was no good, she thought numbly. She would never find her way out of here if she lost her head.

Surely her friends would at least make an effort to find her, she told herself, trying to calm down. They had all earned some success at ferreting out information over this past year, so they could almost certainly uncover what had happened. They would find out. Surely.

As if in response to her thoughts, a door opened somewhere off to her right, followed by footsteps.

"You there!" she croaked, sitting up again. "You have to listen to me! I have friends in the family Yerrin, and they will not be pleased when they find out where I am!"

The footsteps, light and measured, came to a stop in front of her, and hope blossomed in Theren's chest. They did not sound like the heavy boots of the Mystic who had captured her, which could only be a good sign. Had she heard the faint jingling of keys as well? She licked her lips and cleared her throat, trying to force her voice to work properly once again.

"Have you come to set me free?" she demanded, in what she hoped was an imperious tone.

Whoever the light feet belonged to did not answer, though they did indeed produce a bundle of metal keys and unlock the door of Theren's cell. Any hope in her breast was washed away instantly under an icy wave of fear as she heard them step inside and then close the door behind them, shutting themself inside with her. Flesh crawling, she backed herself away from the intruder, every wisp of air on the bare skin of her forearms as sharp as the Mystics' blades in her memory.

The disembodied footsteps remained still for a few moments, their owner silent, before making a wide circuit around her, out of reach but nonetheless too close for comfort. Heart pounding, Theren twisted her body as much as she was able, trying always to face the unbidden visitor.

"What do you want?" she demanded hoarsely, when the silence had grown too much for her to bear.

"What an interesting question."

The voice that responded was almost as rasping and croaky as her own, and she wondered why that would be. It seemed to belong to a woman, at a guess, but not any woman that Theren had heard speaking on her way in.

"Are you going to answer?" she countered, twisting again as the woman took a few steps to her left.

"My, my. You *are* jumpy."

"I know what the Mystics do to people unlucky enough to end up in their care," Theren snarled, jerking back as far as she was able.

"Yes, I heard about that. The family Yerrin does not usually take notice when the Mystics accommodate a girl with no family name or money, but your little visit with us is known to them. And thus, to me."

As the woman continued circling her, a small sound jogged Theren's memory, and she tensed herself further. At one point, so many hours ago that she had almost convinced herself she had imagined it, she had felt she heard someone watching her. She could not be absolutely certain, of course, but the woman's breaths as she walked definitely sounded familiar. If it had indeed been this woman, why would she have come to Theren's cell and then left without a word? If she meant to seek the Yerrins, why not let Theren know? What was it that the Mystics wanted?

"You spoke with them?" she asked eventually, knowing that whatever the risks and uncertainties might turn out to be, this woman was almost certainly still her only way out of this prison.

"Yes, I did," the woman replied, her voice taking on a note of reproach. "They told me enough that I am aware your insistence they would want you freed was greatly exaggerated. Your friend Lilith will doubtless wish to see you again, but she has worn her collection of favors thin these past few months, has she not?"

Theren sighed in exhaustion, chains clinking as she did her best to shrug under their weight. "I had to get your attention *somehow*. If any of you had just spoken to me, I could have explained all you wished to know. If you poked the nest of Yerrins without cause, then it is no fault of mine."

There was a long pause, just long enough to make Theren begin to regret her words, before the woman spoke again.

"Be still a moment."

Alarmed at the sound of movement, Theren tried to lean back out of reach, but a small hand caught her chin in a firm grip while the other deftly undid the fastenings of her blinders. She winced, her eyes squeezed tightly shut, as even the dim light of the prison cells was too much for her after the long period of darkness.

Wary still, she made a show of covering her face with her hands, trying to get her sight back as quickly as possible. She had no idea what this Mystic woman intended to do with her, but if she could pull herself together enough to break her chains with her magic, and then hopefully escape, it would not matter.

"So bright," she muttered, feigning being disoriented, even as her eyes focused sharply enough on her hands for her to get a good look at the irons around her wrists.

They looked far too strong to rip apart with raw strength, but now that she could see the keyholes, she was certain she could form the shape of a key that would fit in the lock, and from there it was just a matter of a small push. Still cringing and covering her face to hide the magelight that would show in her eyes, she painstakingly drew her power into a small, key-shaped form. Just as she was about to try turning it, however, she felt the magic drain away, like sand between her fingers, and looked up at the Mystic woman beside her, whose own eyes were now aglow.

"I am not that easily fooled, little girl," she declared, though there was the ghost of a smile on her lips.

"You are a mage as well, I take it," Theren rasped flatly, defeated.

"Did you think I would have freed your eyes were that not the case?"

Theren sighed heavily, taking stock of her visitor for the first time. Despite being at least several hands shorter than Theren, she held herself as though she were the tallest woman in all the nine lands. She had long, black hair that hung down past her shoulders, with dark eyes and dainty features. There was a gauntness to her face, and a kind of hunger in her eyes, that set Theren on edge, not helped by the fact that her skin was the kind of pale white that put Theren more in mind of an Elf than a person.

As Theren watched, another door opened somewhere along the corridor, and the woman's head turned in the direction of the sound. This slight movement shifted her hair, and revealed that beneath it, the right side of her face was covered with a painful-looking, bruise-colored mass of what seemed to be burned flesh, the twisted and scarred remains of some terrible wound.

"Vivien?" a man called out from along the corridor, presumably to the woman standing before Theren. "Is the mage-girl giving you trouble?"

"All is well, Naro," she replied, calmly, and after a pause, the door was shut again.

Bristling at the idea that this Vivien thought she was no threat, Theren ran a more critical eye over the Mystic, noting the rich fabric of her red cloak and the fine cut of her clothes beneath it. And she had gone straight to the Yerrins on hearing Theren's pleas? A goldbag then, or worse, a crony of them. Theren's top lip curled unconsciously into a contemptuous sneer as she extended her wrists, keyholes first, and she jingled the chains in a wordless command to be released.

Vivien met her gaze with a cool stare, and made no move to unlock the irons.

"You would not be here if you did not mean to set me free," Theren growled, shaking the chains again. "If it was payment you wanted, you would have gone to Lilith, and if she had nothing to give you, you would not have come to me."

Vivien smiled faintly, though it did not reach her eyes. "You are sharper than you look. Though in this case, not quite as sharp as necessary. Your friend Lilith does not have anything that I would take as payment; truly, my interest lies in you."

Suspicious, Theren rocked back on her heels, removing her wrists from Vivien's reach. "Why?"

"I have a proposal for you, Theren," Vivien replied, weighing the bundle of keys meaningfully in one hand. "You have nowhere to go, and the Mystics are always in need of skilled mages to join our ranks—"

Theren was unable to keep herself from bursting out laughing, chains shivering as she doubled over. Even the look on Vivien's face could not silence her. *Join*? Join the Mystics? The very idea was ludicrous.

"After all that you have done to me and Lilith, did you really think I would agree?" she asked, still grinning with the madness of it. "Why would I wish anything more to do with you than what I cannot avoid?"

"I suspect that your patron Imara could provide you with a great number of reasons," Vivien replied sternly, cutting Theren's amusement short. "My proposal is generous, but I cannot give something for nothing. If you will not deign to join our order, then the next time you are caught, you *will* be taken home to her."

Theren shook her head furiously, unbelieving. "How could I ever trust any Mystic, after what I have been through? How could you ask me to? This deal is weighted entirely for your benefit, redcloak, and I see it clearly. You must think very little of me to believe that I could ever stoop to take this offer."

"Not even to win your freedom?" Vivien snapped, eyes flashing. "If I overestimated your ability to reason, then that reflects more poorly on you than it does me."

Theren hesitated, uncertain. The idea that she might meet—might be forced to *work alongside*—the Mystics who had tortured her made her feel sick. But so too did the idea of being sent back to Cabrus to wait at Imara's side like a pet. And if joining the redcloaks would allow her to stay on the High King's Seat, close to Lilith and her friends, did she really have any choice?

Vivien must have seen the conflict on her face, because her own expression softened to something like pity. "I may have spoken too harshly. What you endured was regrettable, and I can see that it affected you deeply. But I truly believe that you could do great things, if given the chance to grow, away from the threat of your patron."

To Theren's surprise, Vivien took the key and wordlessly unlocked the irons, letting them fall heavily to the floor.

"I release you from the custody of the Mystics, Theren. I suggest you take the rest of the day to make your decision, but no longer, for by nightfall this offer shall no longer be available to you."

"Why must I decide so quickly?" Theren demanded, resentful. "Surely you see this is a momentous choice to make."

"I am not without sympathy, but the larger part of our order on the Seat, including me, departs tonight for Feldemar," Vivien answered smoothly, returning the bundle of keys to somewhere inside her cloak. "I cannot extend amnesty to you while I am not on the Seat. Ilya—you met her and her spear yesterday, if you recall—will remain for several weeks, if you would prefer to try your luck with her."

Theren remained silent, rubbing idly at the skin on her wrists, which was raw and bruised after straining against the irons. This offer was sounding worse and worse by the moment, but also more and more like the only option available to her.

"I will see what my friends have to say," she mumbled faintly, after a weighty pause.

"Is there no one else you could speak to? No adults?" Vivien asked her, not unkindly, and then pursed her lips thoughtfully when Theren shook her head. "When I attended the Academy, it was one of my instructors, a woman named Jia, who first recommended to me that I join the Mystics. If you wished to hear it, I am sure she could tell you why, and whether she recommends the same for you."

Theren nodded mutely as Vivien swung the cell door open, unwilling to say that she did not know if Jia would even speak to her after how her time at the Academy had ended. She made her way out into the corridor on shaky legs, feeling her spirits lift only when a gust of fresh air from outside blew across her face, blessedly carrying away some of the lingering stench of the prison.

She turned back to look for Vivien, to see if she was truly free to go, but the Mystic woman was already gone, the corridor empty. Hastily she ducked outside, not wanting to give any of the others any reason to ask her to stay.

It was difficult to estimate the exact time of day from the sky alone as she hurried down into the city, but it seemed to not be midday yet—that, at least, was a relief. With luck, that would leave enough time before tonight for her to find the others and cook up some masterful scheme to get out of all this. There would have to be something they could do. Anything would be better than joining the Mystics, of that she was certain.

She still hurried, however. Just in case she really did need to be back here by nightfall.

FOUR

Various patrons were scattered around the dining room of the Crimson Jib inn, mostly buried deep in their cups, when Theren entered. It was a sailors' tavern in one of the rougher parts of the city, down near the docks, and she and Lilith had specifically chosen it as one of their safer meeting places for this reason. She attracted few looks, even bedraggled and haggard as she was, which suited her just fine. The food here was terrible, and the ale watery and sour, but she could accept that in exchange for not being troubled.

Her stomach rumbled longingly at the thought of

food, even the tavern's ominously named "mystery stew," as she trudged her way through the common room towards the stairs. There was a room on the top floor kept in Lilith's name, and though none of her friends liked the place, it at least had the advantage of being cheap. Her other two compatriots, Ebon and Kalem, had argued vehemently against the Crimson Jib from the start, with Kalem often refusing to sit on the furniture and both boys turning up their noses at any of the food and drink on offer. Lilith, on the other hand, understood the value of anonymity, and had eventually won them over, though even she still hated visiting.

Theren had slept on cobbles, and in rainy gutters, during her time living on the streets of Cabrus. A straw pallet, like the ones the inn provided, would have been a luxury. It was still always jarring, listening to the children of merchants and royals talk about a roof to sleep under as though it was an easy thing to come by.

She knocked on the door four times, and then twice more in quick succession, the signal that would tell them it was her—if any of them were indeed there—and immediately heard the scraping of chairs across the floor and hurried footsteps from inside. Before she could turn the knob, the door was ripped open from within, and Kalem burst out, catching her around the midriff in a tight hug.

"Watch the stomach!" she groaned, as her still-tender bruises from the spear butt she had met the previous morning were reawakened with a vengeance.

"Are you hurt?" Lilith asked worriedly, also coming to the doorway, and Theren felt tears sting in her eyes to see that Ebon was there as well. All three of her friends had been waiting anxiously for her to return.

In response, she lifted the hem of her shirt, displaying the impressive purple-black ring of pain she had acquired, and waved them all back inside the room with her other hand. Characteristically modest, Kalem turned beet-red and looked away, but Lilith gasped in shock, covering her mouth with her hands, and even Ebon seemed taken aback.

"Sky above," he muttered, as Theren closed the door behind her. "What happened?"

She paused for a moment, wondering where she could possibly start. "That . . . is a very long story. Do any of you have any food?"

Lilith fussed over her, pushing her towards the table in the corner, as Ebon and Kalem went down into the tavern to buy what meals they would deem edible. Relenting, Theren let herself be deposited into the closest chair, and watched Lilith as she continued to fret, wringing her hands nervously and muttering about how she would call for a bath if she thought the innkeeper could even provide clean water. She was, as ever, achingly beautiful, as elegant and proud as the day they had met. The long summer had burnished her smooth, black skin in the sun till it seemed all underlaid with shining bronze, like a glowing mirror, and the rich green of her silken dress was a perfect match with the kohl that rimmed her wide, brown eyes.

Theren hated to see her so worried, however; Lilith had lost so much weight over the past year that she seemed almost as though she might fade away entirely. Her once plump, girlish face was now thin, almost pointed, and her dresses hung loose on her frame, as though part of her had been stolen away. Also gone were her long black curls, which had been cruelly shorn off, and, worst of all, the softness in her eyes that Theren remembered so fondly.

All of these ills, Theren thought to herself darkly, had been inflicted upon Lilith by the Mystics. Of all of the things that she might have wished the two of them to share, a knowledge of what it was like to be tortured was not high on her list, and yet it was what they had been given. And Lilith, who had been framed for the murders that had turned all of their lives upside-down, had suffered far worse, for far longer, than Theren had had to endure—a fact which still made her blood boil.

More than whatever they might have done to *her*, how could she countenance joining the redcloaks after everything they had taken from Lilith? Her own pain she could stomach, but not Lilith's. Never Lilith's.

Theren sighed glumly, staring at the tabletop, and barely noticed Lilith come over to pick up one of her wrists, turning it over carefully to inspect it.

"Theren . . ." she began, horrified, looking at the cuts and markings that were unmistakably from a pair of manacles.

Theren forced a smile she did not feel, though that

only seemed to worry Lilith more. "I will explain soon. Only I . . . exerted myself a lot this past day, and I have not eaten enough."

Wordlessly, Lilith took the seat beside her and reached out to take her hands, twining their fingers together. Small though the gesture was, Theren felt her anxiety ease just a little. She thought with fleeting regret of the bouquet of zinnias, but it was likely too late now to try retrieving them—and anyway, they all had more pressing things to worry about.

Ebon and Kalem returned soon, the one tall and tawny and the other small and pale, bearing flagons of the Crimson Jib's less than appetizing ale and a bowl of a stew that seemed slightly less mysterious and grey than usual.

"Kalem pressed the innkeeper to name the meat in it for a few pennies extra," Ebon explained dryly, passing out the tankards. "Enjoy your lamb."

Theren ate as though she had been starved for weeks, the bruises on her abdomen protesting as she hunched over her bowl, while Ebon and Lilith exchanged worried glances and Kalem leaned against the wall, still not keen to touch any of the furniture. The lamb stew was heavy and glutinous, but it was like the finest of meals to her empty stomach.

"Well," she said eventually, pushing the bowl aside. "I suppose I should just . . . start at the beginning."

She described the events of everything she had been through since she last saw them as best she could, though she left out some of the parts that she felt were overly embarrassing. Mention of the Mystic who had chased her down caused Lilith's fingers to tighten their grip on the handle of her mug, and Theren faltered momentarily, not wanting to recount the blind panic that had overtaken her at the sight of the woman's red cloak.

"Why would the Mystics be involved?" Ebon asked, worried, as she fell silent. "They were not there to investigate some aspect of the murders once more, were they?"

Theren shook her head, though she shuddered at the idea. "No, they were sent by my patron. She apparently convinced them that she feared I was too dangerous for her guards, and tasked them to set a mage-hunter after me."

"Sky above!" Ebon exclaimed, while Kalem gasped in horror. "Surely they cannot believe that! What did you do?"

"I wish I could say I eluded my pursuers," she continued, indicating her stomach again with a grimace. "But unfortunately, I have spent the better part of a day or so in the Mystics' cells, blindfolded and chained to the floor."

Lilith shot to her feet, incensed, sending her empty flagon tumbling as she slammed her fists on the table. "How dare they? My family—my family will—"

Theren placed a calming hand on Lilith's arm, feeling the frightened tremble that was running through her.

"One of the Mystics has already spoken to your family about me. She seemed to think that because you were safe, they were not greatly concerned."

"That does sound like them," Lilith murmured faintly, sinking back into her chair. "I am sorry."

"Do not be," Theren replied, softly. "If not for invoking your family's name, I do not know that I would be here, but rather on a ship bound for Cabrus already."

"They let you go?" Kalem asked, surprised, and Theren grinned at him somewhat ruefully.

"Did you imagine that I fought my way free of an entire garrison, my young alchemist friend? Such faith you have in my abilities."

He shrugged casually, bright red hair spilling over his eyes. "When it comes to you, my dear Theren, I will believe almost anything."

"That is well," she responded, sighing, "for now I must ask you to believe something much more far-fetched. The redcloaks have extended me an offer to join their ranks."

Ebon blinked several times, seemingly confused, and Kalem's mouth hung open in shock, but Lilith had gone tense immediately, staring at Theren in horror.

"In fact, they are rather insisting upon it. Unless I agree to enlist by tonight, they will have me sent straight back to Imara."

"Then you have no choice?" Lilith asked quietly, in a small voice that broke Theren's heart.

"Why?" Ebon interjected bluntly, as she opened her mouth to try finding an answer. "Not that they should not want you, but it seems so . . . convenient. Did they say why they wished to recruit you?"

She spread her arms helplessly. "The closest I was given to an explanation is that they are looking for mages. They are apparently sailing for Feldemar tonight in great numbers. It must be in aid of their preparations for the war."

Lilith shook her head vehemently, standing up again. "They cannot! They cannot ask this of you. To stand alongside those—those monsters, only to be sent to the war in Dulmun! Darkness take them all!"

She turned away, wringing her hands in distress.

"I think you should consider it, at least," Kalem said slowly, surprising them all. "In fact, I think this is the first piece of good news we have heard in some time."

"Good news?" Lilith cried, whirling to face him. "To be shipped off to die alongside torturers and toadies of people like Imara, this seems good to you?"

"We do not know that they are going straight to a battlefront!" Kalem replied defensively, his voice squeaking, though he did his best to stand his ground under Lilith's gaze. "The High King holds many strongholds all across the nine lands. And even if it was true, they would not send untested recruits to the front lines to face the armies of Dulmun. I think we *must* consider it, or the only other thing to consider will be visiting Cabrus when we can find time to travel."

Nostrils flaring, Lilith glared at him for a few moments. "There must be some other solution! Something less cruel!"

"Do not speak to Kalem so!" Ebon snapped at her. "We have been stretched thin as it is! And she would be free of her patron for good!"

Theren hung her head, ashamed that her friends were being tasked so heavily simply by her remaining in the city. For them to be openly shouting at each other like this must have meant that all of them were keenly feeling the strain of their predicament.

"Could we buy you passage off the Seat before tonight?" Ebon asked eventually, bringing himself back under control with some effort while Lilith worked to unclench her jaw. "I know you would not wish to leave, but it may be the only way."

Theren shook her head miserably. "The docks are full of redcloaks even now, loading their ships in preparation for their departure tonight. I would surely be seen in daylight, and another mage-hunter would be sent after me."

"I could appeal to my family," Lilith suggested, her voice tinged with desperation. "Beg them to shelter you even just for a day. You could leave once the Mystics are gone!"

"It would be the first place they would look if they already know about the family's interest in her," Ebon countered glumly, slouching in his chair.

"At any rate, one of the few Mystics that will

remain in the city is the very same one who chased me down," Theren added, gingerly placing a hand on her stomach. "And I do not fancy facing her again if I can avoid it."

"I know it seems dire," Kalem said quietly, his eyes downcast as though he expected to be shouted at again. "But we cannot overlook this opportunity. The Mystics are respected, paid good wages, and honored wherever they travel! You might return from Feldemar in a year to serve on the Seat and have things return to how they were before all this. How can it be worse than living on stale bread and skulking through the streets, looking over your shoulder the rest of your life?"

"I would not expect you to understand," Lilith muttered, darkly.

But Kalem's words hung in the air before Theren as she looked around at them all, at what they had all been driven to. She had already been considering leaving, had she not? If she really could return sometime—there was indeed a garrison of Mystics stationed on the Seat—then things might unfold better than she had dared dream. She had survived on the streets alone, and had managed to keep to herself for most of her time at the Academy. How much more difficult could joining the order be?

She cleared her throat, feeling awkward. "The Mystic who spoke to me suggested that Instructor Jia might have some advice. We could ask her what she knows, but I fear she would not see me. I can hardly walk onto the Academy grounds to make an appointment."

Ebon made a thoughtful noise, tapping at his chin with one long finger. "We could ask Dean Forredar to grant you special permission to enter, this once. He may refuse, but we can try."

"Let us do so, then," Theren responded, though she still felt uncertain. "The more information we have, the better I will feel about making this choice. Or at least I hope so."

"This will all work out for the better," Kalem told her, smiling, and patted her on the arm. "You will see. I will go and seek out the dean straight away, since time is of the essence."

Ebon stood hurriedly, obviously keen to spend as little time in the Crimson Jib as possible, and offered Theren a weak grin as he made his way towards the door. Theren watched as the two boys gathered their cloaks and left, and then felt Lilith's fingers creep back into her own, still trembling slightly.

"I am sorry if this seems a betrayal to you," she managed to say around the lump in her throat, turning to gaze into Lilith's eyes.

"I only worry about you," Lilith answered softly, shaking her head.

Theren managed a genuine smile this time, her heart touched by Lilith's concern. "I will survive. Do not fear."

Lilith gave her a fond look, and then stood up.

"We should go after the others. I am in no mood to sit around idly."

Though Theren's bruised stomach did not necessarily agree, she sighed and fell in step behind Lilith, wishing that she could have more time to make this choice. It seemed that rest would have to wait, at least until after tonight.

FIVE

It felt strange to stand beside the tall, black granite walls of the Academy once again. For years Theren had come and gone over them in the darkness of night, seeking freedom and adventure when her instructors would have insisted she remain in bed. Now it was as though they had been heightened in her absence; although she knew it was all in her head, they seemed insurmountable, a hundred times taller than she remembered.

She and Ebon were waiting outside, lurking some way away from the entrance while Kalem and Lilith went to find the dean. Like Theren, Ebon had been expelled from the Academy after their efforts to stop the murders, and now they were both barred from entry. She did not know how hard it was for Ebon to deal with being excluded, but as she stood there looking at the walls, she thought that she could feel an aching hole inside of her, a hole that had once held the closest thing she knew to belonging.

The Academy had been her haven, the place where she had first been introduced to regular meals, comfortable beds, and clean clothes. It was also the place where she had first met Lilith; somehow, though she would never admit it to any of the others, most of Theren's best memories were linked to places within these high stone walls.

She took a deep, steadying breath and turned to Ebon, who was scuffing his boots against the cobbles beside her. "How go your studies? I fear I have forgotten to ask in all the commotion."

He smiled sadly at her, looking as though he appreciated the light nature of her question. "Well enough, all things considered. It is strange to no longer be the eldest student in a classroom full of children—but strange in a good way, at least."

"I only hope you do not suddenly receive a large increase in homework, now that your lessons are not tailored for the young ones," she commented wryly, winning a laugh.

"Not so far, thankfully."

Some days Theren was envious of whatever clandestine task Dean Forredar had recruited Ebon for, as it allowed him to continue his studies with a private tutor and stay in close proximity to the Academy. Whenever she asked him about what the dean wanted of him, however, a dark expression would cross his face that would make her reconsider her envy. It must have been grave indeed, she knew, to keep him from revealing its true nature to his closest friends, of all people.

She hoped that it would not prove too dangerous for him, especially without her there to look out for him.

With a jolt, she realized that she had already begun thinking about her future in terms of leaving the Seat and her friends, though whether this was because she had accepted the idea of joining the Mystics or because she was afraid she could no longer evade being taken back to Cabrus, she could not tell. Ebon apparently noticed that something had just crossed her mind, and he raised his eyebrows questioningly at her.

Luckily, she was saved from having to explain the feelings she did not want to speak of by the arrival of Dean Forredar, trailed on either side by Kalem and Lilith. He was no longer quite so gaunt as she remembered him; his eyes were less sunken and his skin less pallid, no doubt due in part to the return of his son and the lifting of that burden from his shoulders. He still wore the same plain—almost severe—dark grey robes, however, and his hair was also the same, shoulder length and black, though less disheveled now. For a brief moment, she wondered if she would soon surpass him in height, and marveled that she could already think such a thing of her former instructors some months shy of her eighteenth year.

"Well met, Theren," he said courteously, and she ducked her head quickly in respect, somewhat surprised he had even agreed to come.

"Good day to you, Dean Forredar. Thank you for agreeing to speak with me."

He pursed his thin lips, curious eyes searching her face. "It is not every day that I am called to a meeting just outside my own walls, but you four have earned at least some measure of trust from me. I hope I will not regret indulging you in light of that."

"N-no, of course not," she stammered, her heart fluttering with embarrassment as she hoped she was telling the truth. "It is but a simple thing we wish to ask of you, only a moment's concern."

His gaze swept over her, inspecting her more closely, and though his expression remained the same, his voice seemed less stern when he spoke again. "You look less hale than last I saw you, though I daresay I should not be surprised. I must warn you, if this is about the matter of your expulsion, I am in no position to rescind—"

"No!" She swallowed hard, and then cleared her throat. "No, no, I would never ask that. I accepted the decision that was made. I only wish for your permission to enter the Academy, just this once, to speak with Instructor Jia, if I may."

He made a thoughtful noise, but did not immediately decline, and Theren noticed that this seemed to be enough to bring hope into Kalem's eyes, where he still lurked off to the dean's left-hand side.

"May I ask why?" Dean Forredar asked, after what seemed a weighty pause.

"I—I wish for her advice," she blurted out, knowing how feeble it sounded. "I have been offered a position with the Mystics, though I have no love of them, as you might imagine. In exchange, they will free me from service to my patron, but the choices before me seem both equally shrouded in darkness. I was told that Instructor Jia has recommended some students to the Mystics in the past, and that she might have wisdom that could set my mind at ease, one way or the other. They leave for Feldemar on some errand for the High King tonight, or we would not have needed so urgently to see you."

"Ah," he said gravely in response, his face falling. "That indeed seems a fine dilemma."

Theren's stomach seemed to turn itself inside out as she watched him, wondering what he was thinking. His mood had changed so dramatically that she feared he would not only send her away, but chastise Kalem and Lilith for bringing her to him, so she mumbled an apology while he rubbed at his eyes with his hands, clearly still considering.

"I believe that allowances can be made for past students to enter the grounds seeking wisdom from instructors to whom they are known, so I see no reason to deny your request," he declared, eventually. "However, I hope you will not mind if I insist on escorting you."

Feeling almost light-headed with relief, she thanked him profusely, as did Lilith, and the four of them fell in step behind him as he strode back towards the entrance to the Academy grounds. Kalem seemed almost buoyant with delight at this development, as though it was their greatest obstacle overcome already, but Theren had been put ill at ease by the dean's reaction. She did, however, feel her spirits lift just a little with the nostalgic sweetness of memory as they all stepped through the great front doors together for the first time in what felt like an eternity—though she also had to endure a particularly wide-eyed stare from door-warden, Mellie.

The ostentatious black marble floor glittered in the familiar way that she remembered under the tinted light spilling through the colored glass windows, but with everything else being so much the same, she felt even more out of place as one of the few there not wearing the standard-issue Academy robes. She felt the gaze of the other students keenly as they passed through the halls, and not wanting to draw any more attention to herself than was necessary, she stared firmly at the ground.

Dean Forredar attempted to make genial conversation as they walked behind him, asking Lilith and Kalem both about their studies, but it seemed that he, too, had noticed Theren's mood turning mournful.

"All students are called to leave the Academy at one time or another," he told her gently, stopping at a wide corridor bordered by arches that opened onto the gardens. "By all accounts your graduation would soon have been upon you, even had the events of the last year gone differently. In fact, several of your instructors expressed surprise that you had remained so long."

She shrugged, unable to meet his eyes. "It just seems that I am doomed to forever be as a ship at sea, tossed about on restless waves in a storm. I have never had a choice in—well, anything."

"The fates are ever thus," he responded, but he sounded more sympathetic than the dismissiveness she had expected. "I have seen my own share of storms. There is one piece of wisdom that I can give you, though you may do with it what you wish: try not to dismiss charity that is offered merely because it seems burdensome. I thought my appointment as dean was a grave mistake, a punishment and a leash together in one package, but though things have not been easy, I now feel that I have been set on this path for a reason. Someday you may be able to look at yourself and think the same."

"Do you think that she should take the Mystics' offer and leave the Seat? Leave us?" Lilith asked quietly, from just behind Theren's right shoulder, startling her.

The dean surveyed the two of them gravely for a few moments, and then sighed heavily. Birds twittered and chattered outside just beyond the arches, and the fitful breeze graced them with the sweet scent of flowering jasmine and orange blossoms, but the garden and its sunlit pleasures seemed a thousand leagues removed from where they stood. Kalem and Ebon both seemed to be trying to shuffle away awkwardly, as though they were simply nearby and not part of the conversation.

When at last the dean looked up at them again, his eyes were misty, veiled by faraway memories. "Only each of us knows our own strength, our own boundaries. I cannot tell you what you should do. I can say only that the two of you have already endured things beyond what most people might see in a lifetime. I cannot imagine that the foes of either distance or time would be a match for you both, not if you wished to face them together.

"But come, we must make haste if we are to reach Jia's office before the study period ends."

He set off once again, with Kalem and Ebon hurrying after him like geese riding on the slipstream of their forerunner, while Lilith and Theren followed slightly behind. Her cheeks burning with embarrassment, Theren wondered if the teachers often knew about what was going on in their students' love lives. She felt that she might have been more appreciative of his words if they did not suddenly make her feel like all of her emotions had been on display for everyone to see.

Lilith was silent, but Theren could sense her there, following close behind, the whole rest of the way to Instructor Jia's office.

"Have you known many Mystics, Dean Forredar?" Ebon asked as they approached the tall, plain brown door that was their goal. "They are not so common in Idris as in the other kingdoms, so all of my experience has been with those on the Seat."

The dean grunted in a way that seemed to be an unsuccessful attempt to sound non-committal. "I have known many fine Mystics in my time, some even that I counted among my family. I had not heard that they were so few in Idris, though knowing what I do of the family Drayden, I should not be surprised."

Ebon made a face at the dean's back as though he regretted mentioning it.

"It might be that in twenty years, the two of you will be reunited in Idris, Drayden patriarch and Mystic chancellor, free to cause as much havoc as you can as far away from Academy property as possible," Dean Forredar continued, dryly, and both Theren and Kalem laughed.

"Here we are at last."

The laughter on Theren's lips died instantly as the dean, having knocked quickly and not waited for a proper response, froze midway through the act of opening the door. It was not Jia who stood in her office, but instead a middle-aged, pale-skinned man with a close-cropped beard and greying black hair, a man who blanched in terror at the mere sight of Theren's face.

Dasko.

SIX

Instructor Dasko was a weremagic teacher chiefly associated with the higher-level students of that branch of magic, and for most of her schooling Theren had not given the man a second thought. Unlike many instructors, he had been kind and unassuming, never going out of his way to punish her despite her reputation as a troublemaker.

That had all been brought to an abrupt end during their attempts to stop the mastermind behind the murders at the Academy, when Dasko had had the misfortune to stumble across Theren and her friends at a crime scene that the killer had just fled. With all the evidence—including the fact that they now possessed a dangerous magical artifact that had been stolen from the Academy vaults—pointing to them as the culprits, Theren had panicked, and done something incredibly selfish, something unforgivable.

The Amulet of Kekhit, the artifact that they had found themselves in possession of at the time, had contained the power to grant wizards the strength of magestones. For mindmages, this meant unlocking a technique known as mindwyrd, where the wizard in question could force another's mind to direct them to move and act and think according to the mentalist's will. It was a monstrous crime, one that left a lasting effect on its victims as their minds struggled to reclaim control of themselves.

And in her foolish attempts at self-preservation, Theren had used mindwyrd on Dasko in order to make him forget that he had seen them that night. And again, when they had needed him to lie on their behalf. And again, and again, every time some new need had arisen. No matter how much she had wanted to stop, she had still done it.

She still woke sometimes from nightmares, haunted by the ghastly blank expression that had always crossed his face whenever she had used the mindwyrd. She could only imagine how bad it was for Dasko.

Self-loathing choked her, and she turned her head away in shame, feeling smaller than the tiny squeaking noise that Kalem had made upon seeing him. Behind her, she heard Lilith inhale sharply, and Ebon's face was plastered with an expression of horror.

"My mistake, my mistake," Dean Forredar muttered hurriedly, shooing them out of the doorway. "Wait over there, if you please."

He waved them towards a small alcove a short way away, equipped with a low table and several tall, padded chairs, and disappeared inside the office, shutting the door behind him. Numbly, Theren let Ebon practically push her down into one of the chairs, and rubbed at her eyes, half hoping that when she opened them this would all have turned out to be one long bad dream. She sighed, feeling ill, and feeling worse that she had the gall to feel sorry for herself after what she had put Dasko through.

A short while later, the door opened again, and after a brief moment of hesitation, Dasko left. He was no longer shaking, at least, but he walked in the complete opposite direction from them all, and held himself rigid, his shoulders hunched around his chin, as though unwilling to turn his body even slightly for fear of seeing her again.

"You had better come inside," the dean said wearily from the doorway.

They all filed into Instructor Jia's office, any levity they might have gained on the way there now fully drained from them. Dean Forredar quickly finished tidying some of the papers on her desk, which Dasko had made a mess of in his distress when the door had opened, and then turned to leave himself.

"I will go and seek Jia. It would be for the best if you remained in here while I am gone."

"That was ill luck," Kalem murmured, as they all found seats again.

Theren nodded mutely, wondering if the reaction from Instructor Jia would be any better.

"At least we were spared having to argue our way inside past Mellie," Ebon joked, trying to lighten the mood once more, but Theren just sighed.

Lilith reached over to take her hand once more as the time ebbed away. Theren grew gradually more and more agitated, twisting the hem of her shirt and tapping one of her feet against the floor as they waited, until Kalem's scowl at her fidgeting was so intense that she thought he might have turned her to stone had she been within his reach. Fortunately, she was saved the effort of having to try to bring herself under control when the door opened again, and Instructor Jia finally entered.

She swept into the room, pausing for a moment to acknowledge Theren with a cool glance of disapproval, and then went over to her desk to sit down, leafing through some paperwork.

"Instructor—" Ebon began, but subsided when Jia made an irritated tutting noise, not lifting her attention from her papers.

"Now," she said, after quite some time of reading,

putting down her work at last. "I hope you will understand that I am quite busy. What is it you wish to ask of me?"

Theren tried not to wince. The instructor was distinctly cooler and less friendly than she had been the last time that Theren had spoken to her, though she still maintained at least a façade of politeness. Theren knew in her heart that she should have expected this, that Instructor Jia's attitude was justified after Theren's actions, but she still had to struggle internally against her immediate instinct, which was to say something snide and then storm out the door.

That was always the easiest answer: to turn away, and run until the problem was so far behind you that it no longer mattered. A pity then that it seemed that there would be no outrunning either Imara or Ilya and her spear.

Theren took a deep, steadying breath before speaking, and clutched tightly at the arms of her chair to make sure that her body could not flee against her own wishes. "Instructor, it was a Mystic named Vivien who directed me to seek your advice."

The change in Jia's demeanor was instant, her eyes widening in what seemed to be pleased surprise. "Truly? It has been some time since last I saw her, though we do exchange letters as regularly as we can both manage. How did you come to meet her, for her to send you to me?"

"It is a long tale, and surely of no great interest at a

time like this," Theren muttered, fidgeting in her chair as she balked at the idea of explaining her childhood in Cabrus and her day spent in the Mystics' jail. "Suffice it to say that, when we spoke, she extended an offer to me to join the order."

"Ah, then you are very lucky indeed," Jia replied, a small smile lighting her face. "Vivien would likely never have given you a second glance if she did not think you worthy of her attention."

Theren frowned momentarily, not sure whether to take that as a positive or negative statement. "That is my dilemma, Instructor. You see, I am not yet sure whether it *is* lucky. I am hesitant to swear my life to the redcloaks, as I am sure you can understand, after . . . the events of the recent past."

Pursing her lips, the instructor leaned forwards a little in her seat, inspecting Theren. Her gaze was as piercing as ever, her small brown eyes scrutinizing Theren's face and taking in her dirty, stained clothes and the markings on her arms from the manacles. Theren examined her in turn, for lack of anything better to do, noting that her chestnut hair was greying slightly at the temples now, and that she seemed very tired, the dark circles around her eyes starkly visible against her pale skin.

"I have known Vivien for a very long time," Instructor Jia said quietly, apparently having found what she sought in her inspection. "She is a good woman, good and fair, and never afraid to do what must be done or say what must be said. If you had any fears about her personally, I hope I can lay them to rest. She will do you no harm, as long as you can resist escapades such as those you undertook here at the Academy."

Theren cleared her throat, trying to hide the shame she felt. "I do not think that will be a problem, Instructor. But she said that you might tell me what made you think that she should join the Mystics, if I asked."

"Ah," Jia responded, smiling broader this time. "Well, Vivien was always somewhat precocious during her schooling. She was charming enough to cultivate quite a large group of friends, including some among the instructors. She was quite famous for being a bender of the rules, always knowing how to twist them to get her way. I suppose she looked at you and saw some parallel between your situations. You have not quite the subtlety that she did, but I can see you fitting in a similar mold."

"So would you recommend to me that I should take their offer?" Theren pressed, wishing that any of this was making her feel any better.

Jia gave her another long look. "I would, yes, for three reasons. Firstly because you do not look as though you will have an easy time if you refuse, if the bruising on your wrists is anything to go by. And secondly because it is likely the best offer you will receive as far as careers go."

"And thirdly?" Theren asked, weakly.

"Thirdly, if there is one thing I have learned about you, it is that you are bold. Boldness is a quality that the Mystics—and the people whose lives they save—value highly."

The compliment surprised her. She had never thought of herself as bold. She might have said rash, or impulsive, or even reckless. "Bold" did sound nicer, though.

"Do you think it would truly be wise, Instructor Jia?" Lilith asked, gripping Theren's hand tightly. "Even after what we—what *she* went through at their hands?"

Theren could see the undisguised pity in the look that the instructor leveled at Lilith; Jia thought that Lilith was naïve, that such a thing should not matter, not when one's future was at stake.

"I do not think she will be asked to work alongside any of the order that she may have encountered previously," came the answer, eventually, once Jia had managed to formulate a response that she deemed neutral enough.

She seemed to realize that both Theren and Lilith could see through her attempt at obfuscation, however, because she sighed once again.

"Forgive me. I only wished to avoid giving you the idea that it would be easy. Like all those who serve the High King, the Mystics are often tested both physically and mentally. But if it is of any comfort to you, I believe that Vivien may be able to shield you from any . . . past acquaintances you might have made. She was ever the chaperone and protector of her friends during her time at the Academy. I would imagine that she might do the same for a new Mystic recruit in her care."

Theren and Lilith exchanged a glance, with Theren feeling relief wash away her tension for the first time since entering the office. "That would be welcome, if it were so."

"That does not mean you will be coddled, I hasten to add," Jia continued, somewhat more sharply. "Once you are of the order you will be counted as a woman grown, and part of adulthood is accepting the consequences of your actions, however unintended."

Theren bowed her head solemnly. "I understand, Instructor."

"Very well. Now, if you have no other questions, I do have work I need to see to."

They thanked her, standing up from their chairs, but paused when Jia held up a hand suddenly, as if remembering something.

"Instructor?"

She opened a drawer in her desk and sifted through some of the papers inside for a moment, before sighing in resignation. "If it is not too inconvenient, could I trouble you to deliver a message to Vivien for me? I do not have time to write a full response to her last letter, but please . . . bid her be safe, for my sake. And remind her to spend some time attending to her own concerns instead of jumping to please everyone else at the first opportunity, as she usually does."

Theren nodded wordlessly, wondering how Vivien would respond, and then hesitated at the door after the others exited, unsure as to whether they would need to be escorted as they had done on their way in.

"You can show yourselves out," Jia said, seemingly reading her mind, but then added, sternly, "as long as you avoid Instructor Dasko's classroom."

Ducking her head in humiliation again, Theren hurried out, not even thinking to close the door behind her.

SEVEN

"That could certainly have gone worse," Kalem said brightly, once they were all out in the hallway again.

Theren gave him a dark look. "I fail to see how."

"Ah, well, she has become very protective of Dasko since—well, you can imagine. I half expected her not to see us at all. Or for the dean to deny us entry. Getting the information we came for despite all of that seems like a victory of sorts, does it not?"

"The information was but the first step," Lilith countered gravely. "The greater task, the decision, remains."

Theren had to admit, though, even if only to herself, that the burden seemed lessened somewhat now that they were actively confronting it. The sunlight playing across the tapestries on the walls seemed brighter, and the atmosphere in the halls less oppressive; she was glad that they could leave at their own pace, because part of her wanted nothing more than to linger. She would have to try to make peace with the fact that she would likely never visit the Academy again once she passed beyond its walls this time.

There had not been time to say farewell when last she had left. It seemed a strange notion, saying farewell to a building, but it had been her home, more than anywhere else she had ever lived.

"It was good to see this place one more time," she said softly, without meaning to, and then pulled herself together as she noticed Ebon giving her a knowing look. "Even if it *is* nothing but a testament to the goldbags' complete lack of sense. I mean, marble floors? What a stupendous waste of coin."

He grinned at her. "I will pass your criticisms to Dean Forredar. I must hurry home for now, to let Adara know of all that has transpired so that she can stop worrying. Shall we meet back at that awful tavern when I am done?"

"No, come to my apartment," she replied, thinking. "Whatever I decide, it would be wise to gather my things while I am able to move freely through the city."

He nodded, clapped her on the shoulder genially,

and then set off in the direction of the entrance hall. Theren scanned the corridor briefly for instructors, and then turned back to Lilith and Kalem, hoping to delay their departure at least a little.

"Would you mind if we walked through the gardens before we leave? I have heard it said that fresh air is good for clear thinking, and there is scarcely a prettier stretch of open air on the Seat than in the Academy's gardens."

"Well, I—" Kalem's gaze focused past Theren, over her left shoulder. "I, um. Oh, no, I have just remembered. I have some books. To read. And such. I will see you both later."

He scurried away as fast as his legs could carry him, and Theren turned slowly to her left, finding Lilith standing at her shoulder once more, this time wearing an expression that occupied some space halfway between the qualities of "impish" and "smug."

"And what of you, Mistress Yerrin?" she asked, unable to keep the grin from her face.

"I could do with some sun," Lilith replied, smiling warmly.

"You seem in a better mood than I have seen in some time," Theren noted, as they wandered leisurely along one of the paths, tall golden sunflowers rustling gently in the breeze beside them.

"As do you."

"I have missed this place," she admitted, kicking at the gravel pathway. "The classes not so much, but I called the Academy home for . . . most of the years I care to remember."

"I am sorry that you must leave it behind," Lilith said, sighing.

Theren shrugged, though she herself was thinking much the same thing. "There will be other gardens. I am sure that the flowers will grow just as nicely in Calentin."

Lilith turned to face her, curious. "Calentin?"

Theren licked her lips nervously, cursing herself for letting mention of her silly fantasy slip out. "Oh, I—it is nothing. Only I considered, just as an option you understand, that if I could find an opportunity to escape, Calentin might be far enough away to deter Imara and her guards from pursuing me. And that you might visit me, if you were of a mind. With the others, if you wished."

"That is a lot of 'ifs' and 'mights' for a plan," Lilith teased playfully, but Theren could summon no pithy remark with which to reply.

Her heart thumped in her ears, louder than the birdsong and the lazy buzzing of the fat bees that were taking their own stroll through the gardens. She remembered—it seemed like a lifetime ago—when they had last been this at ease with one another, lying on the floor of the bell tower watching the moons and holding hands, or spending their afternoons in the library, Theren asleep with her head in Lilith's lap in a corner behind piles of books.

Emboldened by Lilith's response, she angled herself in closer as they walked, until they were side by side, shoulders grazing against each other. "I would have asked you outright to come with me to Calentin, but I fear I am rather taken with the dean's suggestion of finding out how much of Idris Ebon and I can wreak havoc on together. When I have the invitations prepared, you will be the first to know."

The giggle this elicited was extremely infectious, and Theren had to fight hard to keep herself from grinning inanely as Lilith reached down and took her hand again.

"I am glad to hear it."

Unfortunately, they soon reached the other end of the garden where it folded back into the arched wing of the Academy, their sunny walk apparently at an end. Theren hesitated, not wanting to let go just yet, but after a moment Lilith set off inside, pulling Theren after her.

"Come. Let us visit the bell tower one last time before you must go."

They threaded their way through the maze of corridors, up flights of stairs and past classrooms, giggling with conspiratorial glee as they avoided instructors, though Theren did not think that they would really have been chastised had they been seen. She unlocked the door to the tower easily using the same key trick she had tried on her manacles, and they slipped inside, rushing up the long spiral staircase to the top since they knew they would have to be gone by the next bell.

Panting with the exertion, Theren took a few moments to catch her breath, surveying the view. It was as spectacular as ever, though she had rarely had the chance to see it in daylight; from up here even the Academy itself looked small, squatting like a black beetle in the midst of the ivory-colored stone that the rest of the High King's Seat favored. That was one thing she had always loved about this tower: being able to see over the Academy's walls. It was strange to think that she had once treasured the idea of being able to reach the outside world, and here she was now, wishing she could remain within.

Lilith came to stand beside her, leaning her hands on the guardrail, and closed her eyes, breathing deeply as if to savor the moment. They had stood here together a thousand times before, and now the memories hung in the air like ghosts around them, memories of passion and comfort that seemed both devastatingly far away and tantalizingly near.

"Do you have any idea yet what path you will choose?" Lilith asked her, eyes still closed.

Theren turned to face her, watching her intently. Her voice was neutral, and seemingly not in a forced way, but as though she truly would accept either decision. Both options pained Theren, and in different ways, so she was glad at least that Lilith would not judge her for whichever she eventually chose. And though the thought of the Mystics still made her skin crawl, some part of her felt the need to continually remind herself that her efforts to evade Imara had come to naught in the end, even after all the effort she had spent. She was already inside the cage that she had feared for so long, just waiting for the door to close. It nagged at her, gnawing on her confidence and causing her to want to look over her shoulder for pursuers even now, despite knowing that she was safe until the evening.

"I think I could almost accept going with the redcloaks, if not for what they have done to you," she said eventually, though the words felt heavy and wrong to say out loud.

Lilith opened her eyes, looking shocked. "Me? I would think you would worry more about what they have done to *you*, since it is you who would be working with them. I will not be faced with the memory of them each day."

"They did not attend to me so determinedly as they did you," Theren replied, darkly. "I bear them far more ill will over your injuries than mine. And unlike me, *you* were innocent. No law can justify their actions against you, and none should."

Lilith reached out and touched Theren's cheek softly, surprising her. "You asked me before if I thought this was a betrayal, but I have no stake in this to feel betrayed over. Either way you will leave the Seat, and my grief is for that, above all the other misfortunes. But if you must go, I would wish you safe, not surrounded by darkness."

"I fear darkness lies in both directions," Theren muttered, the image of the cage in which she was trapped once again surfacing in her mind.

Lilith shook her head stubbornly. "Not even the High King herself would have the right to ask Dasko to work alongside you every day after what happened to him. By the same logic, no one should be able to ask you to work alongside those who wronged you."

"I fear you do your argument no favors by bringing up my crimes against Dasko," Theren countered, amused, and Lilith fixed her with a cool glare, removing her hand.

"You saved many lives when you stopped Isra, which you could not have done otherwise," she insisted. "If the instructors had been less stubborn, or the dean had been less suspicious of Ebon, it might not have been necessary. But as it was, there was no other way to stop the murders. And what do the Mystics have to show for their actions? A few night's sadistic pleasure, at the utmost."

She took a few steps away, looking frustrated, and Theren leaned an elbow on the guardrail, still watching her. It was a strange feeling, hearing Lilith speak up on her behalf once again, after all this time. Stranger still that she was being defended from her own accusations.

"I wish I saw myself the way you do," she said quietly, after a long pause.

Lilith seemed to soften straightaway, coming back over towards her. "I have known that ache before. Often did I wish, after we . . . parted company, that I was able to see in myself the way I should have been, the version of me that you saw."

"Sometimes I wish I had never done it," Theren managed to say, her voice thick with emotion as she admitted what was close to her greatest secret, something she had never told anybody before. "I wish I had never left you."

"Not I," Lilith answered, smiling sadly. "I might never have changed if you had stayed."

She closed what little distance between them as remained, wrapping her small arms around Theren's waist in an embrace, and Theren clung to her tightly, almost afraid to let go.

"Was it hard?" she asked, softly, as they remained in each other's arms, neither of them willing to draw apart. "Changing? Believing in yourself again?"

Lilith shivered against her, burying her face in Theren's neck. "It was agony. But then I was only brave enough to try after the Mystics—after everything was stripped away from me. I am certain you can do it more easily."

Theren made a doubtful noise, not wanting to contradict her, and released her grip when Lilith pulled away, though she moved only just far enough apart for them to be able to meet each other's gaze.

"I am *certain*, if for no other reason than I will nag

you until it is done," she teased, her eyes shining, and Theren grinned again.

"Nag? Why with a sweet voice such as yours, I would not even call it . . ."

She had instinctively reached up to cup Lilith's face in her hands, as though they had not just spent all that time apart. Breathless, she met Lilith's eyes for a few moments, feeling dazzled by the warmth of the sun and the cool breeze that ruffled their hair as they stood there, and every other sensation that imprinted itself on her mind in that moment, until she could resist no more, leaning into the kiss they both craved.

She was dimly aware of Lilith's hands in her hair, and of the guardrail against her hip, but everything else was drowned out, washed away by more important things.

By the time they had both surfaced from that wave of passion, Theren feared that it was getting perilously close to the time for the next bell. She rubbed her nose against Lilith's, reluctant to let go, but she realized in that moment that she had made her decision.

"I knew in my heart which choice I had to make, right from the beginning," she said softly, and Lilith raised her eyebrows questioningly. "It was always the only choice. I must become a Mystic, but . . . I kept telling myself that I could remain on the Seat, so that I could stay with you. If only they were not sailing for Feldemar, darkness take them."

"You heard the dean earlier," Lilith replied softly,

though her voice was sad. "What hope does distance have against us? It is the least of our foes thus far."

Theren gazed at her longingly for a moment, wishing that she could believe those words. "I suppose they will have parchment in their garrisons, for writing letters."

"Exactly," Lilith replied, making an effort to smile, and kissed her again.

As they drew apart, something seemed to change in Lilith's eyes, like a spark being kindled. Almost as soon as Theren noticed it, however, it disappeared, and she wondered what Lilith was thinking about. Whatever mote of hope it might have been that had crossed her mind, Theren thought she would feel better for hearing it.

"What is it?" she asked, but Lilith shook her head, though her smile seemed more genuine this time.

"We should go and give them your answer at once," she replied, as she meticulously straightened her dress. "Who knows what preparations they might ask of you? It would not do to start our road to Calentin by being too late for you to enlist."

"I fear we may have to race to avoid being discovered, as well," Theren added, feeling resignation settle on her shoulders like a dull, well-worn coat. "The next bell must be nearly upon us, and many teachers will soon be out in the halls."

"We have never been caught yet," Lilith answered, laughing, and Theren marveled at the sound as they descended the stairs, marbled golden sunlight shining around them where it reflected down off the bell.

She held onto that laugh, in her mind, like an anchor to keep herself steady. Despite everything, it seemed that there was some light left in the darkness after all.

EIGHT

"Vivien!"

Not looking up from the letter she was writing despite Ilya looming over her, Vivien made a small, polite, but uninterested noise of acknowledgment. It had the intended effect, causing Ilya to heave an angry sigh and fold her arms.

"Vivien, why is the little wizard girl that I ran down yesterday now in the entrance hall asking to speak with you?"

That caused her to take notice, setting down her quill and turning her attention to the larger woman.

She had not expected Theren back so quickly; it was only just gone midday.

"I have extended her an offer to join our forces," she explained mildly, aiming to sound as though this were common knowledge, and she was not sure why Ilya had forgotten it.

"You *what*?" The incredulous demand was accompanied by an angry flare of nostrils, and a bullish stare.

Vivien smiled. "Come now. You do not truly believe her to be dangerous, surely. My contacts in Cabrus did not have kind things to say about her patron, this Imara, who set you on her trail, even before this business came up."

"I do not care a whit for what your contacts think," Ilya shot back, stamping a foot angrily. "I serve the King's law! We all do!"

"Ah, of course," Vivien replied, her smile turning even sweeter. "I do so admire your dedication to Her Majesty, Ilya. But then tell me: what was the latest edict from Lord-Chancellor Konnel, as told to her by the High King herself?"

Ilya leveled a wrathful glare at her that she wholly ignored, unfazed. Though she was a tempestuous woman, Vivien knew that Ilya would never resort to violence, especially not against a fellow Mystic. Why would she need to, when she could simply do enough damage by following the law?

Ilya was one of the old guard in the Mystic order,

the traditionalists who believed firmly that the only way to truly serve the people of the nine lands was through fanatical service to the High King and rigid adherence to her laws. There was no room for nuance in their approach; Theren was legally bound to serve her patron, and so therefore back she should go, in Ilya's mind. And yet, given what Vivien had heard about Imara, that would be neither kind to the girl nor the most useful outcome to the High King, not when they were mustering troops in the northern kingdoms.

But Ilya's belief, it seemed, was that compromise was a sign of weakness. Let the High King's law decide every aspect of every life, as though any one person's mandates could truly solve every problem.

For all Vivien's ability to ferret out the strings of schemes and intrigue in which her fellow Mystics partook, she had somehow never been able to find anything on Ilya. Which made it even more puzzling—and frustrating—to her that, despite their having served for the same amount of time with roughly the same amount of success in their endeavors, Ilya was being considered for a promotion to the rank of captain, while Vivien was not. She had borne a similar indignity several years ago with a man named Jordel, and though he was more intelligent than Ilya, Vivien still did not know why she herself had been overlooked.

Originally, she had suspected that it was because she was a mage, but she had now begun to realize that those who rose to any real rank of command in the order were often handpicked for their devotion to the High King above all other qualities.

And so, wishing to conclude her business with Theren and return to her letter, Vivien brought to bear the one weapon she had that was certain to cow Ilya: the words of the High King herself.

"It may be that you have forgotten," Vivien suggested kindly, when Ilya did not answer her question about the Lord-Chancellor's last edict. "You have been so very busy, hunting down young girls. I will remind you! By order of High King Enalyn, in light of the war, we are to expand our recruitment efforts."

"I know it!" Ilya retorted, furious now. "I am merely trying to discern what you saw in a malnourished stray that made you think she was worthy of joining the order! She did not even put up a fight when I apprehended her, only tried to run!"

Vivien's lips spread into a wide grin despite her efforts. "Now your contention is that she would not fight an agent of the High King? How very contradictory of you."

Ilya threw her hands in the air and stormed out of the room, muttering under her breath. Vivien, for her part, tidied away her things fastidiously, smiling to herself, and went to the entrance hall to greet the order's newest recruit.

To her surprise, Theren was not alone. Hovering anxiously at her side was a waifish, black-skinned girl dressed in green, a girl whom Vivien recognized as

Lilith of the family Yerrin. The two stood together in the foyer, occasionally glaring at any of the younger Mystics who happened to pass too close, and Vivien noted the familiarity between them. The Yerrin spokesperson that she had made inquiries with had skirted around the topic of what exactly Theren meant to the family, so it was both amusing and a little disappointing to Vivien to have the answer announced so clearly to her here, watching the two young women trying to hold hands surreptitiously.

She called out to them and watched as they swiveled in unison to face her, both so young and frail-looking. She thought, however, as she had in the prison cell, that she could see something dark and hard behind Theren's eyes, like a shard of flint, while the Yerrin girl could barely contain the fire behind hers.

Vivien waved them over, and they crossed the hall warily, as if afraid that they would be attacked at any moment.

"Welcome back!" she said, warmly, hoping to put them at ease. "And welcome to your friend, as well."

"I am Lilith," the Yerrin girl declared defiantly, taking a step forwards, obviously not recognizing the Mystic. "Lilith of the family Yerrin. I have come to ensure her safety."

"I assure you, that is unnecessary," Vivien replied smoothly, motioning with one hand towards the room she had been using as an office. "Please, come this way."

She shepherded them inside, closing the door to

block out the bustle of the garrison. It was small and cramped and had never been meant as an office, but it had a table in it that was not rickety, which was as close to ideal as she had been able to find in this place. On the corner of the table, weighted down by the chancellor's crimson wax seal that Vivien had taken the liberty of acquiring while Theren was in the city, was a notice of enlistment.

"You need but sign your name, and you will belong to the order," she said, pushing the document towards the two girls. "You may read it first, of course."

Theren snatched up the notice suspiciously, appearing to read through it, while Lilith looked on over her shoulder. "Do all redcloaks have to sign these?"

Vivien smiled, amused by the derisive name. "Indeed we do. There is also an oath that must be sworn before a chancellor, but there will be no time here upon the Seat. You will take it in Feldemar, and if any question the legitimacy of your title as a Mystic, that document will serve as proof enough until you can take your badge. Do not lose it."

Theren gave her a startled look, and handled the parchment more carefully after that.

"It all seems to be in order," she grated eventually, every syllable enunciated slowly, as though she was hoping for something to happen that would give her a chance to turn back.

Though she was not unsympathetic to the girl's plight, Vivien nonetheless handed her a quill with which to make her signature. She needed the matter settled as quickly as possible, regardless of everyone's feelings. It would have been easier had the order not been mobilizing for the war in northern Dulmun—but the fates were ever impatient and capricious. Vivien herself would have wished to return to her hometown of Wellmont, which was yet to recover fully from the recent attack it had suffered at Dorsea's hands, but such was not to be. Both she and Theren had appointments to keep in Feldemar, or so it seemed.

"Wait!" Lilith interjected, just as Theren was about to sign.

Theren, Vivien was interested to see, seemed just as confused by Lilith's interruption as she was.

"Do not sign that yet!" Lilith commanded, and Theren immediately put the quill down.

"Is there a problem?" Vivien asked mildly.

"She will not go with you unless you agree to take me as well," Lilith responded, raising her chin boldly. "*Not* as one of you, of course. But if you travel to Feldemar, you will be within reach of many strongholds of my family. And I do not think I need to remind you of how . . . displeased the family Yerrin has been with the redcloaks of late."

"What of it?" Vivien asked, narrowing her eyes.

"You know what the family Yerrin does when it is displeased," Lilith answered, grinning triumphantly. "Would you rather face probing merchants sent to spy on your activities to ensure you mean no harm to our business and heightening prices on your supplies due to ill will, or simply bring me with you to act as a liaison? I will be their eyes on your activities, and in doing so, be your order's shield from their mistrust."

Vivien inspected the girl's face thoroughly, looking for some sign of a bluff, but she did not find it. She drummed her fingers on the edge of her table, thoughts racing furiously. It was true that the family Yerrin had been much less accommodating of late, due to what seemed to be a confluence of many reasons. Though war had not quite yet come to Feldemar, it shared borders with both Dulmun and Dorsea, and King Alim was said to be asking much of the nobles and richer merchant families in his kingdom in an attempt to be prepared, should fighting actually break out. And now the Mystics would ride to reinforce their own strongholds in the region, rather than help Feldemar's troops.

She admitted to herself that she could see how people in the region might feel abandoned by the High King, especially since the Mystics would be purchasing food grown on their farms, food that their own soldiers might have needed. And she would not have put it past the family Yerrin to conduct the exact kind of espionage that Lilith was threatening, especially if they felt cornered.

Theren, meanwhile, was gaping in shock, clearly taken completely by surprise. That at least meant that this whole situation had not been a Yerrin trap in order to plant Lilith within their ranks, which meant therefore that the girl could instead be an incredibly useful bargaining chip with the family if ever one was needed.

After a long pause, Vivien spoke. "I see the logic in what you have said, and I am inclined to agree."

She was gratified to see the eyes of both girls light up like dancing fireflies as they grabbed at each other's arms in glee.

"But," she insisted, cutting through their revelry, "I can only guarantee you passage to the Mystic fortress of Ammon. Once there, you will have to convince the chancellor in command to allow you to stay. Once you are inside the fortress, his word is law. But I believe that you make good points about your family, so he may welcome you gladly. He may also want nothing to do with you, but if so, I am certain he will convey you either to your family's holdings in Feldemar or back to the Seat."

The defiant look returned to Lilith's face. "I am sure either I or my family will convince this chancellor that my presence will be helpful."

Vivien resisted the urge to laugh. They were both so young, so unaware of how the real world worked outside their schooling. It would almost be a shame to watch them realize how things truly were and how naïve they had been all this time.

Instead she smiled more gently, so as not to set them on edge. "I do not doubt it. But there remains the matter of the signature?"

Not long later the two girls hurried out of the garrison, chattering excitedly and practically dancing with glee. Vivien, on the other hand, discarded her previous letter and began drawing up a new, far more important one to her Yerrin contact in the city, wondering at the great boon that had just fallen into her lap. This trip to Feldemar suddenly seemed as though it would be more interesting than she had ever dared dream.

NINE

"And I shall need to cancel all the reservations I hold with inns around the city as well," Lilith was saying, as she bustled around Theren's apartment, picking up items and examining them to decide whether or not they should be packed.

Theren made a vague noise of agreement, though truthfully her mind was leagues away, her thoughts still somewhere in Feldemar. In her hands, she turned over the notice of enlistment that she had signed, a worryingly flimsy piece of paper for something that would apparently decide the course of her entire future.

"Theren? Theren!"

She looked up, finally shocked out of her contemplation, as Lilith clicked her fingers to get Theren's attention.

"Forgive me, I was just . . . thinking."

"Are you having second thoughts?" Lilith frowned, concerned, but Theren shook her head.

"It all just seems so unreal. Would you have imagined yesterday that this was where we would be now? It feels like an Elf-tale, only everything seems to be going well, which worries me even more."

Lilith came over and placed a hand on her cheek, her fingers cool and calming. "It seems time that something in your life went well, my dear. You shall have to get used to it, or at the very least appreciate it while you have it."

Theren grinned as she nuzzled against her hand. "It may well be that it will feel less like a cunning trick when we ride into the war and things become terrible again. We shall see. But in the meantime, I will try this 'appreciation' you speak of."

"You should," Lilith retorted, but smiled coquettishly.

Theren had just slid a hand around Lilith's waist when a familiar creak told them the downstairs door into the apartment was being opened, followed by footsteps clomping up the stairs. They both sighed disappointedly.

Theren swung the door open midway through Ebon conducting their special coded knock, shocking him, but it was—she felt her heart leap with a small burst of excitement as the thought occurred to her—entirely unnecessary now. Imara herself could have walked into the building, and the notice of enlistment would have been enough to send her packing. Theren hoped it would not come to that, however, since the day had been overwhelming enough already.

"Come in," she told him, seeing that Kalem was behind him on the stairs as well.

The two boys entered dutifully, both looking on in mild bewilderment at Lilith, who was still taking things down off shelves and packing them into one of two trunks.

"You have reached a decision, I take it?" Ebon looked at her curiously as he removed his cloak.

"There was only ever one real option to take," Theren answered wryly, but she indicated the enlistment notice still in her hand. "I am now an agent of the High King, or will be, when I am sworn in at the stronghold in Feldemar."

"This is wondrous news!" Kalem clapped his hands excitedly, but then stopped abruptly, struck by some realization. "But—does this mean—?"

"Yes, I am leaving the Seat," she replied, carefully rolling up her documentation and placing it on a table nearby. "Or rather, we both are. Lilith somehow managed to convince them that the family Yerrin would be very upset if she was not brought along as well."

Lilith snorted, though her voice did sound smug when next she spoke. "There are those in the redcloaks who would jump off a bridge if it seemed it would please my family. It was a small task."

"You might have told me first," Theren shot back, amused. "I thought I had gone there to sign my life away. I almost fled, twice!"

Lilith came over and patted her on the cheek again, smiling sweetly. "And miss seeing the look on your face? Never."

Kalem's small brown eyes had immediately glistened with tears upon hearing the news, and he now ran over and hugged them each in turn.

"I—I cannot believe that you are—that you will be so far away! How can they—But you must—Oh, I will miss both of you!"

Lilith looked shocked to be included in his affection, and even more so at his embrace, but Theren patted him on the head fondly, touched by his words. In contrast to Kalem, Ebon was more subdued, his expression a combination of surprise, wonderment, and regret all at once.

"When do you leave?" he asked brightly, obviously trying to force himself to appear more cheerful than he felt.

"Tonight," Lilith responded, shaking her head. "I have so much to do, but they expect us there by sunset! I may have to leave instructions."

Kalem gasped. "Tonight? Truly? I had not thought

all the Mystics would sail at once! You cannot be gone by tomorrow! Will we even get a chance to say farewell?"

The shock was great enough to cause his tears to stop, leaving him gaping in horrified astonishment, and Theren felt a lump rise in her throat as he spoke. For the first time, the reality of having to leave her friends began to sink in. There would be no more time spent together in the mornings here at the apartment, no more trips to Ebon's family estate in the city . . . not even laughing at the two boys as they turned up their noses at the Crimson Jib's food.

"Well," Theren began, and then cleared her throat, trying to keep her voice from cracking. "Well, you are here now, are you not?"

"This is hardly a proper farewell!" Kalem wailed, hugging her again.

She scowled over his head, not just because her bruises still pained her, but also in an attempt to stop tears from springing to her own eyes.

"I hardly think you need to worry," she told him, gruffly. "I shall write to you if you wish, when I think of you. Whenever I see overlarge stacks of books and am reminded of your face behind them, for example."

"Oh, yes! Please write! You must tell us all about Feldemar!" he bubbled, caught up in the emotion.

"Kalem is right, though," Ebon interrupted, moving aside for Lilith to pass with one of the trunks. "We *should* have a proper farewell. We could fetch Adara and go down into the city, have a proper celebration for your newfound freedom from your patron!"

"Oh, yes, a party!" Lilith cooed, looking more excited than Theren had seen her in a long while. "I still have so much to do, but if you give me a few hours, we could all meet up at a tavern in the city?"

"I hardly think that I will make a good impression on my new colleagues if I show up to the harbor drunk," Theren pointed out, sardonically.

"Oh, hush," Lilith teased, obviously already set on the idea. "Only enlisted for an hour and already you have turned into a stick in the mud! You can refrain from drinking if it bothers you so much. They will *have* to take me, whether drunken or no."

"You can at least eat," Ebon added, amused. "I am sure the rations the Mystics will feed you will pale in comparison to the food available here on the Seat. You should savor good meals while you still have them!"

For the second time in less than an hour, Theren had been encouraged to throw herself into the appreciation of what she already possessed. In some ways that frightened her, as though both Lilith and Ebon feared that she might lose it all at any moment—and they would have been within their rights to do so, given where she was traveling to and what her new profession would be. But it was also comforting, this knowledge that the people in her life truly wanted to be there.

"I am rather hungry," she admitted eventually.

Kalem wrinkled his nose. "Not that awful sailors' tavern, though. Anywhere else would be better!"

"Well, now that I no longer need to hide, we can go wherever you would like, my picky young friend," Theren told him, grinning. "As long as it is your coin that will pay the innkeeper."

He grimaced at the thought. "Suddenly I do not miss you quite so much."

Ebon, who had up until that point been watching Lilith folding clothes, suddenly stood up straighter, as though he had just remembered something. He came over and hugged Theren, kissing her on both cheeks as was the Idrisian custom, and hurriedly collected his cloak.

"Well, that is settled then!" he said, pulling it around his shoulders. "I must go and find Adara. What say we meet at the Silver Stag, where I brought you all to meet her first? In several hours, did you say, Lilith?"

"Yes, I have to speak with my instructors at the Academy still to formally request a leave of—"

"I shall see you all then!" he called out, as he fairly bolted down the stairs and out the door.

"Do you think he knows that he is as subtle as a battering ram?" Lilith asked, dryly, and Kalem snorted in amusement.

"It is a pity we did not bring him to the Mystics as well, that they might deploy him against Dulmun," Theren added, and they all dissolved into laughter.

On the top floor of the Silver Stag inn, alongside its most luxurious rooms, the proprietors had seen fit to have several private dining areas installed. They mostly lay unused during the winter months, because they were open to the sky, set out on balconies framed with trellises of delicate climbing roses and honeysuckle vines to ensure privacy. But now, in summer, they were highly sought after, especially by travelers from Idris or Wavemount where dining in the open air was considerably more common due to the climate.

Theren could not even begin to imagine how much coin Ebon and his lover Adara must have offered the staff in order to secure the use of one of them that afternoon.

The food, she did have to admit, was entirely worth it, with a rich spread of crisp meats and roasted vegetables, soft Idrisian flatbread, and spicy stew from Feldemar that made everyone's mouths burn, followed by a sumptuous array of candied fruit and nuts from Calentin for dessert. There was nowhere in all of the nine lands, the tavern master Canda assured them smoothly, that could procure such a varied banquet of foods from so many different cultures.

She thought about this as they all lay around on the balcony, bellies groaning under the weight of all the food they had eaten. She realized that she did not truly know much about anywhere else in all of Underrealm; even Selvan, where she had lived as a child, was a distant memory to her, just dirty streets and high walls and uncaring adults busy with their own concerns. She had a fleeting wish to see as much of it as possible, although she would prefer to only visit Hedgemond in the summer, being no great fan of frigid winters.

She wondered briefly if her time with the Mystics would take her all over the nine kingdoms, for it was often said that the redcloaks traveled far and wide dispensing the King's justice. It seemed possible, but so did being mired in Feldemar for as many years as it took the High King's armies to defeat Dulmun. The scope of possibilities that her future might hold had been widened beyond what she had ever dreamed, but also narrowed immeasurably by her newfound duty.

If she was lucky, she thought, that duty might bring her back to the High King's Seat someday, to these cream-colored buildings that glowed in the light of the setting sun and the ubiquitous smell of the sea and the views of the palace in the distance, to this place that was almost all that she had ever known.

"I feel I have eaten nearly my own weight in chestnuts." Kalem moaned and clutched at his stomach, curling up in a ball. "You will need to roll me home, for I fear I cannot walk."

Theren laughed, but in truth she, too, was feeling extremely full. "I hope you will not bounce too many times down the stairs."

They had spent the time talking and laughing, occasionally busying themselves with food when the conversation threatened to focus too much on the inevitable parting that was to come. She had felt tears spring into her eyes often, and was glad that her reaction to the peppery Feldemarian food made her eyes water enough to hide that fact. After all, she had a reputation to maintain.

She could see Lilith glancing at the skyline every now and then, obviously judging the time and how long they had before they would have to leave. So, it seemed, did Adara, since she eventually took pity on them all and stood, being the one to call their meal to a close when no one else was willing.

Laying her fine, brown hands upon Kalem's shoulders, Adara helped him to struggle to his feet. "Come, young lord. You and I, and mistress Yerrin, shall go and settle our account with the tavern master. I believe that Ebon has something he wishes to speak with Theren about in private."

Lilith raised her eyebrows at Theren, who shrugged. Kalem, still complaining, stumbled his way to the stairwell at Adara's side, and Lilith joined them, while Ebon came over to sit beside her, the two of them looking out over the city.

"I wish you all the best with the Mystics," he said morosely, looking at the ground, and she nudged him gently with an elbow, though his tone of voice made her wish for more spicy food.

"Sky above, Ebon, you have been mysterious and mournful all day. What is the matter?"

"Other than you leaving?" he pointed out, dryly, and she shrugged again.

"It just seems more than that. Do you think I have made a mistake?"

"No, not at all." He paused, looking away for a moment before once again meeting her eyes. "But I fear I have made many. Some that led to this. I did not think . . . I feel shame that my wrongdoings have set you on this path, when it is so perilous. Especially given what you have already endured."

She stared at him for a moment and then sighed. "I will carry the weight of my own actions, Ebon. You have enough to deal with without punishing yourself over me as well."

He smiled, but shook his head. "I knew you would say that. I only hope you will be safe. Promise me that you will write, even if only to complain?"

"Did you really think that I would not have written you letters detailing my complaints about my new life?" A grin softened her retort. "I expect I shall begin drafting one several heartbeats after I board the ship for Feldemar. I have never liked ships."

He laughed, but his eyes were still sad. "I just . . . hope there will be good in your new life also. I hope you make many new friends, even though I would not wish you to forget us."

She snorted. "I hardly think I will fit in with the redcloaks."

"Ah, but remember you did not think you would fit in with us, either." He chuckled, and she spread her hands helplessly.

"It is hardly my fault that you and Kalem would not leave me alone!"

He laughed again, more genuine this time. "I have something for you."

From inside the small satchel he had brought with him, he pulled out a thick bundle wrapped in plain brown paper. She took it curiously, trying to discern what it might be through the wrapping, and thought that it had the weight and texture of something made from cloth.

"I hope you like it," he continued, anxiously. "I did not know what to do with the idea I had, so Adara picked the style of it."

She paused in unwrapping the paper to smile at him. "Was this why you dashed out of my apartment earlier? You did not have to get me anything, truly."

She gasped as she removed the last of the paper, awestruck. It was a cloak, a red cloak like all those in the order wore. But she had rarely seen a cloak so fine as this one, and especially not on a Mystic, though differing styles and materials were common enough. It was made of a heavy fabric, almost like canvas, but of such fine cut that she knew it must have been expensive. Strangely, it seemed to be not quite as wide as she would have expected for its length, and though it had a buttoned sleeve for an armhole, there was only one.

"It is for dueling, the tailor said," Ebon explained, holding it up to show how it should hang. "The sword arm is kept free, but the heavy cloth around the other can be used to catch a blade or redirect it, in imitation of a shield. I thought if you should see any fighting, that it might be of assistance."

She stood up and struggled into it, fumbling with setting the collar comfortably and fastening the tie that would keep it in place. It felt oddly heavy at first, and it would likely not be much use as a warm traveling cloak, but it was almost regal in how much it swayed and flourished when she moved.

"Let us hope that the enemies will not target me first, out of jealousy for my excellent sense of fashion." She grinned once more as she swished the cape around dramatically, and he sighed in exasperation and rolled his eyes.

"If you do not like it—"

"It is a marvelous gift," she interrupted, relenting, and then hugged him. "Truly. I will wear it in honor of you and Kalem, and Adara. It is perfect."

"This seemed more practical than having an entire suit of armor forged for you," he joked as they broke apart, and she smiled once more.

"I will be fine, Ebon. Remember to take care of yourself as well, wherever your mission with Dean Forredar will take you."

He made a face. "So far it has led only to libraries. But I will watch for particularly vicious dust mites, if that will set your heart at ease."

She laughed, thinking that it would be just Ebon's

luck to discover the world's only dangerous dust mites, as the others returned. Lilith gazed in wonder at the cloak, as did Kalem, while Adara clasped Theren's hands fondly and kissed her on both cheeks, smiling.

"I fear it is now time for us to leave," Theren said, smiling sadly as she turned to look at the view of the Seat in all its sunlit splendor, just one last time.

TEN

Though the late afternoon was still balmy from the heat of the sun, the breeze blowing in off the sea was uncommonly cold as Theren and the others made their way down to the pier where they had been told to meet Vivien. It seemed an ill omen, but Kalem assured her that the sea was often thus, and that cold air would mean stronger winds, which would make their journey shorter. She perked up a bit at the idea of that, not keen to spend more than a week trapped on board a floating death trap, but none of the sailors seemed to share Kalem's optimism.

"They certainly seem a dour lot," Ebon noted, as if reading her mind, as they passed a group of dockhands loading weapons onto one of the ships.

"They are afraid," Adara explained softly, as they stood aside to let a group of men struggle past, carrying a large, heavy crate. "Many sailors from Selvan were contracted to carry the Mystics to Feldemar, when Dulmun even now raids the Selvan coast to the east. Most wish to return and defend their homes."

Kalem raised an eyebrow at her. "I did not know that you were so well informed on matters of the war, Adara."

The sly smile she gave him in return made Theren laugh. "Why, young lord, I did not think I would have to educate you on the habits of sailors and soldiers. Many consider the Guild of Lovers a first stop in any town they visit."

He muttered something inaudible, cheeks turning bright red with embarrassment, and pulled the hood of his cloak up to hide his face.

They passed by long, wide ships into which the deckhands were loading horses, having to coax the animals gently to get them to put hooves to the wooden ramps, and smaller ships with fewer sails that appeared to be for scouting ahead of the rest of the fleet. All around them, members of the order scurried about on errands with a strange kind of shared zeal, like ants in a nest; Theren could not imagine how chaotic it would be disembarking, once they all reached Feldemar.

They eventually found Vivien standing only a few berths from the far end of the harbor, where they were sheltered somewhat from the chill of the cold sea air by the rocky face of this end of the inlet. She smiled brightly at their approach, her cheer a stark contrast to the rest of the Mystics, and waved at a nearby dockhand to take their luggage from them.

Theren's stomach lurched once more as she realized that this was it. Some of the ships, particularly the smaller ones, were already making headway, the wind billowing in their sails and the sailors sounding their horns as they made their departure. Vivien gave her a knowing look and then took her leave, disappearing in the direction of the gangplank.

"Well," Theren said, turning to face her friends. "I suppose this is farewell."

Kalem dashed forwards to hug her once more, his bottom lip trembling heavily as tears glistened in his eyes. "Take care of yourselves."

She mustered a smirk as she ruffled his hair. "Considering all that has happened since we met, I think it would be fair to say the same to you."

"At least I do not seek out trouble deliberately!" he countered, somehow managing to sniffle and look affronted at the same time.

Adara, smiling sadly, hugged Theren somewhat more gently, and then kissed her again on each cheek. "I wish you fair weather, my friends, and good luck."

Ebon seemed to be rooted to the spot by misery,

staring glumly at the ground, so Theren went over to stand beside him while Adara kissed Lilith on both cheeks as well. It was an important custom for Idrisians, indicative of true friendship, and Theren was somewhat surprised, as she thought this might be the first time that Adara had honored Lilith in such a manner. However, she also realized the likely reason for this: there was every chance, now, that they would never be all in one place like this again. Adara clearly did not want to let Lilith leave without making sure that she knew she was considered a part of the family they had made together.

The growing lump in Theren's throat threatened to overcome her attempts to remain stoic, so she turned to Ebon and patted him stolidly on the shoulder, hoping to avoid anything more emotional.

"Stay safe," she told him, the lingering fear of whatever task he was undertaking with the dean still gnawing at her, and he gave her a look that was half-knowing, half-heartbroken.

"You as well," he replied, before engulfing her in a hug, and then kissing her on both cheeks just as Adara had done.

And then, suddenly, Theren found herself with no more words to say. There was no going back; there was nothing she could say that would change what was to come, whether they would meet again or not. It seemed that their time together had ended, and that thought was enough to render her speechless with grief.

Tears prickling in her eyes, she nodded at them all one last time, and then took Lilith's hand, following Vivien's path onto the ship. Though loath to look back, for fear that she would stop altogether, Theren did pause on the edge of the deck to gaze down at Ebon, Adara, and Kalem where they stood huddled together, still watching. Thankfully she was saved from having to remain there, waving like a fool, by the cry that rang out across the docks.

"All aboard! All hands aboard! Set the sails!"

The sailors hurried her out of the way, and Theren struggled to keep her balance, already unnerved by the ship's movements. Lilith immediately headed belowdecks, seeking refuge partially from the cold wind and partially from the melancholy situation, but Theren moved to the stern, still reluctant to truly say goodbye to everything she had known for so long.

The docks were almost cleared, save for little knots of people being left behind, her friends among them. They looked very small from the height of the deck, but Theren could still clearly see the tears running down Kalem's face, and Ebon's arm around Adara's shoulders, squeezing more tightly than he usually would have. As she stood there, Lilith called out to her from the stairway, telling her to hurry below so as not to catch her death of cold, and Theren felt relief once again that the two of them had not had to part ways as well. She could not imagine that she would have been even half this composed had she been leaving Lilith behind.

She did not, or possibly *could* not, take Lilith's advice, however. She remained on deck while they departed, and watched her friends turn to tiny smudges in the distance as the ship slowly cleared the bay.

The sun set rapidly, and the sailors lit lanterns, but the vast expanse of sea around them seemed dark enough to suck away all the light, with even the moons being shrouded by clouds. Despite the dimness, and her growing queasiness, Theren stood on the prow watching the High King's Seat retreat farther and farther into the distance, until not even a speck of it remained on the horizon.

She was afraid to admit, even to herself, that she was not sure she would ever see it again.

The sea journey from Selvan to the High King's Seat that Theren had taken when she first made her way to the Academy had been much shorter than the passage across the Great Bay to Feldemar. She remembered that first trip vividly, the terror that she had felt with every wave, but mercifully it had not been so long that she had been expected to sleep on board. If it meant never having to set foot on a ship again, she thought that she would almost be glad to never return to the Seat, despite how much she missed it.

Theren had barely slept at all the night on which they had set out, dozing off for a few hours in the morning and nothing more. Vivien had invited her to come up to the deck and be introduced to some of the other Mystics, but it had only resulted in Theren getting a few steps out into the open air and then immediately rushing to the edge to relieve herself of her last meal.

She lay currently in a pile of ropes at the very back end of the ship, curled into a miserable ball of churning unpleasantness. Lilith, who was in contrast quite happy to enjoy the late afternoon sunshine, sat beside her, idly reading a book that she had brought with her. Occasionally, she would reach over and rub Theren's back gently, which almost made everything worth it.

After what seemed like an eternity, Theren felt her insides settle a little, helped by the new wisps of cloud scudding across the sun and dampening its bright glare. Gradually, afraid that even the slightest movement might set her stomach off again, she sat up, glad to be smelling fresh air instead of the musty oiled ropes.

"Not much of a one for sailing, I take it," a cheerful voice said as she was getting her bearings, and she looked up to her right to see the captain.

He towered over her, a muscular black-skinned man from Feldemar, but despite his intimidating size, his eyes were kind and he smiled often. She had overheard from chatter that he was usually a merchant sailor, running trade between Feldemar, the High King's Seat, and Dorsea, but she could scarcely imagine the idea of someone spending most of their life at sea. She squinted up at him where he stood, looking out over the edge, and mustered a weak grin.

"If there were a tiny spot of land beside us now, I would descend onto it and never leave."

He laughed jovially. "I have never heard anyone volunteer to be marooned before, but if we find any sandbars, I shall keep it in mind!"

"You will have to forgive her," Lilith chimed in, dryly. "This is only her second time traveling by sea, and the only other journey she made was between Selvan and the High King's Seat."

"Ah, so I placed the accent aright. Well, fear not, my little tortoise, you will adjust to it after a time."

She raised her eyebrows. "Tortoise?"

Lilith laughed beside her. "A name commonly given in Feldemar to those who prefer the land. Those who love the sea are called turtles, because of where the two creatures live."

Theren had only seen such animals in picture books, although she thought there might have been a weremage at the Academy at one time who favored the form of one or the other. She was struck suddenly by the realization that there were a great many animals she had only ever read about with which she might potentially come face to face in the jungles of Feldemar. Thinking of snakes and scorpions, she shuddered, wondering how people could ever feel safe.

"Do you know how long the voyage will be?" she asked him, standing up cautiously.

He shrugged. "That is what I am here to find out. We have had fine weather thus far, but there is a storm behind us, and I fear it will overtake us later today."

He pointed out behind her towards a swell of dark clouds gathering over what seemed to be a vast area, and Theren felt her stomach lurch again momentarily as she realized that she could not see land in any direction from here.

"And the rain will slow us down?" she inquired, her heart sinking at the thought of spending more time at sea.

He clapped her on the shoulder, amused. "No more than a day or two. We will be in Bandar before four days from now, that is certain."

Lilith looked up from her book in surprise. "Bandar? Would it not be faster to sail to Ulande? That is where I have always disembarked when returning home from the Seat."

"Oh, yes, most of the Mystics will be docking west of Ulande," the captain explained, his gaze returning to the clouds. "A special landing area was constructed—for unloading the horses, and the weapons, you see. The locals were none too happy about it, I can tell you. But the bulk of the order's forces are being carried by ships contracted from Selvan, with captains who are eager to return as soon as possible. The few of us who had business in Feldemar before being called upon by Her Majesty were given permission to keep to our usual trade routes, no doubt as a way to try to lower our transport fees."

Theren made an uninterested noise, more concerned with her stomach than trade matters, but Lilith frowned deeply, closing her book with a snap. "Why would people in Ulande be upset with the construction of the landing? Will it not open new trading opportunities or docking space?"

The captain gave her a sideways look, assessing, and then eventually let out a deep rumbling sigh. "You have not seen much of the world beyond your wealthy caravans, that is certain. The landing was constructed with wood purchased—at a discount, for the sake of Her Majesty—from local lumberyards, and it will be dismantled and carted off to Ammon when the order is finished with it, so they cannot even recoup the loss. But it also makes them a target. When last I passed by Ulande, they had already been raided at least once by soldiers from Dulmun. Who knows if it has happened again."

Theren leaned back against the wall behind her, appalled. The High King had truly ordered these installations built solely for the benefit of her army? And surely they could have picked some empty stretch of coastland, if it was likely to attract Dulmun's raiders, rather than the outskirts of a town full of people.

While she was musing, a piercing cry rang out from the sky above them, and she looked up to see a great seabird, with wings longer than she was tall, circling its way slowly down towards the ship.

"Finally," the captain muttered, waving at it, and

the massive bird, which was pure white except for the black tips of its wings, dived down towards them.

It looked as though it was coming in too fast and would collide heavily with the deck, but at the last moment, it beat its great wings several times and then transformed, revealing a young, tanned weremage wearing a tight red coat that marked him as a Mystic. He landed solidly on his feet as he alighted on the deck, as casually as someone else might dismount a horse. Blinking, Theren watched him make his way up to where they were standing, wondering what he had been doing.

"Did you get a good look at the storm?" the captain asked the newcomer, squinting at the sky once again.

"Yes, and it is not good," the weremage replied, and then grinned at Theren, whose mouth was still slightly agape in shock. "Have you never seen an albatross before?"

She snapped her mouth closed, trying to regain some semblance of dignity. "No, I . . . never."

"You were right," he said, turning back to the captain. "I suspect it will be upon us by sunset. A fierce little summer squall."

The captain sighed again. "Thank you, Tinun. I was hoping we could outrun it. Ah, well, a day or so longer will not do us any great harm."

Theren made a face, and both men laughed at her.

"Except you, of course, my little tortoise. Best you get belowdecks before the storm is upon us. Do not fear, this ship is sturdy and summer storms are loud, but small. We will be in no danger."

Lilith laughed at the expression on her face as well as she got to her feet. "Come, you should listen to him. Storms happen all the time. If they were truly so dangerous, how would any ship make the journey across the Great Bay?"

"It seems far more sensible not to try at all," Theren muttered, stomping down the stairs.

She paused down on the main deck, peering out to the west, where she could see the distant smudges of other ships, and shivered as a sudden gust of cold wind brushed past her. At least there would be allies within range to come to their aid if the storm went badly, she told herself, but she was unconvinced by her own efforts at comfort. Luckily for her, Lilith was there, and put an arm around her waist.

"I have sailed through many storms," she said, softly, and Theren snorted.

"And I have survived many things that are no more pleasant in hindsight for having lived through them."

Lilith rolled her eyes. "At least the weather will likely not have a temper to rival yours."

Theren sighed. "I am sorry. I just feel a great sense of foreboding. It may only be the blackness of the clouds, but I have never been so far away from land that I could not see it in any direction before."

"That is what the cabins are for," Lilith countered, smiling. "You cannot see how far out we are if you cannot see the empty horizon. I stayed in my room belowdecks many times before I became comfortable out in the open air."

"I could use some rest," Theren admitted, feeling the great weight of her exhaustion pressing down on her, and Lilith laughed.

"Really? All that tossing and turning was not you attempting to dance in your sleep?"

"Not on purpose," she answered, and then squared her shoulders, turning her back on the oncoming storm. "All right, then. Let me try again. All the times I deliberately set out to nap during my library sessions at the Academy were training for this moment—sky preserve me, I *will* sleep through this storm!"

Giggling, Lilith put her arm through Theren's, and they walked back towards the stairway that led to the lower areas. Theren tried not to look at the growing bank of billowing clouds in the distance as they did so, but they had a way of demanding notice. She hoped that Lilith and the captain would be right about them being harmless, even if only for her stomach's sake.

ELEVEN

THE STORM RAGED FROM SHORTLY AFTER SUNSET UNTIL morning, only dissipating sometime after the sun had already risen. Theren had lain awake for what seemed like the whole night, gripping her pallet in unbridled terror with every lurch of the ship, and dozing only fitfully. Lilith took one look at her face that morning and told her in no uncertain terms to go back to bed immediately. But even now sleep eluded her, as though she was so tired that she had passed beyond the need for rest.

After a few more hours of sleeplessness, she began to hear—though muffled by the multiple levels of the ship above her—a great commotion on the main deck: footsteps interspersed occasionally with shouting. Already on edge, she strained her ears as she tried to find out what was going on, and was shocked to hear several people run down the corridor right outside her door, heavy boots thudding.

"Is it Dulmun?"

"We do not know yet. The captain says—"

Theren lay still for a moment, gripped by sudden fear. The war with Dulmun had seemed so far away until now, and she had certainly not thought to encounter them at sea. There was still trade passing between Dulmun and the High King's Seat, was there not? How could Dulmun risk attacking ships on this route, if they needed the trade from Dorsea and Selvan still? Unless they knew that these were Mystic ships bound for the war.

Her throat dry, memories of the attack on the Seat rose unbidden in her mind: the fire and the chaos, dead bodies in the streets, and buildings aflame. And here there would be nowhere to run but into the cold, black depths of the sea.

She sat bolt upright, pulling her shirt on over her head and scrabbling into her new cloak. Lilith was likely somewhere up on deck investigating the same disturbance that had roused her, in the direct firing line of any Dulmish soldiers that they might run across. Shaking off her light-headedness, she stumbled out the door and made her way quickly up the stairs.

The air grew colder the higher she went, and she emerged into a thick blanket of fog. The Mystics were milling around, most of them peering out over the sides, and many of them had weapons clutched tightly in their hands. Sailors were crawling all over the rigging, tying up most of the sails and tightening ropes, while the captain stood at the front of the ship, barking orders. Beside him were Lilith and Vivien, so Theren made her way over as well, heart pounding at the sound of several splashes in the water below them.

"What is happening?" she asked when she had arrived, and Lilith turned to look at her and made a face.

"You look *terrible*. Why are you out of bed?"

"The commotion woke me." It was almost the truth. "What are they dropping into the water?"

She pointed off to the port side, where one sailor was indeed dropping something over the edge, peering intently down at it in the water.

"Captain Jasir has instructed his men to take down sail and check for shoaling," Vivien explained, sounding almost as tired as Theren felt. "They are dropping in a weighted rope, marked along its length with distances, to try to determine if the water here will become unexpectedly shallow."

Theren stared blankly for a moment before accepting this answer. She knew that she would never understand why this was necessary or why shallow water would be a bad thing, especially not while she was in this frame of mind. Her eyes lingered on

Vivien's face; in addition to looking exhausted, she had her hair drawn back for the first time since Theren had met her, in long, neat braids that were looped around each other to form a bun on the back of her head, which fully exposed the ghoulish burn scars on her right side. They ran all the way from her temple down to her neck, a deep purple in the center that lightened to yellowish-grey on the edges.

"Is something wrong?" Vivien asked her, sharply, noticing her observation.

"No, my apologies," she mumbled, looking away. "I did not mean to stare. I am only very tired."

Vivien surveyed her for a few moments, her own gaze cool. "You look it."

There was a loud screech from the air above them, and many of the Mystics jumped, clutching tighter at their weapons, but Theren knew what to expect this time. She watched the weremage, Tinun, land on the deck, noticing that he was more careful this time so as not to slip on the damp timbers.

"What did you see?" The captain leaned forwards, hungry for information.

"The fog is extensive," Tinun replied, out of breath. "But that is not all I must tell you. Some of it, at least, is not natural. I do not doubt that some has been brought on by the storm, but I can sense alchemy in the air. Someone is deliberately thickening the mist. I would have tried to dispel it, but I feared I would give away our position to whoever was building it."

Captain Jasir's face grew grim. "No honest sailor would willingly cause this mire. That means raiders."

At once, Vivien was at the rail overlooking the lower decks, her voice suddenly full and commanding, as if she had not been weary just moments ago. "Mystics! There are raiders in the mist. Prepare to defend against boarding parties and spears. Shields to the fore, on your guard!"

"Do you have an elementalist on board?" Jasir asked her, lifting up a heavy club that had been sitting nearby, obviously his weapon of choice.

Vivien frowned. "Only Lilith. I was just about to tell her and Theren to go below."

"I could use her aid," he said, apologetically.

Lilith lifted her chin proudly, though Theren could see her shaking slightly. "I would rather stay and help than hide. Though if you need winds, I fear I may not be able to fill the sails fully."

Though Vivien gave her an exasperated look, the captain just shook his head. "No, we do not need a tailwind. But, if you can, try to blow off some of this accursed fog. If we cannot see our enemy, we do not stand a chance."

Lilith swallowed hard, obviously intimidated by the importance of the task, but focused herself. Soon her eyes glowed with magelight as she conjured up an eddying swirl of wind that pushed ahead of the ship's prow.

"Did you get a sense of which direction the

alchemist was in?" Vivien asked Tinun. He opened his mouth to answer, but closed it abruptly, as a sound came out of the mists, sending shivers down all of their spines.

It was a high-pitched voice, at first sounding like a wailing cry, but gradually the note changed, and it became apparent that it was a wordless song. Other voices joined it, singing the same haunting melody, layer upon layer of sound until it seemed that it was coming from all around them, as though the sea itself were keening with grief.

"Keep going!" the captain whispered fiercely at Lilith, as her magic faltered. "It is the raiders! Dulmish sailors sing these hymns to pinpoint the other ships in the flotilla. We must see them before they see us!"

Vivien grabbed hold of Theren's arm firmly, steering her towards the stairs, but before they were halfway there, they heard the mad pealing of a bell in the far distance. It was soon followed by barely audible shouts and screams, the unmistakable sounds of battle—not boding well for the Mystics on the other ships in their fleet.

"Darkness take them," Vivien swore, her grip on Theren's arm tightening until it hurt.

Lilith redoubled her efforts as their ship crept forwards through the fog, the Mystics lining the deck all growing tenser by the moment. The eerie, ululating hymn being sung by the raiders permeated the air, and nothing was visible beyond the clinging fog save for the occasional distant flash of fire from the direction of their sister ship.

A yelp from Lilith broke through the hymn's strange melody. Theren whirled towards her, as did Vivien, and noticed that the magelight was gone from her eyes.

"Someone has dispelled my magic!"

Vivien shoved Theren towards the stairs back into the hold, grabbing Lilith as well, but all three women cried out as they felt the gathering of magic off to the starboard side. It was a great blossoming rose of power, one that Theren knew enough to associate with an elementalist's fireball.

"Enemy mage! Brace yourselves, away from the edge!" Vivien screamed, but it was too late.

The flames struck the wooden ship with a force that knocked Theren off her feet, the terrible wave of heat making her retch as it carried the stench of burning flesh and smoke past her.

In the next instant, everything descended into chaos. With raucous laughter the Dulmish raiders seemed to appear out of nowhere, visible now with the fog burned off by the fireball. The Mystics rallied desperately to recover from the opening attack, but the raiders were already hurling thick, barbed spears, not giving any quarter. In response, Tinun leaped into the air in his albatross form, shrieking indignantly, and tore at the Dulmun ship's dark grey sails with his great beak.

Theren struggled to her feet, still coughing.

"Lilith!" she bellowed, trying to be heard over the tumult.

The fireball had been enormous, far bigger than any she had seen the firemages cast at the Academy. The idea that Lilith might have been caught in it . . .

She dodged past the Mystics as they swarmed near the bulwarks, those with bows firing back at the raiders, while others threw their own spears or held shields for defense. The air was thick with smoke, so much so that she could not see along the full length of the ship, and as she stumbled forwards, the charred timber of the deck in front of her fell through, no more than wreckage.

She darted back, arms windmilling to keep her balance, and then gasped as she felt the enemy elementalist drawing in more power. But before the firemage could cast again, a blast of mindmagic rocketed forwards and shook the enemy ship. Theren, dazed, looked up to see that it had come from Vivien, who stood on the balcony once more, her own eyes aglow with magelight.

"I see you now, traitor!" she cried, and Theren shuddered as she felt Vivien gathering her magic.

The elementalist pushed back, and between the two Theren felt more raw power than she had ever witnessed being wasted on nothing more than dispelling burgeoning spells. It made her dizzy, and that coupled with the acrid smoke and coppery scent of blood in the air caused her head to begin aching. She skirted around the hole in the deck, trying to pull herself together, and made for the stairs. She called out for Lilith again, and hope flooded through her when she heard the girl respond, faintly, from somewhere up past Vivien.

Sailors hurried around her with buckets, trying to put out the fires, but Theren fought her way up the steps against her body's wishes. She almost collapsed with relief when she saw that Lilith stood there, looking singed but untroubled, reciting the incantations for her spells under her breath as she tried to aid Vivien. Theren then took a moment to regain her composure, wishing she had had any sleep at all in the past two nights, and hurried over to the edge to join in the fray.

From up here she could see some of the damage the fireball had done to the ship and the Mystics who had caught the brunt of it, and it was not pleasant. Charred bodies smoked where they had fallen across the blackened and blistered wood, while the water beneath the edge was littered with lost shields, the sea-foam stained murk-grey by the ashes.

Furious, she raked claws of her magic along the ranks of the Dulmish soldiers, knocking them into each other, and yanked at them, pulling one or two off the ship into the sea. She, Lilith, and Vivien had been powerless to stop the growing fireball, unable to see the enemy mage in the fog. She wondered how many other ships had fallen prey to this same kind of calculated attack and felt bile rise in her throat as she wondered if the other Mystic ship they had heard in the distance had had any mages on board to try to defend it as they were doing.

One raider, watching his compatriots get pushed around by an invisible force, looked around for the source of the magic and then seized a spear from beside him when he spotted Theren. He hurled it at her with frightening speed, and she backed away, holding up a shield made from her will. Though the weapon bounced off, the impact still knocked her over, but suddenly Lilith was there, growling.

"You will not harm her!" Lilith cried out in fury, and then let fly with a lightning bolt that struck the man square between the eyes.

He keeled over instantly. Beside them, Vivien finally seemed to be overcoming the enemy firemage, with her hands twisted into vicious claws as she crushed the woman in a viselike grip of her power.

Captain Jasir appeared beside Theren, his club sticky with something she did not want to think about, and pulled her to her feet as a shadow passed overhead. "You girls should get away from the fighting!"

Before she could argue, there was an ugly croaking caw from above them, and the shadow that she had at first thought must be Tinun swooped down at the group of them. It was a huge black vulture, its feet armed with clusters of terrible claws, and the fearsome, saw-edged teeth that bristled in its beak made her certain that it had to be a weremage. Vivien was clearly its target, judging by its angle of approach, but on the way towards her it seemed happy to bowl over anyone else unlucky enough to be in its path. Theren tripped and tumbled backwards down the stairs in her attempts to get away from it, crying out as her elbows, knees, and back joined her stomach in being horribly bruised.

She landed prone on the deck, rattled, and then peeled her face slowly off the floor, trying to regain her bearings. Somewhat distantly, she realized that she was face to face with a dead sailor, his lifeless eyes staring at the sky and several thick, black arrows embedded in his chest. Shock gripped her like the claws of some terrible beast, and she struggled to move her limbs to back away. This was different from the attack on the High King's Seat. There had been devastation in the streets then, it was true, but the Academy students had been protected from it for the most part by their instructors. She had not had to smell a dead man's burns or pull herself out of the blackened blood oozing from underneath his corpse.

That horrible cawing rang out again, and she shook off the stupor, forcing herself to stand. The weremage leaped from their ship over towards its allies, drawn away by some other aspect of the battle. Theren gasped as she realized that it was Tinun, who was now leaping about as a great cat, oblivious to the mage's approach. He had all but conquered the back half of the Dulmish ship with his vicious claws, and the enemy weremage obviously meant to stop him from doing any more damage.

"Tinun! Watch out!" she screamed, her voice hoarse, but he did not hear, and the vulture slammed into him.

He yowled in pain as the vulture's claws bit into his flesh and writhed furiously as he tried to escape from its horrible beak. Theren reached out with her magic and grabbed onto one of its legs, flailing wildly in an attempt to shake him free from its grip. Barking gutturally in surprise, the weremage released Tinun, and he sprang away deftly, transforming back into his albatross form to escape. Theren kept her hold on the vulture, straining mightily to keep it off balance, and slammed it down into the deck several times when it tried to take flight.

Unwilling to let the weremage go, she tried pulling it back off the enemy ship and into the ocean, but regretted that idea immediately as the vulture turned itself towards her quicker than she could adjust the direction of her pull. It sprang forwards, claws outstretched, and shrieked triumphantly as it felt her grip slip away. She jumped back and tripped over the dead sailor, too breathless even to scream as the monster bore down on her. But then, with a great screech and a cascade of feathers, Tinun rammed into it from off to her right, clacking his beak angrily, and knocked it into the mast beside them.

She saw immediately that he would not be able to fight the other weremage one on one; there was a heavy spear now protruding from his breast, and already he seemed to be flagging. She struggled back to her feet for what seemed like the thousandth time that morning as the vulture righted itself, and watched in horror as it transformed into a giant boar, its feathers rippling and reforming into thickened grey skin. It began to charge towards the two of them, and Theren struck out desperately with her magic, trying to lift it or turn it away. Bellowing in rage, its raw strength pushed through her feeble reserves of energy like a shark through water, and she stood there gasping as it approached, with nothing left to do.

Out of nowhere, Vivien appeared in its path ahead of them. The Mystic stood her ground as the maddened weremage continued its charge, apparently unperturbed. In a flash she dodged its tusks, and Theren felt her gathering a great deal of magic around one of her hands. Then, before the boar could react, Vivien brought that fist down sharply on the top of its skull, and the extra mentalism force behind her punch sent the creature crashing to the floor with a sickening crack.

The impact had obviously knocked the weremage unconscious, because the boar form was stripped away, leaving only an extremely pasty white-skinned man, covered in blood-red tattoos. Vivien, her lips curled into a snarl, kicked him over the side of the ship.

"Quickly," she commanded, taking hold of Theren's arm. "Help me bring down the mast!"

The crushing weight that Vivien brought down on the mast of the enemy ship stunned Theren for a moment, but she added to it as best she could, concentrating on snapping rigging and smaller beams while Vivien simply let loose with all the power she had left. A bolt of lightning struck the mast midway up its height, and Theren felt relief once more that Lilith was well enough to be casting spells. Eventually, its timbers groaning horribly, the mast gave way, and came crashing down onto the mess of the Dulmish ship's deck, before promptly catching fire at Lilith's command.

Silence fell, or at least relatively. There was coughing and crying and the ever present roar of the sea, but the blood pounding in Theren's ears had died down as her energy seeped away. Boots thudded across the deck as Mystics regrouped, checking on their friends, and the captain shouted for the deckhands to let down the sails and hasten away.

A burbling sound caught her ear, and Theren looked down to see Tinun back in human form, blood spilling from his mouth as he struggled to breathe. She hurried to his side, hoping mayhap she could hold his wounds closed until a healer could see him, but the spearhead was embedded deep in his chest, its cruel barbs warning against any attempts at removing it. The flesh around the wound churned as he tried to heal himself, but with the weapon still inside him, it was a fight he could not win—unlike their greater battle, in which he had done much to secure victory.

"Just stay still," she told him gently, but the look in his eyes made it clear that he knew there was nothing anyone could do.

"At least we . . ." he gurgled, and then broke off to try to draw another breath. "At least we got the bastards."

He let out a hideous, wet, hacking cough, and his body went limp, falling back against the wall. Still the spear protruded from his body, as sharp and as cruel as the weremage's talons of which Theren had been so afraid. Numbly, she realized that she was covered in his blood; it was all over her hands, and she could feel some running down her face as well, from where he had been spluttering.

She stood, woodenly, and looked back at the now blazing remains of the Dulmish ship, watching it burn.

"Yes. We did."

TWELVE

Their ship limped the rest of the way to Bandar, taking six days instead of the four that the captain had predicted thanks to the damage done by the Dulmish raiders. The mood among the sailors was tense, with Captain Jasir prowling up and down the bow at all hours of the day, watching for more attacks. Vivien was grim and silent, her offer of introducing Theren to the other Mystics having evaporated much like the fog.

Theren spent a great deal of the rest of the journey sleeping, partially out of exhaustion and partially because it was easier than dealing with the frayed tempers of everyone else on board. While it was not the way she would have wished for her fears to be assuaged, the sea now seemed less frightening to her, and sleep came easier, to Lilith's relief. Occasionally, in the middle of the night when no light penetrated through the walls of their room, Theren would wake with a vision swimming in her mind of Tinun or the dead sailor she had tripped over—more horrors to add to her growing pile, alongside the murder victims from Isra's rampage at the Academy, and the inside of the blinders she had worn while the Mystics saw to her with knives.

But then Lilith would sigh in her sleep or turn over beside her, reminding Theren that reality was here and now. She could not even imagine how she would have handled any of this had Lilith not been there with her, a small piece of home in her arms.

It was early morning, the pink-tinged sunlight adding to the already stifling late summer heat, when they came within sight of the shores of Feldemar. Theren was woken by the cacophony of boots on the deck again, and feared that they might be under attack once more, though there was none of the shouting from the other day. She slid out of bed, trying and failing not to wake Lilith as she went, and the two of them dressed and made their way up to the outside world, hearts heavy with dread.

As soon as they were out on the deck, though, their

fears eased, as the Mystics all seemed to be in a state of quiet celebration as they stared at the distant coastline.

"At last," Lilith murmured happily, smiling at the shores of her homeland.

As they came closer, they began to see other ships, though Lilith assured Theren that there was a well-used trading route between Bandar and eastern Selvan and that they were not more raiders. There was no sign of any of the other ships in the Mystic fleet that had been headed towards Bandar instead of Ulande, but Theren told herself feebly that they *had* lost a lot of time, and it might have been possible that the others had arrived days ahead of them.

Bandar itself was unlike any place that Theren had ever seen. It was set in the lee of a tall cliff that formed the western edge of a small bay, with much of the city situated out over the water. Some of its buildings were carved into the nooks and crannies in the rock face, and some others sat atop the cliff above, but the majority of it rose out of the ocean on towering stone columns, with delicate bridges passing between the high rows of houses, while the citizens made their way around in small boats that paddled along lanes of water. The top floor of every building seemed to house a garden, with green vines and flowers of all hues draping out lazily over the umber stone, their vibrant blossoms accentuated by the dark yellowish brown; some larger structures even sported lawns and had great trees transplanted on top of them. Lilith laughed at the look of awe on Theren's face.

On the eastern side of the bay, however, the high cliffs descended towards the mouth of a gargantuan river delta, a twisting maze of silt-stained water and mangrove swamps that wound around a great many tiny islands. The vast wash extended so far into the distance that Theren could barely see the other side, but she did notice that, on the very edge of her vision, there squatted a stout black fortress, with a tower that looked impossibly high rising out of it. It was far enough away that all Theren could make out was the shape, like a thick black box, but there seemed to be a fire burning at the top of the tower, and tiny smudges that were boats sailing around the riverways at its skirts.

"Is that . . . Ammon?" she asked, pointing at it, wishing she had had a chance to look at a map before they had set out.

Lilith's eyes narrowed, and she shook her head. "No, Ammon is many days' ride inland. That is Arod, the great northern war-light fortress of Dulmun. It marks the edge of their territory, the border that they share with Feldemar."

"It is so close." Theren shuddered, memories of the battle still fresh in her mind.

"It will come no closer," Captain Jasir said bleakly, appearing behind them. "The foundations of Bandar were laid centuries ago by the last wizard king, Nayala, at the height of her power. They will not be broken by the armies of traitors."

Comforted somewhat, Theren returned to her scrutiny of the approaching city, though it was not much cheerier a landscape. The people of Bandar seemed weighed down by the tension of the war, and many faces glared angrily at their ship from windows and walkways as it passed by on their way to the docks.

The harbormaster was not much friendlier, demanding to know when the Mystics would be leaving and whether the ship was officially sanctioned by the High King or merely a transport vessel. Apparently the captain's responses were enough to satisfy him in the end, but the atmosphere was distinctly chilly as they all disembarked, with Theren and Lilith once again carrying their luggage between them.

Once they were in the city proper, Lilith's green dress drew more than a few glances, but it did not seem to do much to soften the mood. They labored their way up the cliff, along winding paths carved out of the rock, until at last the ground flattened out and the houses made way for stables and military fortifications. There seemed to be a large number of soldiers, including many watchers on the outer walls, and all of them were armed with spears and shields and were giving the Mystics suspicious looks.

Theren could see now why Lilith's insistence that they would need her to mediate with the people of Feldemar had been accepted, watching her smooth everyone's ruffled feathers as she was forced to step in on an argument between Vivien and a stablemaster about buying mounts. Much as Theren hated the idea of Lilith throwing around her weight like a typical goldbag, it would certainly be better than walking the rest of the way to Ammon.

She just hoped that the humidity in the air here on the coast would not follow them as they made their way farther inland.

Three days later Theren sat wilting in her saddle as the blasted heat sapped away all of her energy. The air was warm and sticky, as though they had wandered into a steaming room, and many brightly colored insects went their merry way around them, buzzing insistently. It had passed into autumn the day before, but apparently the sweltering jungle had not received the message, and she found it almost as hard to sleep as she had at sea during the storm.

Vivien seemed to be similarly indisposed by the weather, her pale skin reddened by the sun, and when their group stopped to water the horses both Theren and Vivien waded into the river with their mounts, splashing the water over their faces and arms.

Lilith stayed atop her horse, laughing at them, alongside a stout Mystic from Idris, who was also grinning at their discomfiture.

"My wife is from southern Dorsea, and she was exactly the same when she came home to Almanzil to meet my parents," he commented, amused.

Lilith giggled. "It must be very boring in Selvan if any amount of weather is too much for you all."

Theren groaned, scrubbing at her face with the cold water. "It will not be like this all through the year, will it? I fear I will perish if it is."

"Ammon sits on a wide, flat plain, or so I have heard," Vivien replied wearily, positioning herself so that her horse shielded her from the sun as it drank greedily from the river. "Once we escape from these infernal jungles, it should be less humid, or at least that is my hope."

"How much farther will it be until we reach the fortress?" Theren asked, managing to drag herself back into the saddle with some effort.

"Six days, if the weather holds. The jungle should thin out within three."

"That is not so bad," she responded, though her heart sank in anticipation of three more days of this anguish.

The Idrisian Mystic laughed. "You are assuming the roads will be clear, Vivien! Here in the north, they say that every second day, the roads are covered by mudslides. It is all the rain, you see!"

Theren scowled at the back of his extremely cheerful head, wishing he had remained quiet. It was bad enough that they had to ride at all, as her knowledge of the saddle was thin at best and her fondness for it even thinner, but she was certain she would have been happier were she not handling everything far worse than everyone else. The last thing she needed was to be stranded here if the roads were destroyed—she wondered how anybody could stand to live in Feldemar at all, if they could not even travel reliably.

"I have never seen Ammon," Lilith said brightly, in an attempt to lighten the mood, as they returned to the road that led northwards through the trees. "Can you tell us anything of it?"

"Very little that deals with the fortress specifically," Vivien replied, shading her face with one hand. "I have never been there either. It is some twenty-five leagues or so from the border with Dulmun, though it is some way south of the current engagement between Dulmun's forces and the High King's army. It will be safe, which is why it was chosen as our primary staging ground."

Theren slapped at a whining mosquito that landed on her neck. "Will there be many new recruits?"

"Few as new as you," Vivien answered wryly. "Though, yes, there will be many young Mystics who have not yet been blooded in wars. They—and you—will receive training, and possibly experience, while there. I do not expect many forces to leave the fortress for several months at least after we arrive."

Theren thought about this as she fanned at her face with her hand, musing. It seemed, at least, that she would not be sent immediately to the frontline of the war, which came as a relief. The term 'blooded' made her shiver though; she knew what it meant, and that it was often used to describe more veteran members of the High King's army as well, but after the battle with Dulmun's forces at sea, she certainly *felt* blooded. It did not seem a badge of honor.

"As a mage, you will have more training to undertake than most of the recruits," Vivien continued, not noticing her reaction. "There are several high-ranking mentalists that I know of who will be in Ammon, but I believe that for convenience you will likely be apprenticed to me."

Theren brightened somewhat at that, but then frowned. "More magical training? What for? Is the Academy's education not good enough?"

Vivien laughed. "Most wizards are not trained for real battle. They might learn self-defense, or find ways to apply their ordinary training to war, but they do not train for it specifically. The Mystics will change that."

Lilith made a thoughtful noise. "What about me? Do you think I could learn something like that while in Ammon?"

"Why? Do you expect to need it?" Vivien asked curiously, giving her a look. "We hardly send our ambassadors into the fray."

"I was in the fray on board your ship!" Lilith retorted hotly. "If I am endangered just by traveling with you, why should I not learn?"

Vivien fell silent, apparently considering. "You make a good point, again. I will ask around, once we reach the fortress. Our own recruits will take priority, however."

"Do you know who was appointed chancellor at Ammon after that business in Dorsea?" the Idrisian Mystic broke in, sounding curious, and Vivien grunted in response.

"Karan, of the family Vordith. It will be interesting to see if he is as disagreeable as all the tales tell."

The two Mystics fell into conversation about their new commander, who apparently had quite the reputation for being bad with people, but excellent at war. Theren did not know whether this comforted her or made her feel worse. She caught Lilith looking at her, and flashed a brief, strained smile, suspecting that Lilith's request to be trained for war had more to do with the fact that she intended to follow Theren wherever she would go than any kind of residual fear of danger. That was something that did worry her: the idea of Lilith following her to the battlefield.

Thankfully, they were to have several months of training before it came to any of that. Or at least, they would if both they and the roads could survive this accursed Feldemarian weather. Theren leaned back in her saddle and closed her eyes, wishing she were an alchemist, so that she might cool the air, and suddenly found herself missing Ebon and Kalem keenly, and Adara. She sighed, wondering how she could possibly describe the events of their journey thus far in a letter, and grimaced when she thought about how much of it remained.

She hoped that there would be sufficient amounts of parchment in Ammon.

THIRTEEN

After three and a half days' travel, the jungle gave way to gentler grasslands interspersed with infrequent trees, just as Vivien had promised. Though less overbearingly wet and sticky, the air was still warm, and the landscape was entirely new to Theren. The plains of Selvan that they had passed through briefly on her trip to the High King's Seat were lowlands—long, flat stretches of land that were well watered primarily because of their proximity to the sea. It seemed, conversely, that the entirety of Feldemar was sloped gently upwards, so the air here felt thinner than any she had known before.

Lilith, amused, had assured her that it was perfectly safe to breathe, though she did admit that she preferred the western lowlands of her home kingdom to these steppes. Theren, despite never having seen the rest of Feldemar, was inclined to agree. Despite the overall slope, the land seemed utterly devoid of any kind of drainage, so rain collected in stagnant pools and formed reeking marshland in the hollows between hills, and the turf was often a thin layer of grass over deep mud. No matter how hard she tried, Theren found she could never quite get all of the muck off her clothes.

This was made even worse after a day or so, when they were forced to ride into a heavy rainstorm that had blown in from the east, turning the road into a tiny causeway of solid ground amidst a sea of oozing sludge as the mud overtook the plains. Theren spent the entire time clutching her saddle tightly, petrified that a landslide might occur at any moment.

The water brought with it clouds of tiny stinging midges, and they in turn brought hundreds upon hundreds of incessantly croaking frogs, so that the air was alive with a cacophony at all times. The Idrisian Mystic, whose name was Yarshun, began to have trouble finding them safe places to camp amidst all the boggy ground, so Theren could not even catch up on any of her missed sleep.

All in all, it had been a thoroughly miserable trip by the time their small band caught up with the rest of the Mystics on the road, the larger group having been slowed considerably by the days-long storm. Yarshun, Vivien, and the other adult Mystics who had been with them all seemed to visibly relax upon reuniting with their fellows, but Theren felt herself growing tense as they came upon the giant swath of red cloaks that covered the road as far as the eye could see.

She told herself that someday that splash of color would no longer instinctively make her nervous, but that day did not seem like it would come any time soon.

"Do not take those off just yet," Vivien told her, when they had made camp for the night, and she had just reached down to remove her boots. "Come with me, and I will introduce you to some of the people you will be working with."

Theren made a face, not particularly enthused by that idea, but Lilith nudged her. "Go on. The more names you have for faces, the less overwhelming it will be once we reach the fortress."

Sighing, Theren looked longingly at their tent for a few moments, but eventually gave in, falling in step glumly behind Vivien.

"You should try not to look quite so surly." Vivien frowned in disapproval. "You cannot be a part of the order without acknowledging the rest of us. Someday you may face enemies alongside us, and they may not be uniformed like the soldiers we fought at sea were. You will want to know who is with you and who against, whatever prejudices you may have."

Despite the admonishment about her grumpiness, Theren merely grunted sourly and glowered at Vivien's back. The implication that her misgivings were out of line was frustrating—especially since, for all she knew, Vivien might take her directly to one or both of the Mystics that had been her torturers. But her displeasure lightened somewhat as they went; Vivien was not simply parading her before every Mystic in the vast camp, instead specifically seeking out many of the mages, and purposefully avoiding some others. It seemed that Theren was being introduced only to those who Vivien knew well, which at least had the benefit of often providing common ground, and she was asked many questions about her training at the Academy and which instructors remained there and which had left.

Several of them inquired apprehensively about Vivien's scars, which surprised Theren; it seemed that whatever had caused them must have happened recently, given how many of Vivien's acquaintances were shocked by her appearance. For her part, Vivien smiled sadly at each of their concerns, and told them merely that serving the High King always held its perils.

Another common topic of discussion was the attack by the Dulmish raiders, which many of those in the larger group had not yet heard about. Theren wondered if any of the mages they spoke to might have known Tinun, but Vivien did not mention him, and it seemed presumptuous to ask without knowing them better.

They met up with one particular mage, a short, stout man from Wavemount, who Vivien was delighted to see, going so far as to hug him.

"Theren, this is Maikano, of the family Koura," she said, laughing, as he lifted her off the ground. "He is also a mentalist. We studied in the same year at the Academy."

"How long has it been?" Maikano grinned widely as he set Vivien back on her feet. "I fear I have not seen you once since those days!"

"Rarely did I have cause to go to Wavemount, and it seems you hardly left there," Vivien replied wryly, and he laughed again.

"Well, you know my family. They feel better having me around!"

"He is a cousin to a powerful merchant family," Vivien explained airily, the happiest that Theren had ever heard her. "Maikano, this is Theren, a new recruit. She will likely be training with me once we reach Ammon."

He inspected her closely at that comment, narrowing his wide brown eyes as he looked her over. "She seems like a fine girl! I have no doubt she will fit in perfectly."

Theren smiled at him, embarrassed. She could already see why Vivien liked him so much; she knew it should have rankled her that a goldbag would simply assume that everyone would find the Mystics to be a perfect new home, but his warmth was so genuine that she instead felt reassured. She found herself hoping that she might see him around in the future, and realized suddenly that this was exactly the reason that both Vivien and Lilith had suggested she do this—not that she would admit to them that they had been right, of course.

"Do you have any advice for me, one mentalist to another?" she asked him, and he chuckled.

"Be mindful of the chancellor, Karan. Rumor has it that nobody has ever made him laugh . . . or even crack a smile! Follow his orders to the letter when he gives them, and you should do well."

"He says that as though you should not follow all of the officers' orders," Vivien commented dryly, and he laughed once more.

"Oh, Vivien, you know as well as I that any girl in your tutelage will learn the finer points of politics and which officers can be ignored."

"Do not give her ideas," Vivien chided him gently. "She must learn to follow orders at all before she can know which ones to break."

Theren snorted. "If you had heard anything about my time at the Academy, you would know that I am already proficient at both skills."

"Ah, what a scoundrel she seems!" Maikano exclaimed, enjoying himself. "I see why you have taken her under your wing, Vivien."

Vivien gave Theren a look, but smiled at him. "She certainly shows promise."

"How is the Academy these days?" Maikano took Theren's hands in his own, his eyes sparkling. "Is old Sollen the weremage still the dean? We used to joke that he would never leave!"

She laughed. "No, no. There have been two since him, though I believe he still lives in the city somewhere. First there was Cyrus, of the family Drayden, and then after Dulmun attacked the Seat a new dean had to be found. Currently the position is held by Xain, of the family Forredar. He is—"

Theren broke off, confused, as Vivien shuddered beside her, rocking almost as though she had been struck by a blow. The woman's already pale skin was now as white as moonslight, and she clenched her hands into tightly balled fists. After a moment, she seemed to notice that Theren and Maikano were staring at her, and she determinedly brought herself back under control.

"I am sorry," she grated, taking a deep breath. "It has been a long day."

Theren frowned, not sure what to think. She could have sworn that it was the mention of Dean Forredar's name that had so affected Vivien, and not some sudden onset of exhaustion, but it did not seem like the right time to countermand or question her. She wondered if Vivien and the dean had some kind of history, and vaguely thought of writing to ask Ebon, if she could remember it.

Vivien seemed to rally herself back to cheerfulness, albeit with some difficulty, as they continued talking, aided no doubt by Maikano's radiant kindness. Theren, however, noticed another Mystic, a hooded man sitting off by himself to the side of one of the camps, watching them intently. He was close enough that he might have heard what they had all been talking about, and when his cold eyes met hers for a moment, she was certain that he had been listening.

She shivered, unsure of his motives, and Vivien noticed, following her gaze. A frown crossed her face momentarily, but then she turned back to Maikano, smiling again, somewhat more forced this time.

"I fear we must cut short our visit tonight, my friend. I look forward to seeing you more often once we reach Ammon."

"Of course, of course! You must get yourselves to bed." His smile as he hugged her and shook Theren's hands was genuine. "The scouts say the storm will last another day at least, so go and enjoy your dry tents!"

Vivien took Theren's arm as she was about to turn back towards their section of the camp, and spoke in a low voice, so quiet that even Theren could barely hear.

"That man you were looking at. Was he listening to us?"

Theren nodded, and Vivien made a noise in her throat, small and uncertain, almost like she was afraid. Even under the pervasive cold of the storm, Theren felt her blood chill, alarmed by the idea that there was some member of the order that Vivien—who would face down charging weremages without fear—was perturbed by.

“I see. Let us speak with him, then.”

One hand still clamped firmly around Theren’s arm, Vivien pulled her over towards the mysterious Mystic, who was still alone by the fire. As they approached, he stood up, becoming even more imposing. He was tall—much taller than she had expected, given how he had looked when hunched over—and lean, with an array of knives and curved swords strapped to his belts underneath his thick, red cloak.

His dark brown eyes were set deep in his face, like small beads of jet, and chin-length black hair fell like feathers around his sharp, pointed features. He might have been handsome, if not for his grim expression and the deep air of suspicion about him. As it was, Theren did not appreciate being any closer to him than she had been before, and hung back behind Vivien as much as she was able.

“Is there something you need, Naro?” Vivien asked him, her croaky voice dripping with feigned politeness.

The man gave her a long, cool stare before responding. “You seemed distressed. I was merely making sure that everything was all right.”

If anything, his words appeared to set Vivien even more on edge, and her nostrils flared in anger despite the chilly civility in her voice. “How very astute of you to have picked up on that from over here.”

He smiled at her, though it did not reach his eyes. "Oh, I am quite observant, indeed. You would be surprised to learn what I have seen, I am sure."

Vivien's sharp intake of breath caught Theren off guard, and she wondered what on earth the hidden conversation that the two were really having was about. She shuffled her feet awkwardly, thinking to try to take her leave, as she in this one night had now had more than enough socialization with Mystics to last a lifetime.

"Theren," Vivien said quickly, taking a firmer hold of her arm. "Please let me introduce Naro, who you may or may not remember from your time in the cells. He was acting as warden that day, though he does many things for the order—most of them too dark to mention in polite company. You met some of his compatriots during the business with the murders at the Academy, as I understand it."

Theren's heart thumped into a panic as she immediately understood Vivien's meaning. Her knees felt weak, and once again she felt the phantom pain of the knives as they played across her skin, exacerbated by Vivien's grip on her arm. Trembling, she inspected his face more closely, trying to tell if she had indeed met him before; however, he did not look familiar, nor did his dark-skinned, fine-fingered hands look like those that had held the knives that had tormented her.

She closed her eyes, head swimming, and tried to pull herself back together, focusing on the present to try hauling herself out of those memories. When she opened them again, Naro was staring at her, his expression just as unreadable as before.

"I am tired," she mumbled awkwardly, taking another step away from him. "I should get some rest."

She slipped out of Vivien's grip and hurried back to her tent, quickly removing her boots and ducking inside before anyone could tell her not to. Lilith lay on their bedroll, already dozing, and Theren watched her sleep for a while in an effort to calm herself down. She tried to reassure herself that the evening had at least been fruitful in learning the names of some Mystics that she could trust, but she could not shake the feeling that the more important piece of information had been about one to avoid.

She did not know why Vivien feared Naro precisely, but given what he did for a living, she was willing to believe that it was justified.

FOURTEEN

THE RAIN CLEARED SOMETIME DURING THEIR LAST DAY of travel, which was a cheerful omen, and Theren found herself sitting up straight in her saddle for the first time in some days. Though the fields beside the road were still muddy, the sun was warm and the breeze pleasant, and for a while she could forget that she was traveling with a large convoy of some of her least favorite people in all of the nine lands. The radiant smile on Lilith's face as she drank in the sunlight helped, as well.

At about midday, the pace of their column quickened suddenly, and Vivien perked up too, commenting that the first of them must have come within sight of their destination. The horses, sensing the excitement of their riders, pricked their ears and put their heads forwards eagerly, until the entire band was practically galloping along the road.

The fortress of Ammon, as it appeared swiftly on the horizon, was a welcome sight, even ahead of the long trail of red cloaks. Theren had never been so relieved to see signs of civilization before, but the thin clouds of smoke rising from distant chimneys looked like shining beacons of hope after the long ride they had been through. Vivien forced them to rein in, however, and Theren did see why; the first of the Mystics were approaching the great gate in the outer wall and being stopped, presumably to wait for it to open and the drawbridge to lower.

A long ramp cut its way up the hill on which the keep was situated, towards the first wall, beyond which they could see what looked like a cluster of barracks. Far-off splashes of crimson dashed back and forth between the buildings and along the walls, the fortress seemingly overflowing with soldiers of the order. Past the second wall, which was thick and squat, perched the keep itself, looming on top of the rise like a predator crouched and ready to pounce. It looked like the kind of fortification that Theren's dry old textbooks would have described as 'unassailable,' which suited her just fine after their run-in with the Dulmunsters at sea.

"I never knew something like this was here," Lilith

said, dumbfounded, as she stared at the vast approach. "It is gargantuan!"

"It is not widely spoken of," Vivien replied, matter-of-factly. "The kings of Feldemar know it is here, of course, but I think it likely few have visited or know its size and formidability. Originally it was nothing more than a holdfast of some wealthy family, and once the order acquired it, the royals would not need to pay it any real mind—unless they themselves considered war with the High King."

Lilith bitterly muttered something under her breath about people being allowed to make choices without fear of reprisal, and Theren shuddered, picturing waves of soldiers pouring forth from Ammon to go towards Bandar in retaliation for their suspicion about the Mystics' arrival. Vivien, it seemed, either did not hear the comment or deliberately ignored it.

Nostrils flaring in anger, Lilith leaned across towards Theren, her voice low. "After they have invited Dulmun to their coastline and taken their resources, how am I to convince anybody in Feldemar to welcome these cretins?"

"Let us hope you find a way, or you will be pondering that question from elsewhere," Vivien retorted sharply, evidence that she had indeed heard. "After all, that is the entire purpose for which you would have us accommodate you."

Her lips taut with anger, Lilith spent the rest of the ride towards the outer wall glaring daggers at Vivien's back, and the brief gaiety of their arrival dissipated. The closer they came, the more unwilling Theren was to look upwards at the now ominous-seeming keep, leaving her eyes focused on the smaller buildings and signs of inhabitation, as though that could help her forget that this was no simple village. Their mounts' hooves thudded across the heavy drawbridge—which was more than sturdy enough to support the crossing of many soldiers, she noted—and they emerged into a wide courtyard that was bustling with activity.

Mystics stood clumped in groups throughout the graveled space, some barking orders, while young stablehands scurried around attending to the large number of newly arrived horses. One danced impatiently nearby as Theren dismounted, and whisked the reins from her hand as soon as her boots touched the ground, disappearing away into a large wooden building nestled in the lee of the wall. Feeling out of place, she looked around questioningly, wondering where they were supposed to go.

Some ways away, Lilith had to chase another stablehand, this one a young girl, to stop her from walking off with their luggage, but Vivien seemed calmer and more in control than ever, as though she was in her element. She beckoned to one of the innumerable servants, and then to Theren and Lilith.

"Everyone will be busy settling in, so you will not have any duties to attend to this afternoon," she told them, and then smiled briefly as Theren made a face at the mention of duties. "I will come and find you in the morning, and let you know of any training arrangements that have been made. In the meantime, you both should take this letter of introduction to the chancellor and see what he thinks of Lilith's request."

She held out a small, sealed document, which Lilith took, and though Theren tried, she could not gauge by Vivien's expression whether or not she thought that they were likely to succeed.

The Mystic woman then instructed the servant boy to take them to the chancellor's office, and he nodded quickly, setting off at a brisk pace that they could barely match after their long ride. Hefting the luggage in their aching arms, they trailed after him through a mazelike burrow of corridors and courtyards, up flights of stairs and then down again, and through narrow openings that barely seemed like they should be proper accessways.

"I never thought I would see anywhere more difficult to navigate than the Academy," Theren managed to say, puffing heavily, when their guide finally stopped.

At her mention of the wizarding school his eyes widened in awe, and he pointed at the door to their right. "The chancellor is in here. I have to go now, but just keep going down flights of stairs when you are done, and you should find your way out in the end."

Lilith, also breathing hard, made a face at his retreating back. "I feel a sudden terror that we will be trapped in this building for all eternity, never finding the exit."

"It *would* be a fitting end to this damnable trip," Theren added, groaning, as she leaned against the wall.

Lilith took a moment, standing up straight and gathering herself as she prepared to knock on the door, and Theren reached out and squeezed her hand, giving her a small smile.

"You know nobody can resist your arguments," she said, and Lilith giggled.

"Just because you cannot does not mean the rest of the world is so stricken."

"Just pretend he is me!" Theren suggested, grinning, and Lilith made another face, this one more disgusted. She seemed reassured, though, and knocked twice on the heavy wooden door.

"Come!"

The voice was low and surprisingly quiet, carrying the kind of hoarseness that sounded like it came from infrequent use rather than overzealous shouting. Lilith took a deep breath and then opened the door, Theren following on her heels as they entered the small, dimly lit room.

"Close the door," he commanded, not looking up from his inspection of a map, and Theren did so, nerves jangling.

He was among the tallest people that she had ever seen, dwarfed only by Instructor Perrin from the Academy, with long, thin limbs and a strange air of wildness about him. Though his hair was touched at the temples with grey, he seemed to be still in his prime, his pale, fair skin unlined by age, apart from the calluses on his hands that were explained immediately by the longbow leaning against his desk. Everything about him exuded an aura of weather-beaten weariness—and yet his clothes and cloak were entirely free of wrinkles, as neat as though they had been laid out moments ago. It was mesmerizing to observe, and baffling to contemplate. Theren could not shake the sense that he should be rumpled and travel-stained.

"I . . . have a letter of introduction for you," Lilith said politely, and held it out in front of her. "I believe I can be of some assistance."

Only then did he look up at them, inspecting them both briefly before reaching for the letter. He picked at the seal on it for a moment, grunting in annoyance, and then his eyes suddenly turned white with magelight, and as they watched the fingernail he had been using to scrape at the wax unfolded into a large, curved talon. He easily pierced it then, and Theren thought that his demeanor and appearance made perfect sense now that she could see he was a weremage. All the travel that had presumably made him so weary must have been undertaken in one of his beast forms, leaving his clothing untouched by the journey.

The great claw returned to its more mundane form and he read through the letter, occasionally lowering it to glower at Lilith suspiciously for a moment before returning to the missive.

"So, you want to handle your kingdom's unending complaints, do you?" he asked gruffly once he was done, setting the letter down on his desk. "I cannot say I would not be glad to see the back of every minor noble in the north with a penchant for whining, since you are offering to take them off my hands. But can you do what you promise?"

Lilith blinked a few times, taken aback by his attitude, and then rallied, pulling herself up to her full height. "Well, I already interceded in Bandar when some of the local merchants were unwilling to sell mounts to the group of Mystics that I was traveling with."

He made a low noise in his throat, almost like a growl, that seemed to deflate Lilith, but instead of remonstrating her, he nodded in approval. "Very well, I will entertain your offer. What do you ask in return?"

"I—" she began, and then faltered. "I do not take your meaning, I am afraid."

He grunted sourly. "I cannot think of any reason under the sky that somebody would willingly offer to deal in negotiations with merchants and noblemen. You must be expecting something in payment, surely? Coin, protection, information? I would know what you seek before I agree to anything. The Yerrin name is stained with darker rumors than many."

Looking embarrassed, Lilith cleared her throat

meaningfully and indicated Theren with one hand, while Theren shuffled her feet uneasily, not sure what to say. Further explanation turned out to be unnecessary, however, since he narrowed his eyes shrewdly at the gesture and their awkward hesitation, and then sighed heavily.

"I see. Well, that is a much cheaper price than I expected, though I am unsure whether it will be wise. We do have a room set aside for diplomats, which you may have. Your companion here will of course have a place in the barracks."

"Well, I thought that I would share with . . . her . . ." Theren piped up, and then felt her voice fall away under his piercing, unflinching gaze, feeling completely out of her depth.

"Far be it from me to refuse resources you are returning to me," he said eventually, turning towards the door and holding it open, waving them through. "But in future please keep in mind that what you do other than follow my orders is absolutely none of my business."

He set off, and they hurried after him, his long legs taking him at an even faster pace than that of the boy who had brought them here. Though Theren's face was hot with embarrassment, she forced herself to ignore it, raising her chin and gritting her teeth as she lifted her end of their luggage higher. She would have endured much worse, if it was required, in order to have the chance to have Lilith with her here. Making a fool of herself was, to echo what the chancellor had said, a much cheaper price than expected.

"Here." He stopped at a small door that was slightly lower than most of the rest of those in the building, and more than a head shorter than he was.

Theren reached out to the door, which was set directly in the corner of the building where two walls met, and swung it open, looking in dismay at the room on the other side. A staircase obviously ran above it, since the ceiling was low and sloped, and there was barely enough room for the three pieces of furniture inside. The bed, which was at least a decent size, occupied most of the floor space, while a desk and chair were squeezed into the area behind the door.

"This is your room set aside for diplomats?" Lilith asked faintly, sounding as though she had passed beyond worry into a strange state of detached, calm curiosity.

"I do not particularly put much stock in diplomacy," he replied, a most unnecessary clarification, and then turned on his heel and stalked off.

The two of them exchanged a long look of confusion mingled with apprehension before Theren finally lifted the luggage once more and edged inside.

They managed to stow their things under the bed, after some wrangling and much shuffling around each other while they tried to both fit inside with the door closed, though it took them the better part of the afternoon to really unpack anything. Stomachs growling, they fought their way out into the building when a bell was rung for dinner, following what Mystics they could see to the mess hall, where they were fed meaty stew with hard lumps of bread. Theren had never felt so alone whilst surrounded by so many people; even in her first days at the Academy she had never felt so out of place.

She did not see either Naro or Chancellor Karan in the mess hall, which she was glad of, but neither did she see Vivien or Maikano. Most of the Mystics ignored them, though she could not shake the feeling that she was being watched by eyes that would turn away whenever she looked over her shoulder.

That night, after they had fought their way into bed past the obstacle course created by their luggage, Lilith fell asleep with her usual ease, and Theren burrowed in closer to her, burying her face in Lilith's back and listening to her breathing. She felt terrified, not just for her own sake, but for Lilith's as well. What if the chancellor was unhappy with Lilith's efforts to appease her countrymen? What might he do? She wondered, as the stomping of feet making their way upstairs above her kept her from sleeping, whether they could run away from the Mystics. Calentin was certainly closer to Ammon than it had been to the High King's Seat—but the fortress was so remote, and it would be so easy to see them on the wide, featureless plain surrounding it if they attempted to flee.

Shivering, she drew her arms tighter around Lilith,

wondering what under the sky she had gotten them into now.

FIFTEEN

THEREN WAS STARTLED AWAKE THE NEXT MORNING BY a knock on their door, and sat up, blinking blearily, while Lilith fought to open it. There were no windows in the room, only a small slit near the ceiling for ventilation, so the sole indication that it was morning at all was a tiny sliver of pale light, something like the color of the first few hours after dawn. Vivien raised her eyebrows in surprised concern at the admittedly narrow view of their living quarters through the partially open door, and told them that she would wait outside while they dressed.

“I hope they do not mean to start every morning this early,” Theren muttered angrily, as she fumbled with her breeches.

“At least they seem to end their nights early as well,” Lilith replied, around a yawn, as she struggled to smooth out the back of her skirts in the limited space.

Gently, Theren took hold of the waistline and straightened it, helping her, and then bent to kiss her shoulder. “We will teach them civilized behavior in the end, I am sure.”

Lilith laughed. “I do not know many cultures that are quite as civilized as you, if your idea of civilization involves sleeping until it has passed midday.”

Theren sniffed haughtily, edging around her towards the door. “I am a paragon of refinement, it is true.”

She took her cloak from the peg behind the door, knowing she would not have nearly enough room to sling it around her shoulders while inside, and exited, surprised by the coolness of the air in the corridor outside. Cramped their room may have been, but it was apparently a minor blessing that at least it was small enough for their bodies to heat it adequately. She mumbled a greeting to Vivien as she pulled on her cloak, scrabbling with the ties as the last vestiges of sleep still clung to her.

“I have rarely met anybody who seems so perpetually exhausted as you do,” Vivien commented, sounding amused, and Theren gave her a reproachful look.

"It is the travel!" she countered, defensively. "I am used to staying in one place, not being in more than a thousand in one day. I think my restfulness is several weeks behind us."

Vivien nodded, accepting this. "It can sometimes be like that, yes. If such is the case, I assume that establishing a routine for yourself here will help—which is well, for the military side of the order greatly favors routine."

Lilith emerged at that, closing the door carefully behind her as though she feared that everything within would burst out if she made too many sudden movements. After all their efforts to unpack their clothes the previous night, Theren would not have been surprised.

"Good morning," Lilith said politely to Vivien, fighting another yawn, and the older woman smiled in response.

"I must apologize for my absence last night. I had many people to speak to and much information to receive and pass on."

Theren waved a hand, understanding. "The worst that happened was that we got a little lost. Given what happened during the sea voyage, I can imagine you had many things to recount."

Vivien's smile faded a little, but she nodded. "Indeed. I am glad you seem to understand the vitalness of turning in reports, as once you are settled in, I will need you to write one as well."

Suddenly Theren regretted mentioning the incident at all, her hand already cramping at the thought of all the labored writing that it would undoubtedly require.

"Come, walk with me," Vivien continued, waving an arm in the direction of what Theren vaguely recognized as the route to the exterior of the building. "I take it that your meeting with the chancellor went well, seeing as you are both here."

Theren snorted, while Lilith wrinkled her nose in distaste. "If that is how meetings go well with him, then I never want to see him angry!"

Vivien tutted disapprovingly, but Theren could see the corners of her lips twitching in a secretive smirk. "From what I can tell, Chancellor Karan has always been of an . . . impatient disposition. He is exceptionally busy these days, of course, so he is not at his best—though if rumors are to be believed, his best is not all that much different. But you will be glad to have him in command, should things ever come to fighting."

Her stomach turning at the idea of more battle, Theren shuddered. "Is that likely?"

"I have been wanting to ask the same thing," Lilith said, anxiously. "Ammon is not built like a training facility."

Vivien slowed her pace for a moment, turning back to examine their worried faces, and smiled gently. "The Mystics have many holdfasts across the nine lands that were constructed in times of greater strife even than this. Ammon, and many other keeps like it, are mostly locations of convenience. If you fear some great siege against all the armies of Dulmun, then you need not, I assure you."

This seemed to reassure Lilith, but Theren frowned, still remembering her vision from yesterday of the Mystics issuing forth to attack Feldemarians who protested the High King's actions. "And what of our purpose here? Are we to be forged into an army?"

Vivien laughed at that, and Theren was surprised to see genuine mirth in her eyes. "Oh, Theren, you are so young. There are not even one thousand of us here, all told. It would be a pitiful army indeed that took the field with so few soldiers."

"Is that not the purpose of the redcloaks?" she mumbled, embarrassed once again, but Vivien just shook her head.

"Though we are called the Tenth Kingdom in jest, the order does not have nearly the numbers to call upon that any king does. We merely enforce the High King's law, and that can sometimes necessitate involving ourselves in battle to protect her people, but not often. Many of the newer Mystics here with us now will be dispersed throughout Feldemar or Dorsea, to the end of maintaining peace and order. Some of them may be sent into Dulmun, but any such mission will be one of reconnaissance, not an all-out attack. In truth, Ammon is conveniently placed to receive intelligence from the front of battle against Dulmun's forces, and not much else."

Theren was silent, processing this, while Lilith made a thoughtful noise. "Dispersed throughout Feldemar, you say? Do you think that will be what happens to us?"

"Quite possibly, now that you have offered your services as an ambassador," Vivien answered, wryly. "Though it is far too soon to tell. There will be some months of training at least before any reassignments are made, and who knows how the tide of battle will shift in that time—Dulmun may even surrender by then. Mages are quite highly prized in the order, and I myself was sent back to the High King's Seat following my training. If you behave yourselves well enough, and impress your commanding officers, it might be that you will follow a similar path."

Theren brightened considerably at that, thinking of returning to Ebon and Kalem, and the familiar streets of the Seat. "That would be welcome indeed!"

They emerged into the chilly air of the courtyard, their breath showing as thin plumes of steam, and Theren marveled that autumn seemed to have arrived so quickly outside of the jungles. Feldemar was truly a land of chaotic weather.

"This is the training hall," Vivien told them, as she led them over to a long, flat building set apart from most of the others. "Every day after the midday meal, you will come here to learn physical combat with the other new recruits, Theren. In the mornings, the three of us and an elementalist to teach Lilith will meet in one of the smaller rooms in the back, to practice our magic. These sessions will begin after the morning meal, but Theren has another duty to perform this morning, so I woke you early today."

"You found somebody to train me?" Lilith asked, excited suddenly, and Vivien nodded, though Theren found herself scowling in irritation.

"Hold a moment—why do I need to bother with ordinary fighting? Is the war magic not enough?"

Vivien gave her a cool look, though it seemed to be underlaid with humor. "There are many reasons, not the least of which is because it is ordered. But I believe it will be good for you; it will teach discipline and coordination in a way that you would not learn simply from honing your own magical talents. Besides, you should know better than most that mentalists can be particularly vulnerable and easily put off balance. There may come a time when the ability to fight off an attacker with your fists while blindfolded could save your life."

Grunting, Theren subsided, though inwardly she dreaded the idea of being forced into an entire afternoon's worth of tedium without Lilith to distract her. She longed to spend as little time alone with the redcloaks as she could possibly manage, and even the idea of learning things like how to hit them effectively was not enough to redeem the notion for her.

"What shall I do while Theren is in combat training?" Lilith asked, curious, and Vivien shrugged.

"Most likely, work with Chancellor Karan on

diplomatic matters, though that will not be the case every day. He will send for you if he needs you, and otherwise your time is your own. I would caution you not to get in the way of the other Mystics, however."

Lilith nodded, though Theren could see the dismay on her face at the idea of seeing the chancellor again. If they were lucky, he might warm up to her once he saw how clever she was, as Vivien had seemed to do, but it was quite hard to feel optimistic about that, given how he had acted yesterday.

Vivien, noticing their crestfallen looks at the mention of the chancellor, smirked once more. "And now to the other matter for this morning. Theren, you must swear your oath before the chancellor and receive your badge. Then, you will be a true part of the Mystic order, and your training can begin."

Theren's stomach lurched, though only partially at the thought of the chancellor; in truth, becoming a Mystic officially was almost as nerve-wracking a thought as facing him again. It seemed a point of no return, her last chance to flee, and it had been sprung upon her before breakfast, when she was least prepared and most unable to do anything about it.

"I see," she said faintly, after a small pause, and Lilith reached out and squeezed her hand comfortingly.

"Come, it will not be so bad," Vivien told her, placing a genial hand on her shoulder, though she still sounded amused. "The oath is short enough, and then you can eat afterwards."

"If you say so," Theren muttered in response, but then stopped dead for a moment as she caught a glimpse of something out of the corner of her eye.

She could have sworn that, lurking under the eaves of the building she knew as the stables, she had seen the tall, lean form of Naro. When she looked again, she could see nothing there but shadows, though the unease caused by that glimpse of him lingered. Telling herself that she must have imagined it, what with all the strain she had been under the past few days, she put her head down and hurried after Vivien, towards the chancellor's office.

SIXTEEN

Theren sat waiting in Chancellor Karan's office for a short time while he sifted through sheets of parchment, occasionally making notes or writing reminders for himself on other documents. He seemed to have hardly slept, if at all, and the thick black swath of stubble on his cheeks and chin was even wirier than it had been when last she saw him. Occasionally he would mutter something under his breath, annoyed, and she managed to catch the words "already missing five horses" and had to bite her lip to keep from giggling.

Unpleasant though he might be, she did not envy

anybody the job of keeping an entire fortress of Mystics under control.

Eventually he seemed to give up on wrangling with it all, sighing and rubbing at his eyes. Then, suddenly, he fixated on Theren, seemingly only just now remembering that she was there.

"Ah. Yes. The oath. Come over here."

He fished something out of one of the drawers of his desk, beckoning to her, and she went over dutifully, trying to get a good look at the item in his hand. It was, she realized, a badge, one like those worn by all of the Mystics: a silver token, just larger than the palm of her hand, on a chain. In the center were three upright bars, surrounded by a ring, with what looked like wings extending out from each side to flank them. Many of the Mystics she had seen wore it inside their clothes, especially here, where they did not particularly need to be distinguished from ordinary citizens, but she knew that it was the official sign of office, far more important than a cloak in their colors.

The chancellor inspected her gravely for a moment before passing the badge to her. "I have been told that you were involved in a skirmish with Dulmun during the sea passage."

"Yes," she answered unceremoniously, but then, remembering the lecture about respect that Vivien had given her outside the door, added hastily, "sir."

If he noticed her hesitation, he did not mention it, merely sighing once more. "Then you are more qualified already than some others who have been sworn in. There seems to be no argument against your enlistment, so I will move ahead to the oath itself. Do you see, on the badge I have given you, the rods in the middle?"

She nodded, looking at them more closely. Of the three, the center one was almost half again as long as the outer two, giving the whole shape a pleasing symmetry.

"They represent the three ideals around which the Mystic order was founded," he explained, absently fingering his own badge. "On the right, the tenet of adherence to the law and rule of the High King. That one is self-explanatory. The one on the left is less clear. It has always been recorded as the tenet of the preservation of life itself."

Theren raised an eyebrow. "That seems a strange mandate for an order of soldiers."

He grunted disapprovingly, though seemingly not at her. "It is vague to the point of bloody nuisance, is what it is. There are as many ways of interpreting it as there are Mystics. Some say it encourages pacifism, while others believe that it advocates a more aggressive approach, striking at evildoers before they can do harm in the first place. Personally, I would prefer it if we could rewrite the oath and do away with all the pointless debate, but I have learned that you cannot command people to be sensible."

He walked over to the window, gazing outside for a moment, before continuing.

"The third rod, then, the center one, represents

the tenet of defense of the people of the nine lands. You will notice, I am sure, that this is the longest of the three; this is because it is considered the most crucial. In theory, if there were a conflict between all three tenets, whatever action best helps serve in protecting the people should be the one that wins out. In practicality, our order is as wont to argue over this as over anything else, with some believing that the best way to serve the people is by following the High King's orders, or some such other justification."

Theren looked down at the badge again, surprised by this revelation. "I would have thought that whatever would best help protect people would be the obvious choice."

The smile on his face as he chuckled looked out of place, though it faded quickly. "You will find us nothing if not argumentative."

He reached down once more, and picked up what looked like a small placard made out of brass, handing it to her. On it were engraved four lines of text—the oath, she assumed.

By these three tenets I swear hereby to stand:
I pledge my blade for the order and justice of the High King, above all other kings;
I pledge my shield for the safeguarding of Life, against the enemy;
I pledge my life for the defense of the people of Underrealm, whenever they be in need.

She glanced back up at him curiously. "The enemy . . .?"

He shrugged dispassionately. "Like much of the oath, it is open to personal interpretation. You need not have a specific enemy in mind, just as you need not necessarily have a blade or a shield. Consider it a metaphor, if that is your wish, for greed, or crime, or the chaos of war, or anything else of your desire. That you understand your duty is enough for me. Only swear the oath, and mean it, for you shall be held to it."

She took a deep breath, and then recited the words, her heart thumping loudly. Though her voice faltered somewhat, the chancellor seemed to either not notice or not care, and when she was done, he nodded in approval.

"Welcome, Theren, Mystic of the order. May your service be long, and your road gentle."

She felt a chill at his words, thinking that if things had gone badly against the Dulmish forces on their journey her service might never even have started, and wondered for how many new recruits such a statement would prove untrue.

"I have a warning for you, before you leave," he said suddenly, his golden-brown eyes narrowing slightly. "While I was not here at the time, the chancellor before me, a well-loved man by the name of Kal, also had a Yerrin girl with him in the fortress, giving advice. It is not known exactly what she did to anger him, but to hear him speak of it, she and her companions must have nearly torn down the sky. You may find that many of the Mystics who were present regard your companion with great suspicion, and you as well for associating with her."

Theren swallowed hard against the nausea crawling up her throat. She wondered now if the atmosphere in the mess hall the previous night was due to this unfavorable reputation, and mentally cursed whichever other member of the family Yerrin had brought it upon them. It seemed that goldbags were capable of ruining her life without even trying.

"I thank you for the warning," she said quietly, genuinely grateful, but he dismissed her words with a wave.

"It was not intended as a kindness. There will be no fighting within these walls, even if some of these Mystics attempt to goad you into it. Step one foot out of line, perform any act of insubordination, no matter what led to it, and you will be disciplined, as will any other offenders. But eyes are upon you, in particular, from many directions, and so you must hold yourself to a standard that reflects that."

Her blood ran cold at the thought of what the Mystics might consider discipline, and she pulled herself up straighter, though her hands trembled. "Yes, sir."

"Good. Now, I have much work to do. You are dismissed."

Numb, she left the room and closed the door behind her quietly, barely able to process half of this, let alone all of it. Hands still shaking, she pulled the chain on which her badge hung over her head, the weight of it feeling impossibly heavy for its size. Distantly, she heard the bell ring for the morning meal, but she no longer felt hungry. She trudged wearily down the stairs, hoping to find her way back to her quarters, where Lilith was waiting for her.

A stream of red cloaks passed her by, heading for the mess hall, and she did not have the heart to look at any of their wearers, fearing to see the suspicion and anger that the chancellor had spoken of. Head down, she skulked through the halls, trying to avoid attracting attention, but when she emerged into the courtyard, she yelped in shock, nearly colliding bodily with someone who was leaning against the wall just outside the door.

"I see congratulations are in order," Naro said quietly, looking for all the world as though he had been waiting for her.

Reflexively, she took a few steps back, and considered bolting altogether, but the chancellor's words played in her mind once again, warning her that any insubordination was a bad idea. She took a moment to try calming herself, though this was made difficult by the flash of irritation that appeared in his eyes.

"You need not recoil from me so. I only wish to speak."

She raised her chin in defiance, but tried to keep the tone of her voice even. "You startled me, that is all. What did you wish to talk about?"

He stood up straighter, not helping her nervousness as he loomed over her. "You keep strange company for a penniless orphan from Selvan."

Her skin crawled in sudden horror as she wondered how he could possibly know where she was from, and she cursed herself for being too distracted to avoid him. If he was one of those that Chancellor Karan had warned her would be displeased with Lilith . . . She shivered, taking another step backwards without thinking. How were they supposed to deal with attracting the ire of a man that even Vivien feared? And how had they managed to do it after being here for only one day?

"My company is my own business," she managed to say, faintly, and once again regretted not leaving when he laughed mirthlessly.

"Why, of course it is," he replied, with an impassive tone of voice that contrasted with his intense gaze. "But I think it would be wise for you to tell your friend to make sure she is on her best behavior here in Ammon. Many people will be watching her now, and not only me."

Her mouth dry, Theren gathered up the billowing folds of her cloak around her left arm and made ready to leave.

"I have no idea what you are talking about," she

told him truthfully, and then hurried away, haunted by the vision of his amused smile at her parting words.

She half expected him to follow her, but everything behind her remained silent as she dashed through the corridors towards her room, eager to be anywhere but in the presence of Mystics.

SEVENTEEN

"He said *WHAT?*"

Lilith, unable to pace in the small space of their living quarters, was wringing her hands instead, overflowing with restless energy born of outrage and anxiety. Theren sat perched on the end of the bed, idly fingering her new badge of office as she recounted the tale.

"There is more bad news, I am afraid," she continued glumly. "Apparently there was a member of the family Yerrin staying in the fortress until recently, and something she did has the redcloaks stirred up like an angry nest of hornets. The chancellor warned me that I am being watched for the first sign of misbehavior, and that any transgression will be punished severely. Naro might not even be the worst of our problems."

That seemed to deflate Lilith, and she sat down beside Theren on the bed, staring at her hands. "Is there nothing about these people that is not disagreeable?"

"We will not let them beat us," Theren declared fiercely, her heart breaking at the sadness on Lilith's face, and hugged her tightly. "I do not care what the other Yerrin girl did. I will show them that you cannot judge one goldbag by another. I will make them see how extraordinary you are, and then we will help turn the tide of the war against Dulmun, and everything will turn out fine and we can go home to the Seat and not be stuck cooped up in a fortress full of Mystics. It will be easy, truly."

Lilith giggled at that, though she seemed only partially convinced. "You have a lot of faith in your persuasive abilities."

"Well, with all the physical training I have to do, I will soon be the most muscular woman in all the nine lands," Theren replied airily, twining her fingers with Lilith's and nuzzling against her. "They will be too dazzled by my physical prowess to refuse. You can parade me about when we go to fancy state dinners and people will be in awe of how wondrous we both are. They will tell tales of us everywhere we go!"

Lilith laughed more heartily this time, and Theren

kissed her gently, wishing that she could do more. Even before they broke apart, the bell indicating the end of the morning meal rang, and she sighed, knowing that it would not look good if they were late on their first day. No matter how much she might curse the Mystics, they now had to abide by the order's rules, as much as they could.

"Come," she said, trying to sound enthused, and held out a hand to help Lilith stand. "Now we must impress them with our ability to learn our magical training at lightning speed. Even great legendary heroes must start their tales humbly."

Together they made their way back towards the training hall, passing by many Mystics, and though Theren was careful to keep her expression neutral, she took special notice of the faces of those who seemed to regard Lilith with particular suspicion or distaste. While there was nothing she could do to stop them, at least she would know which of them not to bother trying to win over. Vivien's warning that someday she might not know her enemies by their uniform rang in her mind, and she gritted her teeth, agreeing wholeheartedly, even though this had not been what Vivien had meant at the time.

The training hall's expansive main room was almost entirely empty, save for a few new recruits who were seemingly trying to get a head start. Training dummies lined the walls in great numbers, and the springy softwood floor was covered over with woven matting—made of some kind of reeds, from what Theren could see. Even from a glance, she could tell that the implication was that those being trained would need a soft surface to land on, and probably quite often. She found herself wincing pre-emptively, imagining it.

Beyond the main room, they passed through a long hallway that was lined on either side with small arenas, presumably rings meant for sparring, that were recessed into the floor and padded even more heavily with matting. Several of these were in use, the grunts and heavy thuds of fists impacting bodies filling the air, and Lilith and Theren exchanged surprised glances when they passed by one bout that had an audience, a rowdy group of Mystics placing bets on who would win between one warrior in heavy, padded armor, and a muscular, unarmored woman armed with only her fists.

They continued on until they came to a row of rooms where the walls and floors turned to sturdy grey stone, outside the last of which Vivien was waiting with another female Mystic, clearly the elementalist who was there to train Lilith. A young man with tawny brown hair and olive-tinted skin passed by them towards a different door, and as he opened it, they could hear the guttural roar of a bear from within.

"Weremage training must really be something to see," Theren said to Lilith, who laughed.

"I think I understand why the walls here are made of stone."

On hearing them speak, Vivien turned towards them, and Theren noticed that she was making a series of complicated gestures with her hands, which the other woman seemed to be watching intently. After a few moments, memories of learning sign language at the Academy in her first few years of schooling unearthed themselves in the back of Theren's brain, and she realized that Vivien was speaking to the elementalist in sign. Theren's grasp of sign was rusty, there having been no students who were hard of hearing in any of her year's classes, and it was hard to read with Vivien's body turned side-on, but she managed to recognize a few words as they approached.

"Excellent," Vivien said to them, sounding satisfied, signing at the same time as she spoke. "I feared you might be late, but it appears you are taking things seriously. That is good."

The firemage beside her smiled, a gesture filled with genuine warmth, and signed a greeting to both of them. She was quite tall, and she was extremely beautiful, with delicate cheekbones that swept up towards her kind grey eyes, and a low, flat nose. Her fawn-colored skin was smooth and unlined, and her black hair long and glossy, the tumbled curls spilling out from a clasp at the nape of her neck to drape across her shoulders.

"This is Kaewa," Vivien explained, spelling the name out in sign carefully. "She has taught many young mages in the order, and has very generously offered to help Lilith train while she remains here."

"I thank you," Lilith signed earnestly, and then bobbed a small curtsy. "Hopefully I will learn quickly so that your kindness is not wasted."

"Very rarely is the quality of learning judged by speed," Kaewa signed in response, still smiling. "In truth, I enjoy teaching, so do not trouble yourself to rush away."

Vivien, her head tilted to the side in curiosity, was watching Theren as she squinted at everybody's hands. "They still teach sign at the Academy, do they not? You understand it, yes?"

"Oh, yes," Theren replied hastily, and then remembered only after she spoke to add the sign component to her answer. "I am out of practice, however."

Vivien nodded, apparently accepting this. "Just do your best, then. It will become easier the more you speak it—you must make sure to do so, though. Not just for Kaewa's sake, but because in many situations where silence is necessary, squad leaders and captains may give orders entirely in sign. It is a necessity here."

"Just ask if you need me to slow down or repeat anything," Kaewa added, once again in sign, and Theren realized that, unlike the woman who had taught their class sign language at the Academy, Kaewa did not speak out loud at all.

"I will get used to it, I am sure," she responded, and hoped that her fingers could match up to her declaration.

Vivien waved them towards the nearby door, obviously ready to begin, and they followed Kaewa inside. Theren felt a small thrill of excitement as she wondered what the training would be like. The room was better ventilated than many of those in the barracks, with a bank of high window slits set in the far wall through which flowed both fresh air and the pale morning sunlight. The walls, although stone, were covered with scorch marks from fire and lightning, and many of the bricks were cracked or chipped in places from other magical impacts. Unlike in the rest of the training hall, there was no matting on the floor, which worried her somewhat, but she tried to tell herself that it just meant it was likely there would be less falling down expected in this particular class.

"Now, you asked me the other day why you needed this extra training," Vivien began, still duplicating her words in sign for Kaewa as her voice echoed around the room. "This morning, we will show you. You are both skilled—I saw that clearly during our scuffle with the raiders—so we may try to begin some of the basics today, but your task for now is simply to observe."

She indicated a small, low wooden bench in one of the corners, and both she and Kaewa removed their cloaks in preparation as Theren and Lilith went to sit down. Kaewa selected a long, thin staff from a rack of weapons along one wall, twirling it experimentally to test its weight, while Vivien, whose usual finery had been replaced with plain, rough clothes, presumably just for this, hefted a slightly thicker baton in each hand.

"Come, when you are ready," Kaewa signed to Vivien, with her free hand.

The smaller woman was still for a moment, gathering herself, until suddenly she leaped wildly towards Kaewa, lashing out with the batons with a force that surprised Theren. Kaewa, on the other hand, was unfazed, deftly blocking both with the staff, and then bringing her own attack to bear with a swirl that whipped a gust of wind up towards Vivien.

The mentalist reeled back, nearly losing her footing, but recovered at what seemed like the last instant. Quickly, she spun around, bringing her leg up in a kick that added a small disc of magical force to her heel. Kaewa blocked with her staff once again, but the additional power granted by Vivien's mentalism caused the wood to splinter on impact, and it nearly split in two. Kaewa, grinning, swiftly hooked the end of her staff behind Vivien's other leg and swung it upwards, sending Vivien tumbling heels over head.

They continued like that, back and forth with attacks so blindingly quick as to cause Theren's eyes to water as she tried to keep track of what was going on. The entire thing was enough to overwhelm Theren's senses; she could see why Vivien had told them merely to observe, when that itself was difficult enough, as she tried to understand both the physical movements and the magical manipulation. Their reflexes seemed expertly honed, as they would quickly catch some of each other's spells and dampen or cancel them, but ignore or deflect others with their weapons, and Theren marveled that they could even decide which called for either at the speed they were moving.

They were dogged and unmerciful, each landing several blows on the other, and Theren was quite sure that at least once, Kaewa hit Vivien with a bolt of lightning.

Eventually, Kaewa struck brutally at Vivien's knuckles, managing to get her to drop both batons, but Vivien simply concentrated her magic around her fists. It was just as Theren had seen her do during their fight against the enemy weremage at sea; the excess force behind her punch was enough to smash clear through Kaewa's staff this time, sending it clattering to the floor. In retaliation, Kaewa wreathed her own fists in a halo of ice, and swung a vicious blow at Vivien's stomach. The mindmage caught the attack swiftly and dispelled the ice, while making a counterattack aimed at Kaewa's ribs.

Theren shook her head in amazement, watching them grappling and swinging punches like ordinary brawlers, though ten times as deadly.

After what felt like an eternity of exchanging attacks, Vivien finally disengaged and held up her hands in surrender, both women breathing hard from their exertions. Kaewa leaned back against the wall behind her and fanned her face with her hands, while

Vivien slumped forwards, puffing loudly as she tried to regain her breath.

"Obviously it has been too long since I faced someone with any real skill," Kaewa signed wearily, once Vivien stood back up, and the smaller woman grinned wryly in response.

"Too long for both of us, my friend. I fear I will need the afternoon off to recover."

Theren watched them both with naked awe, and the look on Lilith's face made it plain that she was feeling the same thing. Some of the attacks they had just seen might have killed lesser enemies, and there had been dozens of those maneuvers chained together in less time than it would have taken Theren to describe the first.

"You seem impressed," Vivien said mildly, observing the looks on their faces, and Lilith, who had spent most of the fight agape with wonderment, finally shook herself out of it and snapped her mouth shut.

"Impressed? I am surprised we were not injured just watching you!"

Kaewa laughed, the sound surprisingly loud and melodious. Theren had been greatly enamored with the way she spun her magic during the fight; in the same way that the magic of mentalists depended on sight and being able to see their target, the magic of elementalists was tied to their voices. Since Kaewa did not speak, she seemed to invoke most of her spells with wordless humming and vocalizing, which obviously worked just as well as the incantations that Lilith and other firemages used.

"You switch so quickly between elements!" Lilith signed excitedly to Kaewa, while Vivien turned away to toss their now-broken weapons into a corner. "I have rarely seen anyone fight with ice. At the Academy the element that receives the most focus is fire, since it is so versatile."

"Ah—I can teach you many tricks with fire, if you wish, though not here, and not today," Kaewa replied, her face clouding momentarily. "I do not think it kind to Vivien to bandy fire magic about, not after it has caused her so much pain."

Startled, Theren thought back to Vivien's words about her scars and how serving the High King could be perilous, realizing that she had never considered they could be from fire magic instead of ordinary flames. She again found herself wondering what had happened, but it seemed terribly rude to ask outright.

Vivien, oblivious to the signed conversation that had gone on behind her, beckoned to them to come over, as she still looked quite worn out. "Come, I have changed my mind. We will try to teach the two of you at least a few basic principles today, if only so that I can take a break."

Lilith sprang to her feet, elated, but Theren glanced apprehensively at the rough stone floor, more than somewhat afraid she would be introduced to it. Luckily for her, Vivien had meant it when she had said that they would learn the very basics, and the rest of that morning before the bell for the midday meal was spent learning about the balance of weapons and where best to center magic on them. Theren's arms were sore from holding up a club that Vivien had tasked her to weigh down with her magic, but at least she had not fallen over, so it seemed a victory, in the end.

"I look forward to getting to know the two of you over the coming months," Kaewa signed to them, after she had gathered up her cloak and prepared to leave, and gave one last smile.

Lilith thanked her profusely, and Theren was gladdened to see how much happier she seemed to be, especially after her flagging spirits from earlier. Kaewa seemed uncommonly kind and gentle for a redcloak, and Theren was grateful indeed that she had offered to help, as well as surprised by her generosity. The Mystics that she had encountered had been such a strange mixture of people, seemingly sitting at the extreme ends of the spectrum of good and evil, that she wondered if something about the order pushed people towards one end or the other.

Lucky for her, she thought as they hurried towards the mess hall, stomachs growling after their exertions, she had at least found a small pocket of the good ones to spend all her time with, so that this whole ordeal might turn out to be bearable after all.

EIGHTEEN

By the end of the day, Theren regretted having gone into the midday meal with any optimism. Though she was quite fit compared to many of the merchant's children that she had known on the Seat, and even most of the softer new recruits, the Mystics' physical training seemed to have been specifically designed to exhaust everyone. The captain in charge, Menrad—a horrible, shouty little man for whom Theren had developed an immediate and intense dislike—had threatened that someday soon he would have them jogging around the entire base of the hill on which Ammon was perched, if they did not "shape up."

As far as she could tell, "shape up" was code for whatever he happened to want at any given moment, and their main problem in providing it was that they were not able to read his mind.

By her estimation, there were nearly a hundred newly arrived recruits, all told, and they were divided into units of a dozen each, cycling through all of the various training activities throughout the afternoon. In addition to the bouts with straw dummies that she had expected, they were also set to running the full circumference of the keep to improve their fitness, given rudimentary lessons in various quite simple weapons, trained in riding and caring for horses, and taught how to respond to the most common battlefield commands.

The absolute worst training, however, was learning how to carry a person slung over her shoulders. There were techniques for the best positioning, to lessen the burden on everyone's backs, but somehow Theren always found herself being the one doing the lifting. It became tiresome very quickly, despite Captain Menrad's declaration that it would be one of the most useful skills they would learn; she thought grimly that she would rather keep her comrades from becoming injured in the first place if the alternative was carrying the wounded from the battlefield like this.

Many of her fellows were full of questions, wanting

to know when they would get to choose their weapons and who would decide what role they would play in the order, while others demanded to be told when they would be allowed into the fray, displaying an eagerness for blood that Theren found disgusting. Later, when the Mystic who was assigned to tutor her unit—a distinguished-looking Dorsean man called Junan—asked their group if any of them had seen combat before, to her surprise she was the only one to raise her hand.

She had come to realize, watching the awe and envy on the faces of the others as she recounted the tale of her encounter with Dulmun on the sea, that the Mystics were not recruited quite so heavily from the children of nobles as she had imagined. There were some few, it was true, but the majority were pulled from ordinary families, farmers' daughters or blacksmiths' sons, who had grown up hearing wild stories of the heroism of the mighty red-cloaked servants of the High King. They were completely removed from the Mystics' true nature, the dark and bloody aspects of the order that Theren and Lilith knew so well. These recruits had signed up to find their own glory, their own adventures, and knew nothing of what might await them.

Junan had done his best to answer their questions pragmatically, and he seemed a decent enough man from what Theren could tell so far, but the whole thing had left a bitter taste in her mouth. Vivien's denial that the recruits had been brought to Ammon to be turned into an army was blatantly false, whether she knew it or not; the numbers it would take to engage in real battle were completely irrelevant when the order knew it was deliberately taking impressionable young men and women with very little knowledge of their true dealings, and telling them what and how to think and act. In some ways, Theren considered that to be even worse than what she had originally feared.

Lilith's afternoon had not been any better, with Theren returning to their room to find her fretting over a letter that she was trying to write, chewing on her lip as she stared at the blank parchment in front of her.

"This whole affair is a ridiculous mess," she complained, once Theren had suggested that she take a break.

Unable to argue with that, Theren simply put an arm around her in what was hopefully a soothing way. Boots thudded overhead as several people walked up the stairs just above them, and Theren felt her blood boil, outraged that the chancellor expected Lilith to work in a place like this just because of his own problems with diplomats.

"What were you working on?" she asked, trying to keep her voice light. "I cannot promise I will understand it, but I could probably get away with tripping Karan in public once or twice before people realize it is me, if you need."

That elicited the laughter that Theren had been hoping for, though Lilith shook her head at the offer. "It is not his fault. Or . . . not entirely, at least. The mayor of Mabawa, a city much closer to the war, is asking for financial aid after they assisted the High King's army in crossing over the border into Dulmun. They helped to drain the marshland in the area so that the High King's soldiers could transport siege weapons to the city of Sangard, but now the battle for Sangard has ended and the war has moved on. Without the marsh, however, a lot of the livelihoods of people in Mabawa are suffering—they cannot fish nearly as much as in previous seasons. The mayor fears that people will starve."

Theren stared woodenly at the far wall, her irritation with Chancellor Karan growing by the moment. "What does he expect you to do about all that? Especially from here, so far away."

Lilith sighed, rubbing at her eyes. "What he wants, I think, is for me to make the mayor understand that the High King's army and the Mystics are entirely separate entities. They cannot intercede on behalf of one another, I understand that well enough, and besides which the treasury of Ammon is stretched thin, from what I have seen in his ledgers. But I also know that the mayor contacted the Mystics here because they are the only representatives of the High King within his reach, and he is desperate. How am I to tell him that he did not submit his request to the right people? And while his townsfolk starve? I search for words, but are there even any that could make this seem fair?"

"The chancellor should never have asked such a thing of you," Theren muttered, darkly.

"It is what I volunteered for," Lilith countered, "more or less. I thought this business would involve supplies, and bargaining with my family, but I was naïve. I think we all have been, even some of the commanders. Ammon itself will be in danger if they cannot engender some kind of goodwill from the people of Feldemar, but everyone seems to have marched out here anyway with no thoughts in their heads but those of glory, the High King's army most of all."

"Does the High King know about all this?" Theren asked, bewildered. "I mean, she must . . . she must have *strategists*, and see reports of what happens, must she not? Things are not yet so bad that they cannot get information across the sea to her, are they?"

Lilith shook her head again, spreading her hands helplessly. "I cannot say. There is always the chance that spies may have infiltrated the palace, though if that were the case, I would think that they would use their position for something worse. Yet it pains me to believe the alternative, that she might simply be willing to watch Feldemar crumble."

"Feldemar has not yet fully allied themselves with her cause, have they?" Theren asked faintly, dread sinking over her as she spoke the words. "She might . . . she might be waiting for them to declare allegiance, I suppose, before sending aid."

"That is exactly what I have been fearing to let myself consider."

Though she knew she should not have been surprised, Theren felt as though some pillar holding up her view of the world had been snatched away. For all her hatred of the nobles and merchants and everyone who considered coin and power to be worth more than the lives of other people, somehow she had always considered the High King in a separate category from them before now. The High King Enalyn had been almost more of a symbol than a living, breathing woman: an ideal to aspire to, or a pretty name to invoke.

Theren did not know how to feel about the faint sense of dread that had overcome her while thinking on these matters. On the one hand, it would seem wiser to remind herself that the High King was just as fallible and capable of making bad decisions as any other person, but on the other, this was the woman to whom Theren had just sworn her life in service. How could she perform her duties, if she could not even be sure that she would agree with the High King's orders? She frowned, hoping that she and Lilith were both wrong about the situation, and reminded herself of the oath's third tenet in an attempt to still her troubled thoughts. As long as the High King's edicts would serve the people of the Underrealm, Theren would not have to think about countermanding them.

Lilith laid her head on Theren's shoulder, and they sat there for a while in silence, pondering weightier thoughts than Theren had ever expected to have to wrestle with.

"Do you think we should run away?" she asked, eventually. "Calentin is not so far out of reach as it once was."

Lilith yawned, exhausted, but managed to muster a smile when she noticed Theren watching her closely. "Not tonight, at the very least. We have both missed our dinner, and we will not get far without food."

Theren grunted in assent, remembering, and then sighed as all of her many bruises and sore muscles reminded her of their presence as well. "I suppose it was a fool notion."

Lilith laughed. "It might be the wisest thing either of us has ever said. I find it hard to tell. But . . . for good or ill, I am beginning to feel some responsibility here, now."

Theren frowned, worried. "But it is not your responsibility to bear. Let the High King's agents untangle this mess. You carry enough burdens already!"

"I do not think that option is open to me as of yet," Lilith replied listlessly, as Theren reached over to take her hand. "How could I set this task aside and spend my days in leisure, knowing that no one else may be able to help these people? I will write to the High King, I think, to request that she send some more administrative agents north to help with this sort of thing, but for now the burden must fall to me."

"It is my hope that someday soon this place will stop throwing horrible things at us," Theren grumbled, not sure what else to say, and Lilith laughed again, this one sounding genuine at last.

"I am sure it would be quite pleasant if all of the redcloaks left."

Theren brightened at the thought, imagining it. "We could try to convince the king of Feldemar to buy the fortress! Kings always want more fortifications, do they not?"

"There is a reason I am the diplomat, and not you," Lilith told her dryly, and then kissed her.

"Is it my irresistible charm?"

Unable to keep a straight face, Lilith dissolved into giggles at that, and Theren returned her kisses, incredibly grateful once again that they were together, no matter the rest of the disaster they had wandered into.

NINETEEN

Over the next two and a half months, life at Ammon gradually evened out into a routine. Theren's mornings were spent in training with Vivien and Kaewa, learning many things that she could not imagine she would ever use, and some she did not know how she had managed without. Vivien taught her about deflecting arrows and spears, and how it was much easier to make them glance with a sweeping blow than simply stop them in midair, while Kaewa taught her to recognize many of the more common combat spells that elementalists would use, and when best to strike in order to disperse them.

Then, in the afternoons, she would return to Junan and her unit and deal with more mundane matters, like learning how to form a shield wall and stand in various attack formations. No matter how much she argued that it was unnecessary for her, being a mage, Junan insisted that she should at least learn, so that she would better understand what her allies were doing on the battlefield. Already fitter than many of her fellows, she was hardened even further by the intense training all through the day, and she would often show off her burgeoning muscles to Lilith in the evening—and only partially to make her laugh.

Lilith herself wrote missives to the High King twice, though they did not know if they would ever reach her, and penned at least five letters to Ebon and Kalem, telling them of their exploits. She also contacted a nearby branch of her family to enlist help for getting aid to the city of Mabawa, and was extremely proud to hear that stores of food had been delivered before the oncoming approach of winter. Theren had feared that Chancellor Karan might be angry with Lilith for interfering, but he mostly just seemed glad that the nuisance had been removed.

Now that their travel was over, Lilith finally seemed to be regaining some weight, much to Theren's joy. Though her work liaising between the chancellor and the people of Feldemar was often unforgiving, it was not constant, and she spent many afternoons reading books that Kaewa had loaned her, or watching Theren and her fellows at their physical training with wry amusement. Theren did not notice much change in how most of the older Mystics treated either of them, but Vivien certainly seemed increasingly impressed with Lilith's activities, and even the chancellor seemed to listen to her about as often as he listened to anybody.

Autumn wore on, the air gradually becoming cooler and cooler, until they could rarely go outside even during the day without their breath steaming in the air. Sudden, violent rainstorms were common, turning the plain beneath them into a putrid marsh as the water lingered. Every now and then, reports would reach them of the war front in Dulmun, or of coastal towns that had been raided, and the mood in the fortress would grow grim. Mutterings began to circulate about a plan to send Mystics over the border into Dulmun, as Vivien had suggested might happen, and who would go and what their task would be; Theren could overhear some of the other recruits discussing it avidly in the mess hall at many of their evening meals.

Several of them were greatly competitive over it, trying to outdo each other in training in the hopes of being noticed. Theren did not think their efforts would matter, since it hardly made sense to send raw recruits directly behind enemy lines, and would often shake her head as they all vied for Captain Menrad's attention. Their efforts seemed to only increase his unpleasantness, as the more conscious he became of them, the more he seemed determined to undermine their confidence with shouted insults. Lilith wanted her to encourage some of her fellows, to see what ludicrous lengths they would go to, but Karan was already frustrated with their antics, and Theren feared that making him step in would end poorly.

The atmosphere in the keep grew more and more tense as winter drew closer, and she got the distinct impression that they had all been cooped up for too long. It felt like a storm was brewing, and she was not sure what destruction it would wreak when the clouds finally broke.

Theren and Lilith made their way to the mess hall for lunch on one particularly cold day to find the other Mystics inside buzzing with excited gossip. They had just spent that morning training in cancelling out other mage's spells—lightning bolts were something of a specialty of Kaewa's, and even together they had both utterly failed to contain any of them—and so had missed whatever had set the others aflame with such curiosity.

Theren asked one of the women from her unit what the chatter was about, and was told that smoke from distant fires had been spotted on the horizon, and scouts had been dispatched to find out what was going on. She did not feel the thrill of excitement that many of her fellows seemed to at that news, and returned to Lilith with her heart feeling like it was made out of lead, and her stomach suddenly unsure whether it really wanted food or not. Forest fires were not uncommon in Feldemar, of course, as Lilith told her in an attempt at reassurance. But the looming threat of Dulmun's armies combined with the fact that Lilith did not sound even slightly convinced by her own argument filled Theren with a growing dread of something much worse.

They picked at their meals after that, appetites gone, and left before the bell, ascending to the top of the wall to get a look at the smoke for themselves. It drifted high in the air, greasy and black, so far above them that they could not even smell it on the wind. That meant that it was distant, one of the watchers told them grimly, and fierce, for a hotter fire would drive its smoke further upwards into the sky.

"Where is it coming from?" Theren asked numbly, staring at it. "Can you tell?"

He shrugged, looking as though he had answered the same question many times that day. "Somewhere south. With how far the wind could carry it, we cannot be more specific than that. That is why the scouts were sent out."

"Ulande lies south of here," Lilith said in a small voice, gripping the stone on the parapet so tightly that her knuckles whitened.

"That is the harbor where the bulk of the Mystic forces landed in Feldemar, is it not?" Theren mused, remembering. "Captain Jasir did say that it had already been raided by Dulmun's forces—"

The watcher cut Theren off with a derisive snort and gave Lilith a stern look. "Do not go around spreading stories to frighten the new recruits, Yerrin. If somewhere in this wretched kingdom is truly in danger, I am sure that your family will see armies sent in its defense, even if only to protect their coffers. We will not have you stirring up unfounded rumors of war—not after the debacle with the last of your lot."

Theren's hands balled into fists immediately, and she opened her mouth to respond, but felt Lilith tug on the back of her cape.

"Let us be gone from here."

The watcher laughed at Theren's glare, waving dismissively. "Yes, go on. Do not snap too hard at the end of your master's leash, or she will replace you with another hound."

Theren's body moved before she even had time to think. Anger burned in her heart like a raging bonfire, and her fist struck the watcher full in the face, sending him tumbling backwards. It was only when several other guards along the wall turned towards them, alerted by the sound, that she realized what a mistake she had made.

"You!" one shouted, hurrying over with his spear at the ready. "Stand down!"

"Send for the captain!" another called, while Theren's pulse pounded into a panic.

The man she had punched made a valiant attempt to scramble back to his feet, blood pouring between the fingers of his left hand where he clutched at his nose. Apparently incensed, he launched himself towards her, swinging wildly with his right, only to be pulled back by two of the approaching guards. She herself was seized from behind by several pairs of rough hands, and doubled over as someone elbowed her in the side, breaking her stance.

"Let her go!" Lilith demanded, but her voice shook audibly with fear.

Time seemed to slow to a standstill as Theren attempted to right herself and caught a glimpse of Lilith's face. The terror that Theren saw there made her want to lash out again, this time with magic, to blast every Mystic in the fortress and shove the ones that were restraining her off the parapets. But she knew that that would only make things worse. How would they punish her for this? What would they do if she escalated things even more? She feared that if any of them saw magelight in her eyes she would be put in blinders again, and that was the last thing she wanted. Unbidden, the memory of her time in the dark with the redcloak torturers overcame her, and she shuddered uncontrollably, going limp.

Lilith struggled to keep pace while the Mystics dragged Theren bodily towards the stairs, along with the other watcher, who was now shouting muffled obscenities. The heart-rending horror in Lilith's eyes was enough to finally help Theren recover her sense of equilibrium, galvanizing her.

"Get Vivien," she managed to say, hoping that the Mystic woman would be able to comfort Lilith a little, before being manhandled into the stairwell.

The guards dragged her to a building that she had never entered before, and her heart jolted to see what was clearly a row of cells, divided by thick stone walls and heavy iron bars. She gritted her teeth, having to fight her instincts constantly, to hold herself back from resisting. She could defeat these Mystic guards easily, she knew. Firmly she told herself that she did not have to prove that to anyone, no matter how they treated her. She was letting them think that they could handle her, for Lilith's sake, that was all.

They dumped her on the stone floor alongside her companion, and several of them snapped to a salute as she heard another person enter the room behind her.

"Captain Ilya! These two got into a fight on the wall, sir. We brought them straight here."

Theren looked up and felt her heart drop straight into her boots for at least the third time that day. The woman who was now looking down her tall, broad nose at the two of them was the same golden-haired woman who had apprehended Theren all those weeks ago on the High King's Seat. The fact that she was a captain made Theren's lips twist bitterly as she considered her spectacular ill fortune; there were few

Mystics from whom Theren would expect less mercy than from this one.

Ilya took a few steps towards them, towering over Theren and the watcher as they both knelt on the floor, her eyes narrowed into a disapproving glare.

"She started it!" the man exclaimed, outraged, and Theren could not keep herself from snorting indignantly.

"Well, he said—"

"I do not want to hear it," Ilya interrupted, curtly. "You are both agents of the High King, and must conduct yourselves as such. Do you understand?"

They both muttered something along the lines of "Yes, sir."

Apparently satisfied, Ilya turned to one of the guards that had brought them in, pointing at Theren. "This one is a mage. You had no trouble with her?"

The guard shook her head, looking perplexed. "No, sir, we did not even know. She made no move to resist or cast any spells."

Ilya made a thoughtful noise, considering something, and Theren gritted her teeth once more, bracing for the order for her to be put in the blinders again.

"Very well," the captain said at last, waving the thought away. "Let them cool off overnight in the cells, and then make sure they have only half-rations for three days. That will do."

Any relief that Theren might have felt was

dampened as she was hauled away and thrown into one of the jail cells, and she sighed bitterly as the door was locked behind her. For some reason, Ilya had decided that she trusted Theren not to try to escape using her mindmagic, but whether that reason was respect for her self-restraint, or expectation that the threat of worse punishments would keep her in check, Theren could not say.

She lay down on the pallet in the corner of the cell and put her hands behind her head, listening to the muffled gurgling sounds coming from the guard she had struck, clearly still struggling with his bloody nose. Now that the danger seemed to have passed, the memory of his words resurfaced in her head, and she smirked in satisfaction at the fact that at least he had been punished as well.

"You should learn to control your temper!" she called out to him, and grinned wider when she heard him cursing in response.

He soon became boring, however, and Theren stared at the ceiling for a while, hoping that Lilith was all right.

That was the only thing that she regretted, really; spending the night in a jail cell was no deterrent to her, after everything she had been through. But she hated the idea of Lilith fretting over her, and resolved to keep better control of herself in future, even if only for that reason. She wondered sourly if the man whose nose she had broken was similarly rethinking his actions, and pondered, not for the first time, what the previous member of the family Yerrin that everyone kept mentioning could possibly have done to fill the Mystics with such hatred.

She hoped that she would never have to meet this mysterious Yerrin figure, whoever they were, or her admirable self-control might find itself tested once again.

TWENTY

Later, in what felt like the afternoon, Theren was startled out of her silent stewing over the events of the day by the sound of a bell tolling. It was louder and deeper in tone than the bell that rang to signal their mealtimes, and she had never heard it before. She sat up warily, listening to the commotion that broke out at its sounding, as heavy boots ran across stone and gravel, and doors were opened or slammed shut urgently. She remembered the greasy palls of smoke that they had seen from the battlements and felt sick to her stomach, wondering what had caused them and whether it might be headed their way.

She clambered to her feet and pressed her face against the bars of her cell in an effort to see what was going on, but there were no handy windows to gaze out of, and most of the sound from the courtyard was muffled. Aimlessly, she hovered there for a while, hoping for some scrap of realization, but eventually sighed and went back to sit down again. She thought of Lilith once more, and frowned, hoping that she was not too worried. Briefly, Theren considered picking the lock on the cell door with her magic, but discarded that idea almost immediately as she imagined how Ilya would react.

A door opened nearby, and she bolted back to her feet, hungry for information, while light footsteps made their way towards her cell. To her relief, it was Vivien. The woman looked unworried, so Theren felt herself relax a little.

"I hope you are not expecting me to get you out of there." The disappointment in Vivien's voice made Theren's nose crinkle in annoyance.

"Compared to the last time, this is like a stay in the High King's palace," she retorted, trying to ignore the fact that Vivien's dissatisfaction with her did sting a little.

Vivien raised her eyebrows slightly at that, but nodded, apparently satisfied. "Lilith was quite distressed. I will tell her that you seem to be doing fine."

"Wait!" Theren called, as Vivien went to turn away.

"What is happening? I heard all the noise some time ago."

Vivien sighed, looking very tired suddenly. "I am afraid it is not good news. Some refugees have arrived from Ulande, seeking shelter. It appears as though the armies of Dulmun have taken the city."

Theren's blood turned to ice. She felt faint as she stood there, glad for the support of the bars that she was now clinging to. Though it had only become a target at all because of the Mystic order's staging grounds, Ulande had *fallen* to Dulmun. There was no sense to it, no way to make herself believe that it was real, and she was not even from Feldemar. She could not begin to fathom how Lilith must have been feeling.

Vivien turned to leave again, and Theren sat down heavily, feeling helpless. Before Vivien could go, however, the door into the jail opened, and someone else entered—someone that caused her upper lip to curl into a vicious, mirthless smile.

"Greetings, Naro."

Theren drew in a breath sharply, and then regretted it, hoping that he had not heard her. Pressing her palms together tightly, she tried to keep herself calm, even as her mind insisted that she did not want to be left alone in a jail cell while Naro was around. She tucked herself into the corner of the cell, though she knew that it would do no good if he was determined to interrogate her for some reason, and tried to take deep, steady breaths as Vivien stepped away towards him.

"I asked around about you, you know," Theren heard the Mystic woman say, so quietly that she was sure Vivien had not meant for the words to be overheard.

"Oh, yes?" He spoke just as quietly, and Theren, despite her worry, pressed herself as close to the bars as she dared, ears straining to try to pick up on their words.

"I have heard that you hail from Dulmun originally," Vivien continued, a contemptuous note entering her already-harsh voice, from slightly farther away. "I wonder, is there anyone that you know paying a visit to Ulande right now? I hope you remember whose side you are on, friend."

Theren's blood ran cold at that, and she had to fight herself to keep from gasping. Was Vivien truly insinuating what her words implied? Could part of the reason that she feared Naro be because she believed him to be a traitor? He had not been with their group that had docked in Bandar, so he must have traveled through Ulande like the majority of the Mystic forces. The idea that he might have passed on information about Ulande's fortifications or weak points to soldiers in Dulmun made Theren's guts churn in a mixture of rage and terror.

"You know as well as I do that we give up all allegiance to any ruler but the High King when we take our oaths," Naro responded, coldly. Theren heard Vivien chuckle.

"Of course I know. I just had to be sure that you did, as well."

It seemed to Theren that Vivien left after that, assuming the receding footfalls were hers. For a few heartbeats, everything fell silent before measured steps made their way down the corridor towards her cell. She stood up, heart pounding, as Naro appeared before her, his eyes even darker and more hooded than usual in the gloom of the jail. She pulled herself up to her full height, swallowing hard, and balled her hands into fists, ready to fight if he so much as tried to step inside the cell. He did not move, however, but merely stood watching her. He seemed to be searching for something, assessing her somehow, but she could not tell what he wanted.

He opened his mouth to speak, but was cut off abruptly when the same bell as earlier rang out once more, followed swiftly by the sound of horns being blown from all around the keep. The look of consternation on his face was so earnest that Theren almost asked him what was going on, but before she could think on whether or not that was wise, he had already turned and bolted out the jail door, not even stopping to close it in his haste.

All throughout the keep it seemed that other Mystics were doing just as Naro had done, as even more tumult erupted, the sounds of chairs scraping and things being dropped joining the constant drum of moving feet and slamming doors. Theren felt helpless and trapped, and found herself cursing under her breath at the man in the cell beyond hers for putting her in this situation. It was endlessly frustrating trying to squeeze through the bars a little and listen for anything that her ears could pick up, but it was the best that she could do right now.

She could not make out much specific over the din of general noise, but she did hear a few swords being drawn, something that made her hair stand on end as dread crept over her like a fine mist. Was there to be fighting? What was going on?

Suddenly, she stood stock still, trembling in shock, as she managed to pick out Lilith's voice over the rest of the cacophony.

"—please!" She was pleading, her voice desperate. "You cannot—"

Theren did not need to hear any of the rest of what Lilith was saying. The fear in her chest hardened into rage and she drew in a deep breath, gathering her will together. Whatever the consequences might be, she was not going to sit here and do nothing while Lilith was so distraught. She concentrated all of her magic under the heel of her foot and kicked out, landing a solid blow on the lock on her cell door. It snapped under the force, clattering on the floor, and Theren hurried out of the jail, ignoring the shouts of the other prisoner as she went.

The courtyard was not nearly as full as Theren had expected it to be, but she did not have time to wonder where all of the Mystics had gone. Instead, she moved directly to where she could now see Lilith, standing by the gates alongside Captain Menrad. As Theren came closer it became clear that the two of them were arguing, and he was so angry that his face had turned a worrisome red color, something that did not bode well for anyone.

"You *must* let them in!" Lilith exclaimed as Theren approached, grabbing the captain's arm, but he jerked it away, and then pushed her backwards.

"Get away, Yerrin! We are not all dogs to jump at a master's commands. I will have you cast out of here if you continue to disrespect the order's authority!"

"What is happening?" Theren asked breathlessly as she ran over and grabbed Lilith's hand, hoping to comfort her at least somewhat.

Lilith turned to her in shock and relief, but Theren could see that the situation was still bad by the look in her eyes. "Dulmun's forces are on approach to the fortress. But he will not open the gates to let the refugees in, so they are trapped outside!"

Even through the thick, wooden gates, the panicked cries of the crowd filled their ears, and she stared at Captain Menrad in shock and disgust, unable to believe that he could hear them and decide not to help.

"Forget him," she hissed, advancing towards the gatehouse. "I will open them myself!"

"Do not forget your place, soldier," he snarled, seizing hold of her arm as she passed him. "I may have to tolerate the meddling of civilians, but *you* must follow orders. We cannot risk opening the gates while the enemy is close enough to enter, and until I am ordered to do otherwise by the chancellor, I will see that they remain closed—as will you."

Theren's blood boiled with hate as she stared him down, thinking that he represented everything that she had always feared she would have to deal with upon joining the Mystics. It took every ounce of her strength to keep from starting another fistfight, and it was only the fact that it would not aid the people outside that managed to help her keep control.

"Am I the only one who listened to the lecture about the oath?" she growled, pulling out her Mystic badge from under her shirt. "I swore to give my life for the defense of the people of the nine kingdoms, whenever they were in need! People are in need outside that gate, right now!"

"You will open that gate immediately, or I will burn it down!" Lilith declared hotly beside her, flames springing to her hands, as Captain Menrad opened his mouth to scream at them.

"Do as she says."

The captain, who was now apoplectic with rage, somehow reddened even further as Chancellor Karan's voice rang out across the courtyard, loud and firm. The Mystics who were charged with manning the capstans hesitated, only to flinch when the chancellor raised his voice even further, to a roar.

"*Open the gate*!"

Gears and cables groaned as the capstans were unwound, and jubilation rose from the Feldemarians outside as the drawbridge lowered swiftly. Karan, still wearing the same strangely crisp clothing as he always seemed to, put a hand on Lilith's arm, and she let her fires die, looking terribly small and afraid all of a sudden.

"Go with the refugees," he told her, impassively. "Take them into the fortress itself. Get them away from the battle."

She looked up at him for a moment, as though trying to read his face, and then nodded silently, squaring her shoulders before heading in the direction of the next wall.

The chancellor's eyes then focused on Theren, and narrowed as he observed her hovering there uncertainly. "I thought you were supposed to be in a cell, thinking about your actions."

She winced, having no real lie to tell in order to defend herself. "I—well, yes. But—"

"It does not matter now," he said, though he did not sound pleased. "Your duty to the people of Feldemar is more important. Go, and join the other mentalists on the wall to the east. You will help deploy our troops over the wall while the refugees fill the gate. And make haste, for the enemy will be upon us soon."

Numb with shock, she ran in the direction that he had pointed, though she could hear him growling, a low primal rumbling in his throat, as she left.

"You and I will have words about this later, Menrad," she heard him say, before she bounded into the stairwell.

She sprinted up the stairs and dashed across the wall as fast as her legs could carry her, relieved as she watched the stream of refugees moving gradually towards the keep. There were still a large number out on the plain, however, some struggling with the mud and others seemingly too tired to move any faster, and she realized with a jolt that the Dulmish soldiers would soon fall upon the most distant of them in their advance towards the keep. There were surprisingly few Dulmunsters compared to what Theren's fear had anticipated. It was more like a sortie than an army, she told herself, trying to force herself to think logically as she reached the staging point for the Mystic soldiers.

As she approached, she understood immediately what the chancellor had meant when he spoke of deploying the troops over the wall. A line of mindmages, including Vivien and Maikano, stood at regular intervals along the battlements, lowering the other soldiers down to the ground below them with their magic.

"You are a little young to be joining the offensive, are you not?" one of the mages asked her, looking her up and down, as she stopped to catch her breath.

"She is one of us," Maikano said cheerfully from beside him, and then patted two of the soldiers in front of him on the shoulder, with one hand on each, before heaving them over the edge of the wall. "Down you go!"

The Mystic soldiers, many seeming slightly unnerved by the fall, were gathering into formations on the rock shelf below the wall while several alchemists worked to shift the stone in front of them, smoothing it out until it formed the opening to a secret path. Theren spotted Vivien on the wall, being more delicate with her charges than Maikano, and steadied herself, straightening her back and taking her place in the line.

There seemed to be an unending number of people to help down, even with the half dozen mindmages on the wall all working at once. When she noticed Naro in the line, Theren's stomach lurched, but to her great relief he made no move to come nearer to her.

All along the wall facing the Dulmish soldiers, archers awaited their chance to take their first shots, and several weremages soared overhead in various bird forms, clutching large rocks or buckets of pitch in their talons. Her tutor, Junan, was among the last of those waiting to be helped over the wall, and she felt a wave of fear wash over her at the thought of him not coming back, making sure to be especially careful as she caught him with her magic and lowered him to the ground.

Several of the mindmages, including Maikano, jumped down to join their fellows, but before Theren could ask whether she should go as well, Vivien stopped her with a hand.

"Not you," she declared firmly. "The chancellor has

the younger mages with him, guarding the gate. And besides, you are already in enough trouble. Go and find him now."

Theren hesitated for a moment, torn between feeling resentful about being sent away and relieved that she would not have to go down to fight.

"Be safe," she said, after a pause, and Vivien smiled faintly.

"Safer than you would be. Now go!"

There were only two others standing with the chancellor on top of the gate when she arrived, one of them being Sarnak, the tawny-haired weremage boy that she and Lilith had encountered several times in the halls on the way to their morning training sessions. He nodded at her as she approached, though he was fidgeting nervously, and the other mage stood with her back to the fighting. She was a slim, black-skinned girl that Theren had never seen before—likely an alchemist, since she did not train with any of the others—and she had her arms wrapped around herself protectively. Theren wondered if she was from Feldemar, and tried to give her a reassuring smile.

The chancellor stood stolidly at the wall, looking out over the battlefield, where the Dulmish army was now beginning to square off against the approaching Mystic forces. Theren walked over to stand beside him, her thoughts a roiling mess of emotions that she could not control.

"Why are they here?" The question had been

bothering her. "They did not go to the trouble of taking Ulande just to send such a small force to Ammon, surely?"

He glanced at her as he folded his arms across his chest and scrutinized her face closely for a few moments. "Given the information available to us, it seems likely that they were sent after the people fleeing the city, to try to keep word from reaching us."

"At least we saved some of them," she managed to whisper, thinking of those refugees who had not been so lucky.

As she watched, the two groups of soldiers collided, like waves crashing into each other, their momentum stalling instantly as the lines met. She thought disjointedly that it felt so unreal from up here it could have been a pantomime, even though there were people she knew quite well and saw every day down there, fighting and possibly dying. She clenched her fists tightly, remembering Tinun, and tried not to think about how many more people she might never get a chance to know as more than brief acquaintances now.

"What will we do after this?" she asked, her throat dry, and Chancellor Karan sighed, his eyes fixed on the ongoing battle.

"I have sent messengers to the king of Feldemar, just in case no word has yet passed west to Yota. Once things are tidied up here, we will march southwest, either to meet the forces of Dahab, or wait with them for the king's armies to arrive from the capital. Then, we shall retake Ulande."

TWENTY-ONE

THE PROCESS OF "TIDYING UP," AS THE CHANCELLOR had called it, took much longer than Theren had expected. Though the fighting itself was over in a sickeningly short time, there were many bodies to be burned, many badges to be retrieved, and much mud to be searched through, so the whole of Ammon remained busy throughout the rest of the day and long into the night. The whole of Ammon except for Captain Menrad, of course, who had been relieved of his duties. He had apparently told the chancellor that he had always intended to open the gate, but not while

Lilith was there, so that she did not get the idea that she could give the Mystics orders. It seemed that he had felt that Lilith's suggestions were being given too much consideration, and feared that she would get them into the same kind of trouble as the last Yerrin girl had.

What few garbled details Theren had been able to pry out of anybody about this previous member of the family Yerrin included that she was much younger than Lilith—barely older than a child—and that the previous chancellor had told everyone furiously that she was partially responsible for the rebellion of Dorsea against the High King. Nobody quite knew how she had done this, just that the chancellor, Kal, had ranted and raged about it constantly, and the more accounts Theren heard, the more annoyed she was that any of the Mystics believed it.

A girl barely out of schooling years, affecting the fate of nations? Foolishness, even for the most cunning of goldbags.

The mood of the fortress and its occupants was changed once again, the previous tension replaced with a kind of weary implacability. Everyone was working—packing supplies, bringing what food and blankets they had in surplus to the refugees, digging graves or patrolling the walls, or even mundane things like taking inventory and making account of their losses—and no one thought of rest. Lilith spent half of her time helping the Feldemaran refugees, and the other half in consultation with Chancellor Karan about what extra supplies she believed she could negotiate from her family connections in Dahab.

True to his word, Karan ordered the Mystics to begin preparations to march the very next day, and many of the more experienced among them seemed to have been ready to go at a moment's notice. A weremage in the form of a great, swift falcon arrived in the middle of the day, wearing livery of indigo trimmed in gold, the colors of the royal family of Feldemar. He told them quickly where they would meet the forces of Dahab, and that they would be led by Her Excellency Shorani, the heir to Feldemar's throne, before taking off again almost immediately afterwards.

"Is it wise to send the next king to the front lines?" Theren asked Vivien curiously, as she helped load one of the carts with supplies for the march, using her magic to lift several boxes at once.

Vivien shrugged. "In Dulmun, the current king as well as their heirs will often take the field. And besides, if I am any judge, King Alim is likely feeling like a cornered wildcat. He can scarcely afford to hold back any weapons within his arsenal, if doing so will mean losing the throne itself for Shorani to inherit."

That thought sobered Theren, wondering if the Dulmunsters were planning to push west towards the capital now that they had their foothold in Ulande, and she found herself searching out Lilith in the crowd, where she stood giving instructions to the refugees. When Karan had announced that they would be traveling with the Mystics, so as to be taken into the protection of the king's soldiers before the battle, Lilith had insisted that she would accompany them as well, in order to watch over them. The chancellor had offered no argument to this, and Theren had begun to wonder if he was secretly relieved to have somebody else to handle civilian matters.

It was sunset by the time they were ready to leave, and such was the urgency of their journey that they marched for several hours through the night anyway, their way lit by torches and floating lights conjured by their elementalists. Lilith seemed to have passed into a state of controlled calm that was far more worrying than any emotional outburst could have been, a mask of serenity that did not quite hide the trembling of her hands. Theren had to beg her to come to bed that night instead of continuing to assist the refugees that were marching with them, and when she did sleep, she was as still as death.

Theren, on the contrary, was restless all night, and when she did manage to doze for a few hours, her dreams were filled with horrible screams of the dying Mystics on board their ship from the Seat and visions of battlefields laden with gruesome carnage, like nothing she had ever seen before. She woke with a start just after dawn, only to find to her dismay that they were being called to break camp and continue marching.

Not in all the stories she had read and all the accounts in her dusty old textbooks, she thought bitterly as she struggled out of her bedroll, had anyone ever mentioned that war was so very tiring.

It took three days of hard marching and being beaten down by merciless thunderstorms that made Theren's bones ache with cold and covered the roads with yet more slick mud before they could rendezvous with the armies of Feldemar in their camp to the north of Ulande. They must have looked a sore and sorry lot, she thought, emerging disheveled and travel-worn from the jungles, especially compared to the Feldemaran warriors, who were resplendent in their royal colors and seemed much more used to the climate.

No sooner had they stopped walking than Chancellor Karan appeared before them, beckoning to Lilith. "Come with me. You, too, if you wish." That afterthought came with a nod to Theren.

They exchanged a glance, and Theren saw the worry in Lilith's eyes, reaching out to take her hand as they followed behind him. At his usual breakneck pace, he led them through the Mystic camp and into the Feldemaran one, not even stopping at the border that separated the two, both sets of guards hurrying aside to make way for him. From here, between the lines of deep blue tents, they could see Ulande: much of it was still smoldering, and at this distance the smoke was an acrid and ubiquitous presence on the wind, almost as aggravating as the green and white banners that had been hung from the walls in the direction facing the army camp.

The land below the rise that the camp had been set upon was razed, great swaths of jungle burned to cinders alongside the occasional farmhouses and stone storage buildings, now smoking ruins. Even at this distance, every misshapen clump of ashes made Theren feel nauseous, and the thought that such might have been the fate of the families of the people who had fled to Ammon refused to be dismissed from the forefront of her mind.

Eventually they passed so deep into the camp that they started seeing guards who were even more impressive than the rest of the Feldemaran soldiers, their heads covered by tall helms with golden plumes in them.

"The royal guard," Lilith breathed, clearly in awe, and Theren swallowed hard, wondering where under the sky the chancellor was taking them.

He strode on, unperturbed, towards the largest tent in the camp, outside which many of the royal guard were stationed. The three of them were let in with only a curt nod, though Theren was sure she must have looked suspicious, given the sweat she felt trickling over her temples and down her back.

"Your Excellency," Chancellor Karan said gravely, in greeting, and then, to Theren's surprise, bowed low.

Lilith curtsied deeply, and Theren hastily bowed to

match them both, though her eyes had not yet adjusted to the lamplight well enough to see the prince beyond a vague outline.

"Thank you, chancellor, but that is unnecessary," a calm, authoritative voice said in response. "We do not have time for ceremony."

Theren looked up to see a tall, fit woman in the same armor and indigo surcoat as the guards throughout the camp, though she also wore a wide golden coronet that was framed by a cloudlike bob of curly black hair. Her skin was a deep umber, darker than Lilith's, and her wise brown eyes were rimmed in kohl that matched the color of her hair.

"This is the girl you spoke of in your messages?" the prince asked, directing an elegant hand in Lilith's direction.

The chancellor nodded. "She is Lilith, and is of the family Yerrin, as you can no doubt tell."

Theren risked a sideways glance at Lilith to see that she seemed to be utterly flabbergasted, staring at the prince in wide-eyed awe.

"And the other?"

"A bodyguard, of sorts," Chancellor Karan replied phlegmatically, and Theren had to bite her tongue to keep from laughing out loud at the implausibility of the entire situation.

Prince Shorani gave him a long, steady look, but he maintained his neutral expression, and eventually she nodded, waving to Lilith to step forwards.

"Mistress Yerrin, I am told that you have been acting as chaperone for the refugees we are to take into our care," the prince began, at which Lilith lifted her chin proudly.

"Yes, Your Excellency. I have done my best, at least."

"Have any of them spoken of what happened when Ulande fell?" the prince asked, studying her intensely. "We have conflicting information about the numbers of the Dulmish forces, and I wished to know if any of the people who fled the city could shed any light on the situation."

Lilith frowned, and bit her lip, thinking. "I do not have . . . any definite numbers to give you. Many of the townspeople did not wish to speak of what had happened."

"Anything you could tell us would be of great value," Prince Shorani replied evenly, picking up a quill with which to take notes.

Theren wondered briefly why the prince did not have an aide on hand to write notes for her, and then realized that none of the other people in the tent with them seemed to be servants. Some of them may have been messengers, or simply guards, but they were all soldiers of some kind or other. Prince Shorani did not seem to match very well with the stories of royalty that Theren had been told as a child, and she found herself begrudgingly impressed.

"Well . . ." Lilith's eyes lit up as an idea blossomed.

"They did say that some of the raiders had left the city. Many of the refugees wished to travel west, to Dahab, as their first attempt to seek safety, but apparently some of the raiders took ship and made their way up the river in that direction, so they did not think it would be wise. Do you think that could be where the discrepancy about numbers comes from?"

The prince muttered something under her breath, scribbling rapidly on her parchment, and then turned to one of the men beside her. "Tell General Akomu to take a brigade of men along the river. If Dulmun thinks to attack Dahab while our forces are engaged here, they will learn not to underestimate us."

"Yes, Your Excellency," the man said, and saluted before hurrying out of the tent.

Theren shuddered, wondering what would have happened if Lilith had not been able to recall that information, or indeed if they had not brought her along, and then felt fiercely proud of her and all that she had done on this trip. The prince, too, seemed grateful, inclining her head gracefully in Lilith's direction.

"You have my thanks, Mistress Yerrin. I have no doubt that your family could supply these refugees without feeling any loss if need be, but we have heard that the Mystics are not so rich in these days. Therefore, the crown will reimburse Ammon for their aid in the protection of Feldemar's people, as a gesture of our gratitude."

Chancellor Karan, looking as happy as Theren had ever seen him, bowed low once more. "You and your father are most generous, Your Excellency."

"We honor those who show respect for our nation, Chancellor," Prince Shorani replied, pointedly.

Staidly, he nodded. "I understand, Your Excellency. Please, let us know if there is anything more you need."

She waved a hand graciously, indicating that they could leave, and Theren ducked out of the tent feeling as though she had just had an encounter with a rare creature of legend.

"Why did you bring me along?" Theren asked the chancellor, as she and Lilith hurried to keep up with him on their way back out of the Feldemaran camp.

"Our Mistress Yerrin would have told you everything that happened anyway," he replied, with an exasperated snort. "Better to let the royals know there is another ear in the conversation than let them give away secrets carelessly. You know how they can be."

Theren did not know, not particularly, but her heart lifted a little when Lilith giggled. "I suppose I would have told her, it is true."

He stopped walking for a moment, once they had finally returned to the Mystics' camp, and glared beadily at the two of them, crossing his arms over his chest.

"Now, you listen to me, both of you. You, Theren, have done far more to prove yourself than many of those who have been in the order longer, but I did not bring either of you with us here to Ulande to drag you onto the battlefield. You will remain here in the camp with the rear guard when the armies take the field, do you understand me? If I should catch even the tiniest glimpse of one or both of you tomorrow, I shall personally ship each of you back to the High King's Seat wrapped up in silk and packed in crates full of rice in order to keep you out of trouble!"

Theren could not help but grin at the idea of them packaged up like delicate jade vases, but she tried to control her mirth, because she did not doubt he would do it. "Understood, Chancellor."

Once he had stormed off, Lilith giggled. "That was unexpectedly fatherly of him."

Theren just snorted. "If he lost you, he would have to do his own paperwork again. Not to mention he would have to speak with merchants. I think he fears conversation more than battle."

Lilith sighed, her mood turning morose again at the mention of battle. "If only we could combine our strengths. I feel almost paralyzed by worry about tomorrow, and would welcome some courage in regard to it."

"They will not lose," Theren reassured her lightly, putting an arm around her shoulders. "Her Excellency's forces seem mighty indeed, and with the Mystic mages, they will be unstoppable!"

Lilith smiled wryly at her. "How things have changed, from the days when we would tell ourselves that the redcloaks would not win."

Theren wrinkled her nose. "I know. Embarrassing, is it not? I think they are rubbing off on me."

She shuddered dramatically, making Lilith laugh, and then yawned, feeling all of the exhaustion that she had built up over the past five days or so come crashing down on her.

"This will make a fine letter for Ebon and Kalem," she said wearily, as they began walking back to their tent. "It is not every day that one meets a prince."

The next morning, Theren rose sometime before dawn and walked to the outskirts of the camp, though she made sure not to pass the lines of guards stationed at the edge. The moons shone like the stained glass of the Academy windows in the sky overhead, not dulled in the slightest by the storms or the smoke, and she thought how peaceful it must be, to look down on everything that was happening and be completely unaffected by it.

The thought soured in her mind as she remembered that High King Enalyn had been named after one of the moons, and wondered darkly if the name had been chosen on purpose for that reason. Like the moon of her namesake, Enalyn would look down on the events of tomorrow's battle as nothing more than a few numbers, just a brief report and a final outcome to acknowledge, as distant from the whole thing as the moons were from the land.

Theren had no particular love for any nobles, but she felt that those like Prince Shorani, who were involved in what their people were doing and fighting for, must surely inspire greater confidence and trust than those who simply stayed put in their palaces, any number of leagues away. While the Feldemarians would fight alongside the woman who would one day be their king, the Mystics would go into battle tomorrow with only a distant silhouette and a name to keep them safe.

Theren hoped that it would be enough.

TWENTY-TWO

Unable to return to sleep, Theren wandered around the Mystics' camp, surprised to see so many of them already arisen. Not because she expected them to sleep restfully on a night like this, of course, but because they were all so uncharacteristically quiet—nervously anticipating what was to come, no doubt. Their faces scared her, a hundred masks of resigned determination, eating what they knew might be their last meal with no complaint, just a weary acceptance.

She was about to return to her tent, unsettled, when she spied Vivien standing alone on a small ridge that looked out over the battlefield, her braids shifting idly in the breeze. The view as Theren drew nearer to her was even more grisly than it had been the day before. Under the pale light of foredawn, the blackened husks of tree stumps and withered, ashen ground looked like something out of a nightmare, and the Dulmish soldiers had prepared for the coming assault by lining the approach to the city with vicious wooden spikes.

"Are you nervous?" she asked, after they had stood there together for a while in silence, and Vivien gave a small smile.

"A little, I suppose. I have been involved in large battles before, though I confess I have usually been the defender, rather than making the counterattack."

"I am surprised that no attempt was made to attack the camps," Theren admitted, having realized that she really did not know much about military strategy. "We are not particularly well-fortified here."

Vivien shrugged. "The armies of Dulmun do not act in the same way as those of Dorsea, that I am familiar with."

"You have experience working with the armies of Dorsea?" Theren asked, curious, and Vivien grinned in response.

"With fighting them, not with working alongside them. I hail from Wellmont, in Selvan, right on the border, so I have seen their tactics at work many times. If I had been born on the coast, I have no doubt I would be more familiar with Dulmun's ways."

Theren shook her head, bewildered. "It seems I am among the few from Selvan who knew nothing of war growing up. Cabrus must be positioned ideally for safety from outsiders, but I do not know if that is what makes it such an enemy to itself."

"You will find that most people look for something to do battle with in life," Vivien replied darkly, her statement accentuated by the scene that lay before them. "We seek enemies in disagreeable neighbors or lax city officials, if no other foes present themselves to us. You will hardly find a single person untouched by *some* kind of strife. It keeps us from fighting ourselves, I think."

Theren considered this for a moment, troubled. "You sound as though you think that it will never end. I do not . . . I cannot believe that. Surely, if given the chance, and if the kings and nobles of these lands stopped giving them orders, everyone here would simply go home. These soldiers of Dulmun seem as though they have been left here to die. They cannot *want* that, can they?"

Vivien gazed at her for a moment, smiling fondly. "You are too compassionate for your own good, sometimes, Theren, I swear by the sky. But then, you are still young." She waved her arms at the destruction before them, sighing. "This is not the product of merely following orders. But I agree with you in at least some measure; the royals of the nine kingdoms have fallen into steady decline ever since the death of Roth, it seems, and their decisions only twist their people further and further into knots. Even Her Excellency quibbles over small terms with agents of the High King, and she is one of the more active nobles, especially in the north."

"It irks me that neither the king of Dulmun nor the High King has any real stake in this battle," Theren added, anger bubbling in her chest, and Vivien placed a calming hand on her shoulder.

"I know. But that is why the Mystics are not solely beholden to the High King. We can go where those under the command of kings cannot, and do what is necessary to set the nine kingdoms back on the right path."

The sun was nearly risen now. Theren shivered as a cold wind from the sea snaked its way over the barren wasteland lying before Ulande and tugged at her cloak, causing rows and rows of tents behind them to flap and flutter at its passing. It seemed to carry with it an air of expectant dread, as though even the land itself were afraid of the coming battle. Looking out at the ruin of Ulande, its walls collapsed in places and smoking timbers exposed to the open sky, she pictured Cabrus and wondered if the armies of Selvan's king would have come to defend it, if Dorsea had ever managed to make their way so far across the border.

The legend of red-cloaked heroes standing between the people of Underrealm and the forces of darkness was an exaggeration—Theren knew that better than most—but it did not have to be a total myth, she realized. She thought about the difference it could have made in her life, a childhood spent scrounging for food scraps in the gutters, if someone like the chancellor had been there to yell at people until their storerooms were opened to give out food for the needy. If she returned to her birthplace now as a touted agent of the High King, she could *buy* food for all the children on the streets, a thought that appealed to the small, forlorn part of herself that remembered the miserable nights of sleeping huddled on cobblestones, hoping not to be washed away by the rainwater.

"I am glad that I joined the Mystic order," she said eventually, though she felt that it sounded strained and insincere to hear it in her own voice.

Vivien either did not notice, or understood her conflicted feelings about it, smiling brightly at her and turning back towards the camp. "You should be proud."

"Wait," Theren said suddenly, before she could walk away. "What will happen if things do not go well today? Will we be safe in the camp? Should we flee, with the refugees?"

Vivien gave her a long look, her eyes filled with a mixture of sympathy and uncertainty. "I will tell you something that you likely already know, Theren, even if you have not admitted it to yourself yet. As a mage, you have power far beyond those without magic, even though the Mystics train us rigorously to take orders from those we could easily overcome. You and Lilith are far safer than any of those in the rear guard who are not mages.

"If it comes to pass that the army is defeated and the forces of Dulmun make an attack on this camp, you will indeed be in danger, but still less so than the ordinary soldiers and the people of Feldemar attempting to return to their homes. You have a great power, equal to dozens and dozens of our fellows in the order, but only you can decide what to do with it."

Theren swallowed hard, shivering. "Are you saying that we should stay and fight, to give the others a chance to escape?"

"I am saying not to be afraid," Vivien answered, shaking her head, a faint smile on her lips. "I truly do not think things will come to such an end, though I cannot blame you for being less sure. Just remember that no matter what you choose to do, you are worth a brigade on your own. You are never defenseless."

Theren did not know whether to be reassured or terrified. It seemed she would have to find the answers on her own, however, as the instant the sun broke its way over the horizon, voices began to sound around the camp, calling for everyone to wake, and Vivien excused herself. Theren stayed there on the ridge for only a few more moments, the sight of flashes of green and white on the walls of Ulande making her feel ill with anxiety, before leaving to make her way to find Lilith.

Despite Vivien's declaration that she was worth a brigade in and of herself, she felt extremely alone as the Mystics all around her finished their preparations for war, getting ready to march without her. How many would return?

Most of Theren's clearest memories of the battle for Ulande had little to do with the fighting itself, since she had discovered that you could watch distant lines of people crashing into each other for only so long before they began to blend together. She remembered the sight of the host arrayed before the city, the weak sunlight glinting off the golden accents of the Feldemarians' armor and causing the Mystics' red cloaks to glow like fire, with the frost on the ground and the chain-links of people's armor all glittering like jewels in a treasury about to be emptied.

She remembered the sound of the drums as the army began their approach, and the horns from within the city, and the tramp of a thousand marching feet. She remembered the stench of death on the air, and sweat, and fire, and blood-stained metal. She remembered the tremble in Lilith's fingers where she held them clasped between her own as the first volley of spears flew from the Dulmish lines, and the first soldiers fell.

Beyond that, much of what she could recall was just a blur, an achingly long day of terror and exhaustion as they waited for it all to end. The bloodiest fighting had been inside the city, and thus out of her sight, but that had only made it worse; at least while watching them break through the gates, nerve-wracking as it had been, she had been able to tell that their side was making progress.

The Mystics had acquitted themselves well, or at least she thought that they had. Their gate had been broken down faster than the other, partially because it had been less heavily defended, and partially because there were so many mages in their ranks. The sight of the weremages barreling up the ramp towards the gate, led by Chancellor Karan in the form of a great elk the height of two people with antlers as wide as he was tall simply trampling the defenders, was something she was glad she had only had to observe from a distance.

Though the armies of Dahab had been tasked with the fiercer fighting for their gate, the dismay that had overtaken Dulmun's soldiers when the Mystics broke into the city behind them had given the Feldemarians an edge that they had expertly exploited. The sight of the prince raising her saber high in triumph when their battering ram had crashed through the gate at last had incited the beating of the war drums once more, and elicited a great cheer from the Feldemaran army.

But neither Theren nor Lilith had shared any of the feeling of victory that the soldiers had enjoyed. She supposed that it might have been something you had to participate in to understand. From their perch overlooking the city, all she had been able to see as the army flooded into its streets were those left behind, the dead and the dying, on both sides.

She did not think that anyone had really won: not the Dulmish forces, who had been devastated, and not their own forces, who had taken losses over a pointless battle that should never have happened, and not the people of Ulande, whose homes were now reduced to smoldering ruins painted red with blood.

Lilith wept when they finally managed to clear enough rubble and gory mess to allow the civilians back into the city, tears leaking from the corners of her eyes despite her efforts to wipe them away. She held her head high, and did her best to hide it, as families from Ulande gathered around her, keening and sobbing for their ruined city in the middle of the main avenue beneath great stone arches that must once have been beautiful but were now jagged and broken. Theren, unable to bear Lilith's sadness, hugged her as tightly as she dared.

"Where is the High King's army?" Lilith demanded, her voice muffled by Theren's shoulder as she clung with all her might. "Is this not what they came north to stop?"

Theren did not know the answer, but the question was enough to make her heart sink. She did not want to believe that Dulmun's forces were outwitting the High King with their tactics, but she did not know what other reason there could be that would not seem callous. She reminded herself that she really did not know much about war, and that the High King's army was no doubt fighting to protect other people wherever they were, but it did not make the reality around her any easier to face.

She just hoped that the High King would win soon so this whole thing could be over.

TWENTY-THREE

THE JOURNEY BACK TO AMMON TOOK THEM FIVE DAYS, since they were now all bone-crushingly exhausted. It rained the entire time, and though Theren was glad to be leaving Ulande behind, the miserable weather and stolid silence of the Mystics was hardly any better. Chancellor Karan spent so much time in his elk form that many of the mages grew concerned for him, though all he would say in camp at night was that he had never been much of a one for wading through mud. Theren almost asked him if something was wrong one evening, but she could not forget the sight of him with blood spattered all throughout his magnificent ruff and gobbets of things she did not dare to name hanging from his antlers, so she just shuddered and left him alone.

Their reception at the fortress was far more joyous than Theren felt was justified; the sight of the younger recruits cheering for the victory of the grim, unsmiling warriors that marched through their lines in search of a warm bed and a hot meal was almost comical. She told herself that they might have been nervous, having been left behind in Ammon with only a few veterans to guide them, but she still did not know if she would have cheered, had she been in their place.

After two days of rest ordered by the chancellor, they all tried to return to their routines, but many things had to be shuffled around, since tutors were in some cases dead, or needed temporary replacements while they recovered from injuries. Theren was relieved that Junan, Maikano, and Kaewa had all made it out of Ulande alive, and of course Vivien and even Chancellor Karan. Less-welcome faces that had also returned included Naro and Ilya, as well as any number of the less friendly Mystics she had only met in passing. It was strange, being reminded how many of them she did not like as individuals after all that time she had spent worrying over their safety as a group during the battle.

The weather did not abate as autumn gave way to winter, but it seemed that the pressure from all corners of Feldemar did, with the missives that Lilith was tasked to write often being those of thanks instead of bargaining or haranguing. Theren did not know whether it was because of gratitude for their aid at Ulande, or an effort to keep interactions with the Mystics to a minimum in order to appear a lesser target to Dulmun, but she appreciated it all the same; anything that took strain off Lilith was a blessing, in her mind.

Theren began to notice a growing resentment towards her among her unit as they gradually readjusted to life at the keep, and it was exacerbated every time Junan included her in stories of the fighting the older Mystics had undertaken. After several weeks of being back in Ammon, they had reached the stage of their training where their tutors gave assessment of their abilities, and many of her fellows were ecstatic about the recommendations Junan would give for what weapons they should specialize in. Theren was not expecting much, given that she was a mage, but the others were all tittering with excitement as they were called into the armory one by one, making outlandish guesses about exotic weaponry, despite more than half a dozen of them returning with mail shirts, swords, and shields.

She ignored their glowers as her name was called and hastily ducked into the armory, more thankful for the chance to get inside and out of the cold than anything else. Though there were some slightly rarer weapons hung on the walls, like halberds and battle-axes, and one or two flails, the floor of the armory was nearly packed with racks of swords, shields, and spears—the others would no doubt be disappointed by how ordinary it was. Junan stood at the back, beside a low table, beckoning her to join him.

There was another man with him, swearing under his breath as he tripped over stacks of crates and stands draped in mail, who was introduced to her as Ostran, the chief armorer. He ran a practiced eye over her and then turned to Junan, already pulling something out of one of the crates.

"I would guess leather on this one, eh, lad?"

Theren bristled at the idea that she was not deserving of mail for some reason, giving Junan an annoyed look. "Trying to make the sparring sessions easier on the others by giving me less padding, are you?"

"I would assume his assessment was based on the dueling cloak, Theren," he replied, clearly amused by her expression.

"Oh," she replied, mollified, though she tried not to show it too much. "Well. All right, then."

"You need not wear it at all if you do not wish," Junan continued, laying the pieces that Ostran was giving him on the table. "Many mages do not wear armor, as I am sure you have noticed. But these are . . . troubled times."

She looked at the thick overlapping plates of boiled leather, dyed red and dangling scores of straps, and thought about the many bruises that she had accrued over her time with the Mystics thus far—enough to make the idea of protection sound appealing.

"It could not hurt," she said, after a pause, and Ostran nodded approvingly.

"Take off that cloak and hold out your arms, then."

He hefted the cuirass while she complied, slipping it on over the simple shirt she wore, and showing her how to fasten the buckles so that it would be tight enough to help, but not too tight for her to breathe in. It was bulkier than she had expected, but she found she was still able to twist around and bend down in it fairly easily. With it came a set of bracers for her wrists, leather greaves which strapped onto her boots, and a pair of plain leather gloves.

While she was being fitted, Junan picked up a long, slim blade and brought it over to her. "You do not have to take this, either, although you may find weapons training repetitive otherwise. You are quick, and the rapier is a weapon of speed—but the element of surprise can be even more deadly. Outfitted with a blade and armor, if your enemies are unwise, they will think you just a swordswoman, and they will not expect your magic until it is too late."

She took it from him, weighing it in her hands, and wondered whether the other young mages were being advised to hide their magic in the same way.

"What happens if someone does not like your recommendations?" she asked him, curious, as she strapped it onto her belt.

He chuckled. "Such as if they were hoping for some exotic monstrosity on a chain, you mean? I inform them that they will have to complete their training using the clubs and staves we have been learning with thus far, and find another Mystic to teach them once they are assigned."

She paused, nervous at the realization. "Are we to be assigned our positions soon, then?"

He nodded curtly, his expression grave, and proffered her cloak with one hand. "Before the end of winter, I believe. There are several weeks' worth of training left still, of course. We will not send you out with weapons you do not know how to use."

She frowned, but thanked him for his attempt to reassure her, and he asked her to call for Milos, another of the men in her unit, once she had left the armory. Walking in the armor still felt strange, and the greaves were heavy on her lower legs, but she managed to make her way outside without falling over, at least. Cold stares fixed on her as soon as she opened the door, almost as frigid as the air, and she sighed, not sure what they wanted from her.

"Your turn, Milos," she said impassively, and the man in question, a tall redhead from Hedgemond, barged past her.

"Does she even need a weapon?" she heard one of the others mutter, bitterly.

Once again she ignored them, telling herself that they would be reassigned soon and she would no longer have to worry about them. Instead she focused on getting used to walking around with the rapier on her left hip, since it was throwing off her balance, and settled in the end for placing the palm of her left hand against its pommel to offset the weight, as she had seen many of the older warriors do with their blades.

It was not until the bell for the evening meal had rung and they were dismissed that she found herself wondering if she would even be able to fit through the door into her quarters while wearing her weapon.

Lilith was much more impressed with the rapier than Theren had been, marveling at the caged hilt, and even Kaewa and Vivien seemed taken aback by her new appearance the next morning. Vivien seemed to think the whole thing was quite foolish, though she did agree to try tailoring some of their magical training to the use of the rapier and dueling cape specifically, admitting that she could see how it would work well. Kaewa told her in sign that she looked very dashing, which made Theren's face grow hot with embarrassment and Lilith laugh.

The lessons with the rapier in the afternoons were exhausting, being what she felt was far too concerned with the placement of the feet for training with a sword, but the Academy had instilled in her nothing if not the ability to memorize patterns quickly, and so she seemed to pick it up at a satisfactory pace. The sparring between recruits, however, had opened up into much more serious bouts, and she found herself challenged to many matches over the course of a week or so. Despite her new armor, and the fact that she won more often than not, she ended up covered in bruises. By the time she had acquired a black eye, Junan had had enough and gave the others a dressing down for their attitude, which did not seem to help in the slightest.

Very few of them challenged her more than once, though, she was pleased to see. Clearly they did not want to fight her *too* badly, at least not when there was a good chance she would make them regret it.

Even the older Mystics seemed to have a problem with her as the weeks wore on, however, and she often felt eyes on her in the mess hall, looking up a few times to see Ilya glaring stonily at her from across the room. Unsure whether this was about the previous Yerrin girl who had been at Ammon again, she just kept her head down, knowing that reassignment was not far away and soon she would not have to deal with any of them anymore. That thought scared her at the same time, though—what if she was sent away from Vivien and Kaewa and the few other Mystics she knew? What if she and Lilith were sent somewhere like Dorsea, which was even more embroiled in the politics of war than Feldemar?

There was so little room in their quarters that Lilith always had to help her with her armor in the evenings, and Theren was somewhat surprised with how used to being in each other's space they had become. They had often shared a bed before, of course, but there was something different about living in a tiny closet together; she would never have imagined that they would be here, like this, if she had been asked a year ago.

Of all the things she had accomplished in her time with the Mystics, that was the most unlooked for, and probably the most cherished, although she was also proud of herself just for surviving it all. The mere thought of congratulating herself made her blanch, though, as if it could invite disaster, and so she busied herself instead, pretending to be as demure in her own thoughts as she was brash and boastful in public.

Like a restless squirrel, she eagerly awaited the end of winter and their new assignments, her anticipation over what the outcome might be filling her thoughts at almost every waking moment.

TWENTY-FOUR

One week before the start of spring, Theren dashed back to her quarters through the pouring rain, trying her best to shield the bowls of food she was carrying under her cloak. She and Lilith had taken to eating alone of late, because the constant observation had become too off-putting to stomach sitting down in the mess hall with everyone else. The weather had not exactly made it easy, but once again she reminded herself that there were few spaces in Ammon that were better heated than their diminutive closet.

Shivering and stamping her feet, she hurried

inside, placed the food on the table beside Lilith, and immediately unfastened her sodden cloak to hang on the back of the door.

"Anything?" Lilith asked, looking up from the letter she was reading.

Theren grunted, shaking her head. "No word of any reassignments yet. I am beginning to suspect that the chancellor will wait until the very last day to tell us."

"Kalem sent us a letter," Lilith said, smiling, and Theren brightened at that, pulling off her gloves in order to take it without getting it wet.

She read through it while unbuckling her greaves and shucking off her boots, snickering occasionally at the various complaints the boy made about what Ebon had been doing that annoyed him. Much of it was in response to their meeting the prince of Feldemar, paragraphs of raving about how fierce and respected she was and how envious he was that they had actually spoken with her. Theren counted at least twelve exclamation points.

He ended by talking about his classes and how he was ready to pass the next alchemy test he would be given and progress to the next year, and said that Instructor Jia and many of Theren's former teachers, and even Dean Forredar, had asked after her and how she was doing. She was surprised, though she was not sure why—after all, it had not, technically, been all that long. It felt longer, she supposed, because of all the monumental things that had happened.

"That boy needs someone to drag him out of the library more often," she said, carefully returning the letter to the desk, and then collapsed on their bed while Lilith giggled.

"He seems to be in academic bliss without you and Ebon around to spoil his study time."

Theren sniffed haughtily, dragging herself back upright with much effort to massage her calves, which were aching after another day of dancing back and forth, dueling. "It is his natural state."

Lilith transferred from the chair to the bed, holding their bowls of stew, and Theren made room for her so that they could sit side by side, legs crossed. It was the same stew they always had—mutton and greens, with thick gravy—a far cry from the luxurious food that had been on offer on the Seat, but she still preferred it to marching tack and dried meat. She felt a small thrill of excitement as she realized that once she was reassigned, they might be sent somewhere with better provisions, and for a few moments even entertained the hope of being sent back to the Seat, wondering if Kalem and Ebon would find her strange after how much she had changed.

"Do you think it will always be like this?" Lilith asked when she was done eating, waving her arms at the room around them.

Theren shrugged. "I doubt it. I am not sure where we will be sent exactly, but I think these quarters are mostly just to do with Chancellor Karan's . . . unique charm."

Lilith laughed. "I did not mean like that. I meant . . . all of this. Spending our nights together, sharing letters and books, eating together and listening to the rain. Us."

With a shock, Theren realized that Lilith was asking if they could make a life together, properly, and she nearly dropped her spoon into her stew.

"I think it could be," she said, reaching over to take Lilith's hand. "I mean . . . if that is what you want. Though I would much rather not have all the redcloaks around if I can help it."

Lilith smiled at that, and Theren leaned over to kiss her, savoring the warmth of their mingling breath while Lilith erupted into a fit of giggles, shrinking back from Theren's still-frozen nose.

"I am even more anxious to hear where they will send us now," she said, nuzzling against Lilith's cheek. "I am hopeful that we may go back to the Seat, but I would be pleased to be sent anywhere away from Dulmun."

"Hm." Lilith pondered quietly for a bit. "I would not mind being sent to a larger city in Feldemar. But I long to be away from here, if at all possible. I have no more wish to see great battles. If I could help the people of Feldemar with letters from behind fortified walls, I would be happier."

"I am sorry that you are bound by what they decide as well," Theren said, sighing. "It must be difficult, not being free to act on your own will all the time as you used to."

"I am not so bothered as you are, I think," Lilith replied, and then laughed at Theren's expression. "My mother and father spent so many hours telling me to be elegant and demure, that by the time I could leave the house I had forgotten who I was underneath, and who the girl I had crafted on my parents' behalf was, and where the two met. I was wild at the Academy, because I thought that the opposite of what I had been told must always mean freedom.

"But the truth is . . . I like peace and quiet. I like reading books, and writing letters, and wearing elegant dresses and meeting princes and feeling beautiful. I had almost forgotten, but underneath, with everything my parents tried to force me to be stripped away, it is all still there."

She broke off, grinning wickedly, and kissed Theren once more. "It can be fun to wreak havoc occasionally, but most days I would rather stay at home and be soft and ladylike."

Theren gazed at her for a moment in wonderment, thinking that she did not know herself even half that well. "I shall endeavor to find a posting somewhere with less war and more dresses, then."

Just as Lilith opened her mouth to respond, someone knocked on their door heavily, calling out their names. Lilith, because she was the only one of the two of them wearing shoes, fought her way to the door, and opened it in trepidation.

A messenger stood there stolidly, clutching a spear

in one hand. "You are both summoned to meet with the chancellor in his office. Immediately."

The weather had chosen to grace them with thunder and lightning ominous enough to fit the occasion. The flames in the lamps they passed by guttered and dipped in the ferocious wind, making them feel as distant from their cozy hideaway under the stairs as if they had crossed a continent. Their messenger either had no answers about what was going on or would not tell them, and Theren felt chills running down her spine that had nothing to do with the sheets of icy rain lashing through the open archways leading to the courtyard.

She forced herself to remain calm, taking deep breaths of the frosty air. Neither of them had done anything wrong that she could think of, and so it did not seem as though they should be in trouble. But the chilly mood that had permeated the keep of late had her on guard; what if one of the innumerable pairs of eyes that had been watching her had found an excuse to have her thrown out? What if some of her fellows, jealous of her apparent hastening unto glory, had done something and framed her for it?

Lilith seemed to be thinking along the same lines, her eyes fixed on the ground, so Theren reached down as they were walking and squeezed her hand gently, being rewarded with a small, brief smile. Whatever happened, she thought, they had come this far together, and they would not be parted now.

The messenger knocked on the chancellor's door, far more politely than he had on theirs, and then opened it without waiting for an answer, poking his head inside.

"I have brought them, sir."

"Good. Inside, quickly!"

Theren and Lilith hurried inside, hearing the impatient edge in his voice, and found themselves in a room filled with grim-looking older Mystics, all of whom were watching them intently. Chancellor Karan stood behind his desk, looking as haggard and worried as Theren had ever seen him, with Vivien beside him and Kaewa leaning against the wall a few paces away. Both women wore expressions of worry, though Vivien seemed to be filled with more restless agitation than Kaewa, who merely looked concerned. Of the other half dozen or so Mystics, the two that Theren recognized were Naro, who was paused in the act of making notes on several large maps, and Ilya, who told the messenger to leave and closed the door behind him before folding her arms and glowering.

None of this did anything to dampen Theren's anxiety over what was going on.

"Now, both of you, listen to me carefully," the chancellor began, signing his words also in deference to Kaewa. "What we are about to tell you does not leave this room. It is information of a highly sensitive nature, regarding the war with Dulmun. Repeating it to anybody outside of these few you see here will constitute an act of treason. Do you understand?"

Theren was silent for a moment, taking in the worried stares of most of the Mystics, and Ilya's belligerent glare, before responding. "I do."

"And you, Lilith," he continued, his face drawn and tired. "Most especially, you must never repeat any of this to your family."

Somewhat taken aback, Lilith nonetheless squared her shoulders and nodded graciously. "I understand, Chancellor."

"Very good," he said, sighing, and then waved a hand at Naro. "Tell them."

The younger man stood up, regarding them with cold, emotionless eyes. "You are both aware, no doubt, of the dangers of magestones."

Theren's breath caught in her throat, and she only managed to nod in response, while beside her she could see Lilith clasping her hands together so tightly that her fingers looked fit to break. The reason that they had been called to attend the meeting seemed clear now—the Yerrins were infamous for being the only merchant family that could traffic in magestones—but with such a grave topic being the opening of their conversation, it did not seem that things would be much more pleasant than if they were being punished for a misdeed they had not done.

"Get on with it," Chancellor Karan snarled, impatient.

Naro walked over towards them, holding out a piece of parchment with a likeness of a man's face on it, which Theren took from him, noting that in certain ways it resembled him quite closely; they had the same strong, overhanging brow, the same narrow nose that looked as if it had been broken several times, and the same small mouth, though the eyes on the man in the picture were much less hooded, giving him a friendlier countenance. If Naro's eyes had not been one of his most noticeable features, she might have thought that they were one and the same.

"That is a trader named Armod," he continued, as Theren showed the picture to Lilith, "from the merchant family Kallis, who are most prominent in Rothton, Dulmun's capital. Information gathered by agents of the High King indicates that he has acquired magestones, and seeks to return home with them."

Lilith's breath hissed between her teeth in a shocked gasp, and Theren felt what warmth was left in her body drain away. She had not seen any mages on the walls of Ulande, or in the sortie that had made its way to Ammon, but she remembered well the weremage from their encounter on the sea. Magestones had the power to grant weremages the ability of hellskin, turning them into dark and twisted creatures that were immune to all the spells of other mages. If the weremage that Vivien and Theren had fought could have called on the power of magestones, none of them would have lived to see the shores of Feldemar.

“I see that you understand the gravity of the situation,” the chancellor declared, nostrils flaring. “Good. Obviously the Mystics—we—must do everything in our power to keep those magestones out of the hands of Dulmun's forces. But the order has upcoming business in Dulmun, and we cannot risk simply marching over the border to apprehend this merchant without endangering our other efforts. Therefore, a small group of soldiers must go undercover, sneak across the border, and stop him before he can take ship for Southbreak. He is to be brought back to face the High King's justice, and the stones are to be destroyed.”

Theren swallowed hard, feeling weak, though she lifted her chin and tried to hide it. “And what does this have to do with Lilith and me?”

He gave her a long, piercing look, and she felt the answer before he said it. “You will be a part of this mission, along with those you see here.”

“Much of this task relies on stealth, and blending in,” Vivien explained, clearly seeing the look of shock on Theren's face. “Whatever your methods, your actions during the spate of murders at the Academy demonstrated an affinity for espionage, and you have both the magic talent necessary to go unarmed without peril, and the strength to wear armor, to disguise yourself as a guard. Though you are yet young, Kaewa and I both believe that you are more than ready, Theren, and the chancellor has chosen to listen to our assessment.”

"Your tutor, Junan, also spoke well on your behalf." The speaker was one of the Mystics she did not recognize, and several of the others nodded.

She felt faint, as though she had wandered into a dream, and wondered for a brief, mad instant if she had been struck by lightning on the walk over here and this was all some kind of vision. She could not believe that they had mentioned her actions at the Academy, and what she had done to Dasko, without it being followed immediately by a dismissal, but the stakes of this venture were enough to sober her after a few moments. If anything would be enough to make people willing to take enormous risks, it would be the idea of Dulmun's armies being strengthened by magestones.

"And what of me?" Lilith interjected, sounding stressed. "You have not spoken of my part in this."

"That is because yours is the part I do not agree with," Chancellor Karan answered, sighing heavily. "You are not under my command, and thus I cannot give you orders. But this also means that I cannot forbid you from volunteering your services, and I know there are those in this group who will ask you for aid, even if we discount Theren. I wish to stress that I believe it would be unwise and needlessly dangerous, though I half fear that those words will do more to attract than repel you."

"I still say that you should send her home if you fear she will act against our wishes," Ilya said angrily, and at once at least five Mystics began arguing hotly, both out loud and in sign, making it obvious that this was a conversation they had already had more than once.

"Enough!" the chancellor bellowed, over the din. "We have been over this a thousand times. Lilith must decide for herself."

"Our group needs a cover, a reason to cross the border into northern Dulmun," Vivien explained calmly, coming over to them. "Trade is still passing between Dulmun and the other nations, though it is heavily taxed now, and searched thoroughly. A merchant caravan, especially one with a respected name such as Yerrin attached to it, would make tricking our way over the border much easier than if we were posing as a simple group of travelers."

"I will go, of course," Lilith said immediately, looking at Theren, and Chancellor Karan sighed in exasperation.

"Of course."

Ilya snorted, throwing her arms up in the air. "This is ridiculous! She is only a child!"

"She is a mage," Kaewa signed, frowning at her. "And a skilled one, at that. She can defend herself."

"This is the *only* way, Ilya," Vivien insisted, her tone flat. "Do you want to catch this man, or do you want to alert Dulmun that we are coming because we had to kill a group of border guards?"

Ilya stared at her belligerently, looking furious,

but eventually looked over at the chancellor and nodded sharply, once. "Very well, then. We will leave tomorrow, at first light."

"I will finish making arrangements for the caravan," Vivien said, and Chancellor Karan nodded, waving her away.

"Yes, good, make it happen then. Dismissed, all of you. Get what rest you can."

The other Mystics swept out around them like a whirlwind, full of purpose, leaving Theren feeling like a stone in the middle of a rushing river. She looked down at Lilith, whose eyes were full of the same confusion and fear that she felt, and then noticed Chancellor Karan gazing at them with what seemed to be concern, though he thrust out his jaw pugnaciously and returned his attention to his paperwork when he noticed her eyes on him.

"Go on, begone, the both of you. Hurling yourselves heedlessly into danger requires a great deal of energy, so I suggest you get some sleep."

Though Theren had no idea how she could possibly manage to fall asleep with all that she had to think about, she could not help but grin at his downturned head, before reaching over to take Lilith's hand and doing as he commanded.

TWENTY-FIVE

Theren's dreams were fitful through what sleep she could muster that night, as she ran through never-ending fields of spongy green turf while a thousand watching eyes bore down on her from behind. When a sharp knock on the door woke her sometime before dawn, she was almost glad to be dragged from her bed.

"Good morning," Vivien said, sounding amused, when she managed to open the door still half-asleep.

"Is it?" she mumbled, staring at the pitch blackness outside.

Vivien chuckled. "You need not wake up just yet, I

suppose. Do not bother with your armor this morning, or your cloak, for either would give you away as a Mystic. Bring your blade, though, if you wish. We will eat on the road."

Yawning, Lilith struggled out of bed behind her. "What about me? Do I need to do anything in particular?"

"We have disguises for you both." Vivien tapped her foot impatiently. "We must leave soon, though."

They shut the door for space and Theren pulled on her boots, sighing regretfully as she looked at her cloak. She hated to leave it behind on one of her first important missions, but she supposed that there was no choice. It would hardly do to go to all the trouble of setting up a fake Yerrin caravan, only to stack it full of Mystic cloaks. She helped Lilith settle her skirts, as she did every morning, and then hugged her, wondering if she was nervous, too.

"This would be a better story to tell Ebon and Kalem if it were not treason to divulge it," Lilith said, smiling, and Theren laughed.

"At least I will not have to tell Ebon that I left his gift behind in Ammon this way."

Shivering in the freezing air in only her shirt and breeches, Theren followed Vivien out into the courtyard, hoping that their disguises would come with warm cloaks, and tried to ignore the growling of her stomach. A small group of Mystics had gathered there around a wide, covered wagon, with stablehands darting in and out of view, tweaking at the horses' girths and green caparisons. It really did look for all the world like the Yerrin caravans that Theren had seen in the past, and she wondered with sudden trepidation where exactly they had found it.

"Where did all this come from?" Lilith asked suspiciously, obviously thinking the same thing.

"We purchased it," Vivien replied matter-of-factly, as they walked over to the back of the cart, which was laden heavily with fine fabrics. "Quite some time ago, of course—back when you secured supplies for Mabawa, in fact. The order has always had more than passing interest in this sort of espionage, particularly during times of war. We have one carriage in Feldemaran royal colors as well, though that seemed less useful here."

Lilith wrinkled her nose in distaste behind Vivien's back, clearly disapproving of the underhanded tactics, and Theren waved tiredly at Kaewa, who looked very different in her long, green riding dress.

"Here," Kaewa signed, smiling, and pushed a pile of clothes towards her. "These should fit you, I think."

There was a stiff leather jerkin, laced at the back and dyed a deep shade of brown, along with a set of leather tassets to cover her thighs and a rich green surcoat to go over the top. Best of all, however, was the bronze gorget, which was topped with a furred ruff that Theren immediately longed to bury her face in. It also came with warm, fur-lined leather gauntlets. Clearly the Yerrins did not want their retainers to die from exposure to the cold, a stance with which Theren could very much agree.

"We have something more suitably noble for you, Lilith," Vivien added, indicating farther inside the wagon, and Lilith clambered up into the back, curious.

Wrestling furiously with the laces on her jerkin, Theren grinned fondly as she heard the gasp of wonderment from Lilith upon seeing whatever they had given her. She then dealt as best she could with the rest of her outfit, though she needed Kaewa to help her to settle some pieces in place, and thought idly that she might not even recognize herself if she could see a mirror now. Ilya, who was busy having a final discussion with Chancellor Karan, looked strangely plain in her mail and emerald surcoat, her golden hair pinned up into a severe bun at the nape of her neck, and Vivien was nigh unrecognizable in a plain riding dress similar to Kaewa's and a green silk headscarf restraining her jet-black braids.

"What about our badges?" Theren asked with sudden realization, but Vivien just shrugged.

"Just make sure it stays under your clothes. Not even the Dulmunsters will force you to bare skin against your will, so you will be safe as long as you do not show it to them."

"We may need them later to identify ourselves, depending on how things go," Naro added, startling her as he appeared out of nowhere.

Like the rest of them he was outfitted in Yerrin green,

and something about his disguise made him seem even more dangerous than usual—though whether it was the heavier scale armor and pauldrons he was sporting or the lack of uniform that signified he was an ally, she could not precisely tell. An ominous thought flashed in her mind: that if given a shield with a white cresting wave painted on it, he could pass easily as a soldier of Dulmun, for green was their color as well.

If he noticed her standoffishness, he did not react to it, instead turning back towards Chancellor Karan, who was now coming over to join them.

"How is the weather beyond the plain?"

"Clear now, for as far as I could fly," the chancellor replied, looking as though he had not slept at all. "The terrain may be wet, but I do not think it will rain again before you reach the border."

"How long will this mission take?" Theren asked, frowning.

"We have no way of knowing," Ilya said, darkly. "It will take as long as it takes, until we can find those magestones and capture the merchant who dares traffic in them."

"Hm," she said thoughtfully, wondering if it would affect her reassignment if it ran past the end of winter.

It would be just her luck, she thought, to miss her ticket away from Ammon because they could not quite track down this merchant in time.

"Theren, can you help me with the rest of this dress?" Lilith called out, from inside the wagon.

She clambered up onto the back, almost slipping off when the tassets affected her movement more than she had expected, and wove her way between the stacks of crates and chests towards the back. Even without a direct light inside the cart with them, she could still see that the dress was sublime; it had several layers of skirts, and the bodice was embroidered all over in elaborate patterns of golden thread, as were the bell-shaped ends of its long sleeves. The neckline, in service to the Yerrin family's fascination with modesty, was high with a delicate lace collar at the throat, and the fabric of the outer layer was impossibly soft to the touch.

It was the kind of dress made for twirling in, and Lilith clearly loved it.

"It suits you," Theren told her, smiling, as she pulled the lacing on the back closed, and helped line up the various layers of skirts straight with each other.

Lilith giggled, leaning in close to her. "Do not tell the others, but I plan to keep it once we are done."

"I do not know where you will hide it, but we shall find some way, I am sure," Theren replied, grinning again, and then kissed her. "You look beautiful."

She looked Theren's outfit over and then made a face. "It is . . . very strange to see you in the livery of my family."

"You should see Vivien," Theren countered, amused, and then felt her good mood drain away as she remembered Naro. "On the other hand, Naro looks as if he were born to it."

"I wish he were not coming with us," Lilith said quietly, looking down at her hands, and Theren grunted in assent.

"So do I. I am not sure how comfortable I will feel being close to the Dulmish border with him around, when he would barely need to change clothes to slip back into his homeland if he betrayed us."

Lilith took a sharp breath, her eyes widening in fear. "Surely he could not be that bold. Even if Ilya could not stop him, I must believe that Kaewa or Vivien could keep him from hurting any of us."

"I hope so," Theren said grimly, though in her mind, the vision of blades in the dark while people were asleep acted itself out for her like a nightmare.

"Are you ready?"

Vivien appeared in front of them, her voice light, but she frowned for a moment when she saw their faces, sensing their dour mood. "Ah, I am sorry. You must both be nervous. It is indeed an extremely important task laid before us."

Theren exchanged a glance with Lilith, who nodded, and she cleared her throat, trying to find the right way to phrase her concerns. "There are . . . some people traveling with us that we do not know very well. We would feel better if—"

Vivien cut her off, holding up both hands. "Now, I know what this is about. And believe me, I know that Ilya can be argumentative, but she is loyal to the order and will defend you both to the death if it should ever come to that for the good of the mission. You truly need not worry about her. But if you are ready, we will be departing soon. The two of you may stay in the cart, or you can ride, and two others will take your place. Do you have a preference?"

"I do not think I can ride in these skirts," Lilith said, with a faint tone of worry in her voice, and Vivien nodded, smiling reassuringly.

"I would believe that. Very well, you can stay in here, then. We will stop at midmorning, and I shall see you then!"

She climbed back down out of the wagon, and Theren watched her go, crestfallen. She had not even considered for a moment that it might be Naro they were worried about, rather than Ilya. Theren did not know how to feel about that, given that it was Vivien herself who had voiced concern about his ties to his home nation in the first place, and wondered if Vivien simply thought the matter was too grave to worry them over. She had certainly not meant for Theren to overhear her conversation with him in the prison, so that seemed as likely as any other explanation.

She frowned, turning back to Lilith. "I think we will have to keep an eye on him ourselves."

Lilith sighed, making another face. "I suppose it will be easier now that the worry will keep me from sleeping!"

From outside, Theren heard the now-familiar sound of the gates being opened and the drawbridge being let down, while feet crunched over gravel and the horses whickered at all the activity. Before she could react, their wagon lurched forwards suddenly, knocking her off balance. They were away, it seemed, and would soon leave Ammon behind. Lilith busied herself finding a comfortable place to sit, but Theren clambered towards the back of the cart over the goods they were carrying, settling herself and gazing out at the courtyard under the silvery light of dawn.

To her dismay, Naro rode just behind them, his expression characteristically inscrutable. Though she would have preferred to watch Ammon slip away behind them as they traveled, Theren instead scowled as she reached up to lower the flaps of canvas that had been pinned to allow them access into the wagon, and pulled them closed to shut out both the cold wind, and Naro's presence.

TWENTY-SIX

By the time they stopped at midmorning to eat, Theren had had more than enough of travel inside the wagon, which was bumpier and more uncomfortable even than their sea voyage had been. This time, however, it seemed she was not the only one who found the motion sickening, as their attempts to catch up with the merchant at all costs saw them pushing their horses quite hard, and this speed jolted the wagon unbearably. Theren did not particularly feel like riding on her own while Lilith was stuck in the cart without her, and so in the end they settled for taking turns sitting in the open beside Kaewa, who was driving the wagon, since that seat at least had the benefit of fresh air.

The team of horses pulling the wagon did not need all that much direction, seemingly content to follow their fellows being ridden ahead of them, and so Theren passed the time conversing with Kaewa about some of the finer details of their plan that they had not had time to discuss the previous night. From their information, the best guess they could make about the Kallis family merchant's route was that he was headed for the Linked Cities, a trade hub and border city that lay in Feldemar on one side of the river and Dulmun on the other.

The border between the two nations was laid out by a great river that originated in the Flamewarden Peaks, a vast range of mountains making up the very northern edge of the explored reaches of Underrealm. About halfway along its journey, this river converged with three others that watered much of northeastern Feldemar, joining together to form an enormous body of water that at its widest was more than two leagues from shore to shore, eventually emptying out into the river delta that Theren had spotted from Bandar when they had first arrived. It was heavily patrolled by Dulmun's ships all along its length, and so the Linked Cities would be the only place that they—and he, as well as any honest merchants—could cross the border without risking running afoul of the ubiquitous raiders.

It would be roughly three or four days' travel to the border, according to Kaewa, and Theren marveled at the fact that despite Ammon being so close to it, closer even than Ulande had been, the Mystic stronghold had still seen no attacks come from the east. If the armies of Dulmun were bent on seeking strongholds and supporters of the High King, it seemed that Ammon could have been easily engaged, but with its impregnable perch it was certainly a harder target to hit than a simple trading port like Ulande had been. It was not truly a threat, either, since as Vivien had pointed out some time ago, there were limited troops stationed at the keep, and the Mystics could not match the force of a proper army. It seemed that behind Dulmun's campaign of war lay more cunning than Theren had expected, and less rage-fueled, reckless destruction, which worried her greatly.

"How did the High King's agents find out about this Armod and his plans?" Theren signed, as the wagon continued on its way along the rough riding path.

Kaewa pursed her lips for a moment, thinking, and fastened the reins loosely around a peg beside her so that she could sign unimpeded for some time. "I do not have all the details, of course, but as I understand it, suspicion was first raised when he left the High King's Seat some months ago. He was born there, I am told, and left only rarely to travel to Selvan or Dorsea on business. Agents on the Seat became suspicious when he did not return after some time, since his family are very seldom interested in the affairs of kingdoms other than Dulmun, and he was tracked riding north through Dorsea towards Feldemar. I do not know precisely what transpired on the Seat, but many of his associates were interviewed, and one eventually revealed his plans. A young woman, who had been present when he paid for the stones."

The rippling stalks of tall grass on either side of the wagon blurred as Theren's eyes unfocused suddenly, and she felt alarmingly faint, clinging tightly to the railing by her elbow for fear of tumbling off. She had thought lately that it seemed as though her fear, the lingering terror and primal revulsion of her ordeal all those months ago at the hands of Mystic torturers, was fading, as though she was healing finally. But the mere implication behind Kaewa's words—a young woman, interviewed until she had provided answers—was enough to make Theren's skin crawl, the phantom ache of a thousand tiny cuts delivered with precision along the lines of veins and muscles rearing its head like a long dormant monster, now reawakened. Cuts delivered by those she was now tasked to work alongside, as though there was any way she could ever trust them knowing what she knew.

"Are you unwell?" Kaewa signed, looking concerned, after she had tapped Theren's arm gently to get her attention. "You could retire into the wagon."

Theren shook her head, rubbing at her eyes furiously

in an attempt to pull herself back together. She did not want Lilith to see her like this, not least because she would ask what was wrong and then Theren would have to explain it to her.

"This wagon is truly unbearable," she signed, glad that none of them were wearing red cloaks for the time being, as she did not think she could stomach the sight of the color. "The constant lurching is turning my stomach."

Kaewa inspected her face for a few moments, clearly not believing her. "You know you can always talk to me about anything, Theren. I know your time with the order has not been easy, but we are all on the same side."

Theren sighed, not knowing how to explain that she really needed not to be around Mystics right now.

"I think I will switch to riding, at least for a time," she signed, hoping that would be enough to end the conversation.

Kaewa drew the wagon to a brief halt, and one of the Mystics that Theren did not know, a taciturn man from Calentin named Tamah, brought over the spare horse, which had been acting as a makeshift packhorse while not being ridden. Theren mounted as quickly as she was able and then kicked the horse up into a canter, reveling the feeling of the wind blowing through her hair, and tried to forget all of the horrible memories that she was still carrying. She dared to let herself hope that one day, they might finally be gone for good.

"You are worrying Kaewa, you know," Vivien said dryly from behind her, dragging Theren's thoughts back into the present as Vivien's horse drew even with hers.

She shrugged impassively, though she did feel a little bad. "I would only have made her feel worse if I had stayed and explained what the problem was."

"The problem?"

Theren hesitated before answering, but she knew that Vivien, out of all the Mystics there, was the least likely to ask any unnecessary questions. "She said that the information we have on this merchant we are chasing, it was obtained via . . . questioning. I did not wish to speak of why that thought was so distasteful to me."

"Ah," Vivien replied simply, and Theren found herself surprised that she did not laugh, or dismiss the concerns as childish.

They rode together in silence for a while before Vivien sighed heavily, seeming to have come to some decision that she had been wrestling with.

"You do yourself no favors when you avoid asking people not to speak of such things, you know," she said gravely, and Theren looked at her in surprise.

"What do you mean?"

Vivien drew her lips into a thin line, her expression guarded for a moment, and then seemed to force herself to relax. "Ever since my . . . injury, I have been nervous in the presence of fire, and the mention of magestones makes me feel ill. Kaewa has been more than happy to avoid using flame in my presence, and the chancellor spoke to me alone, to carefully warn me about the nature of this mission, so that it was less of a shock to me than it might have been. I am sure people would be willing to respect your needs in the same way, if you only asked."

"That would be a fine thing if it did not mean explaining all of my weaknesses to people," Theren growled, blanching at the idea of someone telling Ilya or Naro that she wished to be treated more softly.

"Suit yourself," Vivien replied, shrugging in seeming indifference, though her tone of voice made it clear that she thought Theren was being unreasonable.

She fell into silence for a while as they rode, unable to keep from thinking on Vivien's words, as much as she hated the idea. What did magestones have to do with Vivien's injury?

With a jolt, she shot up straight as several pieces of information connected in her head. She remembered vividly the talk that Dean Forredar had given them at the Academy about the dangers of the evil stones, as though he had known them all too well, and also Ebon's words about how the dean had recoiled from the sight of magestones like an addict in torment. She also remembered, more recently, the sight of Vivien shaking at the mere mention of Dean Forredar's name.

The idea of the dean being an abomination—of him having eaten magestones and then attacking

Vivien for some reason, possibly while she was tasked by the Mystics to track him down–seemed unreal to Theren. And yet, at the same time, it was a more likely explanation than any other she could think of.

She was a little glad that she was no longer within his reach at the Academy, but that feeling was swiftly replaced by a brief tremor of anxiety. What about Ebon, who was now working closely with Dean Forredar? Was he safe?

"Your recommendation on how to make things easier for myself—is that why you warned me of what duties Naro carried out, when first I met him?" Theren asked, after a time, when her mind felt it had fully wrapped itself around the subject at hand.

Vivien gave her a sideways glance. "I confess I was off balance when I made your introductions. But yes, in essence. Working for the order can sometimes mean dealing with people you would rather not encounter. Better you be warned from the outset, than discover the truth later and feel betrayed."

Theren sighed, unsure whether or not that made her feel better. "I wish he was not coming with us on this journey."

Vivien glanced around warily, seemingly to check if any of the other Mystics were within earshot, and then lowered her voice. "Why do you say that? He has not approached you about anything, has he?"

"Yes," Theren replied, and then felt a small chill of fear as Vivien's expression turned into a dark scowl.

"Well, once, at least. He . . . I do not know what he wanted, in truth. He said something about Lilith, and about watching her to make sure she did nothing wrong. I did not know how to respond."

Vivien exhaled in a sharp, irritated hiss, and her eyes darted around to search for eavesdroppers once more. "I wish you had told me. He is—or can be—a very dangerous man. I would advise you not to trust anything he says."

Theren's mouth grew dry suddenly, and she felt faint again, Vivien's words seeming to confirm her suspicions. "Are we in danger from him on this mission?"

Vivien looked at her face and seemed to soften a little, obviously noticing Theren's fear. "I do not think so, not with Ilya here, at any rate. I caution you only to avoid him when you can, which I am sure you would have meant to do, anyway."

Theren nodded wordlessly, but she was not sure how convinced she was by Vivien's attempt at reassurance. She seemed to be placing a lot of faith in Ilya's ability to maintain order, and though Theren would not doubt that Ilya would try, she did not know if she trusted Ilya any more than she trusted Naro.

Vivien seemed to notice that Theren's mood had turned glum, and she too fell into silence as they rode. The fields of tall grass undulated rhythmically in the wind, stretching out before them with no end in sight. Theren did not know what to make of any of these revelations, but she did know that she was sick of uncovering the knowledge of terrible deeds when she did not go looking for it. It seemed that lurking behind every shadow was another horrible secret that she might have gone her whole life never hearing about, save for fate's decree that they should be unearthed.

She wondered if she would have been better off not knowing. Ignorance, as one of her instructors had often spitefully told her when she was caught napping in class, must surely be bliss. Whether or not that was true, she found herself wishing that she could try it and find out.

TWENTY-SEVEN

True to the chancellor's word, there was no rain for the rest of that day, and they even managed to find a relatively dry area in which to stop for the night, an unimaginable luxury after the sodden ground between Ammon and Ulande. Naro and one of the other new Mystics, a woman from Selvan named Iantha, who was said to be an expert tracker, had ridden ahead while the others made camp, in order to scout the way to the road leading towards the border. Theren found herself unable to shake the faint worry that something might happen, and only Naro would return.

Once the campfire had been set and they were ready to eat, Lilith dug determinedly through the articles of clothing that had come with the Yerrin caravan until she found another, more functional dress, with a high-necked woolen collar and furred gloves to protect against the cold—she did not want to risk dirtying the other's skirts on the ground, she explained. Though Theren believed her, she also thought it likely that Lilith was gaining immense joy from finally having a wardrobe of clothing to choose from again, after so long being stuck in a fortress with only the few things she had been able to pack. Theren did not begrudge Lilith her happiness, especially not when she looked so pretty.

She made a striking contrast against the rest of the Mystics, however; many of them had removed various outer layers of clothing, clearly feeling constrained after the long day of riding, and Ilya in particular was stripped almost entirely to the waist, wearing only a breastband as she labored to chop firewood for them. Lilith averted her eyes from the Heddan's naked, glistening muscles as she found somewhere to sit, looking perplexed and embarrassed at the same time, while Vivien came to sit beside her and patted her arm comfortingly.

"Ah, the famous Yerrin modesty. We shall have to keep your sensibilities in mind for the rest of the trip."

Theren, who was quite used to seeing Lilith in a similar state in private, had also forgotten how discomfited she was by anyone being undressed in public, and wondered briefly how they would ever have coped if she had been living in the barracks with the other recruits instead of in their tiny closet, an entire hall full of people being free with their skin to embarrass Lilith into leaving. They were apparently quite lucky that Chancellor Karan put such little stock in diplomacy.

In contrast to Lilith, Ilya seemed less than pleased with Vivien's words, grunting sourly. "I will wear what I wish when I am doing the work."

"If we truly want to pass ourselves off as a caravan of Yerrin, you may wish to play by their rules," Vivien said sharply.

Ilya snorted indignantly in response, though she disappeared momentarily and returned with a shirt, to Lilith's obvious relief. While Kaewa doled out their food—yet more stew, to the great disappointment of Theren's stomach—Naro returned with Iantha in tow, reporting that despite the recent storms, the road seemed clear, and that wagon tracks had been made within the past several days, possibly those of the merchant they were tracking.

"Did you get any idea of how many guards might be with the caravan?" Vivien asked them once she was done with her meal, but Iantha just shrugged.

"It may not even have been the Kallis caravan. Strange as it is to say, if there had been more rain, it might have been better for us, to get a better look at their numbers based on hoofprints in the mud."

"There seemed to be a dozen sets of hooves at least," Naro added, pausing to both talk and sign between huge mouthfuls of his food, with Iantha nodding in agreement. "A similar-sized caravan to our own, at a very rough guess."

"How long until we reach the city of Hallrand?" Ilya asked them, also signing for Kaewa's benefit.

"We will reach Destor first," Naro corrected her, ignoring her irritated look. "Only the portion of the Linked Cities that lies across the Langhale in Dulmun is known as Hallrand, and the people in Destor will not look kindly on you forgetting."

"How long?" Ilya repeated, obviously not interested in the geography lesson.

"If we continue at this pace, I believe we will reach the border on the day after tomorrow."

Theren grimaced at the idea of them maintaining the ungainly pace they had set that day, but Ilya seemed pleased that they had potentially made up some time, allowing herself to relax a little and nodding in satisfaction.

"Now may be a good time to discuss what our plans will be upon reaching the Linked Cities," Vivien said, breaking the momentary silence that had fallen. "The last thing we want is to be going in unprepared."

"We should pass through this Destor with all speed and cross the border into Dulmun," Ilya declared, firmly. "The longer we remain in one place, the more chance we will have to be observed, and once we are over the border it will be much harder to remove us than it would be to simply stop us in our tracks if we are found out."

Though Iantha, Kaewa, and Tamah nodded in agreement, Vivien frowned, and Naro seemed skeptical.

"I do not believe we should rush so," Vivien countered, sounding worried. "Destor, being located on the border but inhabited by Feldemarians, may be our best chance at information gathering. Surely once we pass into Dulmun, the citizens will be far more suspicious of anyone asking questions about the political goings on in their nation. At least in Destor it can be passed off as concerns held by travelers who wish to arm themselves with knowledge before they enter a warring kingdom."

"I agree," Naro chimed in, nodding. "We could gain much information simply by listening, without even having to ask questions. It would be foolish to let such an opportunity go by."

"And every moment that we are spending listening in taverns is another moment that someone may be tempted to inspect our caravan more thoroughly or ask our shepherd here questions about how her trade deals have been elsewhere," Ilya retorted, waving an arm at Lilith. "There are too many risks. What if there are other Yerrins in the city? Or a contact that the Yerrins commonly use, confused that they were not alerted to our coming? It is safer to simply pass through."

“She has a point,” Lilith admitted, fidgeting as she considered the matter. “While I can fabricate lies about how well or poorly our caravan has fared in terms of trade, I cannot know whether any merchant in the city has seen other Yerrin caravans recently and spoken at length with anyone from them. The slightest detail too similar or different to a previously told tale might set someone on edge—merchants are a suspicious lot, by and large.”

Vivien pursed her lips, seemingly conflicted. “I see both of your points, but I still believe that we need to take every opportunity to look for information. *Anything* we could find out about the Mystics in Dulmun could be a boon to us.”

“Mystics?” Theren broke in, bewildered. “Why would we need to gather information about the Mystics in Dulmun? Surely information about the war would be of more use.”

Everyone fell silent for a moment, with several of the older Mystics exchanging uncertain glances while Theren and Lilith looked on in confusion. Vivien and Ilya seemed to be having some kind of silent argument using only glares, before eventually Ilya nodded sharply, once, and Vivien sighed.

“It is not something that any of the newer recruits have been told about,” Vivien began, sounding very tired. “In fact, a conscious decision was made to keep it a secret from you all, for fear of causing undue worry. The truth is, shortly after the declaration of war, all of the Mystics that were previously stationed in Dulmun . . . vanished, or at least they seemed to. There has been no word, not from a single one, so we have not been able to ascertain whether they were all killed, or imprisoned, or whatever else may have befallen them."

"And it is not just those Mystics stationed on Southbreak, either," Naro added, darkly. "Every town, in every territory, went silent. Whatever happened, not a single member of the order made it out."

Theren felt her blood run cold with fear, wondering how such a thing could be possible. She did not know much about what Dulmun had been like before the war broke out, only that Adara had said she had traveled there; that alone seemed proof that these towns that Naro spoke of could not all have been lawless backwaters that one would expect to be dangerous. There had to be *some* places that were just like any other, ordinary places full of ordinary people, where there were likely Mystics like Kaewa, or Iantha, or Junan, or Maikano—people who did not deserve to be disappeared into thin air, no matter what Theren thought of the order as a whole.

And yet not one person had been able to leave Dulmun to speak of it? Thinking of how formidable the Mystics that she knew all were, Theren shuddered.

"Every possible scenario we could imagine is just as unlikely as the last," Ilya continued, sighing. "And none adequately explain the utter silence about it. Many powerful and honorable Mystics were lost, without a trace. We all owe it to them to discover what happened and bring word to their families if they truly were slain."

The faces of the Mystics around the campfire were grim, all of them worrying about the fate of their colleagues, but Theren frowned. The redcloaks all seemed practically incapable of believing that their own could ever do any wrong, so would they even believe it if any of the missing Mystics had betrayed them? What if the king of Dulmun had simply offered them more than the order did? Was this something they had not considered?

"Could they have turned on the High King?" she asked, ignoring the angry looks she provoked. "It might explain why no word has come from them, if they do not consider themselves on the same side as the rest of us anymore."

"This is another reason that this fact was kept from the younger recruits," Ilya said dismissively, shaking her head. "You think they might have turned on the High King because none of you have known the Mystics that we have lost. I am sure there could be some in far-flung towns with sympathies towards Dulmun, but many of the captains and chancellors within the kingdom were some of our most noble warriors. Chancellor Karan's husband, Captain Shan, was stationed in Handelsen when the war began, and I would sooner believe that the moons could come down from the sky than that he had betrayed the Mystic order."

Vivien nodded fervently, agreeing. "The Grand Chancellor of all Mystics in Dulmun was a woman named Falkari, and a finer woman and warrior I have never met. I cannot imagine anything that could turn her from loyalty to our cause, nor can I entertain the thought that any Mystic who did betray us would be able to stop her from returning to the High King to report. This is why it is so important for us to uncover the truth."

Theren realized she must have been making a sour face when Lilith nudged her, and she made an effort to collect herself. Only the fact that Chancellor Karan's husband had been mentioned kept her from launching into a tirade. She could not believe how willfully blind they all were. They were sitting here with a torturer, talking about how none of their comrades could ever commit the dishonor of treachery. She determinedly buried herself in her food, cursing the redcloaks silently for what felt like the millionth time.

"It has been strange, watching the younger ones compete to try garnering a posting in Dulmun, as if it is a game," Kaewa signed, and many of the others nodded, grumbling.

Theren remembered the fury on Chancellor Karan's face at every further set of antics that the recruits would get up to in the hopes of being noticed and receiving what was seen as a prestigious assignment, and thought that she understood him a little better, at least in this regard. She considered suggesting that they might not have been so eager to vie for it if they had been told the truth, but she also remembered the recruits' hunger for battle that she had found so disconcerting. In the end, she could not say for certain if they would have behaved better or worse had they known the stakes involved.

"Is this the upcoming business in Dulmun that the chancellor spoke of?" Lilith asked, while Theren continued her internal complaints.

Vivien nodded. "Yes, well-spotted, Lilith. This is why our mission must be conducted with the utmost secrecy—if those of our order who have gone silent have been captured, any hint of aggression on our part might cost them their lives. We cannot risk provoking King Bodil in any way by revealing ourselves."

"Which is why we must display all possible caution in Destor," Ilya cut in, her voice firm, and Vivien held up her hands in submission.

"Very well, Ilya. I will not countermand you. I hope that we will not miss out on information we may need later, that is all."

Now that Vivien had capitulated, Ilya's argumentative demeanor gradually fell away, and she instead just seemed worried and tired, like all the rest of them. It was strange to see her so vulnerable and messy, her loose linen shirt and a few stray wisps of her hair fluttering in the cold night wind. Theren was not sure whether the falling of her façade made her seem more relatable or less, that she still behaved as she did despite how she felt underneath.

"Our orders are to ignore all other concerns and intercept the merchant as soon as possible," Ilya said morosely after a brief pause. "I am no more fond of it than the rest of you, but any efforts to locate our people must wait until after we have stopped the delivery of those magestones. We must trust that if they live still, they can survive a little longer for the sake of this more urgent mission."

The other Mystics seemed mostly satisfied by this, except for Naro and Vivien, who both still seemed uncertain. Theren, relenting a little, remembered the many empty tables in the great hall of the Academy after Dulmun's attack upon the High King's Seat, and wondered how she would have felt if they never heard any word about what had happened to those who had once sat around them: whether they had been lost, or taken away, or some other such ill fate. Lilith had been away during the attack, she recalled, and she shuddered once more, reaching out to grasp Lilith's hand and twine their fingers together tightly.

There was very little conversation for the rest of the night with the mood having turned so dour, and shortly many of them went to bed. Theren lay in her bedroll next to Lilith, her mind overflowing with thoughts about how entire garrisons of people separated by vast expanses of ocean could possibly just disappear all at once. This journey into Dulmun was seeming like a worse and worse idea by the day.

TWENTY-EIGHT

THE NEXT DAY REMAINED CLEAR, THOUGH IT SEEMED that their discussion the previous night had tainted the moods of the Mystics traveling with them, so that everyone was silent and determined. Kaewa, like Theren, had evidently had more than her fill of the wagon's jolting, and switched places with Tamah, while everyone else pretended to be very busy with saddle-related things and quite unavailable to drive the wagon.

The countryside seemed to be—Theren knew no other word to describe it—deepening, the vast grass-covered savannah seemingly becoming thicker and wilder as they went, until their wagon could simply no longer handle the terrain off the road. They had been avoiding it for some time, since it meandered across the plains and they wished to cut a straight line towards the border, but now they had no choice; the dense grasses choked the wheels, and even their four-horse team labored to drag the wagon onwards.

They passed by indications of small towns and farmsteads occasionally but ignored them all, though Theren could see the displeasure on Vivien's face every time they did so. She herself was too busy wondering how people could possibly live out here, so far from civilization, when all the land seemed fit to choke down any attempt to tame it, to wonder whether the inhabitants might have known anything about the missing Mystics. She wondered if this was what the land in Dulmun was like, and whether that had anything to do with the way the Dulmunsters behaved.

Sometime in the middle of the afternoon, Naro and Iantha rode ahead again to scout, but it had only been an hour or so before Naro returned alone, his face bleak.

"We have a problem," he said to Ilya gravely as she called them to a halt.

Theren immediately felt a prickle of suspicion, ducking her head inside the wagon briefly to tell Lilith what was going on. Lilith's face echoed the wariness that Theren felt, and she crept up closer to the front of the wagon so that she could peek out at the discussion as it took place.

"Where is Iantha?" Ilya asked, the exact thing that Theren had been wondering, though she did not seem quite so mistrustful as Theren felt.

"Ahead, following some tracks we found beside the road," he answered perfunctorily, and then held up one hand to stave off any other questions. "Let me explain. As I said, we have a problem. There is evidence ahead, some half-hour or so of hard riding, that a caravan was attacked upon the road. We found scraps of blue cloth—the color of the Kallis family—and a few scattered jewels and other pieces of merchandise at the site."

A murmur of shock rippled through the other Mystics, with Tamah making a grave rumbling sound of displeasure from the front of the wagon. Theren, on the other hand, still could not decide whether she believed Naro, though at least Iantha was still alive somewhere ahead of them. If he had come back with news that she had perished, Theren was sure she would never have been convinced.

"Are there any casualties?" Vivien asked, her eyes narrowed, and Naro nodded.

"Three outfitted guards, and six of the attackers. They seem to be bandits, wearing no uniform and bearing no marks or weapons that would indicate sponsorship by any other wealthy families."

"So it is unlikely that the attack was motivated

by the magestones?" Kaewa asked in sign, and Naro nodded once again.

"That is what we concluded. The problem, however, is that the gems and jewelry we found were dropped away from the road, in the direction that the attackers fled after the incident went poorly. They have managed to steal some of the merchant's cargo, and we cannot say for sure whether or not they pilfered the magestones with it."

Ilya and Vivien both swore, while Kaewa rubbed at her eyes with her hands tiredly.

"Iantha is trying to get an idea of how far away from the road the bandits may be making their hideout," Naro added, sounding as weary as the others looked. "If we are lucky, it will not be too far."

"Would the merchant of the family Kallis not return to face them if his most precious cargo had truly been stolen?" This came from the third Mystic that was new to Theren, a Dorsean woman named Cilin.

"He may not even have noticed that they were taken yet," Vivien replied solemnly. "One can hardly search through the secret compartments in one's wagon during an attack, at least not without alerting the bandits to the presence of something particularly worth stealing."

Ilya grunted in frustration and gestured at Naro. "Come. We must see the site before we can decide anything. Iantha may even have good news for us by the time we arrive."

She nudged her horse forwards into a trot, with Naro wheeling to ride beside her and the others following behind at a slower pace. The idea that they might be able to claim the magestones from a den of bandits and not even have to cross the border into Dulmun appealed to Theren greatly, but she could see why the others were worried. A day or two delayed here would mean a day or two extra lead that the Kallis merchant would gain on them, and it was less than a week's journey across northern Dulmun all told, even at a modest speed.

They rode until they came to a stretch of the paved road that was lined with tall, wide poplars—a perfect place for ambushing unsuspecting travelers, and the bandits had obviously agreed. Scattered along the road for several hundreds of paces lay splintered wood and small pieces of debris from the wagon, trails of blood and tattered pieces of cloth, along with the bodies that Naro had spoken of. The first they came across was a guard outfitted in a surcoat of ocean blue, the arrow buried in the back of his skull indicating that the caravan had been taken completely by surprise.

Theren wondered if he had even known what his master was transporting, or if this had been just another job to him, earning coin to feed his family.

They halted some ways away, since their horses were already skittering nervously at the smell of blood. Cilin and Kaewa began setting up a makeshift camp by the side of the road while the others went ahead on foot to scour the way for clues. Tamah, as silent as ever, started digging graves to bury those who had fallen, work that Theren found difficult to watch.

Lilith frowned disapprovingly at one of the dead bandits that they came across, as Vivien inspected his clothing. "There have always been bandits in the wilder areas of Feldemar, but they have been kept mostly in check by local constables. The conflict with Dulmun must have emboldened them, knowing that everybody's resources are focused elsewhere."

"War brings out the worst in many kinds of people," Vivien responded gravely. "At least they do not seem to be highly trained. That should make our job easier, whether we must deal with them or whether it simply means they were not skilled enough to steal the stones."

"Is this one?" Ilya called out suddenly from where she had been searching beneath one of the poplar trees, holding up something small and black in one hand.

Heart pounding madly, Theren came closer to get a better look, but just from a glance she could see that it was not. She had never seen a magestone on its own—only in their packets, waiting for sale, on board the Yerrin ship that had been transporting them for the benefit of Isra—but it was not the right shape, and she felt no real pull from the round, marble-size item in Ilya's hand, no tug of temptation. Lilith, who had better knowledge of them, also shook her head, and Vivien and Naro seemed to know better as well.

"This is a pearl," Naro told her simply, extracting it from her hand and turning it over in the sun, light glittering off its every smoky, luminescent surface.

"Surely you jest," Ilya responded, snorting. "Pearls are white, or creamy gold at the darkest."

"Not in Dulmun," he replied impassively. "The Kallis family has made their fortune off the back of these stormpearls. They can be harvested only from oysters below the waterline on the northern shore of Southbreak, and only Kallis has permission to fish there. They are much sought after by royals and wealthy merchants all across the nine kingdoms, and the pieces they are laid in are of such exquisite craftsmanship that many are buried wearing them. A fine niche our friend Armod had for himself, until he decided to dip into illegal smuggling."

"That just shows you how many gold weights' worth of magestones he must be bringing home," Vivien declared darkly. "No merchant's son would abandon such profits, not unless he was promised something far greater instead."

Theren shivered at that thought, amazed yet again by the lengths that goldbags would go to for coin, even when they already had enough to not need any more.

But Ilya had lost interest as soon as she was certain that the pearl was not what they were seeking, turning back to her search. "I will continue looking, then."

They scoured up and down the road for nearly an hour, gradually widening their search into the grass and bushes on either side, but found very little of consequence before Iantha came riding back from her own investigation, looking unhappy.

"There are many more bandits than I expected," she said as they gathered around her, eager for news. "An entire enclave of them, it seems. I crept as close as I dared to their hideout, but it was clear from some distance that they are celebrating wildly. They appear to consider this heist a great success, despite the fighters they lost."

Ilya swore again, and Vivien sighed. "I take it you could not hear any mention of the stones?"

Iantha shook her head as she dismounted. "No, only coin. They are apparently expecting lots of it."

"Darkness take them." Ilya growled and spat on the ground. "Lawless scum! They deserve the sting of the High King's justice either way."

"We will have to investigate," Naro added quietly, agreeing. "We cannot risk that they might sell the stones elsewhere while we are chasing down a merchant who no longer has them."

"But what if they did not take them?" Kaewa signed, looking worried. "How much time will we lose?"

Naro grimaced, but did not seem deterred. "I cannot say. But if we chase down the Kallis caravan and they no longer have the stones, we will have no definitive proof tying him to any crime, and suddenly our presence is no longer a secret and our colleagues in Dulmun may be in danger."

Once again Theren felt a warning prickle as the hairs on the back of her neck rose up, not liking that Naro was the driving force behind this effort to convince them to stay. While Iantha had gone to scout out the bandits' camp, he had been alone at the site of the attack for who knew how long, and could have removed any number of clues. The other Mystics seemed swayed by his argument about their missing fellows, but that seemed to stick out even more sharply in her mind as suspicious, that he was appealing to their greatest fears to change their minds. The more the others capitulated, the surer she became that it would be a terrible idea to follow his advice.

"What if we were to split up?" she suggested, repeating herself in sign for Kaewa as all eyes swiveled towards her. "Send one group onwards to the Linked Cities to continue tracking the merchant, while the other investigates the bandits?"

"Hm," Ilya said, thinking about it, but Iantha sighed, shaking her head.

"It would be difficult. As I said, the bandits are quite numerous. I do not like the odds that half of our band would have against them."

"So do not send so many in the group seeking the merchant," Theren countered impatiently, as her mind raced with a suddenly burgeoning idea. "They do not necessarily need to *capture* him, not immediately. If, say, Lilith and I went alone, and met up with him, asking to join his caravan as he travels, bargaining on the weight of the Yerrin name, we would only need to delay him a little until the rest of you could catch up. That way we investigate both possibilities, and without running out of time."

"We could tell him that our caravan was attacked by the same bandits!" Lilith suggested brightly, obviously taking to the idea. "He would have no reason to believe otherwise, having met them himself so recently."

"I do not like it," Ilya declared, frowning, and Kaewa nodded, looking concerned.

"It seems far too dangerous to send just you two alone."

Theren rolled her eyes, exasperated. "Well, if we sent any of *you*, they would wonder why you had fled towards the town when you are all so formidable. And we *must* send Lilith, for she is the one with the family mark of Yerrin, to prove her identity if need be, to help us win our way onto his caravan."

There was a pause, during which many of the older Mystics exchanged worried glances, while Vivien stepped forwards, fixing them both with a stern gaze.

"You both understand what is at stake here, yes?"

"I have seen the destruction that magestones can wreak firsthand," Lilith replied, lifting her chin defiantly, though her eyes were sad. "I have lost friends to it. I understand."

"So do I," Theren added firmly, meeting Vivien's gaze.

"And do you truly believe you are capable of doing

what you suggest? That you are ready for this?" Vivien pressed, her stare piercing into Theren's soul.

She thought about the alternative, about them missing the merchant by hours and the devastation that Dulmun's mages would unleash all because nobody would dare to disbelieve Naro, and nodded, drawing herself up to her full height.

"I do."

"What say you, Iantha?" Cilin asked, her eyes narrowed shrewdly. "The seven of us, against the bandits you saw?"

Iantha seemed to weigh the decision in her head for a moment before answering slowly. "With both Vivien and Kaewa with us? I would say we could manage it."

"I could always go with them, if that would make you feel better," Naro told Ilya, who was still looking unconvinced. "I have trained in this kind of spywork, after all."

"But you are the only one with any knowledge of Dulmish geography!" Theren interjected hastily, hoping that her distaste for the idea was not too obvious. "The others may need your help to track us swiftly, to catch up as soon as possible."

Both Tamah and Vivien nodded, agreeing, but there was another long moment of silence as Ilya looked them over, assessing.

"We could possibly send Cilin with them instead," Iantha suggested after some time, but Ilya shook her head, finally coming to a conclusion.

"No. They are right. This is the most prudent course of action."

Theren felt a wave of relief wash over her, only to be replaced instantly with a looming sense of dread. They would be going into Dulmun *alone*. She exchanged a glance with Lilith, whose small smile lightened her heart considerably, and told herself that at least they were going together.

"I can give you a simple description of some of the land beyond the city," Naro offered mildly, and though Theren inspected him closely to see if he was angry about them not following the course he had suggested, she could not see any evidence of it.

Ilya nodded sharply, satisfied by their plan at last. "Very good. Let us prepare, then. We have no time to waste."

TWENTY-NINE

At Ilya's command, the Mystics busied themselves preparing for both halves of the mission, with Cilin artfully ripping through one of their horses' caparisons with a sword to lend weight to the story about having been attacked, and Tamah firmly stabbing one arrow into the thick leather of one of the saddles, where it would not interfere with the comfort of either horse or rider. Naro and Iantha were in consultation about the position of the bandits' camp, while Kaewa, Vivien, and Ilya tried to give Theren and Lilith some final advice.

"Do *not* put yourselves in any unnecessary danger," Vivien said firmly, looking especially at Theren. "Even the best Mystics sometimes let smaller crimes go by unchallenged when they do not have backup available. Do not risk compromising yourselves under any circumstances."

Lilith rolled her eyes at the melodramatic way in which the three older women were talking to them, but Theren was slightly relieved to hear Vivien's command. It was her first real outing as an official servant of the High King, and she did not precisely know what her jurisdiction or authority were, so having proper orders not to interfere with people stealing something or asking for assistance was reassuring. She did not know if she could really stand by if she saw someone committing a murder or some such, but she hoped it would not come to that.

"If you get into trouble, or if you have to leave the caravan for any reason, you can send fire magic into the sky like a beacon, so that we can see it," Kaewa signed to Lilith, seemingly very worried over them. "Hopefully we shall not be too far behind you, especially if you can successfully delay the merchant's caravan."

"If we do find the magestones within the bandits' hideout, we will simply come to find you, and tell the merchant that some of the guards of your caravan made it back to Destor," Ilya added, and Theren nodded.

"We are counting on you both," Vivien said gravely, placing a hand on each of their shoulders.

Cilin came over to them, leading the group's youngest, most energetic horse, outfitted with the ripped caparison and the saddle that had been ornamented with the arrow.

"This is about the best we can do, I think. Any more 'battle damage' and we risk making the ride too difficult. You should be able to reach the Linked Cities by shortly after nightfall, if the weather holds."

"We made good time today as well," Ilya noted, satisfied, but Cilin just shrugged.

"One lone horse will always travel faster than a wagon, even carrying two people."

Cilin then handed Lilith a coin purse in customary Yerrin green, which felt hefty enough to outfit a brigade of men, let alone see them through their assignment.

"Good luck," Vivien said, sounding uncharacteristically anxious, as Cilin handed Theren the reins.

"To you as well," Theren replied, swinging into the saddle, as she tried not to think about how uncertain Iantha had been of their odds of success.

Kaewa hugged Lilith tightly before Ilya interlaced her fingers to help lift Lilith up onto the horse in front of Theren, the voluminous skirts of her fancy dress making it difficult to find a safe perch. It would likely have been quite a romantic situation if not for the dire mission on which they were about to embark, and Theren felt her cheeks growing warm with embarrassment as she momentarily pictured them doing the same thing after their wedding someday.

"Remember what is at stake," Ilya told them sternly, though her eyes were not as hard and piercing as usual. "There can be no room for error."

"I understand," Theren told her gravely, as she wrapped one arm around Lilith's waist and gathered the reins together in her other hand.

"Then go. And may the sky bless you."

Theren felt the brief pressure of Lilith's hand squeezing her own, a small gesture of comfort that nonetheless galvanized her, and she nudged their horse onwards down the road towards the Dulmish border, waiting until they had both sufficiently found their balance to kick the gelding forwards into a canter. Clouds had cleared from around the feeble winter sun just enough to warm the otherwise frosty air when bathed in its light, but Theren could tell that it would be a cold night, and she did not want to be stuck riding for too long once the sun had set. It would be the ultimate ignominy, she thought to herself dryly, to freeze to death in a downpour of cold rain before even reaching Armod of the family Kallis. She maintained as fast a pace as their horse could manage, hoping to avoid that fate, even though it did feel somewhat like they were hurtling towards some unknown destiny.

The first thing that Theren noticed about the Linked Cities, as she looked down over the haphazard sprawl of streets that seemed to have grown to fill every available mote of space in the basin in which it sat, was that it did not really seem to be two places at all. The moons were high and bright enough that she could see the spindly maze of bridges passing over the river to connect both halves almost seamlessly, and some buildings even sat in the middle, jutting out over the water on stilts or situated entirely on floating pontoons. If Naro had not warned them earlier that residents on either side would not react well to having the city names conflated, she would never have guessed at all.

The second thing she noticed, judging by the distant glow of moving torches along the outskirts of the city, was that there was quite a large number of guards stationed at the entrance on the Feldemaran side. She wondered briefly which was the more likely reason for their presence: to watch for Feldemarians trying to cross into Dulmun, or for Dulmunsters trying to cross into Feldemar.

"I hope all this security does not make things too difficult for us," she said anxiously.

Lilith shrugged dismissively, though her voice was more uncertain. "There is no better scheme than the one we have already devised. If it fails us, no one can say they could have done better."

Theren wrinkled her nose in distaste at the idea of riding straight back to the rest of their group with news that they could not even make it into Destor. "I fear that fate may have written that statement on my grave."

Lilith laughed at that, patting her arm gently. "At least this time no one has *eaten* the magestones."

Theren grimaced and then turned their horse's nose towards the road down into the cities, steeling herself. "Very well then, let us put on our best show for the benefit of these nice guards."

"Just pretend they are instructors asking you why your dissertations are not completed," Lilith responded, her grin audible even though Theren could not see it.

Theren felt sorry for their poor mount as he made his way towards the gates of the city, drooping with weariness, his heavy breaths erupting into full clouds of steam. They would likely have to dismount once they were beyond the gates, though she admitted to herself that her backside could use a break from the riding as well. At least, if nothing else, they did look as if they had ridden hard to reach the safety of the Linked Cities, because it was technically true.

"Who goes there?" a harsh voice demanded, once they had reached the gates and were shielding their eyes against the sudden brightness of the torchlit wall.

"Oh, please, good sir," Lilith began, her voice cracking artfully. "I am a daughter of the family Yerrin—Lilith is my name—and as we were traveling along the road, our caravan was attacked by a vicious group of bandits! One leaped into the wagon that I was in, and I only barely managed to scramble out in time to escape. My uncle told the youngest guard here to get me away from the fighting, to ride to Destor and not look back! Oh, please, let us in! I could not stand the thought of sleeping in the wilds when such villains roam the countryside!"

She broke down into huge, dramatic sobs, and Theren's eyes had adjusted enough to the light to see the guards exchanging glances, mostly looking sympathetic. For her part, Theren maintained an expression of exhaustion and fright, which was easier to cultivate than other emotions might have been at that time.

"You are the second caravan within two days to report such an attack," one of them, seemingly the one in charge, said wearily. "We do not usually let folk inside the walls after nightfall, not in these days, but I think we can make an exception in this case. It is the least we can do, what with not being able to go out and hunt the bandits down, I would say."

"Oh, thank you, thank you!" Lilith gushed, still weeping, and the guardsman cleared his throat awkwardly.

"Of course, young mistress. Now you two run along inside, and only make sure you do not tell the mayor we let you in after dark if you see him, all right?"

"Oh, I will not tell a soul! But—sir, you mentioned that another caravan had been attacked before ours? I would feel much safer if I could meet up with another group of merchants rather than being on my own! Do you know where we might find the others, if they are still in the city?"

Theren held her breath for a moment, wondering if the question would make the guards suspicious, but they all seemed unfazed, muttering a brief exchange among themselves about whether anyone had heard any details of where the Kallis caravan had gone. The idea that this sort of behavior was common among merchants both amused and exasperated her, though she could not deny Lilith's ability to play a crowd.

"I heard one of the guards from yesterday say that the other caravan made straight for Hallrand," a woman's voice said after a moment. "Went right to the most expensive inn in the city, he said."

The leader of the guards hesitated for a moment, thinking. "All right. Well, Lisse, you can take these young ladies across the river and ensure they have no trouble finding their way, then. I expect you back quick-smart, though!"

"Yessir!" The woman who had spoken saluted smartly.

Theren felt a small thrill of excited disbelief, thinking of how lucky they were. Vivien and Ilya had spoken of crossing the river into Dulmun as if it would be some great feat, and here they were being taken across for the price of a few fake tears. Lisse took hold of their horse's bridle and led them inside the gates, which closed quickly behind them with an ominous clank. Some of Theren's elation turned to dread as she realized that they were trapped within the city now, though in a pinch she was sure that she could jump the wall. However, that would certainly attract attention.

Lilith continued sniffling theatrically much of the way through the city, and though Theren tried to memorize the way they had come, the winding laneways and strange shifts in slope confused her. She hoped that they would not need to find their own way back for any reason, because she had lost track of their route at about the fourth crossroads.

"Do you have any idea how many bandits attacked you?" Lisse asked them as they went, though she sounded more curious than suspicious.

"More than a score, at least," Theren replied, feigning a remembered fear. "That is why we were ordered to flee—there were more than we guards could deal with all at one time."

"Hm," the guardswoman said, sounding sad, as Lilith whimpered in emphasis. "In days past we would have hunted them down and made the road safe. If only we were not so occupied with—well, I am sure you can guess."

Neither Theren nor Lilith answered her, not wanting to provoke any kind of discussion about the war, as they made their way onto one of the bridges that linked Destor with Hallrand, their horse's hooves thudding hollowly against the hard wood. Theren found herself gazing over the edge of the bridge at the river below them, which seemed impossibly deep and wide from up close; it took some amount of walking, across at least three bridges built onto small, gravelly islands amidst the water or sometimes the raftlike pontoons, to even get halfway. The fact that this was not even its widest point boggled her mind, and she marveled at how well chosen it was as a border, since it would be perilous indeed to cross anywhere else than at the appointed stations.

There was a guard at the end of the last bridge, but he did not pay them more than a cursory glance's worth of attention, seeing Lisse and waving her past without a problem. Theren took a deep breath, her heart pounding frantically; they had reached Dulmun. That left only, well, the entire rest of their mission to deal with. But it was definitely a good start.

THIRTY

Lisse left them outside the Unbroken Shield, politely wishing them a good night and saying that she hoped their fortunes would improve. For a moment, Theren almost felt bad for lying to her and the other guards. Was this something that the Mystics did habitually? She could hardly bear to think of it, spending the rest of her life lying to good people for the sake of the High King's reputation.

While Lilith paid for their now-exhausted gelding to be stabled, Theren busied herself with observing what she could see of Hallrand from here. The inn was quite close to the waterfront, and the building foundations were firmer and laid in stone more often, while the roads were paved neater on this side of the river. Somewhat to her surprise, it did not feel particularly different than Destor had; there was no air of menace, no subtle change in the way people looked at her, nothing. It was just . . . another group of people, on a different side of an imaginary line. She wondered if the Dulmunsters living in Hallrand were as upset about the war as the Feldemarians seemed to be, since they apparently interacted with each other with minimal fuss.

Lilith returned from the stables, tucking their coin purse into some hidden pocket within her skirts, and gave Theren a small smile.

"This has gone much smoother than I expected, thus far."

"Indeed," Theren replied, narrowing her eyes. "I am irrationally occupied with the fear that it is the calm before the storm."

Lilith put a hand against Theren's cheek, turning her head this way and that quickly to check for watchers, and then kissed her gently. "Courage, my love."

Theren could not help but smile, shaking her head in wonderment. "If you had told me a year ago that we would be here together, on a mission for the High King, behind enemy lines in Dulmun, I would have suggested you see a physician."

Lilith grinned at her as they broke apart, squeezing

her hand tightly for a moment. "Just remember that for the moment, we are barely more acquainted than a noblewoman and any guard would be. We must keep up appearances, at least for the time being. If one or both of us happens to be caught doing something suspicious later on, our entanglement makes for a fine decoy secret to unveil, if nothing else."

Theren wrinkled her nose. "'Entanglement?' Is that what merchant families usually call this sort of thing?"

"They might say 'dalliance' instead," Lilith replied wryly, as she stepped out from under the eaves of the stables to head towards the front door of the inn. "Some families are very particular about who their children become romantically involved with. I am lucky that my parents only wish me to be happy."

"Did you acquire any confirmation that the merchant is here?" Theren asked, returning to the matter at hand as she hurried along behind Lilith's sweeping gait.

"Yes. The stablemaster said we will know Armod by his vulgar and ostentatious nature."

Theren grinned, thinking that it seemed at least she would not feel bad about tricking *him*. "How charming."

Lilith stilled herself for a moment in front of the door, eyes closed, before taking a deep breath and changing her posture, clutching at her skirts daintily and acting as though she were afraid to touch anything around her for fear of dirtying herself. Theren shook her head, thinking that she had never seen Lilith act like that once in all the time she had known her, and wondered if the children of merchants hated the affectations of goldbags almost as much as she did.

Inside, the inn was rowdier than she had expected, but it mostly seemed to be convivial singing rather than any kind of fighting. Remembering the battle-hymn that had pierced the fog at sea, she almost shuddered, but this song was a cheery drinking tune, something about swords tempered by mead instead of water when they were forged, and she felt herself relax a little. It was not so different from the Crimson Jib, she thought, looking around at the patrons, except that the food and drink were more expensive, and thus likely more palatable.

Lilith made a show of being demure and dainty as they walked inside, while Theren tried to subtly scan the crowd, looking for someone that matched the appearance of the drawing they had been shown back in Ammon. She did not see that face, but she did spot several men and women in tunics and surcoats of the same ocean blue that they had found at the site of the caravan attack, noting that there still seemed to be quite a few of them, despite those that had died in the bandits' attack. Nonchalantly she leaned against the wall, trying to observe them while Lilith spoke with the innkeeper about securing a room for the night.

They were told that the merchant had already retired to his rooms, but the innkeeper looked at Lilith's teary eyes and offered to send someone to speak with one of his guards, to find out if he would meet with her. Satisfied, Lilith paid for her room, as well as food for both of them, which they collected before promptly heading up the stairs to their lodgings. Theren had been unsure whether staying in the same room was a good idea, based on their cover story, but Lilith assured her that a merchant would rarely be without at least one guard unless absolutely necessary—especially one petrified of bandits, as Lilith was claiming to be.

Theren made herself smile trying to remember the last time that she and Lilith had not shared a bed, and realizing that it was almost half a year ago.

"You will have to remember to try to be as unobtrusive as possible," Lilith said while they were eating, and Theren spread her hands innocently.

"I am always unobtrusive!"

Lilith gave her a look, but she giggled despite herself. "You know what I mean. You try to walk ahead of everyone and stand in the center of every room. Get used to standing against walls for a change."

Theren scoffed at the idea that she liked to be noticed, but she knew that she would have to follow Lilith's advice. The last thing she wanted to do was cause them to be discovered.

Shortly after that, there was a sharp knock on the door, and Theren opened it—as a servant would, Lilith whispered to her, hastily—to find a grey-haired man with fair skin and cold blue eyes, asking to speak with Lilith.

"Do excuse me, Mistress Yerrin," he said smoothly, giving a slight bow once Theren had let him inside. "But my master, Armod of the family Kallis, has heard that you wished to speak with him. He sent me to ask if now is an agreeable time, and to inform you that we will be leaving in the morning, so there is thus a regrettably small window of time in which you might converse."

"I suppose if now is the only time, then it shall have to do," Lilith replied petulantly, while Theren tried not to grin behind the man's back at her acting like a spoiled child.

It seemed to be roughly the reaction that he had been expecting, since he made some attempt to soothe her feigned ruffled feathers as they followed him down a long corridor towards an ornate set of double doors, clearly the most expensive part of the inn. Smoothly the man knocked on the doors, and one of them was opened by a guard, who let them in immediately as soon as she recognized the man leading them. Theren, knowing that she was once again very unlikely to be included in the conversation, took up a position standing on the other side of the doors from the Kallis family guard, and thought about how boring the life of a guard must be.

Ironically, she thought to herself dryly, if she had indeed been sent back to Cabrus to wait on Imara, she might have now had a better idea of how a servant was supposed to act, instead of having none.

She scanned the room carefully while doing her best to project the neutral, uninterested stare that all the other guards she had seen were experts at giving off. Like the rest of the inn, it was floored in polished hardwood, but there were thick, luxurious fur rugs covering much of the floor in what seemed to be the living area, a large open space with many low benches and tables. Sitting on one of these benches was the man who was unmistakably Armod, the master of the caravan; Theren recognized him not because he particularly resembled the illustration they had been shown in Ammon, but because he exuded an air of what she considered to be the very worst kind of wealth, equal measures of reveling in luxury and always hungering for more.

In truth, the picture they had been given was not a very good likeness of him at all, though she admitted to herself that she did not know how any drawing could quite capture this man's essence. She had a vivid memory of thinking that the picture looked a lot like Naro, but Armod himself really did not. While they did have a similar face shape and the same broken nose, Armod's eyes were more angular and his jaw sharper and more defined, and his skin was a warmer golden-brown compared to Naro's deeper ochre coloring. She wondered if the illustrator or whoever had described him had been influenced by Naro's presence, or if it was just her own suspicions of Naro that had affected her perception—the latter was awkward to think about, especially in a situation such as this.

Observing him now, Theren found that she could believe that such a man as Armod of the family Kallis would indeed have decided to smuggle magestones simply for coin. He was gregarious, almost charmingly so, and though his eyes sparkled often with mirth, within them was also a glint of cunning that rarely disappeared. Theren watched it glimmer like gold in the depths of a deep pool as Lilith retold their story, about how their caravan had been scattered and how she wished to join up with another to reach Rothton, and while outwardly he was sympathetic, that same shrewd calculation never left his eyes the entire time that Lilith spoke.

"That truly is a pity," he said airily, waving expansively at one of his servants to bring them wine. "Would you like a drink? As I said, such a pity. We ourselves encountered bandits on the road into Destor as well, but nothing of any real value was lost, and we managed to escape quite easily. I am surprised that a caravan of Yerrin could not do the same."

"Oh, we were only quite a small group," Lilith replied with affected embarrassment as she accepted the wine. "You see, I planned to move to Southbreak to live with some of our family there, so we brought only a small amount of goods, enough to pay our way. I confess I had thought that Feldemar would remain safe. I feel so silly about the whole thing."

Theren tried as best she could to watch him closely without appearing to, her heart pounding as she wondered whether he would believe Lilith's story or not. They were in uncharted territory here—none of them had really thought about whether or not he would question how a Yerrin caravan could be overcome by bandits—but Lilith seemed to be doing quite well at coming up with lies on the spot. Theren was already bristling at his comment about nothing of value being lost, remembering the dead guards who lay upon the road, but it *did* seem to be the best evidence they could gather at this point that he still had the magestones with him, and that she had been right to insist they come after Armod instead of concentrating on the bandits.

"I am sure that my family in Rothton would show you their gratitude if you were able to escort us safely the rest of the way there," Lilith added, in one of the best displays of feigned earnestness that Theren had ever seen. She also saw immediately by the sparkle in Armod's eyes and his sly smile that Lilith had won him over.

"Well, it would hardly do to leave two young people stranded here in the middle of nowhere! I am sure we could find room for both of you among us quite easily, as long as you are prepared to leave by tomorrow."

Theren watched him once more as Lilith burst into an outpouring of gratitude, saying that she just wished for the journey to be over and was more than happy to leave by tomorrow morning. He was smooth and amiable, making airy promises about their families meeting once they had reached the capital, and mentioning discounts he might give them on the Kallis family jewelry, giving Theren no hint that he was suspicious of them. She remembered that cunning gleam in his eyes, however, and knew that they would have to be extremely careful in order to maintain their charade until the other Mystics could catch up.

She did not want to end up dead, left along the side of some road in Dulmun, with him once again proclaiming that nothing of value had been lost.

THIRTY-ONE

"WHAT AN AWFUL MAN," LILITH SAID, SNIFFING, ONCE they had safely returned to their own room to finish eating. "Did you see how pleased he was once he believed that our caravan had really been attacked? I have rarely met anyone that made me feel so glad for my own family. I cannot imagine what my life would be like if my parents had been like him."

Theren shrugged, listless. "He reminds me of Imara in some ways, only more shrewd. I was afraid for a moment that he would not believe us. I wish we did not have to go with him on this journey—how much easier it would be, if we could simply arrest him now and be done with it."

Lilith sighed tiredly, rubbing at her eyes. "That might have been a possibility if we had caught up to him while he was still in Feldemar. Though it is hard to say, given how the war has been going here in the north lately. We will just have to work with what we have, unfortunately."

"Do you think we still could?" Theren asked, frowning, as she picked at her food. "Arrest him ourselves, I mean? Not here, tonight, not in the inn surrounded by so many people of Dulmun, but out on the road?"

Lilith was silent for a while, considering it, though her concerned expression gave away her thoughts. "I do not think it would be the wisest course of action to take. We have yet to find out how many guards he has with him, and I would not want to commit to anything before we knew what we were up against."

Theren sighed, knowing she was right. "It just feels wrong, letting him go on living a life of luxury while we know what he is up to. I hope the others catch up soon."

"I wonder if they will have more trouble getting into the city," Lilith mused, as she rose and walked over to the window. "I have no doubt that Vivien could cry on command, but the guards may not fall for the same trick twice."

Theren grinned at that. "I would love to see anyone try to convince Ilya to act frightened."

Her amusement did not last long, however, as the realities of the situation refused to dissipate under the onset of their jokes. Still bitter that they could not be done with the whole affair here and now, she finished her food while Lilith continued to watch the city outside. What was the point in even becoming a Mystic if she could not do what the Mystics were supposed to do, and protect the people of the nine kingdoms against rampaging abominations from Dulmun? But there would be no point in trying at all, she knew, if all it resulted in was them being apprehended by soldiers and taken as prisoners of war. She felt like a dog on a leash, held back from the hunt; a turtle held just out of reach of the water, straining to reach it with every fiber of her being.

"It does not really look the way I expected Dulmun to look," Lilith said idly, once Theren joined her at the window, leaning against her from behind.

"I find it strange to think that there is a war going on somewhere to the north," Theren added, setting her chin on Lilith's shoulder. "You would not think it, not from the actions of the people here. They are all so . . . cheerful."

"Mm," Lilith said thoughtfully, clasping her hands together tightly. "They seem less worried than most of Feldemar, and even Selvan, if Adara was right about the sailors back on the Seat. What a strange place."

Theren continued to look out the window for a few moments, enjoying the view of the moons reflected in the great river, before sighing and straightening up. "So, Mistress Yerrin, tell me: in what way would you best delay a caravan? We must make sure that our new friends spend as long as possible upon the open road, away from the shelter of any cities."

"Well . . . you could make it snow," Lilith said seriously, and Theren laughed.

"I am no wizard king of old. Do you have any other suggestions?"

Lilith smiled, though she spent some time thinking before she answered. "Damaging one of the wagons might be a safe bet. It would need to be only slightly, however, so that it seems well enough to start out the day on—like loosening an axle, or weakening a wheel. The most common reason that any caravans I have been with have stopped has been due to animals foundering, which is far too cruel to force, so I think causing them to stop for repairs will be our best choice."

"I think I can manage that," Theren replied pensively. "I will go out to the stables under the pretense of checking on our horse before I go to bed, then. Even if I misjudge things and break the wagon too thoroughly, the delay is what is important."

"Good luck," Lilith told her, turning around, and then kissed her. "Hurry back. I am dreadfully afraid of being robbed, if you had not heard."

Theren grinned again, leaning her forehead against Lilith's. "Far be it from me to leave any goldbag in distress."

"You are lucky I enjoy your company," Lilith retorted dryly, and Theren smirked as she made her way out the door.

She went downstairs quietly, noticing that by this time a lot of the revelry had died down. There was no more singing, and there did not seem to be any guards in ocean-blue surcoats in the common room either, for which she was quite grateful. The innkeeper paid her no mind as she made her way towards the door and then outside, shivering in the sudden cold and hurrying towards the musky warmth of the stables. She found their gelding quickly, in one of the stalls nearest the entrance—he looked much better now that he had some food and water in him, and he seemed to have been brushed down thoroughly, which was also good. She wondered if stables were a luxury for him after his time on the road with their party.

Harder to spot were the wagons, but she eventually came across them towards the back of the stable—unfortunately, directly behind one of the stablehands, a young girl who was industriously pitching hay that would presumably be used the next morning. Theren considered her options. She did not want to attack the girl, and hanging around waiting for her to leave would also be suspicious. Instead she sidled up to one of the stalls near the end of the row, one housing a tall bay that flicked its ears curiously at her, and clucked at the horse, cooing and stroking its nose familiarly as though she had known it forever. The stablehand ignored her, as she had hoped, and when the girl's back was turned, Theren fixed her eyes upon the rim of the wagon's right-hand back wheel, forming a shape like a fist with her magic. She swung it at the wheel, gritting her teeth, with a force that she hoped might be enough to splinter the wood.

She felt the impact, but the rim had not seemed to yield at all, so she waited for another chance and then swung again, harder this time. There was a quick, unmistakable crunching sound as the wood cracked just slightly, and the stablehand looked up from her work, confused. Theren turned away quickly, to hide the remnants of magelight in her eyes, but after a few moments, the girl went back to pitching hay. Theren waited a little to see if the stablehand would investigate, but obviously the girl had concluded that it had been a rat or some other nocturnal inhabitant of the stables. When she was satisfied, Theren bid goodnight to her new equine friend, and then more quietly to their own gelding, before hurrying back into the inn. She did not know if it would be enough to stop the caravan, but if not, then she would know better for the next night.

Before she reached the comparative safety of her room, however, Theren was startled to overhear Armod's voice, along with that of the grey-haired man who ran his errands, coming from a room behind the stairs on the ground floor. Her interest piqued, she hovered as close to the wall as she dared, and heard a sloshing sound of water that seemed to explain what they were doing down here—evidently the inn had no facilities for bathing even in the richest of private rooms. She wondered if Lilith minded.

"Do you know anything about which branch of the family Yerrin this Lilith might come from, Hargrim?" the merchant asked his lackey, and she felt her heart grow tight with fear.

She crept a little closer, even though she knew that would make it harder to explain her presence if she was discovered; if Lilith was in danger, it was better to know now than to put themselves completely at Armod's mercy by crossing over into Dulmun with him tomorrow and simply hoping for the best.

"I know of her by name," the grey-haired man, Hargrim, replied, and Theren relaxed a little, hearing how unconcerned his voice sounded. "Though the last I heard it was many years ago, when she was very young. I believe your mother and her parents were acquainted . . . They were a mostly upstanding offshoot of the family centered in Nikolo, in the north of Feldemar, I seem to recall."

"Mostly?"

"Well, you know how the Yerrin family are, master."

Theren felt her mouth twist sourly at that statement, no matter how glad she was that Lilith's parents were considered upstanding.

Armod muttered something that Theren could not quite hear, obviously sharing her view of some of the more corrupt Yerrins, and then sighed. "Very well. That matches with the impression she gave me. She had not the smug, self-satisfied look of those in her family who deal with the darker aspects of their business."

Theren shivered, unnerved by just how much scrutiny Armod was paying Lilith, but reminded herself that this was to be expected. These were exactly the kinds of games that the goldbags were used to playing with each other, often over things that were far more trivial. They were simply lucky that neither man found Lilith's parents suspicious.

She stepped away quickly, resolving to go back to her room, and put extra care into creeping up the stairs so as not to give away her position.

"Things must be in an uproar in Feldemar if even the children of rich merchants are fleeing," a third voice said, this one deep and gravelly, like stones grinding against one another. "It seems our king's campaign of war fares well."

Theren's stomach roiled at the words, thinking of the destruction of Ulande, and she hurried away, not wanting to hear any more. Some things were too dark to think of, darker even than the dealings of the family Yerrin.

The bed that Lilith had paid for was bigger than the one they had shared back in Ammon, but the room was much colder and draftier. Mayhap for this reason Theren's sleep that night was fitful, and she dreamed of being pulled backwards by unseen hands, hauling her away from whatever it was that she was trying desperately to reach.

THIRTY-TWO

THE NEXT MORNING WAS WHAT HER TUTOR JUNAN WOULD have called "crisp" and what Armod of the family Kallis described as "cold as a fish's underclothes," the weather seemingly deciding to make the most of the seven days that were left of winter to indulge in the kind of cold that made Theren's eyes and nose ache from being exposed to the air. Lilith seemed quite happy to be able to ride in one of the wagons in her still-beautiful but now slightly rumpled dress, and Theren was once again extremely grateful for the fur-lined gloves and gorget that the Mystics had acquired from the Yerrins.

Several of the guards introduced themselves to her as they were preparing to move out that morning, and she tried to listen to as much of what was being said as she could, in case they mentioned anything incriminating, but they all seemed to be fairly normal, based on what little she really knew about guards. The greying man whom she had overheard speaking last night was named Hargrim, she had already learned, and there was a guard-captain named Norrik—a tall, bulky man with pale brown skin and a thick, black beard, owner of the deep, gravelly voice she had overheard last night speaking with Armod in the baths—along with more than a dozen other guards. It seemed that Lilith had been right to suggest waiting, rather than rushing to make an arrest, for Theren did not know if they could have easily overcome so many at once. It did not make her feel any less impatient.

There was no sign of the other Mystics, and Theren was disappointed, even though she told herself that she probably should not have expected them to catch up so soon. But the question of their safety worried at her; knowing now that Armod almost certainly still had the magestones, and with her suspicions of Naro still nagging in the back of her mind, she would have felt much better if she could have known how they fared.

There was only one gate leaving the city on this side of the river, and Theren realized as they approached why it had been so easy to cross over into Hallrand last night. Wherever the borderline actually was, it was here, at the gate, where all the guards were positioned to stop trespassers. She counted at least a score of them, all armed with the same barbed spears that she remembered so well, and she licked her lips nervously, hoping that Armod had prepared for this moment.

"What business do you have in the kingdom of Dulmun?" the commander barked gruffly, far less welcoming than the guards on the Feldemaran side had been.

"My master is a member of the great merchant family of Kallis, who live chiefly in Rothton," Hargrim told him smoothly, not perturbed by his unfriendly nature. "He is returning home to them in light of the current conflict and brings many trade goods which the nobility of Southbreak may find desirable."

The commander seemed uninterested in such pleasantries, merely grunting and demanding that everybody submit themselves for inspection. Theren waited with trepidation through the whole process, with everyone giving their names and having their weapons and belongings looked over, and felt a great wave of relief when at last they were waved away, as though they had been wasting the guard commander's time somehow.

The cold air billowed furiously around them as the caravan made its way out of the city, and as the thick iron gates closed ponderously behind them, Theren knew that there was no longer any chance of turning back. She swallowed hard and tried to concentrate on the road ahead of her, wondering what her friends were doing now, and whether it would seem absurdly normal by comparison.

Like much of Feldemar that she had seen, northern Dulmun was wet, and sticky, and full of swarming, biting insects, but it did not feel quite so wild as the countryside west of Destor had. For the first few hours of their ride that day, Theren could have interchanged the landscape that they traversed with some place in Feldemar and not noticed the difference, but gradually a semblance of order seemed to fall over the lands on either side of the road. The sparse trees haphazardly dotting the horizon made way for neatly planted rows of oaks and elms, and the uneven, jagged cliffs to the east of the road were replaced with careful terraces for growing crops—though not this late in the winter, so there were very few farmers out tending to their fields as the caravan went by.

The road itself was deeply rutted with wagon tracks, and looked to have seen a surprising amount of traffic recently. Theren supposed it could have been from transporting local farm goods, but it still felt strange to see signs of the kingdom carrying on with ordinary life. She wondered just how far away the High King's army was, and found herself hoping that Armod would have put some thought into avoiding them; she was still not sure just what the High King's punishment might be for being caught with a Dulmish merchant caravan, and particularly one transporting magestones.

On the bright side, however, the road's heavy usage during what must have been a wet and muddy winter had made it uneven and bumpy. Theren realized she was not even sure her damaging of the wheel last night had been necessary, as she watched the wagons jolting heavily along the craggy ridges on the ground. It certainly could not have hurt, of course, but she would not have been surprised if Armod had been delayed even without their presence. That thought rankled somewhat, as she thought about where she and Lilith could be now instead of here, but she was glad that she had stood up to Naro, all the same. She would feel terribly smug, she knew, when the Mystics caught up with them and found the magestones still in the caravan's possession.

At about midday, Theren had to bite her lip to keep from guffawing out loud when the wagon that Armod was in had a rather unfortunate encounter with a large rock, and the already-weakened wheel rim splintered fully and came apart. A startled yelp issued from within, followed by a series of thuds and crashes as he clearly fell over from the jolt, and Theren snickered into the cover of her furred ruff at the obvious indignity of his collapse. Many of the other guards also seemed to be concealing laughter, though Norrik glared at anybody who was not doing a good job of hiding it.

"Darkness take all of the blasted, mud-splattered

north!" Armod exclaimed from inside the wagon, between bouts of loud swearing.

Hargrim rubbed at his eyes, looking very tired. "Shall we stop and make camp, master?"

"Yes! And make sure the tents are up before it starts to rain!"

Theren busied herself trying to be helpful as the tents were set up, once they had discovered a place beside the road that Norrik was satisfied with, but was relegated to looking after the horses. She decided that they were better company than most of the people, as she listened to Armod complaining loudly, though she did occasionally catch Lilith's eyes and had to suppress a few giggles.

"At least this is better than bandits," he grumbled bitterly as she returned from having led the last of their mounts to a nearby stream for water. "I will say this for our northern reaches: they do not suffer the lawlessness of Feldemar. Imagine how much more peaceful it would be if Dulmish soldiers patrolled along the road leading into Destor! At least in Dulmun, all you need fear is the weather."

Theren felt her eyebrows rise in disbelief, glad that her expression was hidden by the horses surrounding her, and concentrated on the bay she was brushing down at the moment. Nothing sounded less peaceful than the idea of Dulmish soldiers patrolling roads in Feldemar.

"I am sure that King Bodil could offer the aid of

Dulmun's army to King Alim, if he is in need of extra forces," Hargrim replied smoothly, and Theren nearly shuddered. "We might suggest it to her when we arrive at court."

"We must!" Armod continued, still annoyed. "How can there be commerce if the main roads are not even safe? Security *must* be ensured, or civilization itself will suffer!"

"Do you think that Feldemar would be amenable to such a suggestion, Mistress Lilith?" Hargrim asked. Theren froze in sudden alarm.

If Lilith answered affirmatively, it might have dire political consequences for the war, depending on if any information ever reached Rothton about her assessment. But if she answered negatively, it could put them in a dangerous situation or rouse suspicion about their motives for joining the caravan. Leaning down as if to inspect the hooves of the horse she was standing behind, Theren risked a glance under its belly at where Lilith and Armod were sitting, with Hargrim standing nearby, about a dozen paces away. Lilith's back was to her, so she could offer no support, but at least if things got messy, she would be able to use her magic to help.

Lilith sniffed dismissively, clearly still playing out her charade of being a spoiled brat. "I really cannot tell you what the king of Feldemar is thinking these days. Things all across the kingdom have fallen into disarray! It is much of the reason I decided to move to be with my family on Southbreak."

Still tense, Theren waited for a moment while the horse beside her impatiently tried to wrest its hoof from her hands, but to her great relief it seemed that both men accepted Lilith's answer. Armod even made a grunt of assent, followed by a dramatic sigh.

"The royalty truly do not comprehend the importance of the great merchant families and all we do for the stability of the nine lands. I do hope that King Alim will come to his senses. It might be that consultation with our King Bodil will make him see what his leadership has cost Feldemar."

Theren stood up again, a sour taste in her mouth as Lilith agreed graciously and Hargrim changed the subject, asking if Lilith had ever visited Dulmun before and launching into a discussion about Rothton's many luxuries. What kind of person could state that they were helping keep people secure, while actively transporting magestones to an army ready for war? She did not know how Armod could live with himself, even as entirely hypnotized by the lure of coin as he seemed to be. Once more she felt stifled by their orders to simply delay him, and yearned for their Mystic companions to catch up.

"This had best be the last delay before we can reach the capital," Armod declared irritably. "I am anxious for this journey to be at an end at last."

Theren smirked to herself and moved on to the next horse—the one she had met last night in the stables, which whickered in recognition as she stroked its nose once more—and decided that, necessary or not, she would sabotage the wagon again that night as well, if only to see more of Armod's discontent. From what she had heard in these two short days with him, it was far less than he deserved.

THIRTY-THREE

A wild and vicious storm blew in from the east that afternoon, rain beating down on the tents and wind roaring through the creaking rows of trees, even fiercer than most that Theren had seen in Feldemar. Lilith asked Armod and the others about it over their evening meal, apparently also surprised by its ferocity, and enquired as to whether it would delay their travel. Norrik, who it happened was local to the area, told her dourly that the closer they got to the sea, the worse the storms would get, especially at this time of year. Armod, however, assured her that their caravan would not stop. Theren dearly hoped that their journey would not take them too much closer to the coast, if only for the sake of her mud-stiffened boots.

She admitted to herself later that night, though, that the storm provided her with a perfect opportunity. None of the other guards had raised a fuss when she placed her bedroll closest to the tent entrance, citing a weak bladder and the possible need to rise multiple times during the night, since none of them wanted to be within reach of the driving rain. With luck, she thought, the sounds of her creeping about would be muffled by the howling wind as well.

For what seemed like hours, she lay waiting for the guard beside her to fall into a deep enough sleep that the woman would not immediately be awakened by her movement. A few hearty snores were enough to assure her, and she slipped out of the tent into the night. Almost immediately the heavy rain soaked through her shirt, and she mumbled a curse under her breath that it would have looked suspicious to sleep in her armor. Her rapier she had with her, reasoning that if anybody questioned her she could say it was for safety, but she had known, sadly, that sleeping with her gorget and gauntlets on would have raised eyebrows.

The moons were hidden behind a shroud of storm clouds, but some few stars managed to peek through the deluge. It was barely enough light to see by, but any light was better than none. Theren, acting as though she really had risen in the night simply to relieve herself, raised one arm above her head against the rain and hurried into the tree line beyond their camp. She did not see any movement, so she hid herself behind a tall, wide pine, and waited. There were four guards, positioned at the corners of the camp looking outwards; she could only see one from her hiding place, but she could guess where the others would be.

The one she was watching had not even noticed her pass, being heavily wrapped up in his cloak and sullenly stationary. Theren shook her head in amusement, thinking that the instructors at the Academy would put these guards to shame. The number of nights that she had been caught by a prowling alchemy teacher deliberately lurking in the shadows were too many to mention—though the nights she had skillfully eluded them were even more numerous. This particular escapade looked as though it would be much simpler.

Crouching low to the ground, she edged her way around the outside circumference of the camp, towards the area where the wagons were being kept. Just as she had hoped, in all the rain and wind, neither of the two other guards that she passed appeared to see even a flicker of her movement. Still, she made sure to bide her time before approaching the wagons, wary of letting over-confidence get her into trouble. She steeled herself, and then, using the horses as cover, darted towards the nearest wagon. Despite some slipping and sliding, she managed to keep her feet.

She waited, heart pounding, crouched down beside

one of the wheels, for the sound of any guards coming to investigate. There was nothing, though. Nothing but the wind and the rain and the occasional sleepy snorting of the horses. Satisfied, she risked a look under the belly of the wagon and noticed that this was the same one she had sabotaged the night before, the newly fixed wheel rim obvious even in the low light. Grinning at the notion that Armod might ride in it again tomorrow, she angled herself so that light just barely illuminated the wheel axle. She heaved down on it with her magic, just as she had done with Vivien on the mast of the Dulmish ship while at sea.

She strained for several moments, pulling so hard that she feared she might give herself a headache before she could yank it loose, but eventually heard the solid crunching sound as one end of the axle broke away from the frame of the wagon. As on the night before, she waited to see if anybody would come to investigate the sound, one hand over her mouth to hide the obvious steam of her breath, but it seemed that she was once again in the clear.

Relieved, she stood up, looking to find the best way to return to her tent, but paused as a thought occurred to her. Here she was, in probably the best position that she might have for some time to search the caravan properly. The storm was keeping the guards occupied with their misery, and she was already over here by the wagons. Why not look through them, and see if she could find the stones herself? If she did manage to dig them out, she could go and find Lilith, and they could leave straightaway, tonight, and be done with this entire wet, messy business—a thought that kindled a little flame of hope inside her heart, illuminating the desire for this crazy adventure into Dulmun to just be over and done with already.

Excited now, she carefully unhooked the canvas covering from the back of the wagon. She went to climb inside, and then only just realized in time that her muddy footprints would give the game away. Wary of getting mud on her hands as well, she instead scraped off every speck that she could find using her magic, glad indeed that there were no other mages aside from Lilith with the caravan. That done, she clambered inside and pulled the canvas back down as best she could without sealing out all the light, wondering where exactly a merchant might hide some highly illegal cargo.

She pored over every corner of the interior, pushing against the floor to try to find hidden compartments. She spent more time there than she would have liked, digging through boxes of jewelry so fine that each piece could have paid for food and shelter for a dozen orphans in Cabrus, more wealth in one place than she had ever imagined. At the bottom of one such box, she came across a pair of plain golden rings—or as close to plain as any items in this collection could be called. One was covered in delicate, patterned filigree that reminded her of the hilt of her rapier, and the other was a plainer band of thicker gold set with two of the Kallis family's prized stormpearls, in the shape of the two moons chasing each other across the sky.

As she held both rings in her hand, a strange feeling of longing came over her. She remembered Lilith's question about making a life together, though it seemed so long ago, the night before they had left Ammon. Theren had very little to offer Lilith in the way of coin and what it could buy, certainly less than the Yerrin family could, but she still longed, even if futilely, to be able to give Lilith beautiful things, to be able to see her cooing in delight like she had over the dress that the Mystics had acquired for her. And if they were truly going to spend their lives together . . .

Not even a year ago, Theren would have pocketed the rings without a second thought. The Kallis family did not need this wealth, and Armod certainly did not deserve it. She swore under her breath, thinking that all this working for the High King had ruined her, and then remembered, keenly, the doubts about High King Enalyn that had been raised in her mind over the course of her time in Feldemar. The pleas of the people of Mabawa that it had fallen to Lilith to answer; the unfriendly faces in Bandar, angry at their presence; the razing of Ulande, with none of the High King's army to defend it—things that she knew she should never forget. Grimly, she pulled out her Mystic's badge, still on the chain around her neck, and threaded the rings on either side of it, her decision made. She then carefully replaced the other items in the box and hid the badge beneath her shirt once more.

The High King's law had its blind spots, and so did she.

She returned to her search, still not finding the magestones, and was just about to try the other wagon when she heard footsteps outside and the sounds of someone pulling on the canvas behind her. Already somewhat hidden behind a stack of boxes, she flattened herself against the floor, only just resisting the urge to yelp in panic. Her mind raced, wondering how much of the contents of the wagon she had displaced, or whether she had left any obvious signs of her presence. She feared that whichever guard was there might hear the frantic beating of her heart, but the agonizing, uncertain silence merely lengthened into what felt like an eternity.

"Accursed wind," a male voice muttered finally, before the canvas was pulled down across the opening fully, blocking out all the light. "The master will have a fit if the rain ruined any of his books!"

Theren sat there for a short while, dazed by the close call, waiting for her pulse to calm down and trying to force some moisture back into her suddenly dry mouth. Quietly, she edged her way towards the front of the wagon, peeking out through that flap of canvas rather than the one that had attracted the guard's attention. Eventually she judged that it would be safe enough to jump down that way—safer than the alternative, at least. Quick as a flash, she leaped for the ground and dashed towards the cover of the trees, expecting angry shouts behind her at any moment. When none came, she breathed a heavy sigh of relief and leaned against a tree trunk.

She would have to be much more careful with the second wagon, now that at least one guard was on alert, even if it was just for what he thought was the wind. She briefly considered not bothering with it and returning to her tent, but with the stolen rings now tucked inside her shirt and the possible growing suspicion of that particular guard, she wanted more than ever to be done with everything by tonight. As quickly as she could, she picked her way towards the undamaged wagon's front step, repeated the trick of removing the mud from her boots with her magic, and heaved herself up inside.

She immediately regretted it when, upon stepping down onto the floor of the wagon, she accidentally put her weight on what must have been a hidden switch. A clearly audible clattering sound rang out as a section of the floorboards came loose, popping upwards to reveal a secret compartment. Once more she flattened herself hastily behind a stack of boxes, thinking that she could very much do without the stress of this kind of business once they were done with this particular venture, and lay there, tense, as she waited for any reaction to come.

Time passed, and nobody came to the wagon to investigate. She carefully allowed herself to relax, making sure to move as quietly as possible, and pulled herself over to the hidden compartment, from which she extracted a plain wooden box about the width of a dinner plate. Her breath caught in her throat as she flipped the catch and opened the lid to see exactly what she had been looking for: magestones, and a staggering amount of them, row upon row upon row all stacked neatly, like weapons lined up in an armory.

"I could have sworn I heard something!" a voice said, and the canvas was thrown open before Theren even had time to react.

"Surely it was just the wind—" The second guard stopped cold as they both saw her sitting there, still holding the magestones, frozen like a deer in the gaze of a wolf.

Time slowed to a standstill as she watched recognition and realization light up in the eyes of the guards, but she knew in an instant that there would be no talking her way out of this. Dropping the box, she leaped towards them and lashed out with a wave of force. It pushed them both backwards out of the wagon, away from her escape route. One yelped in shock, but she sprang out after them, emboldened by panic, and forced their mouths shut with clamps of her magic. Off balance and in shock, the shorter of the two men fell backwards heavily and hit his head on the ground. One swift blow from Theren's fist as he was trying to regain his footing rendered him unconscious.

The second guard was less easily dispatched, as he

immediately tried to run away and fetch some of his fellows while Theren was preoccupied. She scythed at his ankles with her magic, tripping him, and then dived on top of him, trying to knock him senseless like she had done with his friend. He bucked and railed against her even as she wrestled him into a headlock, and drew a knife from his belt, slashing wildly at her right arm. His blade found its mark, slicing into her forearm, and she gasped in shock.

A thousand memories of the knives of Mystics suddenly flooded through her mind, and she released him without meaning to. In her panic, however, she let loose with another blast of pure force, and it slammed the guard's head forwards into the ground, stilling him.

Clutching at her wounded arm, her breath coming in ragged gasps, she gazed around at what had happened, wondering how on earth she could fix this. With tears stinging in her eyes, she ripped off a part of her sleeve to tie around the slash on her arm and used the rest of it to gag both guards, then tied their hands and feet together with ropes from the wagon and dragged them underneath it. She hoped that they would not be seen there, at least for a while. The one that had cut her was bleeding heavily from his nose, so she stirred up the muddy ground with her booted foot to hide the blood.

There was no way out of this now. They would have to make a run for it, and they would have to do it immediately. She grabbed the magestones from the wagon, holding the box close against her chest with her good arm, and headed directly for Lilith's tent.

THIRTY-FOUR

Lilith sat up instantly as Theren slipped inside the tent, her face a mask of consternation. In just a few instants she seemed to take in the rain-soaked, mud-splattered state of Theren's clothing and the bloodied bandage of linen on her arm, and gasped softly, covering her mouth with her hands.

"What happened?"

Theren struggled to find the right words, instead proffering the chest full of magestones, which Lilith inspected with the horror of someone uncovering a fresh corpse, her lips moving soundlessly as she made calculations.

"This is . . . this is a fortune's worth of these!"

"We have to go," Theren croaked, finally finding her voice. "Two of the guards saw me. We need to leave!"

Lilith's eyes flew to the wound on Theren's arm again. "Are they . . .?"

"Unconscious, and hidden under one of the carts. If we have any luck at all, they will not be discovered while this storm continues. But by tomorrow morning, there will be no doubt."

Lilith stood up, wringing her hands for a moment, and then crossed the distance between them, hugging Theren. She held tight in response, even though it made her injured arm sting, and closed her eyes, trying to shut out all the rest of the world, even for just a moment.

"I thought of getting up to investigate tonight myself," Lilith told her, her voice wavering. "I wish I had, for your sake."

"My arm will heal," Theren replied softly, and then kissed her. "It is done now, at any rate. There is no time for regret. We must leave, and quickly."

Lilith frowned. "Can we afford to leave, though? Stopping the magestones from reaching Dulmun is one thing, but surely Armod needs to be brought to justice, as well."

Theren's heart sank as she realized that Lilith was right. Whatever her personal thoughts about Armod's irrelevance in the greater scheme of things, their party had been ordered to retrieve him. Ilya in particular would be loath to leave Dulmun without him in hand. If they absconded now, the caravan would certainly be on much higher alert upon discovery of the theft, and their group of Mystics might have to spend an even longer amount of time in Dulmun tracking him down again. The expressions that she imagined on Ilya's and Naro's faces upon her returning to tell them that she had blown their cover stung at her pride as well—especially when Ilya's disdain for her was palpable already.

There had to be something they could do.

"What if we took him with us?" she suggested uneasily. "I think I could carry him, with the help of my magic, at least."

Lilith gave her a look of appraisal, tinged underneath with worry. "Are you sure? Even with your arm?"

Theren shrugged, flexing it a few times and trying to ignore how much it hurt. "I do not see that we have a choice. Either we do this, or we wait to be discovered."

Lilith hesitated for a moment, and Theren reached out to grasp her hand, simultaneously looking for comfort and wanting to dispel the fear from her eyes.

"We have done far crazier things than this before," Theren said quietly.

"We have not," Lilith replied, laughing. "Every day I am with you, I fear I have wandered ever deeper into some unfathomable maze of adventure and chaos."

Theren hesitated, regretting having brought her

along and putting her in danger. "I . . . I know you wanted peace and quiet. I am so sorry. I promise that once we are done with this—"

"Hush," Lilith said, smiling, as she gently placed a hand on Theren's cheek. "Do not apologize. We have a saying in Feldemar that we use often during these winter storms: without the rain, we would not miss the sun. I would gladly accompany you through a thousand misadventures for the chance at a day spent together in the sun. I could be back in Ammon, or on the High King's Seat, or anywhere else less perilous, but it would not be worth being there without you. You bring me the best of both things that I want, the storm as well as the sunshine."

Overcome with emotion, Theren embraced her, and held her as tightly as she dared. Lilith may have been right, that this was indeed the most ludicrous and dangerous thing they had ever done, but somehow it did not seem beyond their ability, not when Lilith was in her arms and the thought of lazy afternoons in the keep at Ammon or on a terrace on the High King's Seat was within their grasp, if they could just win this one last fight.

"I love you, you know," she said, once she had let go.

Lilith smiled warmly, eyes sparkling. "I know. I love you, too."

"Let us finish this, then, and go home. I could do with some sun."

Quickly they made their plans, and Lilith, though she seemed very disappointed about it, removed some of the many layers of skirts from her dress, to make it easier to run in. The makeshift bandage on Theren's arm was replaced with a thicker one torn from the blankets from Lilith's bedroll, and she also gratefully accepted an extra cloak that Armod must have provided, glad for even the smallest amount of warmth. There was hardly time for any other preparations; the rain was beginning to ease, and they needed to move now if they wanted to be able to use it as cover.

Theren slipped out of the tent warily, prepared to sell a story about her "dalliance" with Lilith if any guards happened to see her emerge, but the drizzle seemed to still be doing a good job of keeping the sentries preoccupied with their own misery. She reached back inside and motioned for Lilith to follow her, and together they slunk across the camp to Armod's tent. They circled around the outside of it, away from the entrance, and by the light of the moons overhead, Theren carefully gathered up the canvas in claws made of her magic. Viciously she yanked at it, ripping it vertically in a slit long enough for the two of them to shoulder through.

It was too dark to see much of anything inside the tent, but Theren could pinpoint Armod's location by the confused, sleepy noises he made as he was woken by their intrusion. Irritated, she wondered what possible reason someone as spoiled as he could have for being a light sleeper, and quickly darted over to his bedroll, hoping that they could do this without too much noise.

"Hello?"

His voice was still sleep-addled, and he seemed unworried, so Theren moved as quickly as possible, not wanting to give him the chance to come to his senses. She grabbed a rumpled cloak from the floor and wadded it, swiftly covering his mouth to muffle any attempt to cry for help. He writhed and wriggled, trying to break free, so she seized one of his arms and placed her knee on his chest to hold him down. Lilith conjured a small ball of flame for her to see by, and he redoubled his efforts, his eyes flooding with panic when he saw the box of magestones in their possession.

With everything now visible, Theren was able to hold his arms still with her magic and clamp his mouth shut, too, for good measure. She tore strips from what was likely a very expensive doublet in order to bind his wrists, and then tied his ankles as well, and gagged him, hoping her knots would hold. That done, she bent down to heft him up onto her shoulder, but they were suddenly interrupted by shouting from outside.

"Intruders! Hurry! We have been attacked!"

Commotion broke out instantly, and Theren froze in panic as the unmistakable sounds of people being roused from their tents filled the camp outside. A brief, fleeting thought that their fortunes might have changed, that their Mystic companions may have caught up with them, crossed her mind, but there were no sounds of battle. They were on their own.

"They must have found the guards I left trussed up under the cart," she said faintly, regretting her choice to search for the magestones all the more.

Lilith gave her a worried look but peeked out through the slit in the canvas they had made to enter the tent, motioning for Theren to follow. "Quickly! Let us go before they can take stock of the situation!"

Grunting, Theren hauled the still-struggling Armod across her shoulders and lifted him just as she had her squadmates during all that training she had hated so much. Thinking bitterly that he could have done without so many rich dinners on his journey, she battled her way out of the tent and back into the storm, thinking that Captain Menrad had at least taught her one thing that had turned out to be useful.

"We may have to knock him out if he keeps this up," she puffed, as Armod attempted to yell for help through his gag.

"It will do him no good if we hurry," Lilith replied, though the fearsome glare she directed at Armod seemed to quell his struggling a little.

She had extinguished the ball of flame that they had been using for light, to avoid drawing attention to themselves, so the forest was as black as pitch as they dashed for the cover of the trees, still hearing people shouting behind them. They had barely gone a hundred paces when Theren's legs and back began to ache, but she knew they were still far too close to the camp to slow down. Grimacing, she put her head down and continued on, willing her legs not to give out underneath her. Lilith ran about a dozen paces ahead, still holding the magestones, but turned back to check on her constantly, obviously worried that they were not moving fast enough.

The fierce rain had turned the forest floor into a vast expanse of mud, with deep puddles of it collecting in the hollows beneath gnarled tree roots. In the darkness it almost looked like tar, so Theren tried to avoid stepping in it where she could. The idea of her feet sinking into it and getting stuck made her shudder, or as much as was possible under the weight of Armod, anyway. Dimly she realized that they were running away from the direction of the road, and wondered whether that was a good idea or not. While the road itself might have offered a slightly easier escape route, even as potholed and rough as it was, it might also be the first direction that the guards would think to search in.

A thought occurred to her as they splashed their way across a small stream, the water so cold that it chilled right through her boots. "The signal!"

Lilith turned back to face her once again, seeming confused. "What signal?"

"Kaewa said—" She struggled to draw in a deep breath, still running. "Kaewa said to send up a burst of your magic if we strayed from the road, so that the others could find us. More so now than ever, we could use their help."

"Do you think they will even be close enough to see it?" Lilith asked, unconvinced.

"If not, then they should be ashamed to call themselves Mystics," Theren growled, and then could not help but grin when Armod quite obviously repeated the word "Mystics?" through his gag, in a panicked realization of how much trouble he was in.

"And besides, we hardly seem to have a choice. What else will we do? Wander deeper into Dulmun until we have no chance of finding our way back? We will have to signal for them eventually, so why not do it when we could use their aid?"

Lilith frowned, still worried. "But it will alert the guards to our position! If I make the flame high enough to be seen from the road, it will certainly be seen by those hunting us."

Theren considered this for a moment, but her mind was numbed by the cold rain and the agony of forcing herself to keep moving. Her lungs burned, and her wounded arm was a constant pulsing source of pain. She did not know how long she could keep this up, but she did know that once she stopped, she would find it very hard to begin moving again.

"Then we must do it now, while I still have the strength to run." She gasped from the effort of speaking as she labored her way up to the crest of a small hill.

Lilith watched her silently for a few moments and

then nodded, having seemingly weighed their odds in her head. She scrambled up the hill ahead of Theren and then raised her free arm upwards towards the sky, whispering words that Theren could not hear. A lance of fire shot forth from her hand, spearing up through the canopy of the trees and sizzling in the rain, and then burst into a wide halo that illuminated the muddied forest around them briefly in searing orange light. Lilith was right, of course; there was no way that the caravan guards could have missed seeing it, though the wide sunburst at the signal's peak may have masked their exact location at least a little. Wincing, Theren jolted her way down the other side of the hill, trying to keep her breathing regular and make good on her declaration of having the strength to keep going.

Lilith seemed to be waiting to see if there would be any reply to their signal, either from their pursuers or the other Mystics, but Theren was still wary of stopping for any reason, in case her legs refused to start again. She thought of the horse that had carried them to Destor despite his exhaustion and put her head down grimly, managing to plod another fifty or so paces before she heard Lilith cry out from behind her.

"Look!"

She turned her head, heart beating wildly at the note of exultation in Lilith's voice, and saw, very briefly, an answering flash of fire in the still-cloudy sky, not much further beyond where she imagined the camp must be. Hope swelled in her chest like the expanding corona of light from Lilith's magic, and she laughed in triumph, feeling her strides lengthen with renewed vigor. With any luck, Kaewa's flames would also be seen by the guards, and they would have to split their forces to investigate both signals.

"Obviously they did not stop for the storm!" Lilith crowed joyously, catching up, and Theren laughed once more.

Armod seemed less amused, still trying to wriggle himself free of Theren's grip. They once again passed over a small, fast-flowing brook that wound around the bottom of the hill that had been their vantage point, but this time Armod's struggling was enough to cause Theren to lose her balance, and she slipped, landing heavily on the rocky streambed. Lilith growled at their captive and grabbed him as he tried to crawl away, but Theren was busy patting herself to make sure nothing was broken. She could have sworn she had heard something snap when she landed.

It was a struggle just to get back to her feet. She knew for certain that she would not be able to lift Armod across her shoulders again. But as she bent double trying to regain her breath, the clouds cleared from in front of the moons for a brief moment, and their light shone upon the entrance to a cave some distance upstream from them, nestled in the foot of the hill.

"In there!" she gasped, pointing, and then leaned down to help Lilith drag Armod towards it.

It was small enough that neither of them could stand up straight, but it was dry, which was a blessing indeed. Fear turned Theren's blood to ice as they heard heavy hoofbeats thud past at a gallop—right along the route they themselves had been taking mere moments ago. Lilith's hand found hers in the darkness, and she clasped it tightly, trying to breathe as quietly as possible. Two more horses went by shortly after the first, and this time the riders had torches, the faint light reaching up past the mouth of the cave on several occasions.

Clearly, they could not stay here indefinitely—when the guards did not find them, they would surely tighten the net of their search, and the cave was not so well-hidden that it would guarantee them safety, even with Vivien and Kaewa and the others on their way. Theren felt her heart ache at the fear on Lilith's face, visible even in the dark, and knew in that moment what she had to do.

"You stay here with him. I will draw them away."

"You cannot be serious!" Lilith gasped, clutching tighter at Theren's hand.

She edged a little closer to the mouth of the cave, risking a glance outside to check for torchlight, and then up at the moonslit sky to try to gauge whether the rain would be returning.

"In fact, I think I am."

Lilith shook her head vehemently, refusing to accept it. "You cannot. I will not let you go alone!"

"Someone has to stay here with him," Theren countered, nodding at Armod, though the anxiety in the pit of her stomach agreed with Lilith. "Besides, you could not move as fast as me with my magic, and I would tire myself out carrying us both. And if we just stay hiding here, we will eventually—"

Another rider went past, slower this time, and with the torch held lower to the ground. Theren gestured around at their hidey-hole, small as it was and shallow, with nowhere to hide further in.

"This would not be a good place to be caught."

"We could fight them off if they came!" Lilith insisted, though even she did not seem very convinced.

Truthfully, if it were to come to a battle, Theren would be of no use whatsoever if they remained inside the cave, due to the lack of light. This was a large part of what had guided her otherwise unthinkable decision. Even if Lilith could clear a dozen men from the entrance with a fireball, there were more than a dozen guards, and it would take only a single spear to kill an unarmored mage—Theren's memories of Tinun's last moments could attest to that.

"The others are on their way," she said, trying to smile reassuringly. "I only need to keep the guards' attention long enough for them to catch up."

Lilith's eyes glistened with tears, and she would not let go of Theren's hand. "But what if you . . ."

The question hung in the air between them without being voiced, and Theren felt her own eyes stinging.

Still bent double because of the cramped space, she scuttled over so that they were closer together and cupped Lilith's face in her hands, ignoring the exasperated noises coming from Armod's corner of the cave. None of this was how she had imagined facing the possibility of her own death, but the absurdity of their situation seemed to make it all the more real. This was no darkened dungeon staffed by corrupt torturers, no bloody and raucous fight with enemy mages upon the high seas. It was frantic and painful and frightening and the best way out of a bad situation, just like so much of the rest of her life.

"We will go together to Calentin someday, even if I am only there in spirit," she whispered, every muscle in her body trembling in fear and exhaustion. "As long as you are safe, that is enough for me."

"Do you not think I feel the same way?" Lilith demanded tearily as Theren moved away.

Theren smiled sadly, wiping her eyes with the back of her hand. "And if you were born the mentalist and not I, you would likely be going in my place. But fate has its whims, and here I am."

She returned to the entrance of the cave, keenly aware of how much colder everything felt away from Lilith, and made another check to see if she could spot any of the guards. She stepped outside and drew herself up to her full height, against the wishes of many of her muscles. Between all her exertions, her fear, and the icy wind, she could barely keep her hands from shaking, but she ignored them and took a deep breath. There was no time for that sort of thing now.

"Be careful!" Lilith called, her voice cracking, and Theren risked one more glance back at her before setting off into the forest.

She could have stayed, could have promised Lilith that she would indeed be careful, but she did not know if that was a promise that she could keep. If it came down to a choice between her life and Lilith's, Theren knew which she would choose. She would do whatever she had to in order to protect the woman she loved.

THIRTY-FIVE

THEREN RAN DOGGEDLY BETWEEN THE TREES, following the path that the riders who had passed had taken. She could see the distant glow of torches some way ahead of her, so she dodged away into the thicker vegetation, hoping to avoid being seen, at least for now. She also slowed to a walk, trying to get her breath back—if what little of a plan she had come up with was to work, she would need to outrun them long enough to lead them away from the cave. Having functioning lungs was a nice side benefit as well.

The guards were coming back towards her at a

slower pace than she had expected, and once they were within sight she was grimly satisfied to see that she had been correct. They were indeed searching thoroughly for hollows and bolt-holes in the landscape, looking for hiding places. She waited for one to pass by the tree she was lurking behind and then broke into a sprint in the opposite direction, making sure to crash loudly through the bushes to attract their attention. When one of them sounded a horn—evidently to alert their fellows—her surprise nearly caused her to trip. With renewed determination, she willed her legs to move faster as they came thundering after her.

In and out of the trees she dodged, weaving around roots and under low-hanging branches. Being smaller than the horses gave her a slight advantage in that regard, but she was rapidly running out of forest to use as cover. The trees began to thin out, and suddenly she was simply running along the flat, muddy ground in the open, wondering where to go next. Though this whole thing had started as a diversion, it was now taking all of her effort to stay out of reach. Dread wracked her body and shortened her breaths as she heard one of the horses drawing closer and closer behind her; the fear of being trampled spurred her to run even faster, against her legs' wishes.

She swerved off to her left, towards a steep, almost sheer escarpment, with a small valley below. To her chagrin, coming towards her along the ridge from the opposite direction were at least half a dozen guardsmen, as well as what looked like the tall, broad shape of Norrik. Luckily, while running around the very lip of the cliff to deter the rider behind her, she spotted a narrow downwards strip of the ridge solid enough to allow descent on foot some ways ahead. It would be dangerous, for certain, but at this point so was every other course of action she could think of.

She hurtled down over the edge, hopping from rock to rock to avoid the slick mud. Every step was steadied with her magic, and every landing was a new brush with death as she narrowly avoided tripping and breaking her neck. Behind her, the air filled with shouting and cursing as the caravan guards attempted to follow her, crashing their way downhill through the choking undergrowth. At the bottom of the slope was a narrow opening in the rock wall that led to what looked like a small gully. Hoping it might buy her some more time, she squeezed through it.

She dashed along the basin floor but skidded to an abrupt halt not a hundred paces later when the gulch culminated in a dead end. A solid rock wall loomed in front of her, and she was further fenced in by the escarpment on her right and an uneven, ridged slope on her left. She squinted up at the rock wall, wondering if she could leap up to the top, but it was higher than any single jump she had ever made before. Her body also balked at the idea, being concerned with air over anything else. She could barely hold herself upright for her need to gasp for breath.

Before she could recover, the party of guards caught up with her, many of them looking as exhausted as she felt. To her surprise, they did not immediately attack her, but merely seemed glad that the chase was over. She forced herself to straighten but did not make any move yet. She would take any opportunity to regain her energy that they decided to give her.

"This is only one of them," Norrik rumbled, exasperated by the whole business, as he looked her over critically. "We still need to find the Yerrin girl. You three, get back out there and hunt her down!"

The guards he had waved a muscular arm at broke away, heading back towards the narrow entrance to the gully, but Theren knew she could not allow them to escape. She leaped up, buoying herself with her magic, and sailed over the heads of the assembled group to land on the opposite end of the basin, blocking them from leaving.

"I suggest you stay where you are," she declared hotly, trying to make her voice sound commanding.

The others had all turned to face her, and any that had not already drawn their weapons unsheathed them. It seemed that her display of magic had shown them that she was not to be trifled with, whether for good or for ill. She counted eight guards, as well as Hargrim and Norrik, which was roughly half of their full complement. With any luck, the rest were investigating Kaewa's signal rather than out looking for Lilith.

She took a few steps backwards reflexively as several guards moved towards her, but then stopped, swallowing hard, and raised her rapier again. The moonslight glinted dimly off their eyes and the silvered scales of chainmail, leaching the color from their ocean-blue surcoats, but it was at least enough light to see by. She reached out with her magic and grabbed the closest one by his heel, yanking upwards. She tipped him over and dropped him in the mud, and then shoved the legs out from underneath the next guard. The urge to bolt once more was growing stronger, but she fought it down and concentrated on keeping her breathing steady as much as she could.

"You cannot fight us all at once, little mageling," Norrik grated, as he shouldered his way through the rest of the guards.

Theren's injured arm already felt heavy from holding up the rapier, but she flicked it sharply and then aimed it directly at the guard-captain. She hoped that they would not notice her arm trembling.

"I will do whatever has to be done."

She gulped as Norrik drew his sword and swung his black kite shield onto his arm, stepping towards her, but Hargrim appeared at his shoulder, looking frazzled, and put out a hand to calm the taller man down.

"Is this really necessary? Come, surely we can resolve this like civilized people."

Theren eyed them both warily, but lowered her

rapier slowly once Norrik had grunted and stepped back. She made sure to keep it ready, though, just in case.

"Now, I think I may know what this is all about," Hargrim continued hastily, wiping the sweat from his brow even in the winter chill. "We—well, as I am sure you are aware, we had certain transactions with the family Yerrin upon the High King's Seat, and while we were journeying through Dorsea, I discovered that—quite by accident, you understand—our ledgers showed that we had not paid in full the price that the Yerrins had asked for their goods. I was most shocked, I can tell you. We would, of course, be willing to pay the extra that we owe. There was really no need for such dramatics, I assure you."

Theren almost laughed out loud, wondering if the Yerrins had even realized that they had been cheated. Armod's caravan must have been exceptionally lucky to make it through Feldemar relatively unscathed, if they had. Many of the other guards behind them looked surprised at the revelation that they had been involved in cheating the Yerrin family, and several were shifting uneasily or even lowering their weapons. Once again, she found herself wondering if they knew what they had been guarding.

She looked at Hargrim's anxious face and shook her head in disgust. "I am not working for the family Yerrin, I am pleased to say. You are in far worse trouble than that."

“What are you talking about?” Norrik growled, taking a step forwards, and she raised her rapier again to halt him.

“I am an agent of the High King,” she declared, lifting her chin proudly, and smirked when she saw Hargrim’s face blanch. “A Mystic. Surely you must have known that they would find out you were transporting such a large quantity of magestones.”

Many of the guards had gasped when she said the word Mystic, but at the word “magestones,” a ripple seemed to run through the group of them, a wave of sudden realization and fear.

“Your master Armod and these two”—she gestured toward Norrik and Hargrim—“have signed all of your death warrants!” It pleased her to see that some were sheathing or even dropping their weapons.

Norrik, however, just laughed darkly, pushing the ashen-faced Hargrim aside again. “Their death warrants? You have signed your own! You are in the woods, in the middle of the night, in a kingdom with which your organization is at war. No one will ever know if you die here, little Mystic. And all we need do is kill you and your friend in order to become simple blameless merchants once more.”

At his words, the guards seemed to recover, and they quickly formed into a rough phalanx formation behind him. Alarmed, Theren swept her magic forwards in a large blast of force, knocking many of them off their feet, but Norrik seemed to have been expecting something like it and braced himself against her push with his shield.

Without even a pause for breath, he lunged, barreling towards her. She danced quickly backwards into her dueling stance, only to have to move again when he pursued her. She parried three swift thrusts that he unleashed in quick succession, but could find no opening to strike back or push him away. He swung again, twice more, and advanced further, implacable as a bull. Frowning, she concentrated a lever of force behind her rapier's blade, like Vivien had taught her, and feinted with a wild sweep. As she had hoped, he seized what he must have thought was an opportunity to knock her sword from her hands, and struck directly at the rapier—only to cry out in pain as it did not yield, his arm jarred by the impact.

Swiftly, she thrust back, slashing along the inside of his arm twice and drawing blood.

"You will pay for that!" he thundered, bringing his blade down overhand, and she dodged it only narrowly.

Any confidence she had built up with her successful strike vanished as she realized that it had done no real damage to him. She wondered how many blows it would take to bring him down and decided not to count, for fear of discouraging herself further.

He continued to bombard her with heavy swings, and though she attempted to feint again, this time he did not take her bait, obviously seeing the magelight in her eyes as a clue. At the very least she could still use her magic to deflect blows, but without any way to create an opening in his defenses they seemed locked in endless back-and-forth. Apparently Norrik also noticed this, since he made a wide sweep of his own, and when she danced out of his reach, he forced the toe of his booted foot down into the damp soil and kicked it upwards, towards her face. Memories of being blinded by Ilya on the Seat flooded her brain, and she panicked, throwing up a shield of magic against which the dirt splattered wetly. The moment she let her guard down, however, Norrik followed through on his maneuver by swinging his heavy shield like a club, and struck her solidly in the chest.

She felt something crack inside her, probably a rib, as the shield slammed into her and the shock overcame her. Her rapier slipped from her fingers, and she forgot to steady herself as she was thrown backwards, forgot to try to remain upright. She landed unceremoniously in the mud and skidded along the ground, colliding heavily with the base of a tree.

Norrik was laughing. She was aware of it dimly, through the dizzy haze of pain that hung in her rattled brain like a fog, but it seemed very far away. Every breath was agony.

Voices swam in her mind, sounds mingling and overlapping as she tried to gather herself.

Does she even need a weapon? one of her squadmates back in Ammon had asked, and she grunted sourly, trying to sit up, thinking that the rapier had not done her a lot of good.

I am telling you not to be afraid. Vivien told her this once more as she managed to haul herself upright, even though all of her limbs trembled uncontrollably with fear.

At least in Dulmun, all you need to fear is the weather, Armod declared officiously, as she clutched at her side, grimacing, and Norrik began advancing towards her.

She froze suddenly, Armod's voice ringing in her ears as her mind raced. The weather . . .

Her eyes flew to the crest of the ridge behind Norrik, several hundreds of paces away, atop the gentler of the two sides to the gully. She could see even by the moonslight that it was just as muddy as the rest of the forest, and if the soil in Dulmun was anything like that of Feldemar, then—as Yarshun had warned her, what felt like thousands of years ago on their journey to Ammon—*the land would be prone to mudslides after heavy rain.*

She sucked in a deep breath, gathering herself, and then raised her fists into the air. Above them all, at a point high in the sky, she drew together every scrap of her magic that she could muster, shaping the largest construct of pure will she had ever created. She briefly considered simply crushing Norrik into a pulp with it, but knew she would then have no energy left to deal with the rest of his men. The spell dragged at her mind, making her light-headed, and she screamed with the exertion as she swung it downwards at the ground.

She slammed it into the earth, as though hammering the land into shape like a wizard king of old.

Growling, Norrik spun around when he heard the sound of the blow, clearly anticipating some sort of attack. Hargrim's eyes flickered back and forth between her and the ridge, more panicky, and many of the other guards clutched tightly at their weapons. But everything was still. Theren had seen the impact hit, had felt the mud shift under her magic's weight, but the earth could not be hurried, evidently. Dimly, she felt something trickle down her face, and realized that her nose was bleeding.

"Pathetic," Norrik sneered after a few moments, returning his attention to her. "Even with all your power, you cannot put up a decent fight. The redcloaks should know better than to let mages out on their own! They sent you out here to die, defenseless."

He took several more steps towards her and hefted her rapier, obviously planning to kill her with her own blade. But over his shoulder, Theren saw the shelf of mud at the top of the slope begin to slip, slowly at first. It gained speed, collapsing under its own weight after she had shaken it loose, and more and more of the ridge started to crumble away. She grinned savagely, and Hargrim, licking his lips nervously, turned his head to see what she was looking at.

"Sky save us!" he gasped, horrified, as the slope gave way and tumbled inexorably downwards.

"A mage is never defenseless!" she shouted triumphantly as they all twisted to see what was going on, and then took off as fast as her legs would carry her.

She ignored their panicked cries, knowing that she would be in just as much trouble if she stopped to react, and stumbled over towards the largest, thickest tree on the basin floor. The stone around them seemed to groan in agony as the landslide gathered speed, trees being ripped loose and rocks sliding free from their perches, so she ignored the stabbing pain in her ribs and threw herself into a run for the last few steps before she leaped for the safety of a nearby branch.

Her trajectory was not nearly high enough to reach it, so she gritted her teeth and called on her magic again. She wrenched herself upwards towards the branch and then gasped as she felt the magic slip away like sand between her fingers, her reserves of energy almost entirely drained. Miraculously, she caught hold of the branch with her good hand and scrabbled for purchase with the other, while behind her the land itself crashed down upon the guards like a breaking wave.

The tree she was hanging from shivered and creaked as the mud swept down over its roots, but though it leaned slightly, it did not fall. Theren waited until the river of silt flowing below her feet had slowed and the screams behind her had turned to spluttering before she even contemplated letting go.

Though pain wracked her chest with every movement, she dropped from the tree and limped her way through the mess that she had caused. Plant debris and rocks now littered the gully floor in a knee-high morass of squelching mud, along with the moaning guards, and several of their comrades who had been less lucky and were very clearly dead. Norrik, on the other hand, only seemed to be angrier than ever.

He labored to pull himself upright under the weight of all his armor, roaring wordlessly, though the clinging mud did not want to release him. With her last desperate shred of strength, Theren planted a foot on his chest and kicked, shoving him back down into the muck, and ripped her rapier from his grasp. She struggled to grip it, her arm now numb, and then gasped as one of the other guards raised up a spear above his head, ready to hurl it at her.

Before she could even wonder whether she had the energy left to dodge it, an arrow whistled through the air and planted itself in the guard's neck.

His lifeless fingers let the spear drop, and everyone in the gulch, including Theren, turned to look up at where it had come from, on the escarpment above them where they had left the horses. It was Tamah, she saw, elation flooding through her, and he had already nocked another arrow just in case. Beside him, silhouetted against the moons, she saw the bulky form of Ilya holding her own spear; the unmistakable small figure of Vivien, her hair blowing wildly in the wind; and Lilith, whose shape Theren would have recognized anywhere, even if she had not then conjured flames which lit up the night like a beacon.

They could not have arrived at a better time; the

mud was already beginning to ebb away through the gully's entrance, not unlike Theren's ability to stand.

"I would drop your weapons if I were you," Lilith called down fiercely, fire still swirling around her hands. "But then if I were you, I would not wish to be roasted to a crisp!"

The remaining guards who could stand appeared to weigh their chances and give in, letting what weapons they still had to hand fall into the mud. Hargrim, his face pale and bloodied, dropped a dagger that had been clipped onto his belt, and though Norrik hesitated, radiating raw, hot rage for a few long moments, he eventually surrendered too, snarling angrily. Theren watched them all with a kind of detached calm as the effects of everything she had put herself through that night all came crashing down upon her in one swift moment, sounds ringing hollow in her ears and her vision beginning to blur as she carefully sheathed her rapier.

"Thank the sky," she managed to say hoarsely, and then fainted.

THIRTY-SIX

HAZY AWARENESS OF BEING CARRIED BROKE ITS WAY INTO Theren's consciousness, along with the dull ache of pain and the growing discomfort of being wet and caked in mud. She tried to wallow in that barely cognizant state, but her body had too many concerns it apparently wished to raise with her mind, and she gradually drifted awake.

The light from a campfire blinded her briefly, and she flinched her face away from its glare, spotting the golden hair of her bearer. It was Ilya, she realized dimly, carrying her across her broad back with a lot more care than she had done on their first meeting.

"Lay her down here," a voice said, probably Cilin at a guess, and soon Theren lay upon a bedroll beside the fire, still groggy, but mostly all right.

"You arrived just in time," she croaked, and heard Ilya make an amused noise from somewhere above her.

"It is said in Hedgemond that fate favors the bold. You were certainly bold tonight."

Theren smiled weakly, remembering how Instructor Jia had said something similar to her, what felt like a lifetime ago.

Cilin, who obviously had some skill with the ways of healing, was inspecting the wound on her right arm and tutting disapprovingly, when a commotion broke out somewhere on the other side of their makeshift camp and Lilith came running over to kneel at Theren's side. She seemed to be still half-crying, and her eyes flickered between fury, relief, and hurt every moment as she sat there.

"I—" Theren would have said more, but Lilith cut her off, holding up one finger quickly.

"If you think I have forgiven you for running off by yourself, well . . ."

She paused, looking over the injury that Cilin was inspecting and what Theren could only imagine would be a wealth of other smaller scratches and bruises, and then sighed. "If you think I have forgiven you, you are partially correct."

Theren grinned, reaching out with her good hand

to clasp Lilith's fingers. "It all worked out all right, in the end."

Lilith gave her a pointed stare, and Theren had to try not to laugh, since it hurt her ribs. "Never again, do you hear me?"

Theren smiled and then raised her hand to stroke Lilith's cheek, amazed that she could have so much good luck at once. "I promise."

"I must go and make up a poultice for this," Cilin told her, rising to her feet. "Do try not to move too much, please."

"I do not think that will be a problem," she replied gingerly, as all of her muscles clamored painfully in agreement.

She dozed for a while, with Lilith still beside her, as the other Mystics occasionally came and went from around the fire. Some of them seemed to be on watch, while others were out dealing with the remaining guards. She did not see Naro, but Kaewa came by to tell her in sign that she had been very brave, and that she and Vivien had felt from a long way off the magic she used to start the mudslide. Lilith and Kaewa broke into a conversation about how heavy the magic had been, and Theren felt her eyes close once more, drifting off into a deeper, less desperate sleep, feeling safe for the first time since crossing over the border.

Over the next few days, Theren gradually recovered

to the point of being able to walk around without regretting it. She felt guilty, at first, for holding up the progress of the group, but Vivien told her wryly that the other Mystics had ridden hard to reach them in time, and could also do with some rest.

Lilith rarely left her side, and they spent a long time talking about the different aspects of the Kallis caravan that they had each seen during their adventure, as well as the story of how the Mystics had found Lilith and Armod in the cave. Occasionally, Vivien or Ilya would ask Lilith very specific questions about things that Armod had said, as if checking some piece of information he had given them, but the two girls were otherwise not given any duties to perform, except to heal.

Theren did not see Armod himself, or any of his guards, while she was recuperating. They had all been rounded up and taken back to the caravan's last campsite, some ways away from where the Mystics had set up their own camp, which was where she had been brought. She did not think she could stomach the sight of Norrik without becoming irritated, after all the energy that she had put into fighting him, so she was glad that they were out of sight.

It was by now past the end of winter, and Theren thought regretfully that she must have missed whatever her reassignment was supposed to be. Both she and Lilith agreed, however, that after all of this business, they would be happy to return to Ammon.

"So, how did you all make it across the border?" Theren asked Vivien one night as they were eating, and grinned broadly as the Mystic woman grimaced in response.

"Let us not get into that just now. It is a long story, and the number of mistakes we made will undermine any chastisement we have all given you over your latest escapades. Suffice it to say that we will know better for next time."

Ilya grunted in discontent, to Theren's further amusement. "Next time! If the skies are kind, we will not return through the Linked Cities. I hope for there to never be a next time!"

"Hm," Lilith said thoughtfully, frowning. "Will it not be more dangerous to attempt to take ship from somewhere? That is the only other route out of Dulmun that I can think of, and we will certainly be conspicuous while transporting Armod and his friends."

Ilya shrugged, clearly not bothered. "We will have plenty of time later to come up with a plan for leaving. There will no doubt be opportunities to gather information about such things in Eskilgard."

Theren looked up, confused all of a sudden. "Will we not be returning to Ammon? Surely, now that our goal is accomplished, there is no point in lingering behind enemy lines."

Ilya snorted dismissively, returning to her meal. "Did you forget already? We seek to discover what happened to our Mystic brethren who have vanished. We can hardly leave before we find them!"

Theren opened her mouth to speak, but no sound came out. She exchanged a worried look with Lilith, trying to turn over in her mind the memory of every instance that their mission had been spoken about. Try as she might, however, she could not recall any time that she had been told they would return after capturing Armod, and the realization struck her like a blow that they might be here for much longer than she had imagined.

"I—I thought I was going to be reassigned," she said weakly, forgetting the food in her hands.

"Theren," Vivien began, her voice deliberately gentle, "what did you think 'reassignment' meant? You have already been placed with a unit and given a mission. This was your reassignment."

"I suppose I thought that it would be more formal, somehow," she said faintly, after some time. "Like the class placements at the Academy, or something of the sort."

Ilya snorted dismissively, but Vivien smiled, presumably understanding. "No doubt the other new recruits will undergo something more like what you imagine. Unfortunately, our mission called for greater urgency and greater secrecy. If the issue of our friend Armod had not arisen, the transition likely would have been less jarring for you."

Theren nodded at that, seeing the sense in Vivien's

words. The haggard looks on the faces of all of the adult Mystics—her unit, she reminded herself, though the words still felt foreign and strange—on the night before they had departed had certainly spoken of little other than stress. It was no wonder that they had not thought to clarify administrative matters with her, when they were all wrestling with the fear of Dulmun's armies being strengthened by magestones.

Lilith, however, frowned. "And what of me? Am I still involved in this mission, now that the magestones have been recovered?"

"Your role is more important now than ever," Ilya responded gravely, to Theren's surprise. "If we wish to move throughout Dulmun with any kind of ease, the cover of a merchant's caravan will be our most potent defense. People may ask questions about what a Yerrin is doing in this part of the world at a time like this, of course, but if you deceived your way past the border guards then I cannot imagine answering such questions will be a problem for you."

Lilith seemed to relax, glad that she was not going to be sent home, and Theren felt some of the tension in her body ebb away as well. This was manageable, she told herself firmly, and especially if Lilith was going to be here beside her. After all she had done tonight, whatever was coming could hardly be more difficult, could it?

"What was the initial plan for this mission?" Lilith asked, sounding curious. "I know you were adamant that I should not come, and I cannot help but wonder how you planned to move around Dulmun without raising suspicion without me."

Ilya remained silent for a moment, frowning, but eventually seemed to force herself to relent. "I was mistaken. I had no real alternative in mind, but I thought it would be too dangerous, for the both of you. It is clear that I was wrong."

Theren was almost more shocked by this revelation than the last, and had to fight to keep herself from grinning in astonishment. This was only made harder by the fact that she could clearly see Vivien hiding a laugh behind her hand in the background.

"I suggest you get some rest," Ilya continued brusquely, as though nothing had happened, and stood up. "You will need your strength. As I am sure you can imagine, Dulmun holds many perils, and our journey is far from over."

Reflecting on those words, Theren thought that she felt a little less unbalanced now that she had had some time to absorb everything. Lilith reached over and squeezed her hand, and she smiled, unafraid. No matter where their path would lead, from here on out they would face it together. She remembered for a brief moment how this had all started: the fear she had felt at the idea of being cloistered in Imara's house for the rest of her life like a pet, and what that fear had led her to. She took a deep breath of the freezing wintry air and savored its bite as a reminder that she was free.

Adventure awaited, somewhere beyond the mud-choked forest and across the rolling, grassy plains of Dulmun, and it would not find Theren unwilling.

KEEP READING

You have begun the Tenth Kingdom series. But you can read more of Theren's story right now.

The Academy Journals tells the story of Ebon of the family Drayden, another student at the Academy for Wizards. Learn how he and Kalem first befriended Theren. Experience the adventure that led Theren to her desperate decision to join the Mystics.

It's all in The Alchemist's Touch, the first book in the Academy Journals. Get it here:

Underrealm.net/Academy-Journals

ACKNOWLEDGEMENTS

This book could not have been finished without the help and support of many people, too many to fit on a dedications page; first and foremost of course is my family, without whom I wouldn't be here. My parents, my younger brother, and various aunts and uncles who all listened patiently while I went on and on about wanting to be an author, have all helped shape my life and who I am.

My friends–not to brag, but they're some of the best people in the entire world–have always been nearby with words of encouragement and sometimes also cake whenever I faltered or needed help. Emily, Kristen and Rob are people that I can't imagine living without, and I hope they find this book satisfactory as recompense for all the times I couldn't spend with them because I was working. You three, Airi, Tarah, Andrea, Wolf, both Sarahs, friends who appear in later sections of these acknowledgements . . . I love you all. Thank you.

The wonderful developmental editing services of fellow writer and veritable angel Liandra Sy helped to make this book a reality, as did more intangible things like her kind words and her exuberant presence. You will always have my sincere gratitude for everything that you've done for me.

Not everyone is lucky enough to have a publisher

that they can call a friend, but I am such a one. Garrett (and of course Meg) have been with me every step of the way along this journey and I am truly grateful for the opportunities that they've given me . . . and also that one time we played Vampire: the Masquerade. I'm sure we've already said everything else to each other that needs to be said.

And lastly with the publication of my first book I feel it important to thank all the people who didn't laugh at me when I said I wanted to be an author. My teachers Rohan Davis, Kim Scudamore and Vicki Anderson all somehow believed I would do it in the end, and I wouldn't be the same person without them. I hope you all enjoy the book and are aware of just how much your patience and encouragement mean to the young minds that you nurture every day. I am eternally grateful to all of you.

Brenna Gawain
2020

THE BOOKS OF UNDERREALM

THE NIGHTBLADE EPIC

NIGHTBLADE
MYSTIC
DARKFIRE
SHADEBORN
WEREMAGE
YERRIN

THE ACADEMY JOURNALS

THE ALCHEMIST'S TOUCH
THE MINDMAGE'S WRATH
THE FIREMAGE'S VENGEANCE

THE TALES OF THE WANDERER

BLOOD LUST
STONE HEART
HELL SKIN

THE TENTH KINGDOM

A CLOAK OF RED

THE BOOKS OF UNDERREALM

CHRONOLOGICAL ORDER

NIGHTBLADE

MYSTIC

DARKFIRE

SHADEBORN

BLOOD LUST

THE ALCHEMIST'S TOUCH

WEREMAGE

THE MINDMAGE'S WRATH

STONE HEART

THE FIREMAGE'S VENGEANCE

HELL SKIN

YERRIN

A CLOAK OF RED

THE BOOKS OF UNDERREALM

THE CHRONICLES OF UNDERREALM

TAVERN CROSSINGS
THE NIGHT OF TWO KINGS
A NIGHT ON THE SEAT
THE MAN AND THE SATYR
THE BEAST WITHIN
CHASING MOONSLIGHT
BLOOD ON THE SNOW
THE HAMMER OF THE KING
THE TIDES OF WAR
THE LEGEND OF CABRUS
THE SUNMANE PASS

ABOUT THE AUTHOR

Brenna Gawain was born on the same definitely extinct volcano where she still lives today. After spending years of being that child that brought books to family gatherings, everyone was apparently still somehow surprised when she made plans to try and make a career out of writing.

Brenna has a background in almost every kind of art imaginable, from classical music and theatre to writing for video games and dance. She has studied information technology, archaeology and sound engineering at postgraduate levels, and her passion for writing is as broad as her interests in other fields, ranging from horror to fantasy to science fiction and back again.

The chance to work with Legacy Books was a dream come true, for both Brenna and her cat, who greatly appreciates the warm laptop that she writes on.

EPILOGUE

Torid of the family Kallis habitually rose at a time when most other people on Rothton would be eating their midday meals, preferring to stay awake late into the night, to work on her artistic creations in peace. Today was no different, and she emerged blinking into the dining hall of her family's manor house to find her older brother Ulbrand reading letters, as was his usual way.

"Anything interesting?" she asked him, bleary-eyed, as she sat. A servant instantly materialized with a plate of food for her.

"Yes, actually. Quite interesting indeed . . ." He looked at her critically. "Have you made any progress on that piece for the King of Wadeland yet?"

"Some," she answered truthfully around a mouthful of eggs.

It was a jeweled torque—not the usual fashion for Wadeland, but something which would show his court that it was a gift from Dulmun. In truth, it was a gaudier piece than she might have liked, but the filigree was done and much of what work she had left to do would be simple.

"Well, finish it soon," he went on, fixing her with a beady stare. "Things are about to change rather drastically. I am sure you will not want to miss it."

She stopped chewing for a moment, intrigued by his fervor, and then her eyes widened as she realized what he must have been talking about. "Armod managed it?"

"Oh, yes," Ulbrand replied, grinning wolfishly. "He is on his way here, now, with the precious cargo on board. This letter was posted from Yota, and they cannot be too far behind."

"How in the name of the sky did he ever succeed in getting them off the Seat?" Torid asked, faintly impressed despite herself, but her brother just shrugged.

"Oh, the usual way. The redcloaks are always looking one way or the other for coin."

She snorted, returning her attention to her meal. "Oh, how proud the High King must be of her loyal minions."

Ulbrand smiled at that, shaking his head. "If Armod's castellan is correct, it was actually the same Mystic that helped us out with that business smuggling pearls into Idris several years ago. It must be a lucrative thing, to be the most corrupt redcloak in any given city."

"Surely they would be more careful with something like this, though," Torid mused, still chewing. "They will hardly be spared when our king's abominations raze the High King's Seat. Have they no sense of self-preservation?"

Ulbrand simply shrugged, moving on to another letter. "It is hardly any of our business. You should know well enough by now, my dear sister, that the only thing that matters is that the victors see their spoils. The vanquished are beneath our concern."

www.ingramcontent.com/pod-product-compliance
Lightning Source LLC
Chambersburg PA
CBHW020601310726
48979CB00008B/1302/J

* 9 7 8 1 9 4 1 0 7 6 7 2 9 *